MOONLIT DREAMS

The sleep that overtook Leigh was blessed by a most remarkable dream. She was running in the woods. Faster, faster. There was a mist ahead, and as Leigh ran into the mist, she was embraced in warm and comforting arms. And she felt safe. The arms were caressing in their touch, and tingles of delight that Leigh had never before felt ran through her body. And then the mist began to fade, the caressing, gentle hands gone, and Leigh whimpered aloud for their return. It was her own voice that woke her from this dream. And with this awakening, she discovered that she had not been dreaming at all! A stranger, asleep from ale, lay at her side, his arms still holding her naked body!

Leigh lay perfectly still, afraid to move less she arouse this stranger's passions anew. A long time later, the man moaned slightly, turning his face from her and into the moonlight. Had circumstances been different, she might have noted his handsome appearance, but now she saw no more than a stranger who had ravished her. Her scream finally came—and it was loud and long.

The man shot straight up in bed, a startled look on his face. He turned and stared hard and long at Leigh, and she looked into the bluest eyes she'd ever seen. . . .

HISTORICAL ROMANCE IN THE MAKING!

FATE'S PASSION

BY ANNE GAYNOR

ZEBRA BOOKS
KENSINGTON PUBLISHING CORP.

To Don for his love,
Mother for her prayers,
and
Linda for her typing.

ZEBRA BOOKS

are published by

KENSINGTON PUBLISHING CORP.
475 Park Avenue South
New York, N.Y. 10016

Printed in the United States of America

Chapter One

Leigh looked into the hooded eyes of Samuel Jones and a shiver of revulsion ran down her spine. She had seen that admiring, lustful look in men's eyes before, but from someone like Jones, it was especially unnerving. His thin unwashed body and foul breath were enough to disgust any woman, thought Leigh, and his manner and character even less desirable. And those eyes—always hooded, always secretive, and yet cunning.

Leigh watched him out of the corner of her eye as he picked up the jug beside him, removed the cork, and took a long, deep swallow. Ale no doubt! thought Leigh indignantly. She glanced to her father and saw the disapproving look on his face but he said nothing to Jones—and that surprised Leigh. After all Jones was in their employ. Though he was hired as a guide, to Leigh's way of thinking the man was still a servant and he had no right to take such liberties. But, she thought with a sigh, what can one expect from such an uncivilized lot as these Americans.

"I think I shall say goodnight now, father," Leigh said rising and placing a kiss on her father's cheek.

"Very well, dear," her father replied, "goodnight."

"Goodnight, missy," Jones said as his eyes hungrily devoured the shapely form of Leigh's body.

Leigh nodded curtly in Jones' direction before turning and entering the wagon. As she undressed for bed she wished for the thousandth time that they had never left England, that she would wake in the morning in the security of her own bed, and rise to spend a pleasant day tending her rose garden. As she thought of England and the spring, her eyes got a faraway expression and tears began to form. If only she could go back to that fateful day last spring, she thought, and change all that happened since.

She had been working with her roses when her father approached her with a serious expression on his face and flatly announced they would be selling their modest estate outside of London and traveling to America. Leigh remembered how unlike himself her father had been that day, and everyday since, and something deep down inside her told her he was dying, though consciously she would not admit it to herself.

She had grown from baby to woman under her father's tender care and could only recall a blurry image of a smiling face that had been her mother. Perhaps because of her mother's early death her father had always been easy and open in his treatment of her, and that made his behavior these past months all the more puzzling to Leigh.

Thomas Burke was a merchant, a successful one until little more than a year ago. And then suddenly, almost mysteriously, business matters had started to go badly. Things had gone from bad to worse and at the same time he had been told his health was failing.

He was a stubborn man and he was determined to leave this world, and his loving daughter, not a poor man. He had decided to sell the estate before his mounting debts grew even larger and to travel to the young country of America where he knew great fortunes were being made.

He had made what he considered an exceptionally good buy on some land in Virginia through an attorney he had met in Boston where their ship docked. It was developed land, the man assured him, and suitable for growing tobacco. Though its purchase drastically depleted his funds, he was too wise a man not to realize that he was too old, and too ill, to homestead free land, clear it, and make it pay before his death.

They had met Jones at the last river community where they had stopped. He had offered his services as their guide for a very nominal fee and assured Thomas that the land he had purchased lay not more than a fortnight's travel across the land and that to continue on by river would be a needless waste of time and money. So Thomas had hired him, and they had been traveling together for three days now.

The man made Leigh's skin crawl. She could picture him now, sitting by the fire, ale dribbling from his seedy beard, those small dark eyes darting nervously, cunningly, from here to there. She wondered again at her father's lack of actions concerning the man. She knew her father was aware of Jones' appraising glances in her direction, for the two men had exchanged many sour words in the past days, and yet her father seemed to hold a kind of reserve where Jones was concerned that he had never had with other servants.

Leigh finished fastening her nightgown with a sigh, and pulled the blankets snugly about her. She could hear her father and Jones talking, and her brow knitted. It almost sounded as if they were arguing. She sighed heavily again, hoping they would soon see the last of this endless travel, and of Jones.

"Leigh run!"

Leigh's head snapped around at the sound of her father's voice. She saw her father struggling with Jones at the rear of the wagon, a frightened expression on her father's face.

"Run, Leigh!" Thomas urged. "Run and hide in the woods and don't return until I call for you! Quickly, girl!"

Leigh scampered out of the front of the wagon and ran for the trees. When she reached the edge of the clearing she turned and saw her father and Jones struggling on the ground and she hesitated, ready to return and help her father. But then consumed with fear, she whirled and ran into the woods.

She ran blindly, stumbling and falling, as tears ran down her face. It was a black October night, no moon, and she could see nothing as she ran with her arms flung out before her, branches catching at her gown and stinging her face. She stopped, panting for breath, and listened. She thought she heard footsteps close behind her, and with a cry, she changed direction and ran blindly on.

Gasping for breath she again stopped and listened intently. Several moments passed and she heard nothing but the wild beating of her own heart. She sank to the ground at the base of a large tree with a feeling of thankfulness.

She shivered as tears rolled slowly down her face. It was a chilly night, a soft wind blowing carrying the promise of the winter soon to come, the ground cold and damp, and Leigh's thin nightdress did little to ward off the elements. She was still gasping for breath as she looked fearfully about, but all she saw was blackness, as if the earth had somehow swallowed her up and now she sat in some endless void. Her ears were alert for the smallest sound, but with the wind rustling the leaves in the trees, it was difficult to distinguish any other sounds. Still she listened. Jones could be only steps behind her, she told herself.

She shivered again and wiped her tears on the hem of her gown. Please God, she prayed, please let Papa be safe.

An owl hooted in a nearby tree and Leigh let out a startled cry and hugged the tree closely finding some strange security in the rough feeling of the bark next to her cheek. Several times she thought she heard footsteps nearby and she sat literally frozen with fear. Each passing moment seemed an eternity to her, and as the night grew long, Leigh passed it crying for herself and her father, and wondering how much longer it would be before she heard the reassuring voice of her father calling her name.

During the long night Leigh debated returning many times. She was concerned for her father's safety, he being much older than Jones and most likely weaker, but she had never gone against her father's wishes before, and something told her this was not the time to start.

When the sunlight began to filter through the thick growth of the forest a new and horrifying fear was added to the ones Leigh already possessed. What if Indians should find her? She had heard tales of heathens in England, and the more she dwelt on the subject, the more frightened she became.

When the realization struck her that her father was not going to call for her, she felt a deep, chilling terror. He is probably lying injured this very moment, she thought. Oh how could I have been so foolish as to wander so deep into these woods, she scolded herself.

Her legs were growing stiff and cramped and slowly she rose rubbing her arms trying to warm herself, and looking nervously from side to side, studying the brush for the smallest movement. She took a few hesitant steps and then broke into a full run. It did not take her long to realize that she was hopelessly lost, but still she ran aimlessly on until her foot caught in a tree root and she fell to the ground with a thud.

"Oh, Papa," she sobbed, "please come for me, Papa."

She cried as much for her father as herself. She felt a deathlike chill when she again wondered why he had not called for her, but then she told herself he must be looking for her—but where? Should she call out? What if Indians should hear her—or Jones?

She sighed, wiping her tears, and rolled over on her back and lay staring at the bright autumn leaves overhead. Is it my fate to die lost and alone here in these woods? she questioned. If I die, who will care for Papa? I should not have wandered so far, she kept telling herself over and over again.

Slowly she rose. I must remain calm, panic will serve no purpose, she thought. She tried to spot the sun through the leaves and then chose a direction at random and started slowly walking, wishing she at least had her shoes. She wandered for hours jumping at each small sound the forest made, and knowing that behind the next tree, a painted heathen was waiting to jump out at her.

By midday she was so thirsty it felt as if her throat was lined with thorns and her stomach kept growling reminding her that she had not eaten. But still she walked.

By dusk she was exhausted. And as the sunlight began to fade the trees took on grotesque shapes in the shadows and Leigh imagined all kinds of creatures lurking just out of her view.

She came to a small brook and greedily quenched her thirst. She was splashing water on her face when suddenly all the hair on the nape of her neck stood up and she knew she was being watched. Slowly she turned to see a deer hiding in the thicket. They stared at one another for a moment and at first it was hard to tell who was the most frightened. Then a nervous, relieved giggle escaped Leigh's lips and the deer darted away.

Leigh had been so worried about her father and frightened at the thought of Indians, that she had not thought about the animals that might dwell in these woods. America is still a wild and unsettled country, she thought, no doubt these woods contain wild beasts not thought of in England. If she followed the stream it could eventually lead her from the woods, she reasoned—but she would more than likely also encounter more animals coming for water—and next time it may not be something as gentle as a deer.

She sat by the stream in the fading light and worried over her plight. She rose a short time later, refreshed by the cool, clear water, and again she walked, choosing not to follow the stream.

When the blackness of night blanketed the forest

Leigh was assaulted by strange and eerie sounds. She wanted to stop and rest numerous times but feared that once she sat down, she would not get back up, and her mind did not want to accept another cold night spent alone in these woods.

Much later, near complete exhaustion, she came upon a hollow log. Admitting to herself that she had reached the end of her endurance for one day, Leigh carefully peeked inside to make sure the log was not already occupied, and then began scooping handfuls of leaves into the empty space and spreading them for a pallet. She crawled in, and as a mumbled prayer passed her lips, her eyes fluttered closed.

The sounds of the birds awakened her. She opened her eyes and at first was surprised to find herself surrounded by wood, then remembering where she was, she crawled slowly from the log.

Strange, she thought, but this morning she no longer felt cold. She placed her hand to her brow idly wondering if she had a fever. She glanced about trying to remember from which direction she had come last night, but try as she might, she could not. She again chose a direction at random and walked.

This morning she had lost all fear of animals, large or small, and the thought of heathens had been pushed to the back of her mind. Her only conscious thoughts now were placing one foot in front of the other. She found she tired easily this morning, and had only gone a short distance when she had to stop to rest. She leaned her back against a large oak tree deciding it was better not to sit down. A rustling came from the brush to her left and suddenly a fox, small and silver, came darting across her path. Leigh's eyes grew large and she flinched, but otherwise there was no reaction. She sighed and looked down at her aching feet. They were covered with mud and she noted blood in several places. She inspected her torn and dirty gown and then placed her hands before her looking closely at the broken filthy nails. Her arms were covered with scratches, as were her hands and legs. She raked her fingers through her hair removing twigs and leaves as she did.

"What a sight I must be," she mumbled to herself. Then a hysterical laugh escaped her lips and changed slowly to sobbing as she sank to the ground at the base of the tree.

She cried as if all the misery of the world were in her soul alone. She began to feel cold and her body shook with chills as well as sobs, and she knew that she was ill, and wondered how much longer she would have the strength to walk.

When all her tears were spent she leaned her head back against the tree with a sigh. Slowly her eyelids drooped closed and she fell into a fitful, fevered sleep. When she woke it was nearly dusk and her body was shaking violently with chills. She lay huddled against the base of the oak and moaned. It was some time before the chills passed this time.

She sat up licking her parched, dry lips and wishing desperately she knew the direction of the stream. She was so thirsty. She sat staring at the trees surrounding her as her mind raced, flitting from thought to thought—her father, herself—her dismal future should she survive. If she should ever reach civilization how would she find her father—or he her? And if her father was—was—dead— what would become of her? Where would she go? How would she get back to England? But her father could not

13

be dead, she told herself as a shiver of apprehension ran through her body—not her father!

If only they had never left England, she thought. She sat with a faraway look in her eyes as tears rolled slowly down her face. In a moment she brushed the tears away with the back of her hand, and taking a deep breath, pushed herself up. Again she walked.

She had only gone a short distance when she saw a thin column of smoke rising above the trees. At first her joy was unbounded but quickly it was replaced with apprehension. What if it was Indians? Or mayhap it was her father—should she call out? If she retreated back into the woods, it would mean certain death—still to Leigh's mind that was much preferable to being captured by heathens. Finally the crisp autumn air and the emptiness in her stomach won the battle and she crept silently closer.

She saw a clearing and a modest two story house made of logs. There was a woman near the house feeding chickens and Leigh started stumbling toward her whimpering.

Mary thought she heard something and turned to see a young woman walking slowly toward her. The girl's face was covered with dirt and her long, thick hair was full of leaves and twigs. Her face was full of sorrow and Mary felt an immediate sympathy go out to the girl. She dropped the basket she was holding and took a step toward the girl just as Leigh stumbled and fell.

"John!" Mary shouted.

A stocky man with broad shoulders and a rounding belly came running from the house. He took one look at Leigh and rushed to pick her up in his arms. He carried her to the house in strong arms as Mary hurried ahead of him. Leigh was placed before a fire whose warmth was not to be believed and a mug of something warm was placed in her hand.

"Child, my name is Mary O'Malley," the woman said placing a blanket about Leigh's shoulders. "And this be my husband John."

Leigh blinked hard and tried to keep the couple in focus but they kept weaving and bobbing before her.

The woman was medium in height with a trim body and small frame. Her hair was a deep black, almost raven, and she had gray forming at the temples. Her dark blue eyes looked at Leigh with kindness. Leigh knew from the lilt in her voice that she was Irish.

The man appeared close in age to her father. And though he appeared to be somewhat stocky because of his broad shoulders, he was not a short man. He had a full head of red curly hair. Though his hair must have once been flaming red, now it was fading with age. His skin looked tough and his face was lined with deep furrows. The stubble of his beard was white and his eyebrows were large and bushy. His pale blue eyes stared at Leigh intently.

"Please," Leigh begged, "you must find my father, please."

"Yes, child," John said, his Irish brogue stronger than his wife's. "Tell us where he be."

After several minutes of gentle questioning the story unfolded and John promised to go and search for Leigh's father as Mary helped Leigh to bed. No sooner had Mary helped Leigh out of the torn and filthy gown and into bed, then Leigh was asleep.

"Such a pretty thing," Mary said to herself. She placed a hand on Leigh's brow and found her burning with fever.

Mary clicked her tongue and hurried from the room talking to herself.

"I'm believing I still have some of those herbs that help with a fever. I best mix up a brew for that child right away."

Leigh's fever raged for several days. She thrashed and often spoke but her words made no sense to Mary. Only once had she seemed rational when she asked in a hoarse voice if her father was here.

"Not yet, child, but John will find him soon."

John had searched for days now and was taking a short cut home for more supplies when he came upon their camp. His mouth turned down at the corners as he took in the scene before him. The wagon had been searched and its contents lay strewn about the ground. Thomas Burke lay among the rubble, his body stiff with death.

John carefully packed all that remained of their belongings and carefully placed Thomas' body in the wagon. He hitched his horse to the wagon and rode slowly back to the inn.

He wondered why their guide had taken them so far from the well traveled roads. Leigh's father bore no wound of knife or gun, but it was his thinking this Jones had caused his death nonetheless, and he said as much to Mary on his return.

"John, what shall we do? I cannot be bringing myself to tell the child."

John looked at his wife with compassion. "She must be told, sweet. We cannot keep it from her forever. If you like, I will tell the child."

"No," Mary sighed, "it is best it be me. I am the one who has cared for her these past days. The lass does not

16

even know the likes of you."

John smiled at her and patted her hand. When Mary left to tell Leigh, John sighed and went to prepare the body for burial.

Mary informed Leigh as gently as she could of her father's death. She stood watching the girl with tear filled eyes. Leigh's reaction, or rather lack of one, frightened her. Leigh sat staring at Mary with a blank expression on her face. No tears, no words, just a kind of deadly calm.

"John will lay him to rest this afternoon child," Mary added.

"Mrs. O'Malley," Leigh finally said in a soft tone, "could you please help me find one of my gowns?"

"Leigh, sweet, you are still ill and need to be staying in bed."

Leigh slowly, almost mechanically, folded back the cover and rose from the bed with a determined look on her face. "I will be present when my father is buried."

"Very well, child," Mary agreed as she left the room to get Leigh's things.

It was a chilly, overcast, and altogether dreary day that greeted Leigh when she stepped from the house. She glanced to the fresh mound of earth across the clearing and her heart rose up into her throat. Mary took Leigh's hand and gave it a soft squeeze as Leigh straightened her spine and took a deep breath. Slowly the women started walking toward John and the large cloth wrapped bundle that lay at his feet. Leigh pulled her eyes away from the bundle and glanced up. She saw a hawk overhead slowly circling, and then it was diving and as she followed it with her eyes it led her back to John and the grave.

Leigh stood with a bewildered expression on her face as

17

she watched the bundle that was her father lowered slowly into the gaping hole in the earth. She looked away and stared intently at the muscles in John's arms as he strained to lower the heavy body carefully. She swallowed hard and drew her eyes away from the grave and stared at the bright colors of the autumn leaves. How out of place they looked, she thought, and how far away England seemed.

The leaves had been green, the day sunny and warm, when she and her father had boarded the boat to sail from her beloved England. Her father had been nervous and seemed anxious for months prior to their sailing, she remembered, but the day they stepped from English soil onto the gangplank of the waiting ship, he had had a look Leigh had never seen before. His eyes had been those of a defeated man, a beaten man, and his color was pale and drawn, dark circles around his eyes. From that day forward Leigh had worried over his health.

They had had adjoining cabins, their accommodations acceptable, if not lavish. She and her father had dined together during the voyage, and twice dined with the captain, but as a rule Leigh spent most of her time alone. She had been one of few women on board ship and her father had decided it best she spend most of her time below deck. He knew the sailors to be a bawdy bunch, often in a state of half dress, bare chested, and he saw no reason to expose Leigh to such indecency. And Thomas had noted the lusty look in the men's eyes when they looked at his daughter. He judged it better not to tempt the men.

It had been a long, lonely, and seemingly endless voyage to Leigh. Her father's health had worsened, a persistent cough developed, and though Leigh would not admit it to herself consciously, a nagging fear began to grow that mayhap her father would never reach this distant, mysterious land. It soon became habit for Thomas to nap every afternoon, something he had never done in the past, and Leigh would sit quietly, protectively, beside his bunk as he slept. She passed the long hours with dreams of what this new home would mean.

She dared to hope they would acquire a modest home not far from a good size town and live much as they had in England. Of course many had lead her to believe the land would be wild and uncivilized, and though Leigh knew the country was young and that for many years England had sent its undesirables to the colonies, she still hoped to find some type of orderly society, some form of gracious living.

Many men had courted Leigh in the past, all of good station—one even of noble birth, a duke, but none had caught her fancy. Leigh had daydreamed often during the voyage that mayhap she would find the one man she could love in this strange, distant land. Though she knew her choice of husband would be her father's decision, she also knew her father would never wed her to a man she disliked, and though she knew most marriages were ones of convenience and mutually beneficial to both families involved, she still dreamed of marrying for love. She had an image of a home full of warmth and love like the one she had known all of her young years—of a handsome knight, as from a fairy tale, who would sweep her off her feet, and who she would love with all her being. And if fate had decreed that there was one person, one lover, one mate that was right for her, and only her, would she find this man in America—or had she left him behind in England—fate forsaken?

The sound of John's voice startled Leigh from her thoughts and she again looked to her father's grave as John spoke a few quiet words of prayer over the fresh mound of earth. Leigh stared at the grave as if doubting the reality of her surroundings. She realized now how selfish her hopes and dreams for the future had been, and she chided herself, feeling immense guilt.

"Come, child," Mary said placing a comforting arm about the girl, "your father is at peace."

Leigh allowed Mary to lead her from the grave and as they entered the house and climbed the stairs to her room, her mind raced. She felt no tears threatening to spill, no hurt—nothing. In fact, she felt an unreal emptiness, and the feeling surprised her. Then slowly the emptiness began to fill with the deepest feeling of loneliness Leigh had ever felt, so deep her body began to ache, and with ache came panic. She was alone, truly alone, she had no connecting thread anywhere in the world. She felt a sudden anger and bitterness growing inside her. How could her father do this to her—leave her completely alone in a strange land? Almost at once she begged forgiveness of her father, and of God, for her selfish thoughts. I should not have run so deep into the woods that night, she kept telling herself. I should never have left father alone with Jones. It is my fault he is dead! Oh God, help me!

Mary's brow wrinkled with concern as she placed a hand on Leigh's brow. The child still had a fever. She hurried from the room and returned several moments later with a mug in her hand.

"Here, child, drink this. It will help you to sleep," Mary coaxed.

Leigh stared at her with blank eyes.

"Please, child," Mary insisted.

Leigh slowly raised her head and sipped from the mug. She lay back with a sigh and stared at the ceiling.

"Try to rest, child," Mary said softly. "The brew will help."

Leigh did not even look Mary's way as she quietly closed the door behind her. She prayed the drink Mary brought her would help, help her to sleep an endless, blissful sleep from which she would never wake. How could she go on living knowing that because of her her father was dead. And if she could not will herself to die what would she do? Where would she go? Should she return to England alone or travel on to this land her father bought? Her mind raced as Mary's herb tea took effect and Leigh fell into a fitful sleep.

Several days passed and Leigh's fever at last subsided, much to Mary's relief. And though Leigh's health was recovering, her mind was not. She would not venture from the bed but seldom and never left her room. Mary brought her meals to her and John and Mary gave her as much comfort as they could and left her her privacy to grieve in her own way.

Leigh sat by her window one day when a man rode up and strolled into the house. The man appeared to be a well-dressed gentleman and Leigh's curiosity was slightly peaked. She could hear muffled voices below and then Mary's voice and that of the stranger's as they came toward her room. Then she heard their words clearly as they stood just outside her doorway in conversation.

"Mrs. O'Malley," the man was saying, "you know I never pass up a chance to stop at your inn. I swear you make the best stew I have ever tasted."

"It is a lying tongue you have Robert Clark," Mary laughed, "but I thank you for the compliment."

They talked a few minutes more and then Leigh could tell the man was entering the room across from hers. She turned back to the window with a surprised expression on her face. She had not idea this was an inn! She did not even know if she had the proper coins to pay for her lodging! And if she did not, would the O'Malleys throw her out? What would become of her? She had only one place to go, her father's new home, and she did not even know if there was a house or shelter on the property, or for that matter, where the property was. And with no money how would she get there?

Quickly she rose from the chair and started searching through her possessions. For the first time in days her mind started to plan and comprehend her future alone in this country.

Her searching had become frantic when Mary entered the room.

"Mrs. O'Malley," she said glancing toward the woman and then continuing with her search, "have you seen a small oak box? My f-father kept it in his trunk."

Mary gave her a confused look. "No, child, John said your wagon had been searched and that he packed all that remained." She bent and started helping Leigh to fold and repack her few remaining gowns back in the drawers. "I will ask John about it if you wish."

"Please."

Mary smiled and nodded her head and then continued

22

to help Leigh tidy the room. She did not know what had brought on this fever of activity, but she was thankful whatever it was.

That evening when Mary brought Leigh her dinner, John came with her. He reluctantly told Leigh he had seen none of her father's clothing or any small oak box.

"This Jones must have taken everything of value, Leigh. The horse was also gone."

Tears filled Leigh's eyes. "That box contained all my father's money and the deed to our land as well," she sniffed. "Now I have no way to pay you for my lodging."

John smiled at her sad face and tenderly patted her hand. "Leigh, child, Mary and I would not take your coins if you did have them. We only run this inn for the few stray travelers that happen to pass this way. It is a farmer I am." Leigh started to speak but John raised a hand to stop her. "Lass, Mary and I want you to know you are welcome to stay here with us as long as you wish, and we will be hearing no more about paying."

Leigh dabbed at the tears in her eyes and a small smile played around the corners of her mouth as she looked at the kind couple.

John cleared his throat, slightly embarrassed at the soft look he saw in Leigh's eyes, and moved to the fireplace and banked the fire for the night. Mary moved to Leigh and placed a kiss on her brow and looked deep into her eyes with love.

"Now it is goodnight we will be saying," John said motioning to Mary.

When Leigh said her prayers that night the O'Malley's received a large blessing.

*　　　*　　　*

Leigh had been with the O'Malleys for over two weeks now and in that time they had shown her nothing but kindness and consideration. She did now venture from her room and often helped Mary with chores around the inn. But John and Mary had noted her still deep depression and worried often over her state of mind.

Leigh walked to the window and stood looking at the view. Endless wilderness, she thought. It was autumn and the trees were ablaze with color but Leigh did not note nature's beauty. She sighed heavily and started to disrobe.

As she climbed into the warm tub she sighed again leaning her head back against the rim of the old brass tub. The water was soothing and she could feel some of the tension leaving her body. She closed her eyes and immediately she saw her father's image before her.

She had thought about her future much in this past week. She had decided there must be a record of the deed somewhere. She would find it, sell the land, and return to England.

She hated the thought of living with her cousins. They had never been close and Leigh knew they would feel her a burden. Mayhap the land would bring enough that she need not be a financial burden as well.

But first she must settle the matter of the missing deed, alone and with no money, in a strange land. This and the death of her father had kept her awake for many nights. She vowed to think on it no more this night, to sleep, and wake refreshed and with a clear mind.

She quickly finished her bath, and donning her nightdress, climbed into bed. Sleep did at last overtake her exhausted body but it was not untroubled. She was dreaming that she was running in the woods, Samuel Jones close at her heels. She must run faster, faster. There was a mist ahead, and as Leigh ran into the mist she was embraced in warm and comforting arms, and she felt safe. The arms were caressing in their touch and tingles of delight that Leigh had never felt before ran through her body. She relaxed in the embrace, delighting at the caressing touch. And then the mist began to fade, the caressing, gentle hands gone, and Leigh whimpered in her dreams reaching out for their return. Again she was in the woods, running, running, Jones close behind her. She felt him reach for her, his hands grasping, demanding. She could feel his hands on her breast, his hot lips at her throat, the smell of ale on his breath. She must get away! She struggled and tried to scream but a scream would not come. She did not remember Jones as being this large, or would have thought him this strong—for the hands that held her were like steel bands.

With a death-like horror Leigh realized that she was not dreaming! Jones was here! Here in her bed! Her mind raced. How did he find her? Where were the O'Malleys?

She fought hard against his advances and again tried to scream, but still it would not come. He had her gown removed and she could feel his nakedness next to her own, his manhood searching. It felt as if his entire body was covered with hair. Hairy legs pushed against hers forcing them apart and the soft hair covering his massive chest brushed against her nipples. There was a sharp, tearing pain between her legs and she stopped all struggling and lay limp against the sheets staring blankly at the ceiling overhead. She prayed to die with each thrust the man made. He placed passionate kisses on the nape of her neck and murmured something as he moved against her, his hands caressing the soft curves of her body. His passion seemed to build and then Jones let out a sigh and sank down heavily upon her.

Leigh lay perfectly still afraid to move less she arouse the man's passions anew. The minutes seemed to turn to hours to Leigh and still the man did not move. She could feel sweat from his body trickling down on her sides. His body smelled strongly of ale but underneath there was a clean, washed smell. Leigh could feel the stubble of his beard on the soft skin of her shoulder, and the soft mat of hair covering his chest pressed firmly against her naked breast as he rested his weight upon her.

A long time later the man moaned slightly and rolled from her, and for the first time in the moonlight coming through the window Leigh saw his face. It was not Samuel Jones, but a stranger!

His hair was dark and curly, his jaw strong and slightly squared, his lips full and nicely shaped. Had circumstances been different Leigh would have noted the man's handsome appearance, but circumstances as they were she saw only a stranger who had ravished her. The scream finally came—and it was loud and long.

The man shot straight up in bed beside her, a startled look on his face. He turned and stared hard at Leigh and she looked into the bluest eyes she had ever seen. Her scream changed slowly to sobbing as she reached for the sheet to cover her nakedness.

She could hear John's worried voice calling her as he made his way up the stairs. He pounded on the door only an instant and then burst into the room still fastening his pants beneath his nightshirt. He stopped short, his mouth hanging open, as he took in the scene before him.

"What is this?" the stranger snapped in a deep, rich voice. He again turned to stare at Leigh and saw his confusion mirrored in her eyes. He scowled at John. "Innkeeper," he barked, "I paid good coins for this lodging and I did not expect to find a screaming woman sharing my bed or yourself entering my room unbid!"

John gave the man a wide-eyed look and Leigh sat staring at him as if he had grown six heads. John found his tongue and began shouting a string of angry words at the man.

"Whoa!" the stranger shouted. He placed a hand near his ear as if the sound of John's voice pained him and continued to scowl at both of them.

"Leigh," John said reaching for her wrapper and handing it to her, "come with me. And you sir—I will expect to be seeing you below in the common room where we can discuss this in more civil surroundings."

Leigh left the room quietly under the reassuring arm of John. He took her to his room where Mary waited nervously wringing her hands. He glanced toward his wife with troubled eyes and she quickly assisted him in settling Leigh in their bed. The two stood looking worriedly in her direction.

She lay perfectly still, her large eyes looking far away. John gazed at her lovely face. He was sure the young lord had done her harm and he did not know how much more her young body and mind could take. She had already been through so much for one so young and so lovely. And lovely she was, thought John. When he and Mary had met those many years ago in Ireland, he had thought Mary the most beautiful woman he had ever seen. And in twenty-five years he had never changed his mind, that is, until he saw Leigh. He must admit, Leigh Burke was even more lovely than his Mary in her youth.

He motioned to Mary and they walked a small distance from the bed and stood talking in hushed tones. He bid Mary to keep an eye on Leigh, and straightening himself to his full height, he left the room.

He would have to deal with this young buck, he would.

Chapter Two

Byron rose from the bed slowly as the two left the room. He was completely and utterly confused. He knew he had had too much ale the night before in celebration. His mind was still cloudy and his tongue felt as if it were coated with cotton. He remembered finding the small inn. He had been in rare form he knew, but thought he recalled asking the innkeeper to find him some lively wench to share his bed. He wished he could remember more clearly, he thought angrily. He should have celebrated his good fortune just a little less, he mused. Still, the innkeeper had no right to enter his room unbid, and what was that fool woman doing screaming her head off in his bed? The scowl deepened on his face and he clamped his teeth tightly together causing the muscle in his jaw to vibrate. If it was some game to relieve him of some of his wealth, he would have none of it!

He quickly finished dressing and hurried from the room.

It was in this frame of mind that Byron entered the common room. The innkeeper was already there and had just finished poking up the fire, he noted. The man turned to him and indicated a chair near the fire, but Byron's present mood was foul and he preferred to stand and did so glaring at the man.

"Sir, I think an explanation is in order," Byron said, his face rigid.

"Yes, sir, I could not be agreeing more," John replied sticking his chest out proudly.

"Well!" Byron snapped when the man made no move to speak.

The innkeeper's mouth fell open and he stared at Byron for a long moment. "Mr. Marsh, isn't it? Please come and sit by the fire. We have much to discuss."

Byron slowly walked to the fire, chose a chair other than the one John indicated, sat stiffly down, crossed his arms in front of him, and continued to glare at John.

John took a chair and sat searching Byron's face. "Am I right in assuming you violated the young woman in bed with you?" he finally asked.

"Sir, I hardly see how I could violate, as you put it, a paid wench. Though I do not remember settling on a price, I assure you I am well able to pay a fair price for her services." He folded his arms more snugly across his chest and continued to glare at John.

John lowered his head to his hands and spoke so softly that Byron had to strain to hear his words. "The lass was not in your bed, you were in hers. She is not a paid wench but a poor orphaned lass." He looked up to Byron and there was anger in his eyes and in his voice. "If you had not been so far into your cups you would have remembered me telling you I knew of no vixen to warm your sheets!"

The scowl was now gone from Byron's face and he looked to John with disbelief. John studied his more solemn face before continuing.

"I gave you the room across from hers," he said sadly. "It is the only other in the inn. It is a small business my Mary and I do."

As John told Byron about Leigh and how she came to be with them Byron slumped further in the chair and his huge shoulders sagged. My God, he thought, what have I done? Was I so ill of spirits that I did not see her already asleep in the bed and thought she entered later? At first Byron was angry, then contrite, and now that he thought on it his anger rose again.

"It seems, sir, the blame lies with me," Byron said rising and frowning at the man. "I shall, of course, accept full responsibility. You have said the girl wishes to return to England. Then I shall book passage for her and pay all expenses." He looked into John's angry eyes and moved his gaze to the window and saw the first light of dawn. "If you will excuse me now, I will return to my room for some much needed sleep. Goodnight."

He piveted on his heel and strolled from the room under the angry stare of John.

John remained by the fire rubbing the bristles of his whiskers with one hand and watching Byron's ascent up the stairs. He is a handsome lad, he thought. Not as young as Leigh, but young enough for me to consider him a lad with my fifty odd years. Wealthy too, by his manner of speech and dress. Probably use to getting his way, John decided. John didn't know what he could do, just a poor farmer and innkeeper he was, but he knew what should be done. The man had taken Leigh's virginity, of that he had little doubt, and were she his daughter he'd make the man take her to wife. But she is not my daughter, he mused. He and Mary had hoped for children for many years but had finally accepted the fact that the good Lord meant them to have none. Leigh was so lovely, in manner as well as appearance, that in the short time she had been with them, she had stolen a place in John's heart for the child he never had.

He rubbed his whiskers with the back of his hand and squinted his eyes. He did not know how, but somehow, he would see the right thing done by Leigh.

He rose slowly and stretched. With the resolution made in his mind he walked to his bedroom to tell his Mary of what had been said by this Byron Marsh, and the decision he had made.

When Leigh awoke the next morning she was out of sorts at first not remembering where she was. She stretched slowly and then the memory of the night before assaulted her. Her eyes glazed and she lay there a long time staring at the ceiling. Slowly her eyes roamed the room and she saw one of her gowns and shifts laying over the back of a chair. She gingerly pulled back the covers and went to get her clothes.

There was a slight knock at the door and Mary entered carrying a small tray of food. She saw Leigh sitting in a chair staring into space. She was dressed but her hair had not been brushed and her face was void of expression. Tears came to Mary's eyes and she quickly brushed them away and smiled.

"Good morning, sweet," she said with a joy in her voice

she did not feel.

Leigh's eyes raised slowly to hers and a smile played around Leigh's mouth as she gazed at the kind face.

"I've brought you a fine breakfast," Mary said holding a tray out for Leigh to see. She placed the tray in her lap and turned to get a brush. "Try to eat, child, and I will fix your hair for you."

Leigh glanced at her and dutifully started to eat. Mary watched her closely as she brushed her long curls. She tied the thick mass loosely in back with a ribbon and then took the barely touched food from Leigh's lap.

"Come, sweet," she said smiling and taking Leigh's hand.

Leigh was beginning to doubt her mind. Had she dreamt the happenings of the night before? She remembered she had been dreaming. She did not really feel any different upon rising. But it must have happened, she thought, or why was I in the O'Malley's room this morn? She had a small frown on her face as she entered the common room. She stopped short, looking up, as blue eyes stared into green ones and Leigh and Byron looked hard at each other from across the room.

Leigh turned to flee but found Mary's hand on her arm, a gentle smile on Mary's lips, and a look of reassurance in her eyes. Mary patted her arm and Leigh allowed herself to be led across the room to where he stood looking at her. She lowered her eyes and blushed profusely. John came to the table as Leigh weakly sat down and cast her eyes to her tightly held hands in her lap. Even though Leigh had her hands clasped so tightly together that the knuckles were turning white, she still could not stop their violent shaking.

Byron stood admiring the vision that had just entered

33

the room. She was the most beautiful woman he had ever seen. Her hair was the color of chestnuts. It was long and lush and hung about her shoulders in thick curls. Her eyes were emerald in color and they turned up slightly at the corners in a most provocative way. Her cheeks were flushed and it made her lips look even pinker and more perfect. She was of medium height with slender, long limbs. Her waist was tiny and her breasts full and round. Byron was completely taken back by her graceful beauty. He vaguely remembered the well formed body from the night past and that the face had been lovely, but to have forgotten beauty such as hers, he must have indeed been drunk!

As he devoured her with his eyes, he could not believe her to be the same maid that shared his bed. He looked to the innkeeper's wife and could see the hint of once great beauty. Could she mayhap be their daughter, he wondered, and they plan to make me think her the wench that shared my bed, when in fact it was a paid wench?

Byron had risen from his chair as Leigh was led to the table. He wanted to say something to this lovely woman and opened his mouth to speak, but flushing slightly, he quickly closed it realizing he did not quite know the proper greeting for a woman he allegedly ravished. So he said nothing and just stood and continued to stare at her beauty.

John glanced Mary's way and his mouth curled with just the hint of a smile. He cleared his throat and bid Byron be seated as he sat himself. Mary excused herself and left the three alone to discuss what should be done.

John looked compassionately to Leigh and touched her arm causing her to look up at him. "Leigh, lass, do you still wish to be returning to England?" he asked.

Leigh looked at John and then cast a quick glance in the stranger's direction. She was shaking so she feared to test her voice. She lowered her eyes to her folded hands in her lap and nodded her head to the affirmative. John turned his attention to Mr. Marsh, she thought John said, and they started an earnest discussion of her welfare.

Leigh paid less and less attention to what they said. She sat catching a word here, a phrase there. She was humiliated to her very fiber. How could they sit there and discuss her as though she were a horse or other such possession to be haggled over? She knew John meant well, but all she wanted to do was flee the room, and preferably the country, as soon as possible.

As she sat half listening, her mind started to comprehend for the first time how really difficult it was going to be for her to acquire her deed and sell her land alone. The O'Malleys were truly wonderful people and Leigh thought well of them, but they were not relatives and she could not impose on them forever.

Her father had sheltered her well and she knew next to nothing about such things as deeds. It was not a lack of learning, for Leigh could read though few women could, but business matters were simply beyond her domain. She was startled from her thoughts by a loud declaration from the man sitting across from her and she jumped placing her hands over her heart.

Byron leaped up and roughly pushed his chair aside with his foot. He placed his hands palm down on the table and leaned over looking hard into John's face with a scowl.

"If I should take her to wife," he ground out slowly, "and mind you I said if—I will not have her traveling to England to have a mate I will never more see!"

"You admit the fault be yours, sir," John spat at him, a frown on his weathered face, "now you must do what is right and marry the lass!" John rose from his chair and stood looking up to Byron's face and they exchanged angry look for angry look. "As to the matter of her returning to England," John continued, "that can be settled betwix the two of you once you are wed."

Byron glanced at Leigh's startled face and then turned to again frown at John. "Sir, I will not be pushed to a speedy end," he stated flatly. "I will give you my answer when I am ready." He glanced again at Leigh before leaving the room with angry strides.

Mary walked in and stood looking at John. Should they be pleased the man seemed gentle born and a man of means? Mayhap they were doing wrong in trying to make the man wed Leigh. After all it was really none of their affair.

They had taken Leigh in less than three short weeks ago. But in that time they had come to love her as their own, and she needed someone to look after her, if not them, who? And her virginity had been taken under their very roof so they were not without blame themselves.

They looked into each other's eyes as if reading each other's thoughts. Leigh had no one but them. She would be as their own child and John would see the man married to her if he had to hold a gun to the man's head to see the deed done!

Upstairs in Leigh's room Byron paced the floor with a deep scowl on his handsome face. Damn! he thought. Of all the luck! She was extremely beautiful but he would not be forced.

At first he suspected that she was not a virgin, but he

had seen the proof on the sheets of the bed. And she was not their daughter as once he mused. The man asked for nothing for himself and stated plainly that she was not his child or even his kin. Byron stopped his pacing and stood with one hand resting on his chin, a sly look in his eye. She did most likely owe the man money for lodging—he started pacing again—but it could not be a very great sum, true. Perhaps the man just wanted to be rid of her. Byron sighed. He did have to admit that John had a genuinely kind face and that he and his wife did seem to truly care for the girl.

He angrily paced the room as he ran it through his mind and no matter how he put it, he always came back to the fact that he did ravish the girl. But to marry a woman he did not know and not of his choosing—never! In his father's time, and in England where his grandfather had had his start, he knew it was often done for reasons of land or money. But he was an American and needed no land or money. He already had an abundance of both.

At the thought of his home the scowl on his handsome face softened. How he loved that land. It was because of his love for his home, and the desire to see it always improved, that he now found himself in this predicament. He had gone to see old man Simmons and once again try to talk the old, stubborn man into selling him his prize bull. Byron needed the bull badly to improve his own stock. He had tried to get Simmons to sell many times in the past, all with no success. And then two nights ago the stubborn old man had finally agreed. The bull was at this very instant on his way to Byron's home under the care of his man Ephraim.

Byron and Simmons had shared a drink to seal the bargain and the old man had offered Byron the bottle of his homemade brew to keep him company on his long ride home. Byron knew to some it would seem foolish to get so drunk over the buying of a bull, but he had been trying to get that old man to sell for years!

He drank little at first, riding slowly along and thinking about his life. He was now thirty-one years old. It was time to settle down, marry, and sire children he decided as he rode. He desperately wanted a son. He drank and thought. He had had his flings. Yes, he was sure it was time to settle down and produce an heir. The fact that he had met no woman that had captured his heart was of little matter. He was much sought after by the maids. He knew part of his appeal was his great wealth, but he also knew that he was not unpleasant to look upon. He had often wondered about this love people so spoke of. He knew it did indeed exist for he remembered well his parents and the obvious love they had shared. He drank some more. All he had ever found was lust, not love, for a pretty maid who would be forgotten with the next flirting smile. He drank some more and soon the bottle was empty.

He half settled his mind on his drunken ride to ask Ella Borough to marry him. She was a tall, buxom, blond that Byron had known all of his life. They had shared a bed many times in the past and Byron greatly appreciated her experience in the art of love. She was not a virgin when first they slept together, and her morals did give him some small worry, but—he was no angel himself, he mused. Ella was madly in love with him, and his money, he knew.

Now this, he thought stopping his pacing and going to flop down on the bed. He had taken a young girl's virginity against her will. But marry her! A stranger! For all he knew she hadn't a brain in her head. He sat up quickly on the side of the bed, a studious look on his face. Come to think of it, he had never heard her speak. Why she could be mute! he thought. No, he realized flopping back on the bed with a heavy sigh—he had most definitely heard her scream. But beauty such as hers must surely have a flaw. She probably had a voice like chicken scratching and a head that would rattle if you shook it. Of course women need not be learned like a man, but he did have an aversion to empty-headed women.

Byron got up from the bed and again started to pace. I am to blame, but . . .

Leigh returned to the safety of the O'Malley's room shortly after Byron angrily exited the common room. She stood at the window staring out at the surrounding woods, but she did not see the trees, but saw instead steely blue eyes glaring at her from across the common room. Her hands still trembled and tears brimmed and threatened to spill. Her eyes focused on her father's grave, her bottom lip quivered, and she began to weep.

"Oh, Papa," she whimpered, "I need you so."

She sadly turned away resting her head forlornly against the window pane. The tears flowed freely now as she silently wept, her body shaking with the sobs. She sniffed wiping at the tears with the back of her hand and walked to the chair by the bed. She plopped down with a sigh, her head hanging low. There was an expression of complete misery and utter hopelessness on her face. All those years, she thought, that her father had so lovingly sheltered and protected her only to have her virginity taken now by a stranger—*a total stranger!*

Her brow wrinkled as she thought about him. What manner of man was he? she wondered. She knew him to be violent from his foul deed of the past night, and had witnessed his quick temper when he spoke to John earlier. Yet the man showed signs of breeding and culture. His clothing was that of the financially comfortable, tasteful, and not gawdy or colorful as seemed to be the fashion with many men today. And his manner of speech indicated an educated man, she realized.

She rose from the chair chewing at her bottom lip in a puzzled way. Her brow furrowed deeper as she again walked to the window.

She pictured the man again in her mind. She saw a lengthy form, shoulders wide and powerful, features smooth and fine, and she realized for the first time how really handsome the stranger was. She recalled the voice, deep and pleasant in tone, and the odd drawl in his speech. She found if she was truthful with herself she must admit that if she heard that drawl spoken by lips other than his, she would find it most charming.

A fleeting thought flickered and skipped across her brain and she had the strangest sensation of pleasure and warmth, security and—and almost a feeling of being loved. But try as she might, she could remember no deed or person to connect with the feeling, for she did not recall ever having felt thus before. As quickly as it came the feeling was gone again and Leigh dismissed it from her mind.

She began running the events of the past night through her mind over and over again, and no matter how often she wished to change them she knew she could not. The deed was done and there was nothing anyone could do to change that fact.

She turned away from the window but this time her head was held high, shoulders erect. The man would leave the inn soon enough, she told herself, and until he did she would remain in this room.

She walked to the bed and lay down with a sigh, staring at the ceiling overhead. The man would be gone soon, she thought, he will be gone soon . . . soon . . .

When Byron went down to the common room no one else was there. Mary came timidly and put a plate of stew before him.

"Madam, would you ask your husband to come and let me speak with him," Byron said courteously, a frown on his brow.

"Sir, ah, my, ah, husband had to leave on a short journey of some importance. He will return on the morrow." Mary gave him a weak smile and quickly left the room.

The stew was delicious Byron noted but he ate little. Mary peeked from behind the door and saw the deep scowl on his face and nervously wrung her hands.

Byron sat there pushing the stew about his plate. He was angry enough at this entire affair and now he must wait for the innkeeper to return. He had hoped to be on his way this night. He was anxious to get home now that the matter was settled in his mind. He would arrange for the girl's passage home, pay all expenses, and settle a goodly sum on her as well. He was doing the right thing he was sure. He could not marry an empty headed stranger. Other maids had suffered as much and lived to see a better day. And with the money he planned on gifting her with, she would have no trouble finding a suitable husband in England. It was a shame, he thought, that she was not a paid harlot. He would have enjoyed calling on her often in the future.

The matter now settled in his mind, he ate his stew, bid Mary goodnight as she came to clear the table, and retired to his room where he immediately found sleep.

Leigh awoke the next morning when Mary came bustling into the room. Leigh had shared the room with her last night but had not awakened when Mary rose earlier.

"Come, sweet, there is much to do," Mary said with a smile. She fluffed up the pillow behind Leigh as she slowly sat up, then went and got a tray off the dresser and placed it before her.

Leigh looked at the tea and toast on the tray and then to Mary.

"I'll be back shortly to help you dress," Mary said as she brushed back the hair from Leigh's brow, and then she hurried from the room.

Leigh watched her go and thought that she did not really need any help dressing, but if it pleased the kind woman, she would accept her help. She sipped her tea and thought of what wonderful people the O'Malleys were. She would trust in their judgment. They were older and wiser than she. And beside never having handled her own affairs, she was not exactly sure of where to start. Yes, she mused, she would definitely trust in the O'Malley's wisdom concerning the matter of the deed.

She knew they wanted that awful man to marry her, but she had already dismissed that entirely from her mind. She was sure the man was of the same mind as she, and had no more desire to wed with her than she did with him. She had little doubt the marriage would ever come to pass.

She had no sooner finished her light breakfast then Mary returned carrying a gown that Leigh did not recognize as her own.

"Come, dear, and try this on for me," Mary requested holding the gown out in front of her.

As Leigh slipped into the dress she admired the fine cut of the cloth. The gown was a soft blue and had a full flowing skirt and fitted sleeves with a high neck. There was white Irish lace at the throat and cuffs.

"It is a lovely gown, Mrs. O'Malley," Leigh said running her hands over the skirt.

"Thank you, sweet, it be mine." She smiled at Leigh and started walking around her inspecting the gown. She gathered a small bunch of the fabric at the waist and started pinning it as she talked. "I packed it away many years ago for the daughter John and I would have someday. Now I want you to have it. I need only take up the waist one wee bit and it will fit you perfect."

Leigh knew many of her gowns had been ruined but she truly did not feel she needed a new one, and especially one as lovely as this one and obviously cherished by the woman. But she did not wish to appear ungrateful so she gave Mrs. O'Malley a tremendous hug thanking her for the gown. Mary smiled broadly as she helped her to remove the pinned gown.

There was a knock on the door and Mary handed Leigh her wrapper and watched her put it on before she called to them to enter.

John came in carrying two large buckets filled with water. He smiled to them both and then went and filled the old brass tub. Done, he turned and left the room without a word.

"I'll make the alterations while you bathe, Leigh," Mary said with a grin and also hurried from the room.

Leigh frowned, confused, and undressed and climbed into the tub. She did usually bathe everyday, but today everyone seemed most intent that she do so quickly. Leigh had not finished her bath when Mary returned declaring the dress was done. When Leigh climbed out of the tub and finished drying, Mary handed her her shift and insisted she sit down while she fixed her hair for her. Leigh did not know what all the fuss was about. She guessed that John was going to take her to a nearby town to see into the matter of the deed.

The morning was well passed when Leigh finished dressing. The gown was truly lovely and looked very nice on her, she thought, as she looked at herself in the small mirror. And she liked the way Mrs. O'Malley had fixed her hair atop her head and woven ribbons of the same hue as the dress among her shining curls.

"You are indeed the fairest maid I have seen, Leigh," Mary said standing back to get a good look at the girl. Then she walked toward Leigh with a smile as she held a small handbag out in front of her. "Here, dear, I brought you your bag in case there is a small bobble you would like to wear."

"Yes," Leigh said, opening the bag and searching the contents. "There is a cameo that was my mother's that would look well with the gown." She found it and pinned it on the gown just below the collar. "It does look well don't you think?"

"Indeed, yes," Mary agreed with a grin, "and it is thankful we should be that it is one of the few things of value that awful Mr. Jones missed."

The minute Mary said the words she wished she could

have pulled them back. Leigh had seemed light and gay for the first time in her home, but now her face was again sad and lost.

"Sweet, come, we must hurry," Mary said as she gently took Leigh's hand and walked from the room.

Why must we hurry? wondered Leigh. It makes little difference if we start our journey a few minutes later.

As they entered the common room Leigh saw John standing to one side and he was dressed very formally. She glanced to Mary and noticed for the first time that her dress was very formal as well. Her eyes slowly roamed the room and stopped abruptly when she saw the stranger standing near the fireplace. Another stranger stood with him dressed in simple black. Leigh's eyes went back to the handsome stranger and she stared at him with frightened eyes.

He wore the same brown coat he had worn the day before at breakfast. His shirt looked fresh and was flawlessly white with ruffles at the throat and cuffs. He wore a tan vest and trousers that fit snugly and left little doubt as to what lay beneath. High brown riding boots completed his attire. His face was rigid and his eyes seemed to be staring a hole right through her.

John approached her and held out his hand for her to take. She was trembling so with the man so near and his eyes boring into her that she gratefully accepted John's offered hand, but found to her horror that he only led her to the man's side, and bowing stiffly backed away.

She stood on trembling legs as the stranger in black began to speak. His voice sounded as if he was a long way away. She wanted to run and her legs would not take her. She felt rooted to the floor. Why did John or Mary not note how badly she shook and take her from the

45

man's side?

The tall man beside her said something and Leigh turned and looked at his handsome profile with confusion. Then the stranger in black was again speaking and she was having trouble understanding his words so she watched his lips closely and heard him say something about repeating, and she did, though she gave no notice to the words she spoke. To her even greater horror the tall man beside her—was Marsh his name?—took her limp hand in his and placed a large ring with a crest upon it on her finger. She looked at it oddly and then kept her finger bent in two so it would not slip off. She heard a voice from the end of a long tunnel say, "You may kiss the bride," and the man beside her roughly pulled her into his arms and stood glaring into her frightened emerald eyes. His face was void of all expression as Leigh rested limply in his strong arms, tears flowing freely down her face. As his lips lowered slowly to hers Leigh jerked and tried to pull free but the strong arms that held her would offer no release as his lips met hers and he kissed her passionately. She was aware of his lips, soft and warm, the clean scent of his body. Her terror of the man was complete and yet she felt her body grow warm as ripples of pleasure made her skin tingle. Again she tried to pull free but he held her all the tighter, his body molded to hers, her breast pressed tightly to his massive chest. She could not breathe and she opened her eyes wide and then closed them again and saw a small dot of light far away, and it grew smaller and smaller and then it was gone.

When Leigh came to she was on the O'Malley's bed. Mary sat beside her holding her hand, a worried expression on her face. Leigh's eyes slowly roamed the room as she listened to Mary's voice.

"You fainted, sweet," she heard her say. "It must have been the excitement of the . . . the . . ."

Leigh's eyes came to an abrupt halt when she saw him standing leaning his large bulk against the door frame. His arms were crossed over his chest. He stood staring at her, his face void of expression except for the eyes, and they roamed over Leigh's body leisurely from head to toe making her feel as though he were undressing her with his eyes. When their eyes met, she blushed and turned her face from his. She heard the door slam and turned to see him gone. She turned a confused face to Mary.

"I-I hope we have done right, child," Mary said, softly caressing Leigh's limp hand. "John and I were thinking only of your welfare when we brought the marriage about." Mary looked to Leigh with an expression of remorse and continued with a longing for understanding in her voice. "The man took you, child, and we saw no other way. If now you find you still wish to be returning home to England, you need not go a sullied woman."

Mary paused again looking into Leigh's confused eyes. Leigh said nothing, did nothing, but continue to look at her in that odd manner. Though Byron had done Leigh great harm, Mary judged him to be a good man deep down, and Mary O'Malley had seldom been proven wrong in her judgments of people.

"I know he is angry now, Leigh, and that he frightens you," she continued, "but he does not seem such a bad sort." A weak smile crossed Mary's face. "You make a grand looking couple. If you should decide not to return to England, I think one day you could be happy with the man."

*   *   *

Mary left Leigh alone to rest and when it came time for the evening meal Leigh knew she could no longer put off confronting the man. He would be in the common room and Mary had not appeared with any tray this time. She could not avoid the man forever, she told herself. I will speak to this stranger who is my husband and tell him of my intention to return home. Nervously she smoothed the skirt of her gown, patted her hair into place, squared her shoulders, and taking a deep breath, she made her way to the common room.

He was seated at the table near the fireplace and he appeared to be in deep thought. As Leigh entered the room on trembling legs he stood up, a frown wrinkling his brow, and held out a chair for her. Leigh hesitated, took another deep breath, and slowly approached the man. As she reached his side she looked up to him and nervously bit at her lower lip. She saw him studying her with his eyes, and as their eyes met, she quickly reverted her gaze and hurriedly sat down. As he assisted her with the chair she murmured her thanks in a soft tone.

Byron stood staring at the top of her head. He thought she had said something, but he could not be sure, so he seated himself and did not look her way as he pretended to study the view from the window.

Leigh watched him from beneath her lashes and wondered what he found so interesting out the window. It was quite dark and she could see nothing from where she sat.

Mary arrived with what appeared to be a feast for the small inn. Byron had no trouble giving the meal its fair due but he noticed that Leigh ate little and kept picking at her food.

Leigh was much too nervous to eat with him so close and watched him carefully from beneath her lashes. He was not an ugly man, handsome in fact when he wasn't scowling. He seemed clean and well-dressed and his table manners were good, she noted. But he was a rogue none the less, she thought. She felt exceedingly awkward at the silence in which they ate but she did not trust her voice to speak and was not going to be the first to break the silence. Besides, she mused, I am not sure of the man's name and how to address him. With a start she realized it was also her name she was not sure of now. She continued to watch him suspiciously as he ate.

Byron glanced her way from time to time. He was totally captured by her beauty. But he was not going to let her beauty ease his anger at being forced to wed her, and by an innkeeper of all people! He could have escaped anytime he guessed, but he had given the innkeeper his word, as well as the minister, and Byron Marsh never went back on his word.

At first he and the innkeeper had exchanged many angry words, and then the old minister had had his say and made Byron feel the cad. He had finally agreed to the marriage, but only after undo pressure had been brought on his head. And he had small doubt the innkeeper would have carried out his threat and used a gun if necessary.

It did not sit well with him. Him, Byron Marsh, married to a woman he did not know and not of his choosing. He had still heard her speak only those few words at the ceremony, and those she had repeated. Her voice had been so soft he had barely been able to tell she was speaking. He was becoming more and more sure he had married an empty-headed woman. And what would his uncle think when he returned home with a bride after a few days gone? He decided right then to take Leigh to Richmond for a time before departing for his home. He would ask that old minister to send a message on to his home before the minister departed tonight. He would have Leigh suitably clothed for the wife of a Marsh while they were in Richmond, and mayhap by the time they traveled to his home he would find out if she was as simple-minded as she appeared. Mayhap, he sighed, they would at least be on more pleasant terms before he must present her to his uncle.

He glanced at her silent beauty and his anger grew. If only, he thought, I had not traveled to buy the bull. If only old man Simmons had been his usual stubborn self and said no again. If only I had not felt the need to drink so much that night. If only . . .

If only he would say something, thought Leigh. His silence just frightened her all the more. If only we had not come to America. If only Papa were still here. If only . . .

The O'Malleys watched the couple from the doorway. They saw the silence in which they they passed their meal. Mayhap I was not wise in making the man wed her, thought John. Mayhap I should have stayed out of the affair and have done Leigh greater harm when trying to only do right. But he felt the weight of responsibility heavy on his shoulders, he told himself. Leigh had been ravished under his roof. Was he not responsible? He knew the man was well into his cups. He should have shown him the room. If only I had, if only . . .

Mary stood beside John and watched the couple closely. My, but they do look handsome together, she mused. She saw the admiring looks Byron cast Leigh when he knew she would not see. And she saw Leigh peek at him often from beneath her lashes. She wished they could break their silence and be more at ease with one another. But someday, given half a chance, they would be happy together, of that she was sure.

Of the four souls in the inn that night, Mary O'Malley was the only one who had no if onlys.

When the meal was complete, Byron rose, excusing himself saying he needed to see to his horse. Leigh sat and watched him go, tears now in her eyes. It was obvious to her the man shared the feelings for her that she did for him. Hatred! She rose to go to the safety of her room and found Mary there preparing the room for the night. She noticed Byron's saddlebag thrown over the back of a chair and it occurred to her for the first time that she would be sharing the room with him tonight. Not only the room, the bed as well!

Mary saw the frightened look on Leigh's face and rushed to console her. "Leigh, sweet, he is your husband now and due all the rights of that position." She placed an arm about Leigh's shoulder and gave her a small hug. "He does seem a kind man in many ways, Leigh, though I know you cannot see that now. In time you may find it in your heart to feel a kindness for him." She turned Leigh so she could look straight into her sad face. "You know, sweet, many wives do not love their husbands when first they wed."

Leigh said nothing as tears appeared in her eyes.

"Come, child, I'll brush your hair for you and help you with your gown," Mary said giving her arm a pat, tears now in her eyes as well.

When Leigh was settled in bed, her hair brushed till it shone and wearing a pretty white nightdress trimmed with lace at the throat and bodice, Mary gave her a reassuring pat on the hand and placed a kiss on her forehead as she sat beside her on the bed. She wanted so desperately to comfort the girl.

"Leigh, I know that woman's way is sometimes hard. I was not much older than your eighteen years when John and I wed. And it was frightened I was." She looked into Leigh's tear filled eyes and smiled as she gently squeezed her hand. "John is a fine man, Leigh, and I love him dear. Now I look back on those fears and smile at how silly I was." She paused cupping Leigh's chin in her hand. "I realize that you learned about man's rutting ways in a cruel fashion, child, and that the man is a stranger to you, but . . ."

Leigh sniffed and then threw her arms about Mary and hugged her fiercely.

"Forgiving is sometimes a hard task, child," Mary said softly against her brow. "But the man is your husband in the eyes of God, and forgive him you must. His act to you, though most foul, was not deliberate, and Leigh, child, he does seem a good man."

The two women sat embracing each other for a moment and then Mary placed another kiss on her brow and rose to leave.

"M-Must you go?" Leigh asked in a trembling voice.

"Yes, child, but John and I will be only downstairs if you need us." Mary forced back her tears and gave Leigh one more quick hug before hurrying from the room.

The minutes ticked by like hours for Leigh as she waited for her husband to return. When finally Byron did enter the room, she sat up with a startled cry and pulled the covers tightly beneath her chin. He looked surprised to see her there but the look lasted only an instant and Leigh could not be sure it had ever been there at all. He started to pace the room with an ugly scowl on his face. He opened his mouth several times to speak but said nothing. He glanced often in her direction and she sat still as she could watching him. Finally he came and stood at the end of the bed and stared at her for an uncomfortably long time before he spoke.

"Madam, I know the circumstances of our meeting were anything but ideal," he snapped, "and what has followed even less so. But what is done is done, and cannot be undone." He looked at Leigh's startled face, her mouth hanging open slightly, and the scowl on his face deepened. "I have been told you wish to return to England, but you are my wife now and I cannot permit that." He joined his hands behind his back and glared. "There is always the chance, slight though it be, that you could be carrying my seed within you."

My God! thought Leigh, her eyes growing even larger. She had never thought of that, but he was right.

"Therefore," he continued, "on the morrow we will be traveling to Richmond where we will stay a short time before we travel on to my home."

He turned abruptly and started to pace again as Leigh watched him with eyes round as saucers. He looked down at the floor as he paced in angry strides and glanced her way from time to time. He again came and stood at the end of the bed.

"As for now," he barked, "it would please me beyond belief if you would quit goggling at me and go to sleep!" He pivoted on his heel, turning his back to her, and stood leaning against the mantel with one hand and staring into the fireplace.

Leigh let out a huff, fluffed her pillow, and slid deeper under the covers glaring at his back all the while. Just who did he think he was? You'd think he was the one put upon the way he acts! She did not ask the drunken fool to enter her room. How dare he! And she might be carrying his child, might she? Well, she would die first! The arrogant cad. Take her to Richmond indeed!

She did not know what or where Richmond was. She assumed it was a small town nearby. Well, she thought with a sly smile on her face, she would play the meek wife and let him take her to Richmond, and once there she would find a way to leave him and return to England. As to her wifely duties, if the oaf came near her she would bite and scratch and keep her legs tightly together. Just who did he think he was? We will see what he will and won't permit!

Leigh made a face at him, since his back was turned, and snuggled deeper in the covers. She would watch him carefully and not dare fall asleep. She remembered well what happened when this man found you sleeping! She lay perfectly still and as the minutes ticked by she could feel her eyelids growing heavy, but still the man did not move. She fought to keep her eyes open.

A long time later, as her eyes slowly closed, the last thing that she saw was Byron's broad shoulders silhouetted by the dying embers of the fire.

Leigh was cold. She moved slightly in the bed and her eyes flew open. She was pressed close to Byron. Her hand rested on his hairy chest and one of her legs was thrown casually over his. Her gown had ridden up during the night and she could feel his nakedness next to her own. Her face turned crimson.

Very slowly and very carefully she edged away from him and moved as far as the bed would allow. She did not know when he came to bed. It amazed her that anyone as large of frame as he could lower himself so gently into bed as to not awaken her. Then she frowned remembering this particular man had had practice entering her bed. A deep frown furrowed her brow as she thought about him. First he shows his displeasure at taking her for wife, and then he comes to bed quietly and does not wake her. And at no time during the night had he made any husbandly advances!—The man was definitely a mystery.

From the very edge of the bed Leigh studied the man's slumbering face. His features were most pleasant when he was not frowning. His skin was tanned as if he spent a great deal of time working outside. His hair was dark, almost black, and full of soft curls. He wore his sideburns long, and Leigh noted his ears were of nice size and lay against his head not sticking out at odd angles as many men's did. His nose was straight and narrow, his lips full and nicely shaped. He had finely shaped brows and full, thick lashes. She could even see the stubble of his beard. His body was muscular and long. His shoulders were large and his chest powerful and covered with dark hair. Even though she loathed the man, Leigh found she must admit he was extremely handsome. Had he been introduced, she mused, at a ball or other such social function, she would have been quite smitten.

Leigh's stomach started to growl. She had eaten very little the day before and was now quite hungry. Very gingerly she rose from the bed. No sense waking him now, she told herself, she could be made to eat those words about husbandly advances. She picked up her wrapper from beside the bed and tiptoed to the bureau where her shift and gowns were. She glanced at Byron's sleeping face as she picked them up. Just as she placed her hand on the door . . .

"And where are you off to, may I ask?"

Leigh was so startled she nearly jumped out of her skin. She turned slowly and looked into angry blue eyes. It took her several minutes to compose herself and by then the scowl had returned.

"I-I did not mean to awaken you," she managed weakly. "I was only going down for some breakfast." She lowered her head so he would not see the frightened look on her face.

"Do you always go to breakfast in your nightdress?" he sneered.

Leigh's head snapped up, her nose in the air, and her eyes spit fire in his direction. "I'd planned to dress in the room across the hall, sir, so as not to awaken you."

"Well, madam," Byron replied swinging his long legs over the side of the bed and rising, "I am well awake now."

Leigh blushed deeply at his naked body so displayed and quickly reverted her gaze.

Byron swung his arm in front of him as if offering Leigh the room. "Please feel free to dress here in our room, as I am wont to do, and we will go to breakfast together."

Leigh forced her eyes up to his face and glared at him. With as much dignity as she could manage, she strolled back to the chair beside the bed and laid down her clothes. She grabbed her brush and started to do her hair watching him out of the corner of her eye. When all the tangles were gone, she picked up a ribbon and tied the thick mass loosely in back leaving small ringlets to circle her face.

Byron pulled on his pants and was fastening his shirt as

he watched her fix her hair. He stood openly admiring her. He had never seen a more gracefully beautiful woman, her hair, her face—those emerald eyes. He could see the soft curve of her body through the thin veil of her gown, the full breast, tiny waist, inviting hips, and he longed to go to her and take her in his arms—to run his fingers through that thick mass of curls, to caress those tempting breasts, to possess her pink, full lips. He found himself aroused, fully aroused, by the sight of her feminine grooming. That this simple-minded bit of feminine fluff should have such an effect on him made him angry. He cleared his throat, feeling awkward and school-boyish, and clamping his teeth tightly together, he reluctantly looked away.

Leigh reached for her shift, and glancing at him under her lashes, saw that he had no intention of granting her any privacy in which to change. Byron moved to the mirror and started lathering his face to shave watching her in the mirror's reflection.

Leigh turned her back to him and tried to show as little of herself as possible by putting one garment on over another, and then pulling the first off from beneath. It was not easy, and the clothes became tangled many times. She heard Byron chuckle and turned to give him a withering glare. He arched a brow and smiled at her, lather still on one side of his face, and when Leigh saw him openly watching her, she lost all courage and quickly finished dressing. Before she was through he was awaiting her at the door.

"If you are ready, Leigh," he said with a small bow holding the door open wide.

Leigh tossed her curls, put her nose in the air, and walked past him through the door and down the stairs to the common room. When they reached a table, Byron held a chair for her and then seated himself. He smiled in her direction and they sat in silence until Mary arrived and placed tea in front of Leigh and coffee in front of Byron.

As Mary walked away Byron picked up his cup and sipped his coffee, watching Leigh all the while. The frown reappeared on his face and he looked away before he spoke.

"We will be leaving for Richmond as soon as possible. I will see if the O'Malleys have a mount to loan for you. I do not wish to take your wagon and will send someone for it later." He looked her way and arched a brow. "I assume you can ride."

"I can ride, sir," Leigh murmured not looking his way.

"Good. Please gather your things when we finish with our meal for it is a good day's ride to Richmond and the day is already well on its way."

Mary was watching the couple from the doorway. She could not hear what they were saying, but at least they were talking. Leigh looked as if she faired the night well and they appeared somewhat at ease with one another. She returned to her work and when John came in the kitchen later, she was humming a merry tune.

Byron had turned his attention to his meal and seemed completely unaware of Leigh sitting across from him. She watched him as he ate and then made a face at him and stuck out her tongue. Byron looked up and she quickly glanced out the window placing a hand over her mouth and coughing slightly. Byron gave her a puzzled look and again turned his attention to his meal.

The O'Malleys had only one mount and could not

spare him so Byron was forced to take the wagon. The trip would be longer this way and he did not like the idea of his roan pulling it. The roan was much too fine a steed for that, but he saw no other solution, and it did little to improve his mood.

There were tears in both sets of eyes as Mary and Leigh embraced in farewell.

"Leigh, now take care," Mary said brushing the hair from Leigh's brow, "and remember what I said about giving things half a chance," she added softly.

"I will, Mrs. O'Malley. Thank you for all you have done for me and my father," she said looking to her father's grave with tears.

Leigh gave Mary a hug and turned and did the same to John as they both placed a kiss on her cheek. She turned with tears in her eyes and placed one small foot on the step of the wagon and felt herself lifted high into the air by strong arms. She looked over her shoulder and saw Byron's face and jerked her clothes with dignity when he sat her down. Byron seemed not to notice her ire and went to speak a few quiet words with John.

All too soon Leigh was waving goodbye to the kind couple as they stood with arms about one another waving. Leigh could see John patting Mary's shoulder as tears streamed down the woman's face.

Leigh sat next to Byron on the wagon seat and the jolting and bouncing caused her slight frame to bump into his more sturdy one often. She scooted to the very edge of the seat and sat holding on with both hands so she would not fall off.

Byron glanced her way and sighed heavily. Certainly simple-minded, he thought. She does not even have the good sense not to sit on the end of the wagon seat and will most likely end up dusting the road from her rump!

They rode in silence from the inn, the only haven Leigh knew, and with each mile that took her farther away, she became more apprehensive. The ever present frown was on Byron's face and he made no move to speak. Leigh wondered how many women had been married to men they had hardly even spoken with. Why, if it had not been for the few minutes she had had alone with Mrs. O'Malley before they left, she still would not know the man's name! She glanced Byron's way and then looked down. Though she knew many maids wed husbands of their parents choosing, they were at least given time to get acquainted with the man.

As the wagon jolted them along their way Leigh's mind wondered back to England. She thought of the gentlemen she had been acquainted with through her young years. All had been most attentive and courteous, and though Leigh doubted she possessed the beauty they declared they saw in her, she had seen desire and longing in many a man's eye before. Several young men had openly declared their love for her begging a kind word from her in return, and one young and overly exuberant lad had even tried to overstep the boundaries of gentlemanly behavior. But all had cooled their heels, most reluctantly, when Leigh thwarted their advances with a firm look and soft words—that is all but the duke.

She and her father had met the duke on a trip to London. They had been dining at a tavern when the man boldly approached their table and introduced himself. Leigh had immediately felt uneasy with the man.

The duke was well up in years, more than a decade older than her father. His body was thin and brittle looking, the hands snarled and almost claw-like in appearance. When he smiled he revealed missing and rotten teeth, a common affliction of the aged, and his breath was foul, smelling old and almost musty. He dressed in the colorful clothes many found appealing though Leigh considered the fashion foppish and anything but attractive. And though his clothes were of excellent cloth and exquisitely tailored, they were soiled with remains of meals, and both he and his clothing gave off a most unpleasant, and unclean, odor.

The man had insisted they dine with him while in London and Thomas had agreed. Leigh had found the evening long and practically unbearable. It seemed the duke's eyes were forever upon her and he made no effort to hide the desire and lust in his glances.

The man made Leigh terribly uncomfortable and uneasy, for he was more than just unpleasant—he was frightening. There was a cruel, evil gleam in the man's eyes whenever he spoke to her. Leigh was thankful when they departed London for home, thinking she had seen the last of the duke.

They had only been home a short time when the duke came calling. Leigh begged to be excused from seeing the man, claiming a case of vapors, but Thomas was not fooled—he had never known his daughter to suffer from vapors in her life.

That evening after the duke had left Thomas came to Leigh's room to inquire as to her health, and to inform her the duke had plainly and openly asked for her hand.

"Father," Leigh pleaded, "I feel no kindness for the duke—and though I know we are not well acquainted, I fear it will always be so."

Her father had never mentioned the man again nor had the man called again to Leigh's knowledge, and she was extremely thankful. Many fathers would have forced their daughters to marry with a man so rich, and with a title, she knew.

What she and her father did not know, and never would know, was that the duke had put into motion all the circumstances that decided Thomas on traveling to America. The duke had been determined to have Leigh. He thought financial ruin of her father would insure this end, so he carefully and systematically set out to destroy Thomas Burke.

When the duke was informed that Thomas had been forced to sell his estate to settle pressing debts, he again called at the Burke home, this time confident Burke would *offer* him his daughter's hand in marriage. When Thomas not only did not offer Leigh's hand, but again flatly refused the duke's repeated proposal, the duke's mood turned ugly and Thomas saw for the first time the evil aureole that surrounded the duke, and which Leigh had noted almost at once. It set his mind firmly, and finally, upon traveling to America. He would take Leigh far from the reach of this powerful, wicked man.

In many ways, thought Leigh, Jones had reminded her of the duke. They were built much the same, thin and wiry, though Jones was much younger. And she thought with a wrinkle of her slightly up-turned pert nose, they smelled much alike—foul! But what in Jones reminded her most of the duke was his eyes—they both had that same evil, lusty gleam in their eye, the same evil air in their manner.

Leigh was abruptly startled from her thoughts when the wagon wheel struck a rut in the road and she nearly lost her precarious seat. She glanced in Byron's direction and noted he made no movement to catch her should she fall, and he still wore a deep, furrowed frown on his brow. She wondered how her father would feel now seeing her married to a man she loathed and a stranger to boot! Though he was more appealing in appearance than the duke, and his personal hygiene certainly of a better standard, she was quite sure that that was where the favorable comparison stopped. For though her husband was pleasant to look upon, stunningly handsome in fact, no one could accuse him of being witty or charming! She grimaced at him and turned her face and thoughts from him.

The sun hit often on the ring Leigh wore on her finger. Byron noted she had tied it with a ribbon to keep it from slipping from her hand. Looking at it reminded him of the burden he had taken upon himself and he felt as if that ribbon was tied around his neck. She sure does not talk much, he thought. Though he disliked chatty women, this one was far worse with her silence. He had discovered she had a most pleasant speaking voice, but with her continuing silence he was even more convinced that her head was empty and she was rather dull.

They rode on well past midday, each ignoring the other with deliberate purposefullness.

Byron cleared his throat and Leigh quickly glanced his way.

"Leigh, there is food in the back of the wagon, I believe, if you would care to get it. . . ."

Leigh quickly scurried to the rear of the wagon and got the food. Once seated again she looked to Byron expectantly.

"Since we were forced to take the wagon," Byron continued with a frown in her direction, "it is best we not stop to eat. The trip will take long enough as it is. There should be some bread and cheese in the basket if I understood Mrs. O'Malley correctly."

Leigh searched through the basket and handed Byron a piece of bread and a large piece of cheese. She took a small portion for herself and nervously nibbled at it.

They ate in silence as the wagon plotted slowly along. "We will stop around dusk and have a warm meal," Byron explained. Leigh looked at him somewhat bewildered and Byron sighed heavily and rolled his eyes. "You see," he stated as if explaining to a child, "though I said it was a good day's ride to Richmond, now that we are forced to take this blasted wagon the trip is slower and therefore will take longer. We will be lucky to reach Richmond by midday tomorrow."

Leigh nodded her head and then continued to study the view. Byron looked to the heavens and prayed for the patience to deal with this simple-minded creature.

Just before sunset they came to a small clearing and Byron judged it a good place to stop for the night. He helped Leigh down from the wagon and went to gather firewood. Leigh removed the basket of food from the wagon and again searched its contents. She found tea and a small teapot. Byron started a fire and then went to see to his horse as Leigh started preparing the food.

He unhitched the horse and then stood leaning casually against the stallion as he studied his wife. Leigh measured out the tea and then stood, slowly turning, studying the view and searching for a small stream. Byron sighed heavily as he watched her turning in circles with the teapot in her hand.

"Is there something you require?" he called sarcastically.

Leigh looked his way and noted the intense frown on

his face. "W-Water," she replied softly.

Byron swore under his breath and started walking toward her in angry strides. Leigh fearfully backed away, her eyes growing large. When Byron snatched the teapot from her hand, she raised her arm as if to ward off a blow. He walked to the wagon and took the lid off a small barrel, and using the dipper, filled the teapot with water. He turned and practically flung the teapot at Leigh and then again returned to his horse.

Tears threatened to spill over Leigh's eyes. He had no right to be so angry with her just because she forgot that these American wagons were equipped with water barrels. She had seen Samuel Jones filling the water barrel before when she and her father had been traveling in the wagon, but it was something she was unaccustomed to, and she had forgotten it. How did the lout expect her to know such things? People in England hardly rode about with water barrels strapped to their carriages! She angrily slammed the teapot down on the hot coals and went on with her chores.

The sun had set when Byron joined her near the fire. Leigh gracefully poured him a cup of tea and handed him a plate of the warmed stew. Byron took a bit of the stew and then sipped the tea.

"Ugh," he exclaimed. "Tea! I hate tea!"

Leigh looked at him surprised. Being British, she had never before met anyone who didn't like tea.

Byron noted the foolish expression on her face and sighed. "Didn't Mrs. O'Malley pack us any coffee?"

Leigh shook her head to the negative and Byron sighed again and rose to fill his cup with water. When he was seated again he noticed that Leigh was not eating but glancing about in a nervous manner. He sighed heavily several times and tried to ignore her. Finally he could stand it no longer.

"Is there something amiss?" he asked in a loud, sharp tone.

"Mighten there be heathens about?" Leigh asked fearfully. She was surprised when Byron threw back his head and laughed hard. She frowned at him and lowered her eyes chewing at her lower lip.

Byron studied her, amusement in his eyes, but when he saw her fear was real, he spoke gently, "No, Leigh. This is 1801 and the Indians have all but left this part of Virginia. The few that remain need cause you no fear."

Leigh looked to him and studied his face. She was quite aware of the year and felt like telling him so, but his words were gentle and his expression kind, so she said nothing. Byron smiled at her and eventually a soft smile graced her lips as well.

The remainder of the meal was passed in silence and after Leigh cleared away the last of it she walked timidly to the wagon. Byron helped her up.

"I'll just see to the fire. I will not be long."

As he turned and left he did not see the color rising to Leigh's cheeks at the mention of them again sharing a pallet. She removed her gown and shift and quickly folded them neatly and donned her nightdress. She sat brushing her hair and thinking of Byron. She doubted she would escape her wifely duties again. He was not totally unacceptable, she mused. She would still fight him of course, but he was so large, and she so small, she had little doubt as to who the victor would be. Once they reached this Richmond she would find a way to leave him. If she was with child, so be it, the child would not be born a bastard, and he would be born in England!

When Byron entered the wagon, Leigh lay on her side with her back to him, feigning sleep. She could hear him undressing and felt his weight lowered beneath the blankets. She waited for his strong arms to reach and pull her to his side. She waited a long time. And then to her utter amazement she knew they would not, for she could tell by his breathing that he was asleep. She slid closer to share his warmth, a smile on her lips, and was soon asleep herself.

Sometime in the middle of the night Leigh awoke. She lay still listening to see if it had been some strange noise that had awakened her. She heard nothing. She was just beginning to again fall asleep when her eyes flew open wide. She heard nothing! Only the sound of her own breathing. Very slowly Leigh rolled over. Byron was gone!

Leigh was filled with panic. He has left me! she realized. So this was to be her fate. Now that they were a safe distance from the inn, and the O'Malleys, it was small trouble to abandon her. She would most likely never be found. She covered her face with her hands and began to cry. She heard a twig snap close by and was immediately alert. Her hands were trembling as she fearfully called Byron's name in a soft voice. There was no reply. Frantically her hands moved over the contents of the dark wagon searching for something, anything, she could use to protect herself. Her hand touched on the empty teapot and she grasped it firmly and held it high over her head. The minutes ticked by as Leigh listened intently. When several moments passed and she heard no further sounds, she eased toward the opening of the wagon and peeked out. She could just make out the shape of a man coming toward the wagon.

"B-Byron," she called in a hoarse whisper, but he didn't answer. He has not only deserted me, thought Leigh, he has lied to me as well! There are still Indians about!

Leigh eased quietly away from the wagon opening, her body tense with fear. She cursed Byron with one breath, and prayed to God with the next. A slight whimper escaped her lips as the heathen stuck his head into the wagon opening. Leigh shut her eyes tightly and brought the teapot down as hard as she could on the man's head.

"Ow!" Byron shouted. "Wench, have you lost all reasoning?"

Leigh gasped and covered her mouth with her hands. She gave Byron a horrified look and then buried her head in her pillow and began to cry.

Byron studied her as he rubbed his aching head. "Leigh, what is it?" She continued to cry and Byron's anger left him as he watched his wife's delicate body racked with sobbing. "I did not mean to frighten you," Byron offered. "I only went into the woods a small distance."

Leigh looked up to him and her cheeks pinkened when she realized that Byron had gone into the woods to answer a call from nature. Her large emerald eyes were filled with tears and Byron thought she looked like a small frightened animal. He bent over her and gently touched her arm.

"I am sorry if I caused you worry," he said softly.

Leigh wiped her tears on the sleeve of her gown and sniffed. She tried to smile but it looked more like a grimace. "And I am sorry," she sniffed, "I hit you with the teapot."

Byron chuckled and then his face became serious and

his eyes seemed to deepen in color as he gazed into the depths of the emerald pools. Leigh started to feel uncomfortable under his penetrating gaze and quickly rolled over murmuring a goodnight.

Byron frowned at her back. Though Leigh was not the brightest woman he had ever met, she was by far the most beautiful, and he could feel his body yearning for her. He wanted to take her in his arms but found that he felt very awkward with this simple-minded slip of a girl. He laid down with a sigh. He had small doubt she would reject his advances. He could just take her, he thought—she was his wife. But he had already done that once and it weighed heavy on his soul, even if he did have no memory of the act. It was not that he really cared if Leigh desired him, but he had never knowingly forced himself on any woman, there had been no need, and he did not wish to start with his wife.

Once they were in Richmond and he purchased Leigh a new wardrobe, he mused, she would accept him more readily. She may be simple, but she was still a woman, and women loved to get new gowns. He would bide his time, he decided, and soon Leigh would be coyly fluttering her eyelashes at him.

Chapter Three

The following day was passed more pleasantly for Leigh. Byron chatted some and even pointed out the large variety of trees along the road. He was by no means charming, thought Leigh, but at least he was not growling at her.

As the morning progressed they passed several other travelers. Leigh realized that she knew nothing about the geography of her surroundings and that this would greatly hinder her efforts to locate her property. And without the sale of her property she had no funds to return home once she fled from Byron. She studied Byron's mood carefully before she worked up the courage to ask him if Richmond was a large community.

"I'd say it is a fair size place," he answered with a crooked grin.

His smile was easy and his manner light. Leigh studied

him a moment more and then decided to casually pump him for as much information as she dare. Byron seemed unusually delighted with her questions, she noted, and answered them freely, sometimes with a smile and a chuckle.

Byron was watching Leigh closely. The intelligent questions she asked he attributed to a natural curiosity. And as question followed question, he could tell that her mind was quick and bright. He smiled to himself. He had found no flaw to her beauty. She did seem to frighten easily but that was no flaw. Women were meant to be protected. She pleased him well and would make a most suitable mother to his son, he decided. He had noted that when she smiled slightly, small dimples appeared in her cheeks and he longed to see her smile full faced.

When Leigh boldly asked him about his home his mood changed with frightening speed and the frown returned to his handsome features.

"Royal Oaks is its name. It was so called by my grandfather. You may not like it. I doubt it much resembles your beloved England."

His words were clipped and he turned his face from hers as if he wished to talk no more. Leigh did not know what she had said to anger the man, but she could tell by his manner that he was indeed angry. They rode on in silence with Leigh glancing his way from time to time, a puzzled expression on her face.

A man approached them on horseback and as he neared their side his eyes seemed to devour Leigh. He smiled broadly and raised his hat in greeting and then quickly shoved his hat back on his head and hurried on his way when he saw the intense scowl on Byron's face.

When they arrived in Richmond Leigh was greatly

surprised. Byron had said it was of fair size, but Leigh never dreamed it would look like this. The city was much larger and grander than she ever had expected. She had thought it would be small and poorly built like the last community she and her father had stopped in. She had been through so much wilderness of late that she had thought civilization was forever behind her.

Leigh chatted gaily about the large building and crowded streets and Byron nodded, saying little, as he watched the dimples that played in her cheeks. He noted many men's heads turn as they followed Leigh with their eyes and he smiled inwardly.

Byron stopped the wagon in front of a hotel that was quite impressive on outward appearance. Leigh wondered if Byron was aware of how much such lodging cost and if he could afford such accommodations. Byron stepped down from the wagon, and reaching two long, strong arms up, grabbed Leigh about the waist and swung her down and set her on the walk none too gently. Leigh gave his back a sour look as he reached inside the wagon to remove their few belongings.

Several passersby glanced at the couple and Leigh felt her cheeks flush. She and Byron appeared beggars in comparison to the people on the busy walks, and the wagon looked oddly out of place stopped there on the street, for though the streets were busy with fine carriages and passing landaus, theirs was the only wagon in sight. She noted that Byron seemed completely at ease with his surroundings and had an almost pleasant expression on his face as he held the hotel door for her.

Leigh entered the hotel lobby and gasped. She was overwhelmed by the grandness of the place. She had never stayed in lodgings this fine, not even when she had accompanied her father on trips to London.

The lobby was large with very high ceilings. Sofas and chairs were scattered about the room in small groups. The floor was covered with a carpet of no small beauty and the room smelled of men's pipe tobacco and women's cologne—not an unpleasant odor, but warm and inviting. The lobby desk was straight ahead, a wide gracefully curving staircase to the left. Everything about the place bespoke quality and gracious living and Leigh noted there was not a speck of dust or dirt to be seen.

A maid and several porters bustled through the lobby in different directions obviously intent in their duties. Two couples stood speaking in soft tones near the center of the room, an older gentleman with large jowls and a distinguished mustache napped in a chair to one side of the room, his mouth hanging open in a most undignified fashion, and Leigh grinned.

As her eyes roamed the room, the room grew suddenly still and Leigh realized that all heads had turned their way. Two matronly ladies descending the stairs' had stopped to stare before their heads came together in hurried whispers. Leigh was acutely aware of the appearance she and Byron presented. Though Byron's coat was of good quality and well made, covered with the dust and dirt of the road, it was difficult to tell. And she wore her oldest gown.

Byron stood beside her, his arms filled with bundles, and again he seemed unaffected by the curious, disapproving stares they received. He motioned toward the desk with a nod of his head.

"I'll—I'll just wait here," Leigh said timidly.

"Very well," Byron replied easily walking toward the desk.

Standing alone Leigh was now more self-conscious than ever, and though people were no longer gaping, and quiet hushed tones again filled the room, quick glances were still cast in her direction.

Leigh glared at Byron's back. No doubt he did this intentionally, she thought, just to humiliate me! She bit at her lower lip and shyly took several steps toward a corner where the light was less bright and made several swipes at her rumpled, dirty gown. She was mortified when clouds of dust billowed from the gown. She wished desperately she could find a dark hole to hide in and turned pleading eyes, and a crimson face, toward the lobby desk praying Byron would soon finish. She again wondered if he possessed the proper coin for such lodgings and knew her embarrassment would be complete if he did not and they must leave under curious stares. Or more likely, she thought with a groan, they would simply be asked to leave because of their shabby appearance. She gave Byron's back a hateful look. Didn't he know hotels as grand as this accepted only persons of wealth and the highest standing? And she and Byron were certainly not gentry!

She felt tears of anger threatening to spill and she whirled about looking out the window at the passerbys and trying desperately to regain her composure.

"Leigh."

Leigh jumped nervously and turned to see Byron close behind her.

"Our room is this way," he commented indicating the stairs.

Leigh gave him an odd look, truly surprised that he had indeed acquired a room, and then raising her chin a notch, she walked briskly past him toward the stairs where she saw a porter waiting with their bundles.

As they climbed the wide staircase to their room Leigh was aware of Byron close behind her. She chewed her lip nervously at the thought that they would again be sharing a bed—and somehow that was quite different from sharing a blanket spread on the floor of a wagon. And there were no O'Malleys here!

Their room was large and sunny. A double bed flanked by night stands stood on one wall, a bureau on another. There was a table and two chairs placed in front of one window and a wash stand and mirror in the corner by the door. The bedspread and drapes were very nice, she noted, and a lovely carpet of blue covered the floor. Again Leigh noted the cleanliness of the place.

The porter placed their few belongings on the bureau and gave them a disapproving look askew as he did. Leigh blushed and went immediately to the window turning her back to all.

Byron also noted the boy's aloof appraisal and he chuckled inwardly. The boy must be new at the hotel, thought Byron, for he did not remember seeing him before.

As the boy passed Byron heading for the door, his face broke into a smile. "Thank you sir," he said as Byron placed a coin in his hand, and then the porter's smile became a wide grin as he noted the denomination of the coin and he thanked Byron again bobbing his head rapidly as he closed the door softly behind him.

Byron studied Leigh's stiff back a moment before unpacking his few belongings.

"Leigh, I need see to a few errands while here," he commented unpacking his shaving things from his saddle bag. "Is there anything you require before I leave?"

When Leigh turned to face him their eyes met and she quickly looked away before answering, always feeling uncomfortable under the scrutiny of those deep blue eyes.

"Ah, if I may, ah, is it permissible for me to have water sent up to bath?" she asked fearing his reaction to this small, but costly, request.

"Of course," he replied easily. "I'll see to it before I leave."

Leigh murmured a soft thank you as Byron left the room. She turned again to study the city from the window and to watch for Byron to appear on the walk below. She noted the busy activity of the city with interest. Several shops could be seen, people strolling leisurely past studying the wares they had to offer, landaus stopping in the busy street to pick up passengers or leave them off. A small boy came running down the walk rolling a hoop with a stick, a floppy-eared brown dog close at his heels, and Leigh smiled at the pair.

A tall man with broad shoulders caught her eye and Leigh watched him a moment more before she realized it was Byron. He made his way down the walk at a leisurely pace, his step agile and carefree, and Leigh could not help but notice how well the man carried himself. He, indeed, was a handsome man she thought as he disappeared from sight. She was curious as to his errand and just how long he would be absent from the room. She wrung her hands wondering if she should gather her few belongings and leave now. But where would she go? She knew nothing of the city. No—she decided. There would be many opportunities to flee in the near future.

She would bide her time and make some plans before she ran haphazardly out into the busy town.

A short time later two young maids arrived with buckets of bath water. They filled the brass tub carried in by two porters and turned to leave.

"Will there by anything else, Mrs. Marsh?" one asked.

Leigh started to look about for Mrs. Marsh and caught herself just in time. "No, nothing else. Thank you."

Leigh sighed as she eased into the warm bath. The water felt grand after the dust and dirt of the road. She washed her long hair and scrubbed her skin until it was a rosy pink. When the thought occurred to her that Byron could return at any moment she finished her bath with considerable haste.

With her wrapper on she went to sit on the side of the bed where she could look out on the city as she brushed her hair dry.

There was a rap at the door and Leigh bid them enter. It was one of the maids returning to empty the tub. With Byron still absent Leigh decided it was a good opportunity to question the girl and mayhap learn some information about Richmond.

"I have never been to Richmond before," she said trying to sound casual. "It is much larger than I expected."

"Oh, yes, ma'am," the maid replied. "My ma says it ain't stopped growing since it became the capital way back in '79."

Leigh kept the conversation light and asked few questions. She found the maid had the gift of gab, and before the girl had left Leigh had learned much helpful information, not the least of which, that Richmond was on a river. The James River to be exact. Though you could not see it from the hotel, as the maid had pointed out, it was a large river and fed into the ocean. If she could get a voyage to the coast, she thought, surely she could book passage on a voyage sailing for England—that is once she had the money.

It did make her wonder why her father had chosen to take a voyage docking in Boston when he could have booked passage on a ship docking here on the coast and much closer to their new home. He had said something about business, she recalled, that must have been it. She sighed. If only they could have avoided that long journey across land and Samuel Jones, mayhap her father would still be with her.

At the thought of her father tears came to her eyes. How much she loved and missed him. Now she would never have love in her life again. She was married to a man she loathed, and though he had shown her some small kindnesses, she knew he felt no love for her either. She would be returning to England to live with cousins she hardly knew and live out her life as an unloved wife with an ocean separating her from her legal spouse.

As a young girl her father had often told her stories of knights in shining armor and how they always managed to save the fair young damsels. Leigh had had a young girl's dream of one day finding her knight, and like her father's stories, living happily ever after. Now that dream was lost forever. She knew there was no knight for her and that she would never have love in her life again.

The door opened and Byron entered carrying several bundles. Leigh jumped up from the bed as if it were on fire and quickly turned her face from his. Byron noted the tears in her eyes as he laid the packages on the bed. He had always been touched by a woman's tears and wanted to say something to soothe Leigh. He guessed Leigh was still mourning the death of her father and remembering

78

his own parents' passing, his sympathy went out to the girl.

The women Byron kept company with were always light and gay and he found he had no experience in this area. Feeling the need to say something and break the silence, he opened his mouth and said the first thing that popped into his head.

"It is lucky I ordered these clothes sometime back," he commented pointing to the bundles on the bed. "My tailor is here in Richmond and when I ordered these I had no idea I would be needing them so soon or so desperately."

Leigh glanced his way briefly and then continued to study the view from the window.

Byron cleared his throat and continued. "I took only a change of shirt with me when I left home on what I thought to be a short journey. I have grown exceedingly tired of this travel worn coat I wear," he commented holding his coat out wide and looking to Leigh. She did not even glance his way. He cleared his throat again and started to unwrap the bundles. "As soon as I bathe and dress we will go downstairs and dine. I think you will like the food here, Leigh, it is very good."

At Leigh's continued silence Byron felt more awkward than ever. Well, he thought, that certainly lightened her mood, you oaf! A weeping woman always feels much improved after a gentleman has given her the latest of information concerning his wardrobe! Byron was agitated that this slip of a girl could fluster him so, and the room remained silent as water was again brought up for a bath.

Leigh kept her back turned as Byron disrobed and climbed into the tub. She finished brushing her hair dry and went to get her only remaining gown suitable for evening wear. It was soft pink with a round low neck and short puffy sleeves. The skirt was full and flowed generously from the small fitted waist. She no longer possessed the proper amount of petticoats to make the gown stand out as it should, but giving the skirt a pat with her hand, she vowed not to dwell on the matter and started to fix her hair.

Leigh had noted the dress of the women of Richmond and she saw they wore the latest of fashion and that most dressed very well indeed. She took special care with her hair and put it atop her head leaving small curls to fall where they may. She hoped she would be suitably dressed when she and Byron went down to dinner and nervously bit at her lower lip. She had just finished smoothing her stockings into place when Byron asked her if she was ready. She had been so intent on her toilet, she had forgotten he was in the room and flinched at the sound of his voice.

She turned to see him looking quite handsome. His coat was of the latest cut, black in color with gray lapels and trim on the cuffs. His breeches and vest were also gray and his shirt was flawlessly white. He wore black stockings and his shoes were also black. As she stood taking in his appearance, she knew he would draw much attention from the women present tonight.

Byron's eyes shone and deepened in color as he stood looking at her. The dress was most becoming and he liked the way she had fixed her hair. There would be many a man openly admiring his wife this night, he thought. He would have to keep Leigh close by his side if he did not want every young buck tripping over himself to make her acquaintance.

"There is just one thing before we go, Leigh," Byron said looking at her in an odd manner. "If I may have the ring you wear, I've worn it these many long years and I am afraid my hand misses its weight."

So, he does not want anyone to suspect we are married, thought Leigh as she unwrapped the ribbon from the ring. She walked stiffly toward Byron holding the ring out in front of her.

Byron grabbed the ring and then her hand. "Besides," he said placing a small gold band on her finger, "I think this one will be a better fit." There was a gentle smile on his lips as he looked at her surprised face. Leigh looked to the ring, then to Byron, and then back down to the ring. Her mouth was hanging open slightly and Byron reached up with one finger and gently pushed it shut.

"Come, pet," he said offering her his arm, "I don't know about you, but I am famished."

Leigh looked at him slightly confused and then a soft smile graced her lips as she took his arm.

Many heads turned their way as the handsome couple entered the dining room. The room was large with a high ceiling, and there were several crystal chandeliers holding a multitude of candles. The floor was covered with a cranberry carpet and the seats and backs of the chairs were covered in a fabric of the same hue.

They were escorted to a table near a huge fireplace. The table was covered with a white cloth, set with china and sterling and a good quality of crystal, Leigh noted. As Byron assisted her with her chair, she glanced about under her lashes at the other women present. She relaxed some to see that she was suitably dressed. Her gown was not as fine as many she saw, but that was of no matter. She noticed many heads come together in whispers as they looked their way and she blushed. She wondered how many of these people were acquaintances of Byron's.

Byron gazed at the lovely portrait Leigh made sitting there across from him. He had seen the admiring looks she drew from the others present as they entered the dining room and he smiled to himself as the waiter approached the table.

"Mr. Marsh, how good to see you again," the waiter said with a grin.

"How have you been, Ralph?" Byron replied with an easy smile.

"Just fine, sir, and you?"

Byron nodded his head and Leigh quickly lowered hers, her cheeks pinkening, as the waiter glanced her way.

Byron noted the curious look on Ralph's face as he gazed at Leigh, and he chuckled inwardly, surprised that the hotel grapevine had not worked its way to the dining room yet. Soon enough all the employees of the hotel would know that Mr. Marsh was married. He picked up the menu and began giving Ralph their order.

"Is there anything special you desire, pet?"

Leigh glanced his way and then cast a look askew at the waiter. "Whatever you decide will be suitable with me," she replied in a timid voice.

Byron ordered their meal and an excellent wine to accompany it.

"Your steak as usual, sir?" Ralph said curteously.

"Yes, Ralph."

"And the lady's?"

Byron glanced to Leigh's averted face. "Slightly more well done I should judge."

"Yes, sir," the waiter smiled.

Ralph turned to leave wondering where Mr. Marsh had found such a lovely flower as the woman accompanying him this evening. The women he dined with in the past had been quite different in nature. Though all were attractive and of good family, none were as timid or shy as this woman, and none as beautiful.

Byron and Leigh passed the time quietly waiting for the meal to arrive. Leigh hated these awkward moments and was relieved when the food finally arrived.

They were served beef sliced thick and still rare. It had not been boiled, as Leigh was accustomed to, and she found it very tasty. Leigh glanced to Byron from time to time but always found him intent on his food.

"Pet, more wine?"

She looked up to see Byron grinning at her. "Yes, please. Just a small amount."

Byron filled her glass and the meal continued in silence. When it was complete Leigh found she had grown sleepy with her stomach so full and the aid of the wine.

They returned to their room and Byron seated himself in a chair near the bed as Leigh turned her back and started to undress.

Byron lounged quietly in the chair, his long legs stretched out and crossed in front of him, his hands clasped and resting on his stomach. His gaze caressed her back casually as she removed her shift and donned her nightdress. She folded her gown neatly and put it away. She glanced Byron's way, and when their eyes met, hers hurriedly continued on around the room. She got her brush and went to stand by the bed as she brushed her hair with trembling hands.

As Byron watched her it took all of his control not to rush to her and take her into his arms. She is so lovely, he thought, I hope she soon shows some softening toward me. He did not know how much longer he could keep himself in check. Though he planned to be patient, a man's patience was not infinite, and he would not wait forever. He rose from the chair with a sigh, stretched, and started to undress for bed.

"We will be going to the clothier's tomorrow, Leigh," he commented as he removed his coat. "I have noted you have need of some new gowns."

"I am sorry, sir," Leigh snapped, her voice defensive, "if my poor apparel embarrasses you."

Byron turned and looked at her stiff back turned to him. "Leigh, I meant no insult on your gown," he said, "only that you will need a larger selection of gowns before we travel on to my home." A small frown wrinkled his brow as he studied her and then his voice rose in anger. "My home is more than a day's journey from here, madam, and I cannot be running to Richmond whenever you feel the need of a new gown!"

Leigh whirled to face him, her nose in the air. "I do not recall, sir," she quipped arching one fine brow, "having asked you to buy me any new gowns now."

Byron scowled. "Leigh, don't use that tone with me," he growled.

"I'll use any tone I wish," she replied primly.

Byron was at her side in an instant. He roughly grabbed her arms and stood looking hard into her eyes. Leigh realized at once that she had gone too far and was immediately sorry. Byron's teeth were clamped tightly together, his jaw set, and the angry blue eyes bore into her, his strong fingers biting into the soft flesh of her arms.

"Please, Byron," she said in a small voice as tears appeared in her eyes. "You are hurting me."

Byron released her with an oath realizing that she had used his given name for the first time, and it had been with fear. He jerked at his clothes angrily.

"Go to bed," he instructed. "The hour is late and we have a busy day ahead."

Leigh watched him with frightened eyes and without another word climbed into bed. Her hands were shaking violently as she pulled the covers tightly under her chin.

The only other man in Leigh's life, her father, had had an even and easy character. Not like this man, thought Leigh, with his moodiness and impatient manner. And though Leigh's father's discipline of her had always been firm, it had been dealt out in the most gentle of methods, and Byron's quick temper absolutely terrified her.

Byron blew out the candle before removing his pants and then climbed into bed beside her. The minutes ticked by. Leigh was most uncomfortable in her present position, but she did not want to figit and arouse Byron's further anger—or anything else for that matter! She lay perfectly still listening to Byron sigh heavily several times and fearing at any moment he would again turn his anger on her.

The man was a true puzzle to Leigh. One minute he was courteous, even kind, and the next he was impatient and angry. And he obviously possessed some wealth, as the O'Malleys had surmised, for he acquired this room, and by the conversation he carried on with their waiter at dinner, he had stayed at this fine hotel before. Yet he did not dress to the dictates of fashion as most wealthy persons did, but rather seemed to dress to please himself. And he did not appear to have a bloated image of himself as many people of means did. In fact, as much as Leigh hated to admit it, the man had several admirable qualities.

When a long time later Byron's breathing was slow and even, and Leigh thought him asleep, she moved slowly and in small degrees until she was more comfortable. Finally with the help of the wine from dinner, she eventually fell asleep.

Byron laid awake beside her and stared at the ceiling. Women! He would never understand them. He thought she would be thrilled at his offer to buy her the clothes suitable for his wife. But instead she acts insulted! He had not meant to lose his temper with her, he must try and be more patient. With her constant presence and watching her dress and undress, it was sorely testing his moods. He had never been long on patience, he knew, but now he must try to be more pleasant, and damn it, woo his own wife!

He cursed her in his mind and tried hard not to think of her all soft and beautiful beside him. He finally fell asleep with a frown on his brow.

The next morning the sky was clear and bright. Byron roughly shook Leigh awake and turned away as she rose and dressed. She waited until he was done shaving to use the mirror and when he walked away she scurried to it and started doing her hair. She tried arranging it in a bun at the base of her neck but her hands were trembling so, she finally gave up, and tied it with a ribbon.

Leigh noted Byron was not in the best of moods and they passed the morning meal in silence. As they rose from the table Leigh begged to be excused a moment, her cheeks pinkening, and Byron escorted her to the door leading to the convenience behind the hotel and stood patiently waiting for her return.

"Byron!"

Byron turned at the sound of his name and saw Cynthia Motley walking toward him, a bright smile on her face. Though Byron was relieved that it was no one who would carry the news of Leigh to his home, Cynthia being a resident of Richmond, he was not overjoyed to see the woman again.

Cynthia was an attractive young woman of good family and a pleasant enough evening's companion, but to Byron she was just one of many such women, and he felt no special attraction for her. About the same time Byron had begun to tire of her company, finding her increasingly dull, Cynthia had started showing signs of possessiveness. Byron had never called on her again.

"How grand to see you again, Byron," Cynthia said as she reached his side.

"How have you been, Cynthia?" Byron inquired politely.

"Just fine, Byron, though I must admit," Cynthia said coyly lowering her eyes and batting her lashes, "I have been disappointed that you have not found time to visit Richmond for simply months now."

Byron looked at her and arched a brow. He could think of nothing he had done to give the woman the impression that he would call on her every time he happened to be in the city.

"I've been busy," Byron replied, his manner brisk. He glanced toward the door where Leigh would return and casually placed a hand on Cynthia's elbow and steered her away.

"Surely not so busy you can't find time to visit *me*," Cynthia said trying to appear shy yet assured.

Byron felt himself growing truly agitated with the woman and he quickened his step toward the lobby door. "Cynthia, a woman as attractive as yourself must have so many suitors that I truly doubt you have had time to notice my absence."

"Oh, Byron," Cynthia giggled, again fluttering her lashes.

When Leigh returned she was surprised to find Byron gone. Her eyes quickly searched the room and she saw him standing near the lobby door, an attractive woman with him. She could tell they were conversing, and that they obviously were well acquainted, for Byron held the woman's arm and the woman was smiling broadly at him. Well, thought Leigh, her spine growing stiff, he certainly wasted no time! Although she knew that neither she nor Byron had desired their marriage, and that there were no kind feelings in the relationship, she had still somehow expected the man to show her the courtesy of not flaunting his rutting ways in public. She chided herself for being so foolish as to expect any show of decency from this man.

"Cynthia, I'm afraid I must beg your leave," Byron stated. "I have pressing matters to attend."

"Of course," Cynthia replied, her voice sounding hurt. "But you must promise to call," she added placing a hand possessively on his chest.

"Cynthia, I—really doubt I shall find the opportunity. I don't plan to stay long in Richmond," Byron stated as he opened the door wide for her.

"Oh," she said, and there was no mistaking the disappointment written on the woman's face.

They stepped onto the walk and Cynthia gave Byron a look much like a love-sick puppy. Byron bid her a courteous goodday and watched as she turned and walked hurriedly away.

Leigh had watched the entire exchange closely and when she saw that Byron was not going to leave with the woman she quickly spun about and opened and closed the door behind her, as though she were just returning.

Not a moment too soon, thought Byron when he noted Leigh's return. Not that he really owed Leigh any kind of explanation, he thought, it was simply easier if the two women did not meet. He smiled broadly at Leigh as she approached his side.

"Ready, pet?" he asked politely.

Leigh nodded, refusing to look his way.

When they stepped onto the walk Byron commented what a pleasant day it was. "We often have warm spells in October, and even into November," he explained. "It is called Indian Summer."

Leigh didn't care much for the name but she found the idea of warm days into a time she considered to be winter, most charming.

"Since it is such a nice day," Byron continued, "mayhap you would like to walk. It is only a small distance to the clothier's, or if you prefer we can hire a carriage."

"No," Leigh replied rather snippy, "I would enjoy the walk, thank you."

Byron smiled broadly at her and eventually she gave him a timid smile in return, just the hint of dimples in her cheeks. Byron offered her his arm and they strolled off down the street.

Leigh noted many women turned to look at Byron and

though she had no feelings for the man herself, it pleased her somehow that she was the one on his arm.

The walks were full of people and they passed many shops along the way. Cobblers, clothiers, silver shops, candle shops, the list was endless. Leigh had never dreamed the city would be like this and she noted there was very little one could not buy in Richmond if one had the proper coin. They passed a millinery shop and Leigh saw a sign in the window stating a clerk was required within. She made a mental note of the shop's name and location. It could prove helpful when she fled from Byron. Though she had never held a position before, she knew she had a good head on her shoulders, and besides, she thought, how difficult could it be to sell hats?

They turned the corner and Byron led her to a shop specializing in women's gowns. He had been careful not to choose the one he knew Ella Borough to frequent. He knew how gossipy women could be and he had no desire for the news of his marriage to precede him home.

He had been relieved to see no one he knew in the dining room last night. He came to the city several times a year and was fairly well known. Of course he had run into Cynthia this morning but no real harm was done—the two women did not see each other, much less meet. And though they knew him at the hotel, it was well managed and he knew any employee caught gossiping about the guests would be immediately dismissed, and more important, he knew the employees knew it as well. Still, they would be in the city for no less than two weeks to have Leigh properly wardrobed, and he doubted his luck would hold.

As they entered the small shop Leigh noted the costly look of the place. A woman of middle age approached them with a broad smile. Leigh was amazed at the woman's energetic step for she was much overweight and her gown seemed to pull at the seams begging for release.

The owner of the shop herself came to wait on the couple. She noted the fine cut and cloth of Byron's coat and expected an order for several costly gowns for the young woman with him.

"May I be of some service?" she asked smiling brightly at Byron.

"Yes, my wife is in need of several gowns and other items," Byron said glancing about the shop.

"This way, madam," the woman said with a slight bow and a gesture of her arm.

Leigh walked to the table the woman indicated and was handed a stack of sketches.

"These are the latest from Paris," the owner assured her. Leigh glanced to Byron but his face was averted. She went through the sketches slowly, glancing his way from time to time. He stood at the window looking out at the city and appeared to have lost all interest in the matter. She quickly chose several gowns to her liking that did not appear to be too expensive. She sighed dreamily over the sketches of the elaborate gowns. Her father had purchased many fine gowns for her in the past but none as lovely as the exquisite gowns this shop had to offer.

"Would you like to select fabric for matching shifts?" the owner asked after Leigh had finished selecting the fabric for the gowns.

"Mayhap for the one evening gown," said Leigh glancing askew at Byron, "but not for the day gowns."

She finished her selections and turned to join Byron lounging near the door. She hoped he would not be angry that she had selected more than a few gowns. She had been very careful to choose only the plainest the shop had to offer.

"Leigh," Byron snapped walking toward her, "you could not possibly have finished this quickly."

"I chose five gowns, Byron," Leigh said hesitantly.

"I have told you I cannot be running to Richmond every time you feel the need of a new gown," he said with a frown. "Now come and let us complete this and have it done."

She looked to him astonished and the frown wrinkling his brow deepened.

"I can see, madam, that I am going to have to assist you with this matter."

The owner grinned from ear to ear and handed the sketches to Byron.

Leigh stood by in amazement as Byron chose one gown after another. All he indicated must have matching shifts and many were chosen with matching coats for day or capes for evening. Leigh could not believe her eyes. Her father had never bought her more than seven gowns at once and Byron must have chosen over forty! And he paid no mind as to how costly the gowns appeared.

"Now should we choose the cloths," the owner stated merrily looking to Byron.

"My wife will choose," Byron said arching a brow at Leigh. He handed the owner one sketch of an evening gown. "I would prefer this in emerald green however."

The owner glanced to Leigh's eyes, and smiling, nodded her head.

"Leigh, choose from the tables over there," Byron said pointing across the room to table that held bolts of fabric. "The cloths there appear to be of an excellent quality."

The owner's smile deepened as she led Leigh to the tables of costly fabric. She wondered at the young woman's silence. She would have been bubbling at the wardrobe just selected.

Byron stood across the shop watching the two women. Leigh chose well he noted. Had she chosen anything he did not approve of, he would have immediately gone to her aid.

When the women were done with the lengthy selection he strolled casually to their side.

"There will be several social events we will be attending in the coming months," he said to the owner. "We will expect all the gowns completed and delivered to my home before eight weeks time." He glanced to Leigh askew and noted her downcast face. "As for now," he continued, "we will expect ten of the day gowns and half that number of evening gowns delivered to my hotel within a fortnight."

"Oh yes, sir," the owner was quick to assure him nodding her head so briskly that her fat cheeks jiggled. "Everything will be as you desire." Her mind was racing trying to estimate the worth of the order. Why, she would make a small fortune on what the handsome gentleman had ordered! To her further amazement, Byron questioned her about furs to line some of the coats and capes.

"Sir," she grinned, "just let me take your wife to the back and have her measurements taken and I will bring you some samples of what we have." She smiled at Leigh and indicated a curtained doorway at the rear of the shop. "We won't be a moment," she assured Byron.

She returned a moment later, alone, and with an arm full of furs. She placed them on the table with a "whoof!"

"My best seamstress is taking your wife's measurements," she said out of breath as she spread the furs out for Byron to inspect.

Before Leigh returned Byron had chosen the furs, a dozen nightdresses, camisoles, handkerchiefs, and various other items for her, all without her knowledge.

It was very late in the day when they left the small shop. Leigh was hungry. She was relieved when Byron led her to a small tavern for lunch.

There was a frown on her face as Byron assisted her with her chair. She was puzzled by Byron's generosity to her. She knew the O'Malleys had thought him a man of means, but his show of wealth overwhelmed her! Why did he buy me so many gowns? Leigh wondered. He does not love me. I don't even think he likes me. She concluded it was a matter of his vanity. Forever burdened with her on his arm, he was determined to make her a pleasant burden to look upon. He could obviously afford it, so why not? It was not for her he had purchased the gowns, she decided, but for himself.

Leigh was very quiet and Byron watched her closely. She sat eating her lunch in a dainty manner and not glancing his way. She had said nothing about the gowns. He had expected some show of excitement over the clothes he bought for her. What must he do to please her? he wondered.

After lunch, to Leigh's continuing amazement, he again led her from shop to shop. Hats were chosen, many with matching muffs. Gloves and shoes, the list was endless. Leigh, ever the woman, loved to shop, but even she was growing weary of the endless procession.

At last they returned to the hotel, Byron overloaded with packages. When they reached their room Leigh collapsed in a chair with a sigh. Byron noted her tired appearance and left the room to order dinner for them sent up to their room. Leigh was unpacking the many gifts he had bought for her when he returned. He sat in the chair studying her closely, his eyes taking on a hooded appearance.

When their meal arrived, he held her chair for her with a smile, but she refused to look his way. Byron tried several times to engage her in conversation, all to no avail. She spoke only when spoken to and her answers were short and clipped. When the meal was cleared away, Leigh quickly undressed, and not even brushing her hair, climbed into bed.

Byron still sat quietly in the chair. He did not know how much longer he could restrain himself. He thought she would have shown some tenderness toward him after today, but she said nothing and seemed to accept her wardrobe as her due. It was her due as his wife, he thought, but still he had expected some show of gratitude. Why Ella would have been jumping for joy were she the one gifted.

He rose slowly and stretched and walked toward the window glancing at Leigh askew. He realized she was already sleeping and he took several steps closer and stood looking down at her sleeping form. She was so lovely. He wondered at her lack of reaction for his gifts and remembered she had been unusually quiet after they left the clothier's today—almost appearing upset with his generosity.

He frowned as he began removing his clothes and there was a deep scowl on his face by the time he roughly fell into bed jerking the covers. How dare she be so content while he was having his insides torn apart! He turned his back to her, hoping he had awakened her, and tried desperately not to think of her beside him.

The following days flew by for Leigh and crawled by for Byron. Leigh's mind was ever active with her plans to escape him and return home to England. Byron found little to occupy himself other than strolling the streets with Leigh and showing her the city. He was normally a very active man with the running of his plantation and the idleness he now found had him dwelling more and more on Leigh's small waist and round breast. It was sorely testing his moods.

Byron had started to leave Leigh alone in the mornings while she bathed. She had no idea where he went, she assumed he was below in the lobby. That, and the fact that the sun was high, were the only things that kept her from fleeing while he was gone. She wished he would leave her for a short time at night, though she was grateful for the privacy in which to bathe.

Since they had little to occupy their hours, Byron was determined to spend as little time as possible in the hotel room. In the days that followed they would stroll the streets of the city and Byron would point out various things he thought would interest Leigh. They would stop at a tavern or inn for lunch and then spend the afternoons again shopping for Leigh's wardrobe.

Byron had shown Leigh many things he felt interesting.

"This is St. John's Church, Leigh," he said smiling and pointing to the building. "It is where Patrick Henry made his famous speech."

"Patrick Henry?" Leigh said puzzled.

"He was a patriot in our war with Britian. He made a

now famous speech here saying, 'give me liberty or give me death.'"

"Oh," Leigh said showing little interest.

Another time he showed her a spot where Benedict Arnold had burned down a cannon factory when he raided Richmond.

"Was Benedict Arnold a patriot?" she questioned with large, innocent eyes.

"No, Leigh," Byron said exasperated. "Benedict Arnold was a traitor. He fought on the side of the British."

"Oh," Leigh replied showing no interest at all. If this Arnold fought on the side of the British, he was no traitor to her.

She was aware that Byron seemed to always show her things concerning the war between their two countries. She considered it to be insulting and very rude of him, and with each such case, her anger grew.

Byron was doing anything to fill their hours. He thought Leigh would enjoy seeing famous places concerning the war. But she showed little or no interest and Byron felt he was boring her. It served to make his moods more foul.

They had returned to their room after dinner and Byron flopped down on the bed and bending his arm, he rested his head on his hand and watched Leigh undress for bed.

"What do you think of Richmond, Leigh?" he questioned as she stepped out of her gown.

"It is a very nice city," she commented dryly.

"Just a very nice city," he said sitting up on the side of the bed and frowning.

"Yes," she replied glancing over her shoulder at him.

His frown deepened and he rose from the bed and started to undress. He was insulted that she found his tours so boring. He had tried to be a most charming guide and he resented her lack of interest. No matter what he did, she treated him cooly, and he had still seen no fluttering of lashes from her. His anger grew as he jerked off his coat.

"You must forgive us backward Americans," he snapped impatiently. "Our cities are not full of old cathedrals and palaces of kings!"

Leigh glared at him and started to brush her hair.

Byron jerked his stock and then sat down in the chair to remove his shoes. He pulled off one shoe and threw it hard to the floor.

"And you must forgive Richmond as well," he barked. "Though Virginia is one of the oldest colonies, we have not had time to build like your fancy London."

Leigh turned to him and stuck her nose in the air. "At least in London, sir, one does not take a person about and show them memorabilia from the war between our two countries."

Byron pulled off his other shoe, stood and walked toward her holding it in his hand. "That, my dear madam," he shouted, shaking the shoe in her face, "is because you lost the war!"

"That makes not the slightest difference to one's manners," Leigh angrily replied shaking her brush in his face.

Byron stood scowling at her, confused. What had manners to do with it? He threw his shoe to the floor and stomped away. Leigh slammed her brush to the bureau and angrily strolled to the bed.

Byron turned and snarled at her as she climbed into bed. She daintily fluffed her pillow while glaring at him, and then neatly arranged the cover. Then she let out a huff and flopped back on the bed jerking the covers about her.

Byron blew out the candles and removed his pants. He climbed into bed turning his back to her turned back. He jerked the covers and Leigh lay seething with rage but not enough courage to jerk them back. Now he had most of the blanket on his side of the bed!

"There is no one more ill of manners than a poor loser," she heard Byron hiss.

"Unless it is an ungraceful winner," Leigh whispered.

She felt Byron sit up beside her and at first was frightened that he had heard her words, but then he laid back down and jerked the covers again. Now she had no cover at all!

She lay there silent, her eyes moving rapidly back and forth. She marveled at her own bravery and actions toward the man and was thankful he had not raged at her, or mayhap even struck her! She got so cold she eventually scooted slightly closer to him, but found she still had only enough blanket to cover her legs and hips. She wrapped her arms about herself to help ward off the cold and was just beginning to relax when Byron rolled against her.

She was now wide awake but fought to keep her breathing regular, as if she were sleeping. She felt Byron sit up and she panicked. But to her astonishment, he lifted the covers and gently placed them about her, tucking them snugly about her neck. He laid back down with a sigh and moved away from her.

Leigh had a faint memory, as from a dream, of warm caressing hands, tenderness, and pleasure. A tingle went through her body at the faint memory. There was a soft smile on her face as she fell asleep all snug and warm.

The day arrived for Leigh's first fitting. Byron angrily paced the shop while Leigh went to the dressing room with the owner. He chose to wait in the front of the shop rather than be witness to Leigh displayed in the gowns. At the time he had chosen the gowns he had thought how lovely Leigh would look in them, her pink, ripe breasts all but spilling over the bodice. Now he fought hard not to dwell on the matter.

Byron grew more and more agitated as time went by. He felt quite the fool waiting so long alone in the shop. Several young ladies had come and gone with their purchases, and all had glanced at the handsome gentleman pacing to and fro. One young lady had even been so bold as to try to start conversation with him. Byron had paid her little attention, only the common courtesies of a gentleman to a lady, and soon she had left the shop with a last longing look in his direction. The woman had been very attractive and Byron had been unaware of the change in himself. Only a few short weeks ago he would have needed little encouragement to approach the woman and tip his hat.

Finally Leigh emerged from the rear of the shop in deep discussion with the owner. Byron was irritated that she did not even glance his way. When she finally did look at him, he was leaning against the wall, his arms crossed in front of him, and an expression of utter boredom on his face.

"I am sorry to have been so long Byron," she said in a small voice, "but if you will grant me a few minutes more, there are several trimmings I must choose for some of the gowns."

Byron sighed and accepted his fate of endless waiting.

Another week passed and at last Byron saw an end to this constant confinement with Leigh. Leigh noted that the scowl was now almost a constant part of his face. She tried to stay out of his way as much as possible knowing he had a short wick when it came to patience. She did as little as possible to bring his anger down on her. His answers to her occasional questions were short and he often sat and glared at her for long periods. She could remember nothing she had done to cause such meanness and attributed his mood to a growing anger at having her for a wife. It set her mind all the stronger on leaving him as soon as she could.

Leigh had mixed feelings about the man himself. In many ways he was kind and courteous. She actually enjoyed their morning strolls together, except for his insults made about England, his manner on their strolls was gentle and she greatly enjoyed seeing the city. But his constant gifting to her made her wonder if he thought he could purchase her affections along with the gifts, and his quick temper frightened her more than she could bear. She wondered at his reason for not ever making any further advances toward her. She assumed he felt no desire for her because he did not love her—and that suited Leigh just fine. Still, the man did have his good qualities even if he was a kaleidoscope of moods.

Their conversations were always polite, but never

personal. They talked as any two casual acquaintances, and at the end of two weeks, being constantly together day and night, they were still strangers to one another.

Leigh had her final fitting today and Byron was most anxious to leave the city and start for home. He worried often about the state of affairs there. A large plantation could not run itself. Of course Ephraim was there and would have sent word had there been an emergency. That is if the minister had gotten word to his home as he had requested of the man.

When Byron and Leigh arrived at the clothier's, the owner came rushing to greet them with a broad smile on her round face.

"Mr. Marsh, I had feared we would not get all the gowns fitted before you must leave, but I have had five seamstresses working on them and all is going well now. The ones you requested be complete are all but done, and we should have no problem fitting the remainder today."

"Very good," Byron commented showing little interest in the matter. "Please have the completed ones delivered to my hotel in the morning. The others can be sent down river to my home when they are completed." He turned to Leigh. "Madam, I will leave you here a short time and make arrangements for our journey home." He tipped his hat to them both and turned and left the shop.

Leigh watched him go and wished she could think of some excuse to give the owner so she could also leave. But the woman was talking gaily and ushering her to the fitting room in the rear of the shop. She must find time to be alone so she could make her escape, she thought with panic. But soon the owner had her trying on one gown after another and Leigh found that time again had wings.

Byron vowed not to spend another day waiting in the front of the shop, and by no means was he going to the fitting room and watch Leigh displayed. He made his way to the docks along the river. He had decided they would travel home by boat. It would be much more pleasant than taking Leigh's wagon, and quicker too.

His land was bordered on one side by the river, so it would take them almost to his door. He had docks for supplies brought and felt sure there would be some servants about to send to the house for a carriage to take them the remainder of the way to the house.

Byron was walking along the docks inquiring into a boat for hire. He thought about returning home with Leigh as he walked. It had still been only a little over two weeks since he had met her and their hurried marriage was going to be hard to explain. And she still treated him cooly. He had thought the time they spent together these last weeks, and his many gifts to her, would help bring them closer together, but Leigh seemed even more quiet and shy than ever before. Had he given Ella this much of his time, he mused, and been this generous with her, she would have seduced him many times by now.

It was going to be awkward introducing Leigh to his uncle and friends. You would have to be an idiot, indeed, not to notice the lack of warmth the couple shared. Mayhap tonight he would have a long serious talk with Leigh and try to soothe things some between them. He sighed again, thinking of his plight, and heard his name called. He knew his luck had been too good to be true, and he turned to see Jack Cummings walking toward him.

Jack owned the land next to Byron's. His plantation, Allenwood, named after Jack's mother's family, was not as large as Byron's nor did Jack possess Byron's wealth, but few did. Still, Jack was not considered to be wanting, and to all but a select few such as Byron, he was considered quite wealthy himself.

They had grown up together and had always been the best of friends, but right now Byron would have preferred to see just about anyone other than Jack.

Jack reached Byron's side and offered him his hand. "Byron, you old dog, I did not know you were in Richmond. Had I known you were going to be here, I would have left Emily at home," he added with a chuckle.

Until just a few years ago when Jack had met Emily and wed, he and Byron had been the worry of many a father with a pretty daughter. The two of them had roamed the countryside and won many a maiden's heart, only to leave it broken.

Jack stood almost as tall as Byron. His hair was light in color, his face smooth and handsome. His frame was not as large as Byron's, the shoulders not as wide, but he was a striking man and had broken his fair share of hearts. He had a good wit and was extremely charming. He was one of those people you met one minute, and felt the next as if you had known him all of your life.

"Why don't you join Emily and me for dinner, Byron?" he asked. "We will only be here a short time. Emily is being fitted for a new gown for your uncle's gala New Year's Eve ball," he chuckled to himself. "If your uncle does not soon end this annual affair, Emily will have me bankrupt."

Byron was used to Jack's sense of humor and chuckled along with him. He knew how devoted Jack was to Emily. It was the happiness he saw on Jack's face and the two adorable children he now had that had set Byron's mind to marrying the night he had taken his drunken ride and met Leigh.

Jack was one of Byron's closest friends and he wanted to tell him of his recent marriage, but somehow the timing was not right, so he chose to tell him a small lie instead.

"Jack, ah, I have business to attend and must most reluctantly decline your offer of dinner."

"I know you, Byron," Jack laughed. "Let's see, Ella is at home, so tell me the name of your pressing business. No doubt she is a beauty."

Byron laughed but he had a sheepish look on his face and soon Jack left with fond farewells.

Byron found a boat with a small crew that appeared to be trustworthy. You could not be too careful. He made the arrangements and left the docks. With this task behind him, he made his way to a tavern along the docks and had one ale to pass the time.

Why didn't I tell Jack I was married? he thought. We will be arriving home in less than two days, and now the task will be all the harder. Jack will wonder why I kept it from him. But he would have asked questions, Byron mused, it was only natural, and Byron was not prepared to answer them as yet. In his present state he was in no mood to take the ribbing Jack would have given him. For though Leigh was his wife, he was all too painfully aware that she was his wife in name only.

Of late he had started to dream about her in his arms. He could feel her soft flesh next to his, those full ripe breasts pressed next to his chest. In his dreams her kisses were long and hot. If he did not soon bed with her, he was

105

afraid he was going to find himself mad. As much as he hated the thought, he had begun to think of taking her by force. It would take little more before all her protesting would do no good.

Leigh had just finished when Byron entered the shop. He had had more than one ale and paid the owner for the completed gowns in a jovial manner. He placed a hand possessively on Leigh's waist as they left the shop and she nervously glided out of his reach. Once they were on the walk he offered her his arm and she accepted it nervously. As they made their way back to the hotel Leigh watched him warily. They passed the millinery shop and Leigh was relieved to see the sign still in the window.

When Byron and Leigh entered the lobby of the hotel Byron noted one very familiar face and he hesitated momentarily.

"Monsieur Marsh." The woman smiled reaching his side.

"Madame DuVey," Byron replied politely with a nod of his head.

Madame DuVey glanced to the lovely young woman with Byron. Mon Dieu, she thought, but she is a beauty. What I could make with a girl such as her in my employee. Leave it to a man like Monsieur Marsh, she chuckled inwardly, to find her first.

Leigh studied the woman before her. She was of middle age, well dressed, very attractive, and obviously French. She noted the look in the woman's eyes as she smiled at Byron, and Leigh wondered, disgustedly, if all the women in Richmond were infatuated with her husband.

Byron noted the two women appraising one another

and try as he might, he could think of no graceful way to avoid introducing the two women. "Leigh," he said casually placing a hand on her shoulder, "allow me to introduce Madame DuVey. Madame DuVey, my wife."

There was an audible gasp from Madame DuVey and her eyes quickly lowered to Leigh's hand and she noted the gold band Leigh wore. Her eyes roamed over Leigh's form and she was envious of the slender waist, full breast, long limbs. She studied again the lovely face and noted especially Leigh's eyes. Oui, she thought, I can see the shy innocence of the young madame. I always knew it would take a very special woman to capture the heart of Monsieur Marsh. Ahh, she thought with a slight flutter of her heart, she is indeed a lucky woman this Madame Marsh!

"It is a pleasure to meet you, Madame Marsh," Madame DuVey said with a smile.

Leigh smiled shyly in return and then lowered her gaze wondering what this woman's relationship had been with Byron. She doubted they had had a romantic connection, the woman several years older than Byron, but then she thought—one never knows. After all she is French!

"You are a very fortunate man, Monsieur," Madame DuVey said sincerely. "Your wife is most beautiful."

Byron nodded, acknowledging the compliment, and then glanced at Leigh askew as if judging the truth of Madame DuVey's words.

Madame DuVey saw the expression in Byron's eyes as he looked at his wife. Ah, I will miss seeing him, she thought. But with a wife such as this, he will have no need to call at my home in the future. Oui, I see the passion when he gazes at her. Mon Dieu, Mon Dieu—

what a man!

"Ah," Madame DuVey said, her attention caught by some activity outside the hotel, "I see my carriage has arrived. I must hurry. It was very nice meeting you, Madame," she said smiling at Leigh.

Leigh replied politely and Byron held the hotel door for the woman wishing her a goodday.

Before they went to their room, Byron stopped at the desk and ordered their dinner sent up to their room. It better suited his mood of late. He was growing tired of every man in the dining room eyeing his wife. And besides, Jack and Emily stayed at this hotel when they were in the city and he did not want to take the chance of running into them.

Leigh paced the room nervously as she waited for their dinner to arrive. Byron sat quietly in a chair, his eyes hooded, and every time Leigh glanced his way her anxiety grew.

When the meal arrived Leigh was relieved but it was short lived, for Byron ate little but consumed much of the wine, she noted.

"Leigh," he said pushing the food about his plate, "we will be leaving for Royal Oaks on the morrow and I think we need to discuss a few things before then."

"Yes, Byron," she replied glancing his way and then returning to her meal. Though her voice sounded calm, her mind was in panic. Time was running out. She must get him to leave her alone for a small time tonight.

He scowled at her and rose from the table. "I would like to discuss the fact, madam, that you are my wife! And as my wife there are certain things . . ." he stopped and Leigh looked up to his angry face nervously. He had an odd look in his eye, somewhere between desire and discomfort. Then he scowled and walked to the window turning his back to her.

"Leigh, it is very uncomfortable for a man when he . . ." he paused clearing his throat, "when he is constantly with a . . ."

His voice trailed off and Leigh blushed at his turned back. She did not know exactly to what he was referring but she assumed it had something to do with the more intimate life of a husband and wife. She nervously twisted the edge of the table cloth.

He turned and scowled at her. "I have made arrangements to leave by boat. Please have all of your things packed and ready to depart in the morning." He pivoted on his heel and again looked out the window.

"I will be ready at the appointed time, Byron," Leigh said in a small voice.

Though her voice gave no trace of it, her mind was racing. She must leave tonight! She knew little or nothing about Byron's home and its location. If she was ever to leave him and return home, it must be tonight.

Byron had been leaving her alone in the mornings when she bathed, she wondered . . .

"Byron, if I may, ah, since we are leaving on the morrow and with the packing to do and the gowns to be delivered . . . would, ah, it be alright if I had water sent up for a bath tonight?"

"You bathed this morning, did you not?" he snapped, turning to scowl at her.

"Yes, that is true, but with the packing and gowns," she hesitated, not exactly sure of what to say. Then she swallowed hard and summoned all of her courage and frowned back at him. "Sir, you have told me often enough that your home is more than two days journey from here. I will not be able to bathe in the morning, nor on the boat, and I do treasure my baths."

He stared at her for an unusually long time and Leigh felt as if he could read her mind.

"If it is not convenient," Leigh said as casually as she could drawing her eyes from his, "then I withdraw my request."

Byron said nothing and when he took angry strides toward the table Leigh flinched. He roughly pushed back the chair and sat down. He picked up his fork and again pushed the food about his plate. Leigh's heart stood still waiting for him to say something.

"I will request the bath water when they come for the dinner dishes," he growled.

Leigh released her breath and picked at her food watching him askew.

The dishes were cleared, the tub filled, and still Byron sat idly in the chair. Leigh glared at him when he wasn't looking her way. It appeared her plan would fail and all she would get this night was an extra bath.

Sighing and accepting her fate, she started to undress turning her back to him. When Leigh started to remove her shift Byron jumped up from the chair, and murmuring something, quickly grabbed his hat and started for the door.

No sooner was he gone than Leigh was throwing on her clothes and packing her few belongings. She hurried, frantic that he would return at any moment.

At last she was ready and gingerly opened the door and peeked into the hallway. All clear. She scooted out and quickly closed the door behind her. She practically ran down the hall looking over her shoulder to make sure she had not been discovered.

She decided to take the back stairs, the ones used by the maids. It eventually led to the kitchen and Leigh stood at the door for a long time in indecision. She squared her shoulders, took a deep breath, and walked through the place as if she owned it. All heads turned to watch her progress, and many mouths fell open, but no one stopped her or spoke a word.

When she reached the area behind the hotel she let out a sigh and permitted herself a small smile. She wondered what Byron would think when he returned and found her gone, but she did not dwell long on the matter, and doubted that Byron would either. He would most likely be overjoyed to be rid of her. She did smile broadly when she thought of what he would do with all those gowns and other gifts he got for her. Then she found the thought made her angry. He would most likely find someone else to give them to. He really was a handsome man, she thought, though his moodiness left a lot to be desired, no one could fault him on appearance.

She started walking in the direction of the street. It was dark now and she knew the shop where she intended to stop to apply for work would be closed. There was a small inn near there she remembered. She would lodge there for the night and go to the millinery shop first thing in the morning.

She had taken several coins from the place she knew Byron kept them and left her mother's cameo in their place. Tears came to her eyes when she laid it in the drawer. It was the only item she had left of her mother's now, and she hated to part with it. But it was the only item of value that she owned other than the ring Byron had given her. She could hardly take his money and leave an item he had given her in its place, she decided.

As Leigh walked quickly toward the street her hand toyed nervously with the small gold band she wore on her finger.

Chapter Four

When Leigh reached the walk she cautiously peeked before she stepped out of the shadows. She started off in the direction of the inn. So intent was she on her destination, she failed to notice the strange looks she drew from passerbys. It was quite unusual to see a woman alone after dark, unless of course, she was a woman of loose morals, and Leigh had much too much the look of innocence about her to be mistaken for that type of woman.

"Miss, oh Miss," a voice from behind her called.

Leigh's heart jumped into her throat. She had been discovered! she thought. No, maybe not, perhaps they weren't speaking to her. She hesitated only a moment before quickening her step.

"Miss. I say Miss, may I be of some assistance?" she heard the same male voice call.

Now Leigh knew they were definitely speaking to her for she could see a man approaching from behind out of the corner of her eye. She glanced about quickly to see if there was anyone of whom she could ask assistance, and by then it was too late, the man was at her side.

A smile was on the man's face as he tipped his hat. "I am sorry if I frightened you," he apologized. "I could not help but notice that you are alone and thought mayhap I could be of some assistance."

His voice sounded sincere and he did not seem to be sent by Byron. Leigh relaxed slightly and said nothing as she searched the man's face.

"Allow me to introduce myself," he continued. "Thomas Whitefield is my name. I do apologize if I gave you a fright. I mean you no harm, I assure you," he smiled. "A young and beautiful woman such as yourself, if I may say," he paused, his smile growing broader, "should not be wandering the streets alone. There are those about who would do you harm. You are too great a temptation, my dear, for some black heart."

Leigh remained silent and continued to study the man's face.

"If you would care to tell me your destination, I would deem it an honor to escort you," he added with another tip of his hat.

Leigh was uncertain as to what to do. He seemed harmless enough, but how was a girl to know? The fact that the man was older, probably close to her father's age, and not some young buck, eased her mind slightly. He was tall with a trim body, a full head of gray hair, and a most jovial face. And he did speak the truth, she thought. It was not safe, or proper, for her to be wandering the streets alone. Mayhap this gentleman could be of help.

She still had a distance to go and if they stood here chatting much longer Byron could come by.

"I am a silversmith," Mr. Whitefield said. "My shop is not far from here. I assure you again, I mean you no harm," he said with an easy smile. "My only concern is for the welfare of one as young and as lovely as yourself."

That settled it. Leigh would trust the man. "Thank you most kindly, sir. I would greatly appreciate your escort," Leigh said softly and graced the man with a dimpled smile.

With another tip of his hat Mr. Whitefield offered Leigh his arm. She told him of her destination and he commented that the innkeeper there was a friend of his and he offered to see about a room for her as well. Leigh smiled again and thanked him and they chatted casually as they walked. Leigh knew she was being terribly rude not introducing herself in return, but she thought it was best not to just in case Byron should decide to inquire about her. She was thankful that Mr. Whitefield was much too well mannered as to ask.

Good as his word he took her straight to the inn. He excused himself once inside and went to speak with the man behind the tavern bar. Leigh had been in the inn many times in the daylight with Byron but she was surprised to see how different the place looked at night.

The room was filled with smoke and as her eyes casually roamed the room she realized that she was the only woman present except for the bar maid scurrying about. She noted several men glaring at her and swallowed hard. She glanced Mr. Whitefield's way and saw he was in deep discussion with the gentleman behind the bar.

Two men at a nearby table sat with heads close

together speaking in low tones as they looked Leigh's way. She did not care for the gleam she saw in their eyes. Then one of the men rose and started walking her way with a smile revealing missing teeth. Leigh fearfully took several steps back and then gasped and turned at the sound of a loud crack.

The entire inn became deathly still as all heads turned toward the bar.

Thomas Whitefield stood with his cane slapped against the bar and there was a menacing look in his eye.

Leigh stared at him amazed that a person's features could change so drastically. No more was the face jovial—now it was dark and threatening as he glared at the man approaching Leigh. He pointed his cane toward the man and then slapped it against the bar again.

"Take your seat, gent," he said in a low and threatening tone. "The lady is none of your affair."

"Do as he says, Tom," the bartender added.

The man hesitated a moment and then returned to his seat mumbling. The room remained silent for several minutes and then hushed conversation started and rose until again the place was full of the sounds of bawdy men enjoying an evening of relaxation.

Leigh looked to Mr. Whitefield and his friend and they both gave her smiles of reassurance. Thomas came to her side and took her arm.

"I have made all the necessary arrangements for your room," Thomas explained. "My friend assures me you will not be disturbed. Sometimes these places become rather rowdy you know," he added with a grin.

Leigh glanced around with large eyes. Rather rowdy! she thought. She was now indeed thankful she had accepted Mr. Whitefield's escort and she thanked Mr.

Whitefield profusely as he escorted her to her room. When they reached the door Thomas opened it allowing Leigh to enter and remained in the hall.

"Be sure to latch your door securely," he warned her.

"I will, Mr. Whitefield, and thank you again, sir."

"If you should need my assistance further, I will be happy to return on the morrow."

"No, thank you again, sir. I do appreciate your help this night and your kind words with the innkeeper."

"Then I bid you goodnight and farewell," he said with a smile and a tip of his hat.

Leigh watched him stroll away swinging his cane and then closed the door and latched it. She hugged herself. Safe! She had done it! Now if she could get the position at the millinery shop, in time she could save the necessary coin she would need for the voyage home.

Mayhap after she was sure Byron had left the city, she would call on the kindly Mr. Whitefield to see if he could suggest how she should go about the matter of the missing deed. Yes, she thought, things were definitely going well.

She was up before dawn the next day. She carefully fixed her hair and wore her prettiest dress. She was the only person below in the common room when she went down for breakfast. The same sleepy-eyed serving bar maid brought her tea and porridge. After she had finished her meal and settled her bill, she left in the direction of the millinery shop. She walked quickly with her head down in case Byron should be about.

She reached the shop only to find it still closed. She peeked through the window and thought she saw someone moving about inside. She tapped on the window, and after several tries, she saw a woman coming to answer the door.

"I am sorry, miss, but we are not open as of yet," the woman said.

"I have come about the position," Leigh replied pointing to the sign in the window.

"Oh, well, come in then. We will have a few minutes to chat before I must open."

The woman held the door open wide for Leigh to enter. The shop was small. There were several shelves on one wall lined with hats. Tables and chairs were scattered about the tidy room, each overflowing with hats, and the flowers, feathers, and bows covering the hats gave the place a colorful, festive appearance. Though the shop did not have the elegance of the clothier's, it had a warmth and tastefulness about it that bespoke quality.

The woman indicated a curtained doorway near the rear of the shop. "Come this way. I have tea brewing. Would you care for a cup?"

"Yes, please, thank you."

"I am Rose Marrow. I own the shop."

"Leigh, Madam Marrow, Leigh, ah, Burke."

Leigh followed Mrs. Marrow through the small curtained doorway. A desk and chair stood in one corner of the small room. Two Queen Anne chairs and an elegant tea table sat in front of the only window in the room. Swatches of fabrics, ribbons, and other items lay scattered about the room on small benches and tables. Though the room appeared in total chaos Leigh had the feeling that Mrs. Marrow could place her hand on any item needed.

"Sit down, Miss Burke. I'll get the tea."

The woman smiled at Leigh indicating one of the

Queen Anne chairs and then left the room through a small doorway. Leigh could hear a teapot just starting to whistle somewhere closeby.

Leigh judged Mrs. Marrow to be a woman in her middle forties. She had light brown hair she wore in a bun at the back of her head and a blondish streak ran through her hair from front to back. Her figure was attractive and she had a quick and easy smile.

She returned shortly carrying a tray with a teapot and two cups. She poured for them both and then turned to face Leigh.

"Have you worked as a clerk before, Miss Burke?"

"No, but I am quick to learn and I can read and am good with numbers," Leigh said in a rush. "I am sure I can handle the position."

Leigh quickly sat down her teacup so it would not rattle on the saucer and show Mrs. Marrow just how nervous she was.

Rose saw the eagerness in Leigh's face. She had her doubts. She had already had three clerks and none of them had worked out well. She had made up her mind to be very careful in her next choice of employee.

"I really need the job most desperately," Leigh added when she saw the doubt cross Mrs. Marrow's face. "My, ah, husband died recently and we had just arrived in this country. Now I find I must earn my own way and save enough money to return home to England."

Leigh felt terrible guilt lying to the woman. But she could hardly tell her she had fled a husband she hated and had been forced to wed. Besides, she thought, the part about needing the money to return home was true.

Rose glanced down and noted the wedding band on Leigh's hand and she spoke gently to her. "I am truly sorry, Mrs. Burke. I am a widow myself and feel your plight, though I was not as young as you when I lost my dear, sweet, George."

Leigh hung on her every word, her expression changing back and forth from one of hope to one of disappointment.

"I would like to help you and have only one small hesitation. The work here is simple enough, and if you can read, I have small doubt you would do just fine, but . . ." Mrs. Marrow paused and looked into Leigh's eyes before continuing. "To put it bluntly, dear, my only concern is your accent. England is not much loved here since the war even though we do trade with the English."

"I see," Leigh said lowering her eyes, her face full of sadness.

Mrs. Marrow studied the young woman before her. She was so pretty, thought Rose, and how sad to be so young and lose one's husband.

"Still—this is Old Dominion," Rose commented.

"Old Dominion?" Leigh looked up with a puzzled expression in her eyes. "I thought this was Richmond."

Rose roared with laughter. "Oh, Mrs. Burke, forgive me," she said her voice still full of merriment. "Old Dominion is a nickname given to Virginia more than a century ago by Charles the Second when it was the only colony to remain loyal to the crown."

When Leigh heard the explanation she also laughed.

"I like you, Leigh. May I call you Leigh?"

"Yes, please do."

"Well I sell hats, not guns to Federalists, so let us give it a try. Besides, now that I think on it, women are not as foolish as men. I doubt any of my customers will deny themselves a new hat just because the clerk speaks with

120

an English accent. And," she added with a wink, "I have the prettiest hats in all of Richmond."

Rose found that Leigh intended to board at the nearby inn and offered her the use of a small room on the third floor, and for a very nominal rent. Leigh was delighted and quickly accepted the offer thanking the woman over and over. Rose also invited her to take her meals with her. She explained that she lived in the apartment just above the shop and below the room she offered Leigh. Leigh said she would be most grateful and again thanked the woman profusely.

"Nonsense, Leigh. The room is empty anyway. I am afraid it is not very large, but the view is pleasant and the bed comfortable. If the truth be told, it is I who should be thanking you. I hate to eat alone."

She showed Leigh up the stairs to the room and continued chatting as they made their way. "My children are grown and gone now. It will be nice to have your company."

When Leigh saw how nice the room was she again thanked Mrs. Marrow.

"I'll leave you to put your things away," she said with a smile turning to leave. "Come down when you are finished and we will start you in your new position."

Leigh stood looking about after Mrs. Marrow had left. The room was small true, but it was light and cheerful. Really much nicer than she had expected, and much preferable to the inn.

There was one small window and the view was nice as promised. A brass bed with several quilts was against one wall, a wash stand with a bowl and pitcher next to it. There was a chest with three drawers and a small fireplace with a chair nearby. All in all a most pleasant room. And with the little she would pay for room and board she would be able to save the necessary coin just that much sooner.

As Leigh put away her things the sunlight shone on the gold band she wore. Immediately Byron's face floated before her. That was another reason to be grateful to Mrs. Marrow, she thought. Not only had the woman given her the position and a place to live, but with this lodging she would not have to leave the shop and travel to and from her job. That meant even less chance of Byron finding her should he stay in Richmond for long, though Leigh doubted he would waste much time looking for her. She imagined that by now she was completely erased from his thoughts. Out of sight, out of mind, the old saying went. Anytime now he would be boarding a boat and leaving Richmond for his beloved Royal Oaks. Good riddance! she thought.

Quickly she finished putting away her few belongings and went to start her new job.

Leigh learned her job quickly. She was courteous and helpful and in a few short weeks Rose found her indispensible.

The customers also seemed to take a liking to her. Some of the older patrons had her try on hats for them to take home to surprise daughters and granddaughters.

It had been three weeks since Leigh had started working for Rose, and in that time she had grown extremely fond of her employer. She enjoyed sharing small chores with Rose, like cooking and cleaning. Leigh had only blurry memories of her mother and had never lived with another woman other than a servant or governess. She found it most enjoyable, and in many ways began to think of Rose in a daughterly way.

They often sat and talked for long periods in the evening when the shop was closed. Leigh had learned that Rose had two children, a son and a daughter. Her son had gone west several months ago to see what lay there in this vast, still unexplored land. And her daughter was living in Georgia, married to a fine man.

Leigh had asked Mrs. Marrow if Georgia was a large Virginian city and Rose had laughed long and hard explaining that Georgia was the fourth state of the Union. Leigh had said she would never understand this state business. If a person lived in America why not just say so, instead of this Virginia or Georgia, or some other place. They had laughed hard over the matter and often teased about it.

Leigh said little of her husband or her life since she came to this country and Rose attributed it to the fact that she was newly widowed and did not press the matter. But Leigh did tell her charming stories of England and her childhood. Rose grew fonder of Leigh with each passing day and was grateful to the girl for filling an emptiness in her life that she had felt since her son left Richmond.

"Leigh, I just don't know what I would do without you," Rose commented one evening as they sat eating dinner. "You are truly a treasure. If you are as good at numbers as you are at everything else I have asked you to do, I have a favor I would like to request of you. Would you see if you can help me with my books?"

"I would be pleased to try, Mrs. Marrow," Leigh replied, grateful that there might be something she could do for this woman who had done so much for her.

"My son used to do all my accounts before he left to

seek his fortune. What's a mother to do?" Rose said raising her hands into the air in a helpless way and then laughing.

Leigh smiled broadly. She found she smiled very easily these days.

"I am afraid," Rose continued, "I have no head for figures and have made quite a mess of the accounts since James left five months ago. I know I have accounts I have sent no notice of, and just yesterday, a customer insisted they had already settled an account that I thought still owing."

"Would you like for me to look at them tonight?"

"No, no, dear. Tomorrow will be quite soon enough. If you are able to make heads or tails of the mess I have made, I will pay you a higher wage to do the bookwork for me."

"That is not necessary, Mrs. Marrow, really. I expect no increase in salary. You have been more than kind, and I welcome the opportunity to repay you in some small way."

"Now I will hear no more on the matter. It is settled. You are the best worker I have ever had, Leigh. You won't even take a day off. Why, I don't believe you have set foot from this shop since the day you started work here."

Leigh quickly lowered her gaze and murmured something. No, she thought, she had not left the shop, and she would not until she could be absolutely certain that Byron was no longer in the city. Leigh had found herself thinking of the man several times in the past weeks—their morning strolls, pleasant dinners, his occasional kindness. Once she had seen a tall man with dark hair stroll past the millinery shop window and she had rushed to get a better look thinking it was Byron, but the man had disappeared around a corner and she could not be sure. Later she told herself that it was not him, for the man she saw, though tall with broad shoulders and dark hair, had had an unkept look about him, his clothes looking as if he slept in them, and Byron had always been extremely neat. And whenever Leigh caught herself thinking of Byron, his handsome features, his good qualities, she would hurriedly tell herself to remember his quick temper, foul moodiness, and how the man had always frightened her.

Rose studied Leigh's sad profile. She remembered how she had felt after George's death. She had not felt much like going out into the world and facing people either. Again her sympathies went out to the girl. She felt that she and Leigh were close enough now that Leigh would speak to her about her late husband when she felt the need, and until she did, Rose would do nothing to prod the girl. She had noted the melancholy expression Leigh sometimes had and attributed it to the recent loss of her husband. Rose had decided that mayhap the book work would keep Leigh from dwelling too much on her loss— and besides, she thought, she really had made a mess of the job and did truly require help.

"I do truly hate to do the accounts," Rose continued, "and," she laughed, "do a poor job at that. I would much prefer to work in the front of the shop. The reason I required a clerk in the first place was to give me the necessary time I needed to devote to the accounts. If you will take that burden from my shoulders I will be forever grateful."

"I will do my best, Mrs. Marrow," Leigh replied.

"Good! Now that that is settled let us finish the dishes," she winked, "and I shall beat you at a game

125

of cribbage."

Leigh giggled and started clearing the table.

Leigh proved to be as good as her word. She was most definitely good with numbers as she had said when she first applied for the position. It took her almost a week to decipher the mess Mrs. Marrow had made, but now it was all falling into place.

As a rule she worked in the back of the shop at the desk behind the curtained doorway. From there she could work undisturbed and still hear the activity in the front of the shop and go and help Mrs. Marrow when the shop was busy, as it often was these days.

It was nearing the end of November and the store was often crowded with holiday shoppers buying gifts and hats for the parties the season would bring.

Leigh sat working at her figures and sipping tea.

"Ugh. This tea tastes funny," she said to herself. She had brewed it the same as usual, but here of late it often tasted odd. And she had become so clumsy of late, dropping things and bumping into furniture. It puzzled her. She had always been rather graceful. She dismissed it from her thoughts and went back to her figures.

She heard the bell on the door ringing and knew a customer had just entered the shop. She started to rise to see if Mrs. Marrow needed her help. She had been wool gathering, she knew, and not paying attention to the clanging of the little bell. Then she heard Mrs. Marrow helping the newly arrived customer and returned again to her book work.

She kept one ear alert to the front of the shop in case more customers should arrive and was vaguely aware of the conversation taking place in the front of the shop. It was not that the customer was talking overloud, it was just that she had one of those voices that carried well.

Suddenly Leigh dropped her quill and sat very still. The conversation now had her complete attention. The customer had just said something about Byron Marsh!

Leigh tiptoed to the curtain and gently pulled it back just enough to peek through. Mrs. Marrow was talking to an attractive blond woman slightly taller than Leigh. Leigh noticed at once the costly clothes the woman wore. She was dressed in a striking gown of pale yellow and black. The skirt was full and had stripes of the two colors running from waist to hem. The bodice was yellow with cuffs and collar in black. She held a matching coat over one arm and wore a small black hat with feathers. Her figure was nice, breast generous, and she was an elegant picture to behold.

"Yes, Mrs. Marrow," the woman was saying, "Byron and I are still keeping company, though he has been away on business here of late. Confidentially," the woman said leaning closer to Mrs. Marrow, "I expect to be proposed to just anytime."

"Really, how nice, Miss Borough," Mrs. Marrow replied. "Though I have never met Mr. Marsh, I understand he is a most handsome man. You must consider yourself very lucky indeed."

Leigh caught, at once, the small insult Mrs. Marrow had made. She knew Mrs. Marrow quite well now, and it was obvious to her that Mrs. Marrow did not like the customer. But evidently the customer did not catch the slur as to her luck, and by the smile on Mrs. Marrow's face, was unaware of the woman's feelings for her.

"Yes, he is rather handsome," Miss Borough said raising one lily white hand up to pat her hair, "and quite wealthy you know."

Mrs. Marrow gave the woman a withering look when her face was turned and changed the subject.

They talked on but Leigh was no longer listening. No wonder Byron had resented her so, she thought. He had practically been engaged! And the woman, this Miss Borough, was extremely attractive.

Leigh sat down heavily in the chair by the desk. She bit at her lower lip in a nervous manner. She felt a sudden sadness in her heart that she could not explain.

Sometime later Mrs. Marrow came to ask for Leigh's assistance in front and found her crying.

"Why, Leigh, what is it dear?"

"I am sorry, Mrs. Marrow. Pay me no mind. I guess I am just homesick."

"Of course, dear, and losing one's husband such a short time ago. I understand."

Leigh could hear the chatter of customers in front and rose quickly to go and wait on them. But Rose stopped her by placing a hand on her arm.

"Dear, first go press a damp cool cloth to your face and take some time to recover yourself. I can handle things for awhile by myself. Besides," she said placing a comforting arm about Leigh, "it would not do for them to see your tear-streaked face. They would think me a most unpleasant employer," she added with a smile.

Leigh did as she was told and soon she was out front helping Rose.

That evening after the shop had closed, Rose insisted Leigh go and lie down and rest while she started dinner. Leigh protested, but found as usual, it did little good. So she climbed the stairs to her room, laid down on the bed, and stared at the ceiling.

She had thought of Byron often in these past weeks, and since the incident of this afternoon, he had been constantly on her mind. Absently she toyed with the ring on her finger as tears filled her eyes.

She had been right about Byron not searching for her, or at least she guessed that she had, for she had not seen him since the night she ran from the hotel. He was probably, at this very moment at his beloved Royal Oaks planning his life with that woman she had seen today. She sniffed as she wiped the tears from her eyes.

When Rose called from below that dinner was ready, Leigh rose with a sigh and walked to the wash stand. She poured some water into a bowl and splashed it on her face. It would not do for Mrs. Marrow to see she had been crying again. After she dried her face and smoothed her gown she started down stairs. When she was halfway down, the smell of the food assaulted her. She hurriedly placed a hand over her mouth, her eyes round, and raced back up the stairs to her room. She made it just in time. She had vomited several times before Rose entered the room, and was still sitting with her head over the chamber pot.

"Leigh, I heard you running up the stairs and . . . Here dear, let me help you. Sit here on the bed while I get a damp cloth for your head."

Leigh sat on the side of the bed groaning, all the color drained from her face. Mrs. Marrow returned with a cloth, and helping Leigh to sit further back on the bed with her back resting against the headboard, she placed the cool cloth against her brow.

"Really, Mrs. Marrow, I don't know what has come over me. I am seldom ill," Leigh murmured embarrassed.

129

Rose gave Leigh a knowing look and bade her sit still while she emptied the chamber pot. She left the room saying she would return shortly and bring Leigh some tea.

She returned several moments later to find Leigh's color slightly improved. "Here, dear, sip it slowly. Sometimes it helps," she said handing Leigh a cup of tea.

Leigh took small sips of the tea and felt herself some better. "I am truly sorry, Mrs. Marrow. I just don't understand what has come over me."

"Leigh," Rose said in a hesitant manner, "do not think me presumptuous. I don't mean to pry. I know you have been widowed only a short time and . . ." She stopped and took a deep breath and looked Leigh straight in the eye before continuing. "Is there a chance you could be with child?"

Leigh's eyes grew round and she sucked in her breath. Oh no! NO! Leigh panicked. But now that she thought on it, her monthly flow was well overdo. Could she be? . . . The answer was a definite yes!

Almost at once she began to cry. "What will become of me?" she sobbed.

Rose took her hand, patted it, and sitting down beside her on the bed, brushed her curls from her brow. "You are not alone dear, I am here with you. We will talk later when you are feeling better. Now try to rest. I will be below if you need me." She placed a motherly kiss on Leigh's brow, and as Leigh lay down, she covered her with a quilt and tiptoed from the room.

Leigh lay there, her mind in turmoil. She hadn't near enough money to return to England, and in a short time, she would no longer be able to work. What would become of her and the child? She could not possibly return to the

O'Malleys' to request their help, and she would not stay with Mrs. Marrow and be a burden, even if the woman did ask, which Leigh felt sure she would. That left only Byron. He did not want her before, she thought, and it would be doubly so now. Besides, she could hardly go searching for him and ask him to take her back after she had run away. She was much too proud for that. And after she had seen that woman who entered the shop today—she felt sure Byron would not take her back even if she begged on bended knees!

How would she and the child live? Leigh had visions of two urchins standing on a street corner on cold winter days begging for food from passerbys. She sighed heavily as large tears slowly rolled down her cheeks.

"Poor, dear, sweet child," Rose said to herself as she made her way downstairs. "It will be hard to bear a child so young and alone. At least she will always have a part of her dearly departed husband to cherish. I know what a comfort a child can be to a widow."

Chapter Five

Byron did not know what else to do. It had been almost five weeks since he had returned and found Leigh gone. He had been searching for her almost constantly since.

He had returned that night to find the room empty. He had stayed away a long time. He was feeling more and more pressure being with Leigh and not touching her. He had started leaving her alone to bathe because he saw no reason to further torture himself. When he had left her alone that night, his first instinct had been to go to a nearby inn for a few glasses of ale. But then he had decided it was not wise to partake of ale in his present state. Spirits had been the reason that he was now in this condition. And besides, he would need little encouragement to throw Leigh to the bed and have her no matter how she felt, or what effect it had on their future together.

So he had strolled down to the river instead. He loved the river. It somehow always had a calming effect on him. At home, often when something was bothering him, or he had a lot on his mind, he would ride to where the river met his land and sit for hours. Just sit, and think, and watch the river. It always made him feel better somehow.

He had spent more time at the river that night than he had intended and as he was about to leave a woman of the street had approached him.

"Lonely, sweet?" she said walking close to Byron's side and moving her body seductively. Her face was painted heavily and she smelled unwashed. Though Byron desperately wanted a woman, he would not touch this one with a ten foot pole!

"Excuse me please," he said tipping his hat, "I have an appointment to keep."

"I ain't good enough for the likes of you, uh?" the woman replied with a sneer.

"I assure you, madam, I mean no insult, but I must hurry. Good evening." And with that Byron walked away leaving the woman to shout curses at his back.

When Madame DuVey opened her door and saw Byron standing there she had to bite her tongue to keep from exclaiming her surprise.

"Monsieur Marsh," she said opening the door wider, "please come in."

Byron entered the foyer and stood taking in the familiar surroundings. Though Madame DuVey's house was situated in one of the less desirable areas of the city, it was nonetheless lavish. The foyer was wide with shining floors, a staircase to the left, red carpet padding the steps. The drawing room archway was across from the stairs and Byron could see several people talking in soft tones near the doorway.

Madame DuVey escorted Byron to the drawing room and then excused herself. Byron stood looking about the room. It was large, a red carpet covering the floor. Several love seats covered in a plush cream colored velvet were scattered about the room. A French toile pattern wallpaper in cream and red covered the walls and the chairs in the room were upholstered in a matching fabric. Elaborate sconces of brass and crystal were spaced on the wall about the room, the candlelight subdued. Intricately carved tables sat near each seating group, their tops filled with decanters and glasses.

Byron had been a guest here several times in the past and yet he never failed to be slightly taken back by the decor of the rooms. Though everything in the house was of excellent quality, it was a bit too fussy, too lavish—too French, to suit Byron's personal taste.

Byron studied the faces of those present. He recognized several of the women but none of the men. He nodded politely to the two women who looked his way and then made himself comfortable on one of the love seats.

Madame DuVey returned, a young woman at her side, and when the young woman saw Byron she nearly flew to his side.

"Byron, what a pleasant surprise," the young woman said seating herself beside him.

"Vivian," Byron replied with a grin, "you are as ravishing as ever."

Vivian laughed heartily and placed a hand on Byron's arm. "You always were a charmer."

Madame DuVey approached and handed Byron a

snifter of brandy. "All is satisfactory, Monsieur?" she inquired.

"Yes, Madame DuVey," Byron replied easily, "all is satisfactory."

Madame DuVey grinned, and excusing herself, went to see to her other guests.

Byron sipped his brandy as his eyes roamed leisurely over the woman before him. Vivian had long blond hair which she wore in an intricate coil on top of her head. Her face was lovely, her large blue eyes wide set, the lips full and almost poutful. Her figure was nice, waist trim, hips round, and breasts generous. She was a tall woman and carried herself gracefully. The gown she wore was blue, almost matching the color of her eyes, and extremely low cut. Byron found it difficult to keep his eyes from the tempting display. Byron wondered again, as he had on previous occasions, why a woman as attractive and desirable as Vivian would choose the life of a harlot.

Madame DuVey was watching Byron closely out of the corner of her eye. She recalled the first time she had opened her door and seen his smiling, handsome face. She had noted the self-assuredness of the man and knew he would be an experienced and passionate lover, and at that moment Madame DuVey had wished herself twenty years younger. He had chosen Vivian as his evening's companion on his first visit, and on subsequent visits, and though Byron had never been what one could consider a regular customer, he did occasionally call when he was in the city.

She knew any of her girls would have gladly given themselves to Byron, and without benefit of fees, for

Vivian had wasted no time in telling the other women what an excellent night's companion Byron proved to be. She had practically swooned when she informed them that Byron not only knew how to receive pleasure—but how to give it as well. She had gone into great detail explaining how Byron understood what gave a woman pleasure and was able to take her to higher and higher heights of passion. In fact, Vivian's boasting had gone on to such an extent, that for a short time it had caused a rift between her girls.

A concerned frown wrinkled Madame DuVey's face as she thought about him. She could not understand his presence here this night, and that bothered her. Madame DuVey knew and understood men well, it was her job— and she was *very* good at her job. She knew a man like Byron was not only passionate, but would be a tender and sensitive lover, and such a man would be patient and understanding with a young, and virginal wife. And she saw other qualities in Byron that perhaps would have surprised him, for though she knew Byron had much enjoyed the ways of the bachelor and had been free and fickle with his attentions, she also saw one of those rare men that once he did find a woman to love, a very special woman, he would trustingly place his heart in that woman's hand. So why was he here? she questioned. Had the young madame been careless with his heart? She had not appeared so foolish. Was perhaps the young and beautiful Madame Marsh not that special woman? Then why had Byron wed her? He was not the type of man to give up his bachelor ways easily. Why, she questioned, does he leave his beautiful young wife and come to me?

Sometime later when Byron and Vivian passed her on their way upstairs she still had a puzzled frown on her brow.

Vivian opened the bedroom door and preceded Byron into the room. She lit a candle on the nightstand beside the bed and turned to Byron with a smile full of promises.

Byron casually removed his coat as his eyes took in the room. It was a nice size room done in shades of blue and green. The only furniture in the room was a bureau, a long, low chair, the nightstand and a large comfortable looking bed. The bed was covered with satin sheets, numerous pillows tossed casually near the head. The bed hangings were ruffled and lavish in a deep shade of blue, the drapes in a print of dark blue and sea green, and a sea green carpet covered the floor. It was a pleasant room, but again it was too fussy for Byron's taste.

Vivian came to stand before him and uncoiled her long blond hair. With a toss of her head it fell about her shoulders and breasts in soft curls. Slowly and seductively she unfastened her gown allowing it to fall to the floor circling her feet. Byron's eyes seemed to grow deeper in color and cloudy as they roamed over her long, slender body. She stood boldly before him in her thin chemise, it slightly more than a haze covering her fair skin. White, sheer stockings caressed her long legs, blue garters circling her shapely thighs.

Vivian laughed, deep and throaty, when she noted Byron's passion rise and she put her arms about his neck, her look promising pleasurable delights. "Byron, love," she said placing a fleeting kiss on his lips, "how I have missed you."

Byron felt the tension in his body growing, his long denied and frustrated passions building, and he roughly pulled Vivian into his arms covering her mouth with his. Vivian moaned and moved against him as Byron's hands explored her body, caressing a breast, a thigh, pressing her tightly against his body. His lips devoured hers and then moved to her neck where he placed fevered kisses. Vivian clung to him enjoying the feel of his powerful, muscular body next to her own. Her hands began unfastening his waistvest, pulling it open wide, and then moved on to his shirt. She pulled his shirt free of his trousers, and unfastening it, exposed the large powerful chest covered with soft hair. She rubbed her breast against him, enjoying the feel of the soft, downy hair against her skin as her hands caressed his back. Vivian felt his hand clutching her chemise, and with an easy tug, he tore the filmy garment from her body allowing it to float to the floor. Picking her up in strong arms, he carried her to the bed. Vivian looked deep into the dark blue eyes noting the fire she saw kindled there and again his mouth covered hers, his tongue parting her lips. Vivian's hands trembled, their touch clumsy, as she tried to help him remove his trousers.

"Oh, Leigh—Leigh," Byron mumbled, his lips caressing Vivian's neck.

Vivian froze. She pushed hard against Byron, her eyes searching his. "Leigh? Who is Leigh?"

Byron stared at her with unbelieving eyes and felt his passion die. He quickly rose from the bed and walked to the window, turning his back to her. Leigh, he thought seeing her beautiful face floating before him—what have you done to me? Has the wench so bewitched me that now I cannot enjoy the charms of another? Do I so dream of possessing her beauty that now I cannot find pleasure elsewhere? He felt anger, bitter anger, growing inside him and he abruptly took several coins from his waistvest pocket, and not bothering to fasten his vest or his shirt, he angrily snatched up his coat, handed the coins to Vivian, and with mumbled apologies, turned and exited the room leaving Vivian to stare with mouth agape.

When Madame DuVey saw Byron hurrying down the stairs in his half dressed state, she smiled to herself. So— my Vivian is not as appealing as she once was to Monsieur Marsh, she thought. It will be difficult for a man such as he to find he no longer enjoys the rutting ways of the bachelor and that the wee madame holds his heart in her hand. She smiled knowingly as Byron left the house. Ah, Mon Dieu, but I shall miss him. What a man!

As Byron made his way back to the hotel his anger grew. By the time he reached the lobby there was a deep scowl on his face. He would have Leigh no matter how much she protested. She was his wife! And the way he felt at present nothing else would cool his passions, or his temper!

His surprise was great when he opened the door and found the room empty. At first he thought mayhap she had gone to the convenience behind the hotel and he had gone to look for her. Then he went to the lobby deciding she had become frightened by his lengthy absence, and when he asked the man behind the desk about her, the gentleman assured him he had not seen her.

The desk clerk saw the fast growing concern on Byron's face and immediately summoned the maid that serviced their room. When the sleepy-eyed maid arrived she told Byron she had not seen his wife and that when she went to empty the bath water she had found the room empty.

"But there was one thing, Mr. Marsh," she said, a puzzled expression on her face. "That bath water was fresh and clear. Never been used."

Byron thanked them both for their help and asked that the manager be sent to his room immediately.

He paced the room hurriedly waiting for the manager to arrive. He was growing more anxious with each passing moment. Mayhap she had been taken by force. That must be it! Someone took her for her great beauty. There were those that sold women into bondage, Byron knew, and a woman as beautiful as Leigh would bring a high price. Or mayhap they took her knowing of Byron's wealth and would ask a ransom for her return. He realized he would give all the money he possessed if only she were safe.

There was a knock on the door and Byron barked for them to enter. The manager timidly entered the room wringing his hands.

"My wife has been taken from this hotel by force!" Byron stated, the anxiety showing in his voice.

"Mr. Marsh, I fear you are in error. Your . . ."

"What do you know about it! I tell you my wife has been taken from this room by force! She is missing!"

"Sir, please." The manager wanted desperately to flee from the room. Byron stood over six feet tall, and was powerfully built, his shoulders huge. And the manager was slight in comparison. The man knew Byron was extremely upset and feared his reaction when he told him what he must. Byron's hands were already doubled into fists, he noted.

"Mr. Marsh," he said swallowing hard, "your . . ."

Byron came at the man in a rush, and grabbing his coat, lifted the man completely off the floor. His face was furious as he glared into that of the manager's. "If you have something to say man," he shouted at the man, their faces inches apart, "spit it out!"

"Your wife, sir, ah, Mr. Marsh, was, ah, seen leaving the hotel alone by way of the kitchen." The last words came out in a rush.

Byron slowly lowered the man to the floor. He frowned and walked away turning his back so the man could not see his face. "I see. I apologize for my behavior just now," he said in a low voice. The manager stood his ground afraid to move or speak. "My wife, ah, is homesick for England. We quarreled about her returning home for a visit soon. She must have gone to stay at a nearby inn to try to teach me a lesson and better fight her cause," Byron explained. Byron disliked revealing any of his private life to a stranger, even if it was a lie. "I apologize again for my actions," he said turning to face the man. "I thank you for your assistance in this matter. Now if you will excuse me," he said walking to the door and holding it open for the man.

"Yes, sir, goodnight sir," the man said nervously, nearly running from the room.

Byron again began pacing the room. Where could she have gone? She had no money. A sly look came to his face and he went to the drawer where he kept his coins. He found the cameo and knew that she had left it in place of coins. He was not sure of the amount of money that had been in the drawer, but he had an approximate idea, and he estimated that Leigh took very little. In fact, if it had not been for the cameo, he would have never missed the coins at all.

He went to the wardrobe and found that all the items he had purchased for her were still there, but the few things she had when they wed were gone. He noticed a handkerchief on the floor of the wardrobe and he bent and picked it up. It carried the scent of Leigh's hair and

141

Byron stood quietly holding it next to his face, a far away look in his eyes.

So she had left him. Why? Had he not been kind to her? Why the clothes he bought for her alone would have won many a maiden's heart. Had he forced her to bed with him? Had he been unkind in any way?

His worry was fast turning to anger. So she had left! Well, he thought, she would not get far. She had little money and nowhere to go. He would find her, and when he did, she would regret stealing away in the night. He grabbed his hat and left the room with angry strides.

He had checked every inn that night, all to no avail. He did not know that in one particular inn he had been lied to. The woman he searched for was fast asleep upstairs. The innkeeper had promised Thomas Whitefield the maid would not be disturbed, and he would not go back on his word to a friend. Byron could not bring himself to tell anyone he was searching for his wife. He only described Leigh and thought that that would be enough. If anyone had seen her, they would not soon forget.

He had even gone to the inns along the waterfront. He prayed that no one would say they had seen her there because that would mean she was in great danger, or worse. That area of the city was definitely not safe for a woman alone at night.

He passed the night wandering the streets in search of her, his mind in turmoil and anguish.

In the days that followed he frequented all the shops where he and Leigh had made purchases. In each he asked if they had seen his wife, and when they replied that they hadn't, and gave him an inquiring look, he said he must have been mistaken, she must have meant for him to meet her somewhere else. When this too failed to give him any clues, he again went back to the inns to recheck them all once again.

This time when he asked about Leigh in the inn where she did stay, he asked the serving girl. The girl was not overly bright and paid little attention to the women that occasionally entered there. She told him she had seen no such woman, and coyly batted her eyelashes at Byron before he turned and left in a rush.

After the first week went by and nothing, he began to doubt she was still in the city. He had already checked all the means of travel her meager coins would buy, but he checked them all again. When this too failed, he considered the fact that she could have left Richmond by foot. He had doubted this in the past, but it was fast becoming the only solution.

He rode out from the city and circled it in ever widening circles. He stopped everyone he saw and asked if they had seen the maid he described. All said no, and many said with a smile they wished they had. It did little to improve Byron's mood.

When this, too, failed he returned to the city and again walked the streets, looking in every shop, every inn, at every face he passed on the street.

He did not know how often he passed the shop where Leigh worked. Once he entered the shop just as she went to the back to look for a hat a customer had come to pick up. The second time he entered, he quickly looked about, saw an older woman waiting on a customer, and again turned and left not knowing that Leigh sat behind the curtained doorway working on the books. He did not inquire of her in the shop, it was one of the few places he had bought her nothing. That shop, and the one where Ella bought her gowns, he had steered Leigh clear of. It

143

was the millinery shop Ella frequented he knew.

He thought of returning home several times to get help. If he brought some of his men from home, they could take the city apart brick by brick until he found her. But it would take him away from the city for no less than four days, and he worried he would miss her if he left. He felt sure she must still be here somewhere, but where?

The manager of the hotel watched Byron come and go at odd hours. His face was haggard and his normal neat appearance had all but disappeared. His clothes were wrinkled and mussed, as if he slept in them. And he would go several days without shaving. Not at all like Mr. Marsh, he thought. He must love his new wife a great deal.

In the past he had seen Byron bring a lovely lady to dinner at the hotel, and then several days later when they chanced to pass in the lobby, hardly even give her the time of day. Poor, Mr. Marsh, he thought, his wife has left him with a broken heart. And who could blame him, such a beauty she was.

At odd hours Byron would fall into bed for a few hours of badly needed sleep before he would again walk the streets in search of her. He dreamed of her often. Sometimes she was standing, her arms held out to him, a gentle laugh in her voice as she called his name. In others she was screaming at him to save her before it was too late and Byron would wake to find himself covered with sweat.

And now, thought Byron standing at the window in his room and gazing out at the busy street below, it had gone on for almost five weeks. He looked at the now soiled handkerchief he held in his hand, and placing it to his

144

nose, found it still carried the faint scent of her hair. Leigh's image floated before him and his mouth turned down at the corners. He knew it was time to accept the truth of the matter. Either she had found a way to vanish into thin air, or foul play had taken her forever from him. He would never know. He found the not knowing worse than losing her. His mind was in constant torment as to her fate.

Now he would go home. There was nothing else to do. He packed his belongings and could not bring himself to leave the items he had purchased for her behind. It was foolish, he knew, but it was all that he had left of her. He had often found himself fingering one of the gowns and staring off into space. He would have Ephraim pack them away in the attic, he decided, and one day when he was old and gray he would get them down and remember the lovely woman who had been his wife. The many sorrows she had brought him, and the few joys as well. But now all he wanted was to forget her, and those lovely emerald eyes.

With a sad heart Byron rode from Richmond. He had all of her things sent on by river. He rode slowly, long ago losing all interest in returning home. When he was half way home, he decided to leave the road he was on and ride over to the river. He would follow it home. It would be longer that way, but what matter.

It was dawn of the third day of travel when Byron reached his land. He followed the river to one of his favorite spots, and leaving his horse to graze, went to sit on the riverbank and watch the river, unmindful of the cold.

He took Leigh's soiled handkerchief from his pocket and sat staring at the water, his hand caressing the soft linen cloth. Something colorful in the water caught his eye. It almost looks like a woman's gown he mused. But then it disappeared from view and Byron quickly lost interest. A few minutes later he spotted the object again. It was floating atop a log, and the harder Byron stared, the more he was sure it was in fact a woman's gown. And it almost appeared as if someone were still wearing it!

Removing his boots and heavy coat, Byron dove into the icy water and started swimming toward it.

Chapter Six

Leigh rose the next morning to a cold and dreary day. She again was nauseous on rising, but it soon passed. It was Sunday and the shop was closed. She and Rose would have the entire day to talk.

They sat eating breakfast and discussing Leigh's condition.

"Leigh, I insist you stay here with me and I will hear no more of this burden business," Rose said putting down her teacup and looking to Leigh stubbornly.

"If only I had the deed," Leigh commented to herself.

"The deed?"

"My, ah, husband purchased land somewhere near here. When he died the deed was lost. If I had it I could sell the land and have enough money to return home."

"Shouldn't there be a record of the purchase somewhere?"

"I guess, but I do not have the slightest idea of where to begin to look," Leigh said sadly.

"I am afraid my worldly knowledge begins and ends with hats," Rose said looking to Leigh thoughtfully and tapping her fingers on the table. "If James were here I bet he would know where to search. What we need is a man's advice."

"I know a gentleman we can ask," Leigh said excitedly. "I met him the day before I started working here. His name is Thomas Whitefield and he owns a silversmith shop not far from here."

"Mayhap he would help us."

"Mayhap," Leigh agreed with a smile.

"We need go see him today while the shops are closed. Do you know where he lives?"

"No," Leigh replied, her face again sad. They sat in silence and then Leigh again got an excited expression on her face. "But I know of someone who may know where Mr. Whitefield lives. The innkeeper at the tavern close by here is a friend of his."

"Good, let us go and speak to this innkeeper."

"Do you really think that we should?" Leigh questioned, her face now showing doubt.

"Of course," Rose replied with a grin.

They walked to the tavern and found the innkeeper did indeed know where Thomas Whitefield lived. They got directions and hired a landau to take them to his modest home on the outskirts of town. As soon as they stopped in front of his house Leigh again became doubtful.

"Mayhap we should not bother him," she said nervously. "I met him only once and that was weeks ago. I doubt he remembers me."

"Nonsense, Leigh, we have come this far," Rose said as

she climbed down from the landau. She had thought that mayhap the man would be a young man that Leigh had met and perhaps was slightly attracted to, even though she was newly widowed. Now she was beginning to have her doubts and was wondering if mayhap it would have not been better to call on one of the gentlemen she knew in town.

Leigh knocked hesitantly on the door and in a moment Thomas answered. He took one look at Leigh and smiled.

"Mr. Whitefield, ah, I do not know if you remember me, I am Leigh Burke," she said in a small voice.

"Of course, my dear. How nice to see you again."

"This is my employer, Mrs. Marrow." The two exchanged nods. "We have come to speak with you on a matter of which we require the advice of a gentleman. If it would not be . . ."

"Come, come in please," Thomas said smiling and holding the door open wide. Once inside he helped them with their wraps and then extended his arm. "Please come into the parlor."

They entered a small but comfortable room. Thomas bade them be seated near the warmth of the fireplace.

"I was just going to have some tea. Would you lovely ladies care to join me?"

"Yes, thank you, Mr. Whitefield, that would be nice," Rose replied with a smile. "That is if it is not too much trouble."

"No trouble at all. I'll just be a moment. How nice to have two such lovely ladies come to call," he said excusing himself and leaving the room.

Leigh again started to worry over their visit to Mr. Whitefield but Rose shushed her with a wave of her hand.

Thomas returned with the tea moments later and they sat chatting. When he discovered that Mrs. Marrow also owned a business in Richmond, the two chatted easily together.

"Now, my dear," he said sitting down his cup and turning to Leigh, "how can I help you?"

"Well, sir, I need your advice concerning a deed." Leigh went on to explain and he nodded his head in understanding.

"Do you know if your husband had the deed when you left England?"

"I do not know. He did talk of buying land while we were still in England." Leigh's face had a hopeless look. "I am sorry, I truly do not know."

"Hum," he said looking to the ceiling and clasping his hands together. He put his two index fingers to his lips and sat thoughtful for a moment. "When do you recall first seeing the deed?"

"After we left Boston. You see we docked there and," Leigh stopped, an excited look in her eye. "He did mention business while we were there."

"Well then," Thomas smiled, "he most likely dealt through a law firm there. I will check tomorrow to see if there is a record of the deed in Richmond."

"Do you mean the record could be right here?" Leigh asked surprised.

"It could be if the land is not far from here. But many times these things take a long time to record and sometimes it is left to the purchaser to see the proper records are kept. But if he dealt through an attorney, the attorney would handle that for him. I will write to one of the better known law firms there and see if they can inquire into the matter for you."

"How long do you judge it will take?"

"Most likely several months at the least if the record is not here. And then, of course, there is no way of knowing how long it will take to find a buyer."

Leigh's face sagged. "Oh, I see. Well thank you for your offer of help and your advice."

"It is my pleasure, Mrs. Burke," he replied noting her sad face.

They talked on for awhile and then Leigh and Rose thanked him for his time and hospitality and departed.

As they rode back to town Rose tried to cheer Leigh up. "You did not tell me how handsome this Mr. Whitefield was."

"He is very nice too," Leigh replied forlornly.

Rose studied her sad face. "Leigh, I see now how much it means to you to return home. I did not offer before because I wished you would change your mind and stay with me. Now I can see that I can no longer be so selfish in the matter. I will loan you the necessary money to return to England."

"Oh no, Mrs. Marrow. I could not possibly let you."

"Now, dear, let us not quarrel about this," Rose said patting Leigh's hand. "I have little doubt that eventually Mr. Whitefield will find your deed and you will be able to sell your land. But it will take time. By then you will be well along with child and the voyage to England would not be safe for you. If you must go, it is better you go soon." She gave Leigh a motherly smile. "When Mr. Whitefield calls tomorrow to let us know about the records here in Richmond, we will tell him of our decision. And I think," she added with a wink, "I will invite him to dinner."

*   *   *

151

The next day Thomas came to say there was no record of the purchase in Richmond. Mrs. Marrow did invite him to dinner and they discussed what the two women had decided. He seemed to greatly enjoy the meal and their company as well. They talked long into the evening.

Thomas vowed to do all he could to find the record of Leigh's land, to sell it for her, and to forward the money on to her in England after Mrs. Marrow recovered her loan. Leigh insisted on at least that. When Leigh reached home she was to write to Mr. Whitefield if she should gain any helpful information concerning her husband's purchase.

It was all settled so quickly that two days later Leigh had booked passage on a small boat to take her down river to the coast.

The day Leigh left was harder for her than she had ever expected. She had thought that she would feel only joy at leaving America and returning home. This land had brought her so much misery. But she found it had also brought her friends she would miss and cherish all of her life. The O'Malleys, Thomas Whitefield, and most of all, Rose Marrow.

Rose and Thomas went with her to the docks and stayed to say farewell.

"Now write often, Leigh, promise," Rose said as Leigh made ready to board the small boat.

"I will, Mrs. Marrow, I promise. I do not know how I shall ever thank you. I will never forget your kindness, never."

There were tears in Leigh's eyes and in many ways she regretted leaving this woman and her other friends.

"You take care now, and remember what I said about the tea if your stomach becomes upset," Rose added in a whisper.

"I will." The tears were still in Leigh's eyes but now there was also a grin on her face as she looked at Rose's concerned face. She turned to Mr. Whitefield. "And thank you, sir. I know it is no small favor I ask of you. I am eternally in your debt."

"Now, Mrs. Burke, I do nothing any gentleman would not do for a lady in need." He gave Leigh a warm smile. "And especially one as lovely as you, my dear."

Leigh stood on tiptoes and placed a kiss on his cheek. Then turning to Rose she embraced the woman fiercely. Quickly she turned with tears streaming down her face and practically ran aboard the boat.

The boat was really little more than a raft with a waist high railing about it and a small cabin used sometimes for passengers. The captain of the boat had been sternly questioned by Thomas Whitefield and finally approved as a suitable person with which to entrust such a delicate flower as Leigh. There were two crew members and only one other passenger, the captain told Mr. Whitefield, and the other passenger had not booked passage all the way to the coast. The small boat was loaded with supplies for homes down river.

There were tears in Leigh's eyes, and Rose's as well, as the boat pulled away from the dock. She waved to the couple thinking how nice they looked together standing there. Thomas placed a comforting arm about Rose's shoulder and Leigh smiled thinking that perhaps someday this widow and life long bachelor would find happiness together. She hoped they would. She watched them and waved until they became small pin points on the horizon, and then sadly she walked to the shelter of the so-called cabin and passed the long afternoon in tears.

Leigh found to her dismay that she was seasick for the first time in her life. She attributed it to her pregnancy and hoped it would not continue on the long voyage home.

The sun had set when one of the crew members brought her a light dinner that looked unappetizing at best. He was a young boy, extremely shy. He stuttered and stumbled over his feet when Leigh thanked him with a smile. She ate nothing, and when no one returned to take the untouched food, she decided to go out on deck away from the aroma of the food and get some fresh air.

There were crates of supplies piled everywhere and she made her way around them and walked to the side of the boat seeing no one along the way.

She thought about her future. There would be no O'Malleys, Mr. Whitefield, or motherly Mrs. Marrow to comfort her. When she reached the coast she would book passage and sail for home alone. She dreaded the long voyage with no one to help her pass the time. It would be difficult remembering the last one shared with her father.

She found herself thinking of Byron. In many ways she now regretted leaving him. If only they had met differently, she mused. In the past weeks Leigh had grown much in wisdom and maturity. She thought of the kindnesses Byron had shown her. All those weeks they shared a bed and he never acted the husband. Of course it most likely was as she first thought, the man simply did not care for her and found her undesirable. But now for some reason, Leigh also felt it was because he had felt concern for his young wife—She would never know.

She shivered as the cold air whipped around her skirts. The shawl she wore was not very warm and she slightly regretted not taking the warm cloak Byron had purchased for her.

She wondered what her life would be like right now if she had stayed with Byron. Lord knew, she told herself, she did not for one instant miss him, but she was curious as to what her life, and that of her unborn child's, may have been with the man. She released a sigh and pulled the shawl more snugly about her.

"Well look who it is."

Leigh flinched and her body grew suddenly cold as if the blood in her veins had turned to ice. Her pulse quickened, her body tense, and all her senses became keenly alert. She knew that voice! Slowly she turned and looked straight into the face of Samuel Jones!

"I thought sure you was dead," he said with mock sorrow, his face twisted in a sneerlike grin. "I had great plans for the two of us, missy. There is this gent I know who was to give me a lot of money for the likes of you." He laughed a wicked laugh and Leigh quickly glanced about and realized that the crew could not possibly see them in the blackness of the night and with the crates piled high around them. There was an expression of total horror on Leigh's face as she stared at the man.

"Of course I would have took you to him after you and me got better acquainted and had some fun," Jones continued. He leered at her with that same evil look she had seen before. "I spent a long time searching for you in them woods, missy," he sneered and then threw his head back and laughed, "and now I find you without no looking at all."

"You—You killed my father!" Leigh gasped.

He smiled revealing rotten teeth. "He was a sick old man, missy. 'Sides, how else was I gonna take you to sell."

Leigh stared at the man with unbelieving eyes. Had the man no morals, no conscience? Her body began to tremble violently and she drew her eyes from his leering, evil face. She made as if to step around the man but he quickly blocked her path.

"L-Let me pass or—I'll scream," she said trying to hide the fear in her voice and sound self-assured.

"You ain't gonna scream 'cause I ain't gonna let you." And with that he grabbed her and pressed his mouth over hers.

His breath was foul and Leigh thought she would be sick by the repulsiveness of the man. She fought with all her might and pushed the man from her. He smiled at her terrified face and reaching out one clawlike hand tore at her gown ripping it open at the bodice and giving him a glimpse of one of Leigh's full breasts. Leigh opened her mouth to scream but Jones quickly grabbed her placing a hand over her mouth. He pulled her close and again covered her mouth with his. Leigh fought him with every ounce of strength she possessed but the man just held her tighter. He was forcing her back against the railing of the boat and it was pressing into the small of her back causing great pain. Leigh brought up one leg and stomped down as hard as she could and caught his foot in the arch. He released her with a curse.

"Why you little bitch," he growled. "I'll teach you!"

He brought back his hand and struck her hard across the face. Her body went reeling and she looked down and saw only black water below her. She fought desperately to regain her balance and waved her hands in the air reaching for a hand hold that was not there. A small squeal escaped her as she began to fall. She hit the water with a splash. It was ice cold and took her breath away.

She choked and sputtered for several minutes and when she recovered her breath she looked frantically for the boat and yelled for help in a weak voice.

There was no moon and the night was black. With panic she realized she could see nothing, not even the shore, and she had no idea in which direction the closest shore was. She could swim so all was not lost, but with her heavy skirts weighing her down and tangling around her legs, she would have to choose a direction soon. She tried to float to feel the flow of the water but her skirts kept pulling her under. She chose a direction at random and slowly started swimming. She prayed the shore was not far. The water was so cold, and were things not bad enough, the cold made her movements jerky.

She could only hope and pray the crew had heard her fall or would miss her soon and return to search for her. She held no hope that Jones would tell anyone. He was a thief and a murderer, and Leigh knew that. He would want her dead if he could not have her for his own sick reasons. She knew he would do his best to make sure she was not missed.

She swam for what seemed like hours in the icy water. Her hands and feet felt numb and she was crying so hard she found it difficult to breathe. She went under several times and each time she thought it would be her last, but somehow her exhausted body would fight its way back to the surface.

If only she could remove the gown, she thought. It would ease her way without its weight and the constant tangling.

She choked and went under again and this time she knew it would be her last. She was just too tired. She fought hard to live and again her hands reached for a hold that was not there. As she choked and fought for breath, her mind remained calm. It was as though she were standing back out of her body and watching her own struggle. So this is what it is like to drown, she thought calmly. She realized that she was sadder at the thought of the child that would never be born, than at the thought that she would die so young and alone.

When it felt as if her lungs would burst her hand brushed against something hard. Leigh frantically clawed at it and caught on to something that felt like a log. She held tight to a small branch and it pulled her along with it. She managed to get her head above the water and gasped as her lungs took in the wonderful, wonderful air.

She lost all trace of time and had no idea how long she floated supported by the log. She wept thanking God for his mercy in saving her life and the life of her child.

Eventually she tried to pull herself up on the log and out of the freezing water. The log kept rolling and she feared she would lose it altogether. Finally she managed to get herself over the log from the waist up. She hugged it tightly and closed her eyes.

Chapter Seven

Byron reached the log and saw there was a woman atop it, and she looked to be dead! He found a branch for a hand hold and started swimming for shore dragging the log behind him. It was very heavy and not easily changed in direction, and he lost his hold several times. When he finally reached the shore he quickly exited the water and turned and lifted the woman in his arms. As she rolled over and he saw her face he gasped.

"Leigh!" came the startled cry. Her skin was nearly blue and she had a nasty bruise on the side of her face.

He placed his ear to her breast. "Thank God she still lives," he whispered. He reached for his heavy coat and wrapped it snugly about her and then hurriedly put on his boots watching her face all the while. He lifted her gently and carried her to his horse and placed her limp body over the stallion's back in front of the saddle. He mounted, and lifting her into his arms, he leaned her against his chest and placed one arm snuggly about her. With his free hand he grabbed the reins and rode for home as if all the devils of hell were after him.

When Byron reached the house Ephraim was standing on the veranda, his hands shading his eyes. "Master Byron?" he called seeing Byron nearly run the huge stallion up on the steps. Then he noted the woman in his arms and rushed to help him.

Byron gently handed Leigh to Ephraim, dismounted and took her back in his arms, barking orders the entire time.

Byron entered the house and ran up the stairs taking them two at a time. He rushed to the bedroom and had just laid Leigh on the bed when Ephraim and Annie entered. The two walked to the bed and stood wide-eyed looking at the lovely lady's limp form.

"Ephraim, quick, build a fire, and make it a big one!" Byron ordered. "Annie, get me a gown for her, or my robe, anything that is warm and dry!"

They both rushed to do his bidding and when Annie returned with Byron's robe he had the woman rolled on her stomach and was starting to unfasten her gown.

"Masser Byron," Annie said, "you best let me do that."

Byron didn't even look her way. "Annie, this is my wife. There was an accident on the river. Now quick go get Aunt Mary and see if she knows of an herb to help with her rattled breathing!"

Annie gave him a startled look and hurried to the cook-house to find Aunt Mary.

When Leigh awoke she did not know where she was,

only that she was warm and dry. She opened her eyes and tried to look about but her eyes would not focus. She could see someone near but not make out their features. She closed her eyes tightly and looked again. Her voice was weak and hoarse as she spoke his name.

"You are safe now, Leigh," Byron said gently. "Just rest. Everything will be fine now." He placed a cool hand upon her brow and she closed her eyes and was immediately asleep.

Leigh's fever raged for days and she often thrashed in her sleep mumbling. When she awoke again several days later, Byron's was again the first face she saw.

"How do you feel?" he asked touching her brow with the back of his hand, a concerned look on his face. Thank God her fever has finally broken, he thought.

"Ah, I am not sure."

She moved and tried to sit up in the bed and Byron immediately placed an arm about her and helped her, placing another pillow behind her back. He sat down on the side of the bed studying her face.

"Where am I? How did I get here?" she questioned looking about.

"You are home, pet, at Royal Oaks. I found you afloat a log in the river." His voice was soft and caressing as he devoured her with his eyes. "You have been here five days now. You were very ill."

"Five days!" She looked to him confused.

Byron smiled softly and patted her hand. "I don't mind telling you those first few days we did not know if . . ."

Suddenly Leigh's face drained of color as she covered her face with her hands and began to cry.

"Leigh," Byron said in a comforting tone, "you are safe now. There is nothing to fear."

"I've lost the child," she sobbed.

Byron's brow knitted as he studied her sorrowful face. Then his eyes grew large and unbelieving as her meaning became clear to him. "You are with child, Leigh!"

Leigh looked up to his surprised face and immediately stopped her crying. He did not know?—She had not lost the child! She quickly looked away from those penetrating blue eyes and murmured a soft yes, wiping her tears away with her hand.

Byron sat staring at her with his mouth hanging open, then he rose from the bed and started pacing the room. He stopped a few feet from the bed and turned to look hard at her, a frown now on his face. "Is the child mine?"

Leigh gave him a wide-eyed look, her mouth now hanging open. "Is the child mine?" she mimicked. Byron noted the anger in her eyes as she doubled her small fists and raised them high into the air. "How dare you!" she said bringing her fist down hard on the bed. "Ooh! How can you ask such a question?"

"Answer me!" he snapped, his face rigid.

"I will not!" She glared at him, clamped her teeth tightly together, and stuck her chin in the air.

"Leigh Marsh, I will not put up with your shows of temper, ill or no!" he shouted. "Now answer me or I'll, I'll . . ."

"You will what?" she said arching a brow. "Beat me?"

"Do not try me, Leigh," Byron warned. "I do not approve of striking women—but I have no quarrel with spanking naughty children!"

"You would not dare," she ground out slowly.

He took several steps toward her and Leigh's anger changed quickly to fear. Byron noted the look on her face and stood his ground scowling at her. She looked especially pitiful sitting there in the large bed, a bruise still on one side of her face. Then with an oath he turned and started pacing again.

"Leigh, it has been almost six weeks since we parted ways in Richmond." He stopped to face her and looked deep into her eyes. "You seem to attract trouble like a magnet, madam, and I do not feel my question unjust."

Leigh glared at him a long time before she spoke. "I am not some strumpet to fall into bed with any man, sir— and yes, the child is yours." She turned her face from his and started to cry again. She heard the door close and looked to see him gone. She turned pleading eyes to the ceiling. "Whatever have I done to deserve to be put upon by this man?"

There was a knock on the door and then it was opened by a trim negro woman wearing a checkered dress and matching kerchief on her head. She walked to the bed carrying a tray, a warm smile on her face.

"I am Annie, Miss Leigh," she said placing the tray in front of Leigh. "The masser says I to be your personal maid now. We sore is glad you is feeling better child."

Leigh smiled at the woman in return. Annie had a contagious smile. She puttered about the room talking all the while.

"The masser, he sore was in one terrible fit when he brung you home so sick. Why, he stay rights here in this room almost every minute. We all thought sore you gonna die, but I guess Masser Byron not permit it." She turned and smiled at Leigh with a chuckle. "He is a good man, Masser Byron."

Well that is certainly a matter of opinion, thought Leigh, but she said nothing and continued to study the woman as she tidied the room.

"Try to eat some of that there broth, child," she said pointing to the tray.

Leigh picked up the spoon and though she did not feel hungry, she took a small taste to please the woman. It was delicious and Leigh felt her hunger grow. Soon she had eaten every morsel under the watchful eyes of Annie.

"Yes, sir," Annie chuckled, "you be up and about in no time." Smiling, she removed the tray and walked to the door. "You rests now, Miss Leigh. I comes back later. If you wants anything, you just pull that there cord aside the bed and I be here quick as can be." She gave Leigh another one of her beautiful smiles and left the room closing the door softly behind her.

Leigh looked about the room with interest. It was large with high ceilings edged with elaborate crown molding. The walls were covered with a dark grayish blue wallpaper with a diamond print of white upon it. The woodwork was deep and also painted white and the floor was wide oak planking. There were numerous rugs from the Orient scattered about the shining floors.

The bed was huge with four post and had carvings of what appeared to be rice and tobacco climbing up the post. There was a flat canopy on the bed and it was edged with a pleated blue fabric that matched the bedspread. The bed was flanked by windows, a small chest below each. The windows went almost ceiling to floor, were shuttered, and had drapes of muted blue matching the wallpaper.

The wall to her left contained two more windows with a lovely highboy in between. The shell carvings on the little drawers shined in the sunlight.

The door Annie had used was across from the bed in the far left corner of the room. Next to it stood a small chest with several drawers, and next to it was two large wing back chairs covered with the same fabric as the drapes. Directly across from the bed stood a fireplace with an oversized opening and Leigh could feel the warmth of the fire burning there. To the right of the fireplace was a wardrobe with mirrors on the doors.

To the right of the bed was another door and a small table with a white chair close by. There was a lovely mirror with carvings of birds and flowers over the table and these few items were the only things in the room that were the least bit feminine. The room was definitely masculine, no ruffles or frills, but Leigh found she liked it very much and for some strange reason, felt very much at home in it.

When Annie came to check on Leigh later, she found her sleeping. After carefully covering her she tiptoed from the room.

Three days passed and Leigh did not see Byron and was determined not to ask Annie as to his whereabouts.

"Annie, I don't care what you say, I am getting up," Leigh said stubbornly to the woman. "I know I am still weak, but I will grow no stronger lying abed." Leigh rose from the bed and stood staring at the stubborn woman with her hands on her hips. Annie opened her mouth to argue, but Leigh would not listen. "Now, Annie, please see if you can find me something to wear."

"Why, Miss Leigh, you gots a whole wardrobe full of clothes rights here," Annie replied. "They come while you was sick. And Masser Byron says there be more acoming in a fortnight."

"Well please pick out a gown for me and, Annie, I would greatly love a bath." Leigh wanted to give the woman little chance to change her mind about letting her out of bed.

"I go and gets the water rights now," Annie replied scurrying from the room.

Leigh walked to the windows beside the bed and stood looking out. There were rolling hills and trees as far as the eye could see. The day was clear and standing in the second story window she judged that she could see a great distance. She frowned and walked to the windows next to the highboy. The view was the same. She did however see a roll of small cottages and a barn in the distance, but that was all. She stood at the window, a puzzled look on her face, when Annie returned.

"Annie, why can't I see any of our neighbors' homes in the distance? Do these windows face away from their homes?"

"Lordy no, Miss Leigh," Annie said with a chuckle. "These here windows face Masser Jonathan's place. That Masser Byron's uncle. And them," she said pointing to the windows by the bed, "they face the Cummings' plantation. But you can't see them from here. They a long way off."

Leigh looked to her with some amazement and when Annie saw her surprise she laughed.

"Royal Oaks a big place, Miss Leigh. I guess it about the largest plantation in all Virginy," she added proudly.

Leigh's bath was ready and after Annie helped her with her hair and scrubbed her back for her, she went to lay out her clothes.

She assisted Leigh from the tub and into a shift matching the gown she had chosen. She placed a robe, luxurious and warm about Leigh's shoulders. Leigh fingered the robe and frowned. She did not remember Byron buying this for her, but then she dismissed it. He had bought her so many clothes she doubted she would recognize many of them.

Annie bid Leigh sit down in the small white chair in front of the table so she could fix her hair. When Leigh's thick hair was brushed dry, Annie opened a little drawer in the table and took out a peach colored ribbon. She tied Leigh's shining curls loosely at the back of her head.

"My, you sore got pretty hair, Miss Leigh. Long and thick and full of curls. It gonna be a pleasure to fix your hair for them fancy parties Masser Byron go to with the holidays."

"I may not go, Annie," Leigh said in a small voice.

"Why, child, of course you go. Whatever make you think you not?"

The two women looked at each other in the mirror's reflection.

"They weeks away yet," Annie continued. "You be strong by then." Annie gave Leigh a scolding look in the mirror. "That is if you don't overdo."

Leigh let the matter be. No sense telling the woman Byron would not want to take her, she would find out soon enough. A thought occurred to Leigh and she bit her bottom lip wondering if she should open the subject.

"Annie, ah, weren't you surprised to see that Byron had married?"

"Some I guess. But the masser, he always be one not to linger long on a matter once his mind made up." She smiled at Leigh softly in the mirror and again Leigh caught her smile and returned it. "I guess first time he seen you, child, pretty as you are, he made up his mind to marry with you. I bet he swooped you right off your feet," she chuckled. "Knowing Masser Byron he gave you little say in the matter."

Leigh quickly lowered her eyes. Annie did not know how close she was to the truth. "Y—Yes he did," Leigh murmured softly.

"That be Masser Byron, once he get his mind on a matter, ain't no changing his mind or any peace till he gets his way. He been that way since he was a child." She patted Leigh's arm and smiled at her. "Now let's get you dressed, child. The masser have my hide I lets you get sick again." She chuckled and went to the bed to get the gown she had laid out for Leigh.

The gown was a dark peach made of taffeta. It had long fitted sleeves with six small buttons on the cuffs and a high neck with a small round collar. The bodice was inset with a lighter peach taffeta pleated into small French pleats, and the color matched her hair ribbons. The skirt was full and Leigh now had enough petticoats to make it stand out as it should. Leigh had to admit, the new clothes did feel and look grand.

"If it is permissible, Annie, I would like to go downstairs. I have grown exceedingly tired of this room, handsome though it is."

"Miss Leigh," Annie said smiling and standing back to see how pretty Leigh looked in the dress, "you is mistress of this house and I reckon you can go wherever you like." Then she gave Leigh a warning look. "As long as you don't tire yourself."

"I promise, Annie."

Leigh smiled and left the room and started down the long winding stairs to the foyer below. Annie stood at the top of the stairs watching her.

"Now you mind what I say."

"I hear, Annie. I promise not to overdo."

The stairs were wide and gracefully curved. There was

a large brass chandelier hanging from the high ceiling and Leigh admired its beauty. There was a love seat on the wall to her left at the bottom of the steps and a set of double doors beside it. On the right wall was a small table with a mirror above and another set of double doors. The walls were papered in a gold and cream print of flur de le pattern. The entrance door was large and had a fan window above it and Leigh walked to it and stepped out onto the veranda.

The house was extremely large and painted white. There were several white columns supporting the high roof over the long expanse of the front of the house. Leigh walked back inside and stood looking at the foyer. The hallway appeared to curve behind the steps and she could see several portraits hanging along the hallway. She walked to the set of double doors next to the small table and gingerly opened them. She gasped at the room before her.

It was the drawing room and it was very large. There was a large fireplace facing her with a portrait of a woman above. There were two love seats facing each other before the fireplace and a larger sofa facing the fireplace with them. They all were of Mr. Chippendale's design Leigh noted, and extremely handsome. To her right there were two sets of French doors with the fan windows above them and a beautiful French armoire between them. Leigh walked to it and stroked the wood admiring the intricate carvings in the wood. Two large wing back chairs stood in one corner, a small round table between them, and a lovely piano stood in another. The room was done in soft golds and muted blues with bits of cinnamon here and there. Again there were many rugs from the Orient scattered on the shining oak floors. Leigh walked about the room with large eyes. It was the most beautiful room she had ever seen.

She walked around the tea table between the two love seats and studied the portrait of the woman over the mantel. She was striking but did not much resemble Byron, except for the eyes. They were the same deep shade of blue.

Another pair of doors were on the wall near the piano and Leigh walked to them and carefully peeked inside. It was the dining room and it too was large and held a long table with twelve chairs around it and more still lining the walls. It was done in the same soft blues and golds of the drawing room and there were two large windows in the room, with the fan windows above, that looked out upon a view of rolling hills and trees. There was a huntboard on one wall and Leigh admired the lovely tea service upon it and the sets of candlesticks as well. A china cabinet stood at one end of the room and Leigh saw it held a good quantity and quality of china and crystal.

She returned to the foyer and walked to the set of doors next to the love seat. This room was paneled in cherry and lined with shelves. Many books and other objects of interest filled the shelves and Leigh timidly entered the room and stood looking about. The mantel was especially nice and elaborately carved. The fireplace was directly in front of her and she walked toward it studying the portrait of the man above it. This had to be Byron's father. The likeness was unmistakable. The jaw was slightly different and the mouth a little more stern, but the shape of the face and brows were Byron's. He was quite handsome, Leigh thought, but not as handsome as Byron. Few men were.

There were two sets of double doors with the fan

windows to her right, and they led to the veranda the same as the ones in the drawing room. There was a large desk to her left with a comfortable looking leather chair behind it. Two more leather wing backs stood near the fireplace and there was a long high table on one wall.

Leigh assumed this was Byron's room and turned to leave only to find herself face to face with him.

"Are you sure you feel well enough to be up, Leigh?" he asked from the doorway.

"Yes, thank you, I feel much improved." She lowered her eyes and folded her hands in front of her.

"Very well," he said moving into the room and walking past her to the desk. "I have just returned from a visit with my uncle. Had I known you would be about this morn, I would have put off the visit to another day."

Leigh said nothing and started to leave the room.

"Wait, Leigh. We have a few things we need discuss." He motioned to one of the wing backs near the fireplace for Leigh to be seated, and she quickly returned and settled herself nervously on the edge of the seat. As soon as she was settled in the chair Byron sat down behind his desk and looked sternly at her.

"I wish to make some things clear," he said. "First, the room in which you sleep is mine." Leigh quickly looked to her lap as he continued. "I have been sleeping in one of the guest rooms while you were ill, but in the future you will be sharing the room with me."

Leigh blushed and tightened her grip on her folded hands. He continued with a sterner tone in his voice. "Do not plan to steal away in the night again, Leigh. Royal Oaks is a large plantation and you would not get far before myself or one of my men found you."

Leigh said nothing and nodded her head still looking

171

down. She felt very much as she had as a small child when her father had corrected her for some wrong.

Byron looked at how lovely she looked sitting there. She was so small and delicate. She stood just below his shoulder and her bones were finely shaped. Sitting there with her head bowed, she reminded him very much of a young girl just out of childhood. She was nearly, Byron thought. He had never asked her age, it was not a gentlemanly question, even from a husband, but he judged her to be eighteen or nineteen. As he sat looking at her, he thought how much he yearned to go to her and take her into his arms and tell her everything would be alright now. He would never let anything ugly touch her life again. He did not know what happened to her before he found her in the river, but he intended to find out. But not today, he told himself, she looked much too lovely sitting there in her new gown for any more sad words today.

He rose from the chair and cleared his throat. "Leigh, if you will grant me time to wash, we will lunch and then I will take you on a tour of the house if you like."

"Yes, I would like that," she said looking up at him, her mouth twitching with a small smile.

Leigh went into the drawing room and sat on one of the love seats to await Byron. He entered shortly, followed by a black man with gray hair at his temples and dressed in butler's livery.

"Leigh, this is Ephraim," Byron said placing a hand on the man's shoulder and smiling. "He is the butler and runs this house like a stern sea captain. He sometimes manages the field crews, knows more about good horseflesh and cattle than any man I know, and I guess is about the best friend a body could have."

172

"I am most pleased to meet you, Miss Leigh," the man said making a small bow. His voice was rich and cultured and he had a broad grin on his face. "I am very happy to see you recovered from your recent illness." He turned and smiled at Byron. "You pay no mind to Master Byron's words, he has not been quite right every since Annie dropped him on his head when he was a babe."

Leigh covered her mouth with one hand and burst into giggles. Byron laughed hard and Ephraim chuckled at his own wit. Leigh could tell the men shared a friendship to be envied by the looks they gave one another.

"This old man," Byron said in mock anger, "still thinks me the boy he used to turn across his knee. One of these days I will show him differently."

Ephraim chuckled and went to open the dining room doors wide announcing lunch was ready. Byron offered Leigh his arm and she took it, a smile still on her face. Byron seated her at one end of the long table and himself at the other. A delicious meal was placed before them and they began to eat in silence.

Byron looked up to her many times and wanted to say something to her to break this damn awkward silence. He opened his mouth several times but each time closed it with a frown. What could they discuss? He could say, "Oh, by the way, Leigh, tell me what you did in Richmond when we were apart?" That would start an argument for sure. They could not discuss friends—they didn't share any. He looked up at her and frowned. He'd be damned if he'd discuss the weather!

With each silent moment Leigh racked her brain for something to say. When the meal was half over she felt so uncomfortable she wanted to jump up and scream.

"I, ah, have already seen part of the house, Byron."

Leigh looked up but Byron was studying the food before him and there was a deep frown on his face. Leigh quickly looked down and continued in a meek tone. "I am afraid I looked about some on my own."

Byron glanced her way but she was looking down. "Nothing to be afeared about, pet." He again turned his attention to his food. "This is your house now too, please feel free to look about."

Leigh looked up at the top of Byron's head. "The furniture is lovely and the house is much bigger than I expected."

Byron looked her way but again Leigh was looking down. "The sofas are of Mr. Chippendale's design." He returned to his food.

"Yes, I know," he heard her say. Byron smiled and laid down his fork resting his elbows on the table. "My grandfather built the home originally. Royal Oaks was a land grant from the crown." As Leigh looked up and they at last had each other's attention, he smiled at her and continued. "My mother saw to its present furnishing. All the pieces were sent for from Europe, many from England."

Leigh smiled timidly at him, and they stared at each other for an awkward moment before again returning to their meal. After the meal was complete Byron took her on a complete tour of the house.

The ballroom was enormous. Several chandeliers hung from the ceiling and there were eight windows in the room. The floor sparkled as the sun shone on the well waxed oak. Chairs lined the walls and there was an alcove for musicians.

There was a large spotlessly clean cookhouse to the rear of the house. You entered it by way of a long closed hallway. Byron commented he had had the hallway built, disliking cold food. Leigh was introduced to a robust negro woman Byron called Aunt Mary.

There were five bedrooms upstairs not counting their own, and each was done in a different color and style of furniture. Some were French in design and full of ruffles and soft colors. None were as large as the master bedroom and Leigh still liked that room best of any in the house. Everywhere they went she was introduced to servants. She would never remember all of their names she commented to Byron and he smiled softly placing a hand on her waist as they entered the drawing room.

"May we have tea, Byron?" she questioned softly.

"Of course, Leigh. Let me go and search for Ephraim."

Byron left the room and Leigh sat down on one of the love seats with a sigh. She was overwhelmed by the beauty of his home and had much enjoyed the tour with Byron. When they had something to discuss, they were relaxed with each other, she noted. Then when the subject was spent they again would sit in silence for long awkward periods. Leigh realized how very little she really knew about Byron.

Byron returned and sat down across from her on the other love seat and in a moment Ephraim entered carrying a large silver tea service. Leigh recognized it as the one from the huntboard in the dining room. Ephraim smiled to her and placed the set on the table between them and then left the room. Byron watched as Leigh gracefully poured a cup and handed it to him and then poured one for herself and leaned back looking at him with a timid smile.

"The house is truly lovely, Byron. You must be very proud of it." Her voice was soft and she smiled as she looked at Byron's huge hands delicately holding the small tea cup.

"Thank you, pet. I am glad you like it so well." His manner was easy as he sipped the tea though it took all of his self-control not to grimace. He hated tea and only had the stuff to please Leigh and give himself an excuse to spend more time with her.

A long awkward silence followed before Leigh asked if he would care for more tea.

"No, thank you. One cup is quite enough," Byron said sitting his cup on the table. Leigh noted the tea had barely been touched and smiled to herself. Now she remembered, Byron does not like tea.

Byron insisted Leigh lay down and rest before dinner and when she awoke Annie was there waiting to help her dress.

The gown Annie chose this time was a rich aqua in color. It had a large ruffle along the neckline that fell in soft folds about the shoulders and across the bodice. The skirt hung fairly straight in front and was bunched full in the back giving the gown a gentle swinging motion as she walked.

Annie pulled Leigh's hair to one side and wrapped it in a bun behind her ear leaving small curls to fall over her shoulder. With the deep, rich color of the gown and her hair fixed in this manner, accentuating the slant of her eyes, Leigh looked very seductive.

As she entered the drawing room Byron stood by the fire sipping some refreshment. He turned at the sound of the swish of her skirt and stood admiring her beauty, a smile on his face, and his blue eyes growing deeper in color.

"The gown looks lovely on you, Leigh," he commented

walking toward her, "but then I knew that it would."

"Thank you," she murmured lowering her eyes, a slight blush on her cheeks. She walked to one of the love seats and sat down.

"Would you care for a glass of wine before dinner?" Byron inquired when he realized that he was standing staring at her.

"No, thank you."

Byron sat down across from her and from time to time they looked each other's way and smiled but nothing was said until Ephraim came to announce dinner. Byron escorted Leigh to the table and a delicious baked ham was placed before them. Leigh found it very good and had never eaten ham prepared this way. There was also a vegetable she was not familiar with and when she questioned Byron about it he laughed hard, a twinkle in his eye.

"It is a yam, Leigh. I am very fond of them. Do you like it?"

"Yes, it is very good, as is the remainder of the meal. I especially like the way the ham was prepared," she said looking up to him with a smile.

They sat staring at each other for a moment and when neither spoke, they both quickly looked down to their plates. Byron scowled at his food. Are we ever to be strangers? he mused. We may as well discuss the weather now! He vowed to end this awkward chit chat between them. They must learn about each other and end this mood of strangers that they shared.

Leigh could not bear the thought of another long awkward evening and returned to the bedroom shortly after dinner. Annie was there and helped her undress and handed her a lovely blue nightdress. Again Leigh did not remember it as one of the items they had bought in Richmond. A small frown wrinkled her brow as she put it on and climbed into bed wishing Annie a goodnight.

Byron entered the room and told Annie goodnight as she passed him on her way out of the room. He glanced Leigh's way and smiled. When he started to undress Leigh quickly laid down and nervously looked to the ceiling. Byron blew out the candle before removing his pants though the light from the fireplace was more than ample to see his silhouette across the room. There was a full moon and the window on Byron's side of the bed was open, the drapes and shutters wide, allowing the moonlight to shine on the foot of the bed.

The bed was over large and Leigh was relieved to see that there was a great deal of room between she and Byron. Byron said nothing as he climbed into bed, and when several moments passed, Leigh assumed he was falling asleep and was just beginning to relax when the sound of his voice startled her.

"Tell me about your home, Leigh," he said softly.

"What do you wish to know?" she inquired nervously.

He raised up on one elbow and frowned at her. "About your home—your father—your childhood," he snapped.

Leigh drew her eyes from his and blinked hard several times before she spoke. "My mother died when I was young. I do not really remember much about her except the soft smile she always had on her face—Our home was not far from London and . . ."

She continued in a dry voice, as if reading a list, and Byron lay back with his hands beneath his head frowning as he watched the firelight dance on the canopy. Eventually Leigh's voice took on a softer tone and she relaxed slightly seeing that Byron was truly interested and not making sport of her.

"Is there anyone you especially miss in England?" he asked when she finished.

She turned and frowned at him. "There are a great many people I long to see."

"I mean a man you yearn to see," he snapped. "A suitor—someone that courted you."

"No," Leigh snapped back. She turned on her side away from him ending the conversation.

Why did I not tell him I had a beau in England? Leigh asked herself. There were many young men who had escorted her to various places, and more than one had asked for her hand. But not one of them did she especially long to see again, she mused. But I should have told Byron there were many men I missed and yearned to see again. She knew Byron was thinking of that Borough woman when he asked the question and she wondered how long it would be before she saw the woman being openly courted in her home. She remembered well the attractive woman from the millinery shop.

Byron lay awake long after Leigh was sleeping, thinking of what she had said. Though they had not talked long, or on the personal level he had hoped for, at least it was a start. It pleased him that Leigh was not longing for some man in England, and he was most pleased at the thought of the coming heir. He didn't like being forced to wed the girl, but if he was truthful with himself, the force had not been too great.

It was that old preacher that had finally changed his mind. By some dumb luck John O'Malley would have to bring a man that had been acquainted with Byron's father. The minister had pointed out to Byron several times that his father would turn over in his grave to know the foul deed Byron had done if he refused to marry the girl. But when the old man said there was always the chance that she could be with child—that had been the final blow. Byron had already decided to marry and sire children—now the deed was done.

He glanced at Leigh's sleeping form and sighed. He had his wife and his son was on his way. That he did not love Leigh was of little matter. He had planned to ask Ella to marry him, and he did not love her. He did not choose freely in the matter, true, but now that he thought on it, neither did Leigh. Had she asked the drunken fool to enter her room? NO! Had he courted her with a soft and gentle manner? NO! Had he asked her to be his bride? NO! He did not love Leigh, Byron Marsh loved no woman, but she was his wife and the mother of his child, and for some strange reason it was very important to him that Leigh care for him—mayhap even love him.

He would bide his time and treat her kindly, and in time she would grow to care for him. He had never had any problem attracting the maids before. It would not be easy to not act the husband, he mused. Her graceful beauty did greatly arouse his more basic nature. But, he thought with a sigh, he would have to control himself if they were ever to have any kind of marriage. He liked not the thought of the mother of his son not caring one wit for the father!

He sighed and turned his back to her and went to sleep thinking of her all soft and full of beautiful curves close beside him.

The next morning Byron was gone when Leigh awoke. Annie brought her breakfast in bed and laid out her clothes as she ate. Leigh passed the morning again going from room to room and admiring the beautiful house. She talked to Annie and Ephraim trying to make herself familiar with some of the other servants. She especially liked Aunt Mary, the cook. When Leigh asked Ephraim who's aunt she was, he grinned.

"Why, Master Byron's of course."

Leigh looked to him confused and was surprised to see he was very serious.

Ephraim chuckled and went on to explain. "We are one large family here, Miss Leigh. Annie is my wife, and Henry who takes care of the stables and drives the carriages is my son. Some of the other Negroes are also related, but we are all Master Byron's family."

Leigh smiled broadly at the charming man thanking him for his information.

Byron joined Leigh for lunch and offered to take her for a ride after lunch and show her some of the grounds. Leigh readily agreed and Byron chuckled as she rushed from the dining room to get a wrap.

"Be sure and dress warmly, Leigh," he called after her. "It is a chilly day."

When Leigh descended the stairs dressed in a warm cloak Byron was awaiting her in the foyer. He smiled offering her his arm and escorted her to the waiting carriage in front of the house. A handsome Negro man was waiting for them and opened the carriage door as they approached.

"Leigh, this is Henry," Byron said.

"Miss Leigh," Henry smiled with a nod of his head.

Leigh returned the man's smile noting that he had his mother's grin. "It is very nice to meet you Henry."

Byron handed Leigh into the carriage and made sure she wrapped the lap robe snuggly about her. Henry secured the carriage door and then took his seat on top. Once they were settled, Byron tapped on the carriage roof with his walking cane to let Henry know they were ready and slowly the carriage pulled away from the veranda steps.

Leigh was keenly aware of Byron so close beside her. She glanced at him askew and saw the deep blue eyes studying her. Her cheeks flushed and she felt her composure slip. She quickly turned to the carriage window and studied the passing scenery.

They passed the large barn Leigh had seen from the bedroom window and then entered a small lane lined with cottages. Leigh realized these were the slave quarters she had seen from the bedroom and she sat forward in the seat to inspect them more closely. She saw white frame houses of good size and in excellent repair. Some of the small yards in front of the homes had picket fences and all the homes looked comfortable and warm. She saw two Negro women chatting casually in one yard and made special note of their clothing. They wore dresses of good cloth, well made, and had warm wraps to hold back the winter cold.

Byron noted her interest in the homes and tapped the carriage roof again, a signal for Henry to stop. "This house," he said pointing to a frame house larger than the others, "is where Annie and Ephraim live, and that . . ."

Byron was interrupted by a small black face that suddenly appeared in the window, a young boy pressing his nose against the glass. Byron motioned to the boy to step down from the carriage step and as the boy did, he opened the carriage door.

Leigh saw a small black boy of nine or ten looking in at them, a large smile on the boy's face.

"James Lee," Byron said with a frown on his face, "hasn't anyone ever told you it is not polite to go about peeking in carriage windows."

The boy nodded his head vigorously, acknowledging that they had, but the smile never faltered.

"And," Byron continued, his voice gruff, "I did not invite you to open the carriage door, but merely to step down."

Leigh adjusted her position on the seat to get a better view of Byron's face. She knew well Byron's foul temper and she feared he would turn it on the smiling child at any moment.

"Well," Byron commented arching a brow at the boy.

The boy cast a quick glance Leigh's way and then looked again at Byron, cocking his head. "Well what?"

Just the hint of a smile turned at the corners of Byron's mouth. "Kindly close the door," he instructed.

"Yes, sir," James Lee replied. He made to close the door, but then hesitated a moment, his smiling face still directed at Byron. "The new Miz Marsh is sore enough pretty," he commented before closing the door.

Byron chuckled. He heard Henry telling the boy he best learn to mind his own business, and when Henry commented that if he caught the boy behaving as such again, he would tell Ephraim, Byron laughed hard for James Lee disappeared in a flash.

Byron turned to Leigh and found a soft smile on her lips and a tender expression in her eyes that he had never seen before. He gazed deep into the depth of the emerald pools before Leigh shyly lowered her eyes.

Byron signaled for Henry to continue and the carriage started forward with a lurch. Byron threw out a hand to catch Leigh should she fall and Leigh murmured a polite thank you, refusing to look his way.

They passed a large plowed field and Byron leaned Leigh's way pointing out the window. "This field," he said placing an arm on the seat behind Leigh, "will be filled with tobacco blooms come the summer."

"Tobacco plants produce a flower?" Leigh questioned.

"Indeed yes, and this field will be full of them for as far as the eye can see."

Leigh looked to the field judging its size and decided Annie was correct. Royal Oaks was a large plantation.

The ride continued and Byron pointed out various items of interest. Fields of cattle, more barns, more areas for planting, and yet she noted there were still vast areas left unspoiled. She was amazed by the size of the place.

When Byron signaled to Henry that it was time to start back toward the house Leigh commented how much she had enjoyed seeing the plantation.

"When the weather is warmer," Byron said, "I'll take you on a complete tour of the grounds."

"You mean there is more?" Leigh asked surprised.

"Indeed there is." Byron smiled. "You have seen only one section of Royal Oaks this day."

Leigh sat back with her mouth hanging open. She knew America was supposed to be a vast land, but she had no idea any one man could lay claim to so much land, and the fact that that man was her husband astounded her.

The carriage remained quiet as they made their way back to the house. Leigh became acutely aware of Byron's silent presence beside her. She felt as if the man surrounded her, his arm still resting on the back of the seat behind her. Nervously she folded her hands primly in her lap and tried to keep her gaze on the window. The few times she dared to glance Byron's way she found the deep blue eyes watching her closely.

She found the man was more of a puzzle to her than ever. She had found that not only did he possess some wealth, he possessed a *great* deal of wealth. Why, she thought with some surprise, at home in England Byron would be considered gentry! And his home was not only fine, it was gracious, and even warm. She also noted the mutual respect shared by Byron and his servants. Her brow wrinkled as she wondered if it was only she who brought out his foul temper and bad moods, for it was evident that his servants did not fear him, or his sudden wrath. And she was confused by his behavior toward her since she had awakened to find herself in his home. Granted, he had insulted her that first day when he questioned her about the father of the child, but now that Leigh thought about it she did have to admit the question was not totally unfair. After all Byron knew little of her and her character, and she thought, it was only by the grace of God that she had again escaped the clutches of Samuel Jones.

An involuntary shudder ran through Leigh's body at the thought of Jones and Byron quickly adjusted the lap robe around her thinking she was cold.

Leigh studied his handsome profile. She had never expected to see the man again, but she mused, if I had, I would have expected him to behave completely differently than he has. He had shown no wrath over her leaving in Richmond, in fact he had not even mentioned it. And he had not seemed upset to find himself again burdened with her, but instead, seemed almost pleased to have her in his home. He had been gentlemanly, gracious, and even kind. It was as though two people dwelled within the handsome form she saw. The kind, courteous, and even charming man that sat beside her now, and the man who could at a moment's notice become angry for no apparent reason and turn his foul temper at her in rage.

When the carriage stopped in front of the veranda steps Byron exited first and then turned to assist Leigh. Leigh made as if to take his hand, lifting her skirts to descend from the carriage but Byron's hands slid to her waist and he lifted her down gently. Their eyes met and Byron's hands remained on her trim waist seeming reluctant to loose their hold. Leigh's cheeks pinkened as she shyly drew her eyes from his.

"Thank you, Byron, for taking me for the carriage ride," she said in a soft tone. "I enjoyed it much."

"You are most welcome, pet," Byron replied easily.

When they entered the foyer Leigh continued on making her way up the stairs. When she reached the top she turned and found Byron still standing below in the foyer, his eyes focused on her. She smiled timidly and hurried on toward the bedroom.

Byron came in as Leigh was dressing for dinner and smiled at her and Annie as he gathered his clothes and walked toward the adjoining bedroom.

"Byron," Leigh offered meekly, "this is your room. Do not let me run you from it. Annie can finish with my hair after you have bathed and changed."

"No, pet," he said smiling to her and then to Annie. "I never interrupt a master at her work."

Annie laughed hard and winked at Leigh as Byron left the room. Annie braided Leigh's hair into two large braids at the back of her neck and then looped them there, letting the large braids lay on her back slightly over lapping one another.

The gown she chose this time was a soft cream in color. It was made of silk and the neck was cut low and round with small puffy sleeves that were worn off the shoulders. The skirt had just enough of the extra fullness in the back to give it the gentle swinging motion as Leigh walked.

When Leigh finished smoothing her stockings and putting on the small cream colored slippers that matched the gown, Annie walked toward her offering her her mother's cameo saying it would look well with the dress. Leigh looked at it a long time in the woman's hand before she took and pinned it carefully on the center of the bodice of the gown.

Leigh made her way to the drawing room, her skirts swishing about her. When she reached the doorway, she stopped, taking in the scene before her and her heart skipped a beat.

Byron stood talking to an older man nearly as tall as himself, and the man's features much resembled Byron's.

"Leigh, dear, come in," Byron said turning and seeing her framed in the doorway.

As Leigh entered the room on trembling legs Byron walked to greet her with a smile and placed a hand on her waist as he introduced her to their guest.

"Leigh, I would like for you to meet my Uncle Jonathan," he said.

Leigh was startled, and though she knew that Byron had an uncle from Annie, and the fact that Byron himself had mentioned the man only yesterday, she had not expected to meet him tonight. She nervously bit at her lower lip wondering how much the man knew of their marriage.

"Leigh," Jonathan said taking her hand and placing a gentlemanly kiss upon it. "I am very pleased to meet you. I have been most anxious ever since Byron came over and told me he had wed." He smiled at Leigh. "I don't mind telling you I was surprised, to say the least." He glanced to Byron and grinned. "But it is about time Byron settled down, and he has chosen a most charming wife I see."

Leigh blushed and murmured her thanks as she nervously sat on the edge of one of the love seats. The men each had a glass of wine, and Leigh quickly nodded her head when Byron inquired if she would also care for a glass. As Byron handed her the wine she nervously gulped a mouth full.

"I have a daughter close in age to you, Leigh," Jonathan said. "She is married now and living in the Carolinas. Being a widower, Byron is the only other family I have. It will be a pleasure having such a lovely niece as well."

Leigh smiled timidly at the man and tried to talk politely with him, but her voice kept cracking with nervousness. She could have kissed Ephraim when he came to announce dinner.

Jonathan winked at Byron and went to offer Leigh his arm. She accepted it with a jerky smile and he escorted her to the dining table. Leigh and Byron sat at opposite ends of the long table, as usual, and Jonathan sat in the middle to Leigh's right.

Leigh was glad the table was so long and hoped they sat far enough apart that Byron's uncle could not see how badly her hand shook as she tried to eat.

Jonathan attempted several times to engage Leigh in conversation, but her answers were short, though polite, and not lending themselves to further discussion.

As soon as the meal was over Leigh excused herself on the pretext that she was tired and still not recovered from her recent illness. Jonathan said he hoped she would feel better soon and again told her how happy he was to meet her and have her in the family.

As Byron walked with Leigh to the foyer, Jonathan watched the couple closely. How good they looked together, he thought. He wondered where Byron had found someone as shy and innocent as Leigh. Byron had always been lucky at wagers and gaming, and now it appeared he was also lucky when it came to choosing a wife. Jonathan had little doubt that luck had a great deal to do with it, for though he knew Byron to be bright, he had never shown much wisdom in his choice of women. Byron seemed to favor women of a rather loose nature in the past. He had given Jonathan's old heart a bad time when he thought that he might marry Ella Borough. Though the Boroughs were neighbors, and Fred Borough was a very dear friend of his, he had never much cared for Ella. She was a spoiled brat as a child and he saw little difference in her now that she was grown. He seriously doubted Ella to be a lady in the strictest meaning of the word. Yes, luck, he mused, most definitely played a part in Byron's choosing a wife as sweet and lovely as Leigh appeared to be.

Byron had told him on his visit yesterday that Leigh's father had recently died and that she was quite alone when first they met. He had said he had fallen in love with her almost at first sight and he swept her off her feet giving her little chance to decline his offer of marriage. Jonathan knew Byron well enough to know that he was hiding something and not telling him the complete truth, but he would not pry. Though Byron was his brother's

189

son and he loved him like his own, Byron was a man full grown and Jonathan felt he had no right to interfere.

Now that he saw Leigh, he wondered. It would not be hard to fall in love with a woman on first sight who was as striking as Leigh. Watching the couple closely in the foyer, he saw Byron's gentleness with her and the admiring look in his nephew's eye. He smiled to himself. It did indeed appear Byron had at last been struck by cupid's arrow.

Byron stood looking at Leigh and his face was full of concern. "Leigh, if you feel ill I can . . ."

"No," Leigh interrupted in a cool voice, "I am just tired. Goodnight." She turned and started up the stairs and Byron stood a moment watching her skirt swinging jauntily as she climbed the stairs.

Annie was in the bedroom preparing the room for the night and once she helped Leigh out of her gown, Leigh told her she would brush out her own hair and wished Annie a goodnight. Annie frowned slightly but soon left the room, a worried expression on her face as to Leigh's mood.

Once Annie closed the door Leigh raged. How dare he invite his uncle and not tell her the man was coming! She flopped down on the white chair in front of the mirror and started angrily yanking the brush through her hair. How was she to answer the man's casual questions? She sat in front of the mirror making coy faces at her own reflection.

"Oh yes," she said to her own reflection, "Byron and I met only a short time ago."

She jerked the brush angrily and then again looked in the mirror.

"No, we did not know each other long before we wed."

She jerked the brush again and looking at herself, coyly fluttered her lashes.

"You see, Byron ravished me and the innkeeper where I was staying forced him to marry me!"

She threw the brush across the room with an oath, and rising from the chair, she started to pace the room in angry strides. Ooh! She was furious! The very least Byron could have done was tell her the man was coming to dinner and how much he knew of their marriage.

She had been so quiet at dinner, afraid to say too much less she put her foot firmly in her mouth, that now she was sure Byron's uncle thought her a fool. She gasped, eyes wide. What if Byron told the man the truth! She would never face the man again. Ooh, how could Byron be so cruel!

When Byron entered the room much later after Jonathan had left, Leigh was sitting up in bed with an odd look on her face.

"Not asleep yet, pet?" he asked unbuttoning his shirt and starting to get ready for bed. At her continued silence he turned to her with concern. "Leigh, do you feel very ill? Is there anything wrong?"

"No Byron, there is nothing wrong," Leigh replied, sarcasm dripping off of each word.

"I see," Byron said arching a brow.

"You see, sir, a wife made to look the fool!" Leigh flounced out of bed giving Byron a quick peek at one nicely shaped thigh before her gown fell down into place. She started to pace to and fro before him.

"How could you?" she raved throwing her hands in the air. "Why did you not tell me your uncle was coming?" She stopped her pacing and turned to glare at him. "I did not know what to say, or how to answer his casual questions. Or," she said with a toss of her head, "how much you had told him about our blissful courtship." She stretched her neck out and stuck her face as close to his as she could manage on tiptoes. "I imagine I was made the villian of your tale!" she hissed. She turned and started pacing again.

At first Byron had been greatly surprised by her anger, but as he stood quietly listening to her rant and rave, his own fury grew.

"This is my-y-y-y house, madam," he snarled, "and I think I may invite my-y-y-y uncle to dinner without your permission!"

"Ooh!" Leigh fumed stomping one small foot on the floor.

"Leigh!" Byron snapped. "I have told you before I will not put up with these shows of temper of yours. If you insist upon acting like a child, I shall turn you across my knee!"

They stood staring hard at one another for a long time. Then Leigh stuck her nose in the air and walked to the door of the adjoining bedroom. She turned and gave Byron a hateful look and then opened the door.

"And just where do you think you are going, madam?"

"I am going, sir, to spend the night in this room," she said pointing her finger toward the guest room. "I don't intend to pass the night with a husband who threatens to beat me, and who does not have the common courtesy to tell me there will be a guest for dinner!" She put her nose in the air, walked through the door, and slammed it hard behind her.

Byron stomped to the door. "Leigh, you open this door at once!" he yelled.

"I will not!" came the sharp reply.

Byron tried the door but found it was locked and the key was on Leigh's side. He scowled at the offending portal and again yelled for her to open it. This time there was no reply at all!

A low growl escaped Byron's throat and he turned quickly and went to the door leading to the hallway, down the hall to the room's other door, but it too was locked.

Byron pounded on the door with his fist, shouting. "Leigh open this door this very instant or I shall break it down!"

"No!" he heard her shout.

He laid his shoulder to the solid oak door several times and Leigh's anger was fast turning to fear. She could hear his angry curses and decided she best open the door now before he DID break it down and his anger would be all the greater.

Quietly she tiptoed to the door, and unlocking it, quickly scurried away.

Byron opened the door the second he heard the key turn in the lock. He was furious! He walked toward Leigh, a fierce scowl on his face. Leigh backed away cautiously with large, frightened eyes and moved to put a chair between them.

"Byron if you lay hand on me, I'll—I'll run away again, I swear," she said in a small fearful voice.

Byron reached out and grabbed the chair and sent it flying across the room. "Very well, madam," he growled, "I warned you."

He reached out one long arm and snatched Leigh around the waist. Lifting her off the floor and holding her in one strong arm like a sack of potatoes, he smacked her hard several times on the bottom. Leigh kicked and screamed and tried to wiggle free. He then proceeded to carry her to their room still in the same position and Leigh kicked and beat on his back with her small fists the entire way.

He carried her to the soft downy mattress on the bed and roughly deposited her on it. Tears streamed down her face as she glared at him. He had not really hurt her, though her bottom did sting some, but her pride had never been more injured. She was humiliated to her very soul.

"I hate you!" she screamed at him.

"Right now, madam, I don't care for you much either," Byron said arching a brow at her.

He took long angry strides to the door and then turned to glare at her. "Now be a good little girl," he snapped, his voice growing louder with each word, "and go to sleep!" He left the room and slammed the door hard behind him.

"Oooh," Leigh hissed. "If I had a gun right now I would shoot him!"

She sat and glared at the door, then turning her face to the pillow she started to cry in earnest, and just like any small child, she eventually cried herself to sleep.

Chapter Eight

The next morning when Leigh awoke the sun was high and Byron was not in bed. She had not awakened if he ever did come to bed last night.

Annie appeared carrying a breakfast tray. She told Leigh Byron had risen long ago and gone to the barn, and she thought Leigh needed to rest and have breakfast in bed.

Leigh thanked her and as she sat eating her breakfast, she wondered if Annie or Ephraim had witnessed their angry words of the night before. Though she knew that all the servants had their own cottages, one of them could have still been below tidying up when she and Byron quarreled. She desperately hoped not.

Annie bustled about the room laying out Leigh's clothes and talking all the while.

"Masser Byron sore do love that there bull he brung

home," she said. "He spend half his day with it. You'd think it made of gold or somthin' the way he carry on," she chuckled.

Leigh did not have the slightest idea to what Annie was referring, but she smiled at the woman, enjoying listening to her talk.

When Leigh climbed into the tub Annie took the breakfast tray leaving Leigh to soak for awhile. Leigh sat in the tub thinking of the past night. She was not one to carry a grudge for long. She would behave today as if nothing had happened. By no means would she apologize to Byron, but perhaps if she was pleasant the affair would soon be put behind them and things would again be as pleasant as they had the day Byron had shown her the house. She had greatly enjoyed the tour, his company as much as seeing the beautiful home.

Annie returned and made the bed while Leigh extracted herself from the tub. Once in her shift and robe, Annie came to help her with her hair. She brushed the thick mass and then braided her hair into two long braids on each side of her head looping the braids above her ears. It looked most charming as the heavy braids brushed against her shoulders whenever she turned her head.

Annie assisted Leigh into a gown of rich, soft, gray. The skirt was full and pleated in large French pleats. When one walked the pleats opened to reveal insets of a darker gray fabric. The bodice buttoned from waist to collar and the buttons, collar, and cuffs were all in the darker gray of the insets. It was a beautifully designed gown and with Leigh's dark hair and creamy complexion, she looked ravishing in it.

"Miss Leigh you gets prettier ever' day," Annie said

with a grin.

Leigh gave the woman a small curtsy and a tremendous smile. "Annie I fear you do yourself small justice. It is this lovely gown and your careful grooming you see before you."

"Oh, go on," Annie replied with a swish of her hand, but Leigh knew the woman was pleased with the compliment by the deep grin on her face.

Leigh found she had little to occupy her with all the servants, and Annie would hear nothing of Leigh doing small chores around the house. She decided to go to Byron's study since she knew he was absent from the house, and see if she could find a book to her liking.

Leigh spent several hours in the study and found no less than twenty books she wished to read. She finally decided on one and went to the drawing room.

She had just settled down in one of the wing back chairs, her feet tucked beneath her, when she heard someone come in the front door. She laid down her book on a nearby table and started for the foyer.

Byron had probably returned, she thought, and she wanted to greet him following her resolve to mend the quarrel of the night before. As she reached the doorway she almost collided with the woman entering the room.

"Who are you?" the woman asked with a look of complete surprise on her face.

"It appears I could ask the same of you," Leigh replied. Leigh knew quite well who the woman was. She recognized her the moment she laid eyes on her, and while the advantage was on her side, she decided to make full use of it.

"I am Ella Borough," the woman said brushing past Leigh and entering the drawing room. She had already removed her cloak in the foyer and stood now removing her gloves and looking Leigh up and down.

"I am very happy to meet you Miss Borough," Leigh replied sweetly making no effort to introduce herself in return.

Leigh slowly walked to one of the love seats and sat down demurely, carefully arranging her skirts. She knew this woman had planned on marrying Byron and no doubt would be greatly shocked to discover that Leigh had already done so. She felt sure Byron loved this woman and Leigh took an instant disliking to her seeing in Ella all that she feared she lacked. Ella was lovely in appearance and seemed self-assured. All too soon Ella would learn the circumstances of their marriage and the fact that Byron felt no love for her, or she for him. But that did not prevent Leigh from acting the secure wife now—that is if she ever decided to tell the woman who she was.

Ella stood glaring at Leigh. She did not like what she saw. This girl was much too young and attractive to be here in Byron's home. Byron had been away an unusually long time on business, thought Ella. This girl was most likely a guest along with her father who had business with Byron, Ella decided. Still, the sooner that she was gone, the better Ella would like it. Although now that Ella thought about it, Byron could not possibly be attracted to the girl. She did not even have the good breeding to introduce herself!

Ella opened her mouth to speak and Ephraim appeared in the doorway.

"I am brewing your tea now, Miss Leigh. Would you like it served in here?"

Leigh looked to the man puzzled. She had not asked for

198

tea. And besides, it was too early for tea, she had not even had lunch yet! Then she realized that Ephraim also knew Miss Borough and had come to see how Leigh faired and if he could ease the tension between the two women. The man is a jewel, thought Leigh.

"Yes, please Ephraim, serve in here," she replied smiling broadly at the man.

Ephraim grinned and nodded his head and then turned to face Ella. "The child you sent to fetch Master Byron returned to say he will be here directly." He smiled again in Leigh's direction and turned and left the room.

Ella noted the respect Ephraim had shown this Leigh what-ever-her-name-was. The man had never shown her such respect. He had not been rude, he was much too good a servant for that, but Ella knew the man did not like her. Oh well, she thought, it is of little matter, he is only a servant.

Ella seated herself just as demurely and just as carefully arranged her skirts glancing at Leigh askew. She noted Leigh's lovely gown and her dislike for the girl grew.

"I know Byron has been away on business. Is your father a business acquaintance of his?" she asked looking Leigh up and down.

"No," Leigh replied with a smile and again carefully arranged the full skirt of her gown.

Well she certainly doesn't talk much, thought Ella. She was becoming quite agitated with the girl. Best to put her in her place right away, she decided.

"Please do not think me presumptuous," Ella said in a sweet, cooing tone, "but Byron and I have known each other a long time. He has very few acquaintances we do not share. As a matter of fact," she cooed reaching a hand up to pat her hair, "we plan to be married soon."

"Really," Leigh replied making large eyes at the woman.

"Yes, we have . . ."

Ella's voice trailed away when she heard Byron's boots clicking against the floor as he made his way down the foyer to the drawing room. When he walked in he was looking down fastening the sleeves of his shirt.

"One of the children came to say we have a guest. You must excuse my appearance, I . . ." He stopped in midsentence when he looked up and took in the scene before him. A small groan escaped his lips.

"Byron, love, I have missed you," Ella said rising and rushing to his side. She grabbed his arm and hugged it tightly to her generous bosom as Byron cast a wary eye in Leigh's direction. "Byron I do believe you get more handsome with each passing day," Ella exclaimed smiling broadly at him and fluttering her lashes.

Leigh thought she felt ill watching the woman hang on Byron, but she did have to agree with Ella concerning Byron's appearance. He was dressed in fawn colored breeches that fit very snugly and left little to the imagination. He wore a white shirt open at the throat and some of the hair covering his massive chest was showing. His riding boots were of the best leather and came high up on the muscular calfs of his legs. Whoever had said clothes make the man, reflected Leigh, had never met Byron! He looked handsome no matter what he wore, but Leigh decided she rather liked him best dressed as he was now, casually. The deep tan of his skin and the slightly rugged clothes made his handsome features even more striking and his masculinity seemed to fill the room.

"Byron, love, I have missed you terribly," Ella purred.

Byron made a non-committal grunt and Ella turned to face Leigh still clinging to Byron's arm. "Love, I have not met your house guest," she commented stressing the word guest and giving Leigh a "poor dear" look.

Byron cleared his throat and pried his arm free of Ella's grip. He walked to stand behind Leigh placing his hands on the back of the love seat. Leigh could not see his face from where she sat and she watched Ella's closely.

Byron had not meant Ella to find out like this and he feared she would make a terrible scene. He sighed heavily seeing no escape, and plainly and simply stated the facts.

"Ella, this is my wife, Leigh. We were married outside of Richmond over eight weeks ago."

Ella's mouth flew open and she sucked in a great deal of air. Just then Ephraim entered with the tea, as if on cue, and placed it on the tea table before Leigh. He glanced to Leigh askew and they exchanged a look. Then without a word he turned and left the room.

"Tea, Miss Borough?" Leigh asked sweetly. Her hands were trembling so waiting for Byron to continue and tell the rest of the tale, and she fought hard not to show her anxiety.

Byron stared at the back of Leigh's head as she poured the tea. He did not know what had been said between the two women before he entered the room, but he decided it could not have been much. Ella did not know who Leigh was, and Leigh was much too at ease and the perfect hostess. He sighed inwardly when he realized that Ella must not have said anything about their past relationship.

"Your wife!" Ella finally gasped looking from one to the other. "I do not believe it!

"I assure you Ella, it is quite true," Byron stated. "I

201

would not be so cruel as to jest on something of this importance."

"Why you little harlot," Ella sneered taking a step toward Leigh with a fierce look in her eyes.

"Ella!" Byron said sharply. "This is Leigh's home now too, and I will not see a guest insult her in her own home!"

"Byron, darling," Leigh said smiling to herself, "I am sure Miss Borough meant no insult. She is no doubt shocked that such an old and dear friend," she said arching a brow at Ella, "has married without her knowledge."

Now Byron was shocked. He looked to the back of Leigh's head and mentally shook himself. What was this darling business? Leigh never used endearments where he was concerned! Something had most definitely been said before he entered the room—but he'd be damned if he knew what! He looked from woman to woman, confusion on his face.

"You most likely have much to discuss," Leigh commented glancing to Ella, "so I will excuse myself now. I need to talk with Aunt Mary concerning dinner anyway." She rose, and turning to Byron, patted his hand resting on the back of the love seat, and then she turned again to face Ella. "It was very nice to meet you Miss Borough. Please feel free to call again."

Ella let out a low growl as Leigh daintily exited the room. Leigh could hear angry words exchanged as she made her way to the cookhouse. She passed Ephraim on the way and smiled at him, dimples deep.

"Why, Miss Leigh, you look like the cat that swallowed the canary," he commented with a grin.

"Do I, Ephraim? I cannot imagine why," she said with

a grin as she continued on her way. "Thank you for the tea, Ephraim," she called over her shoulder. "It was quite delicious."

"You are most welcome, Miss Leigh," Ephraim replied with a chuckle.

That night at dinner Byron noticed that Leigh and Ephraim seemed to be sharing some kind of secret. They kept exchanging knowing glances whenever the man was in the room. Byron watched them closely and was truly puzzled. He wished desperately to know what went on between the two women this afternoon, and what in the devil was going on between Leigh and Ephraim now!

He thought how refreshing Leigh looked at the far end of the table. She had conducted herself most properly today and it was a pleasure to share her gentle, quiet, graceful, beauty after the harsh and bitter words he had exchanged with Ella this afternoon. Ella was a shrew, and to think I actually thought of asking her to marry me once, he thought—No wonder I got so drunk that night!

Leigh glanced at Byron under her lashes. She wondered what all had been said after she had left Ella and Byron alone. She knew they had quarreled, she heard that much on the way to the cookhouse. Mayhap later Byron had calmed her down and told her the truth of the matter. She hoped not, but she doubted that hoping made it true. However, she was very pleased with Byron's behavior toward Ella today when she was present and she vowed to think on it no more and ruin the day.

A smile crossed her face as she thought of the look on Ella's face when Byron told her they were married.

"What have you found so amusing, Leigh?"

She glanced up and saw Byron carefully studying her.

203

"Nothing, Byron. Pay me no mind."

Byron frowned, more puzzled than ever.

When dinner was over they retired to the drawing room. Leigh seated herself and watched Byron begin to pace. She had come to realize that Byron did this whenever he had something on his mind, and she smiled at him as he walked to and fro.

Finally he stopped and faced her. "Leigh, I do not know what Ella said today, but sometimes she exaggerates greatly."

He looked to Leigh with anticipation, and folding his arms across his chest, waited for her to speak, but she just looked at him smiling.

"I have known her all my life," he prompted. "We are good friends," he said emphasizing the word friends.

He again waited for her to offer some information about Ella's visit, but she again looked at him in that charming way and smiled. Byron turned with a curse and again started to pace.

"Byron," Leigh finally said sweetly, "you owe me no explanation."

He frowned at her and arched a brow. "I was not aware, madam, that I was offering one."

He mumbled something under his breath and flopped down in one of the wing back chairs. He saw the book Leigh had left on the table that afternoon and he picked it up studying the cover.

"How did this get here?" he said more to himself than to her. "I do not recall leaving this book here."

"I left it Byron. I am sorry," she quickly added. "I did not mean to be careless with the book."

"You left it!" He glanced to the book and then back to Leigh. Was this entire day to be a puzzle? "Whatever for Leigh?"

"I had planned to start reading it when . . ."

"You can read?" he asked amazed.

"Yes," she smiled shyly, "and I . . ."

"I did not know you could read," he said standing and walking toward her with admiration in his eyes.

"There are a great many things you do not know about me, Byron," she said coyly, still smiling at him. "I hope you do not mind me making use of your library."

"No, of course not. I only regret that it is not larger. I love books and there are a great number I still wish to own. They are one item still hard to come by here in America."

"I found a great number I wish to read," she said brightly.

"Really, which ones?"

Byron came and sat beside her on the love seat and for the firt time Leigh and Byron found a subject that they shared—their love of books. They talked late into the night and their words came easy and unguarded. They both truly relaxed with one another for the first time.

Leigh found she enjoyed the closeness of him. His occasional jesting and easy laugh made her feel slightly lightheaded in his presence. Once when their hands chanced to touch, Leigh felt a tingle go through her body, almost as if it had been shocked. She felt her composure slip slightly when she raised her eyes slowly to his and saw those blue eyes looking even bluer, and slightly hooded as he stared at her intently.

Ephraim passed the doorway and could hear the couple talking. He could not help but eavesedrop slightly and he smiled as he listened. He knew the couple had their problems. He could not put his finger on the exact trouble with the marriage—but he knew there was something. Listening to them talking like this, he felt hope for the marriage. As he strolled to his cottage that night, he was whistling.

That night before Byron climbed into bed he wished Leigh a goodnight.

"Goodnight Byron, pleasant dreams," she replied smiling and pulling the covers up under her chin.

Byron stood warmly gazing down at her for several moments before he blew out the candles, removed his pants, and climbed into bed. It would not be long now, he told himself, before she accepts me as husband. Byron grinned to himself.

He did have very pleasant dreams that night. Now if only they would come true, he thought upon wakening.

The next day was Sunday and Byron, dressed and ready for church, paced the floor in the foyer awaiting Leigh. If she did not hurry they were going to be late.

"Leigh, pet, are you almost ready?" he called up the stairs. "The hour is late."

"I am hurrying, Byron," he heard her reply.

When Leigh had found they were going to church, she nervously helped Annie to choose a gown for her. She knew she would be meeting many of Byron's friends today and she wanted to look her very best.

Leigh appeared at the top of the steps and Byron's eyes glistened as he looked up at her. She smiled timidly and started slowly down the wide staircase.

She wore a gown of dark mauve. It was made of silk and had ruffles at the cuffs and throat in a soft gray fabric. There was a wide band of gray circling the full skirt halfway down. Her hair was wrapped in a large bun at the base of her neck. She wore a gray fox hat and carried a matching muff. A mauve coat was thrown over one arm, the gray lining showing.

"You look very lovely, Leigh," Byron said as she handed him her coat. She thanked him, blushing, and said she could say the same of him.

"That I look lovely?" Byron replied, merriment in his eyes.

"No, silly," Leigh giggled, "that you look handsome."

As Byron helped Leigh on with her coat he commented that they would most likely be the most handsome couple present at church today. When Leigh turned to give him a shameful look, he winked.

The carriage was waiting at the front door. Byron handed Leigh in and then took special care that the lap robe was tucked snugly about her.

"I do not want you ill again," he said. "Mayhap we should not go, it is a rather cold day."

Leigh searched his face thinking he was anxious about introducing her to his friends. She saw only concern for her in his eyes and promised herself not to be so belittling of him in the future.

"I am fine, Byron, please let us go. I do not think we should linger much longer or we will be late."

"Anything you say, pet." He winked at her again and tapped the top of the carriage with his cane so Henry would know they were ready.

They were the last to arrive. As they entered the church Byron placed a hand on Leigh's arm and escorted her quickly to the Marsh family pew. Whispering seemed to follow them as they made their way down the aisle and many heads turned to stare. Uncle Jonathan awaited them at the pew and rose as they came to sit beside him.

"Good day," he said smiling to them both. "My Leigh, but you do look lovely today."

"T-Thank you," Leigh murmured, slightly embarrassed at seeing the man again. "You look quite handsome yourself," she added.

Byron chuckled and Jonathan gave him a bemused look. He had heard nothing amusing. Leigh glanced at her husband and her eyes were also full of merriment. No sooner had Byron helped Leigh with her coat, and they sat down, than the service began.

Ella sat to their left and a few rows back. She had seen the merry looks the couple exchanged and the gentle attention Byron paid his wife. Byron's uncle seemed acquainted with the girl as well, she noted, and she stared at the back of Leigh's head through the majority of the service. If looks could kill, Leigh most certainly would have died. Ella had noticed Leigh's lovely gown and matching coat, not to mention the fox hat and muff. She was green with envy thinking those things rightfully belonged to her. This little Leigh will rue the day she met Byron before I am done, she thought spitefully.

After services were over many came to be introduced to Leigh. Leigh saw Ella standing to one side with an older man and the look she gave Leigh made her feel extremely uncomfortable to say the least. Ella turned to enter her carriage but the man with her walked toward them, a smile on his face. He was introduced as Fred Borough and Leigh discovered he was Ella's father. He was very polite and wished them both well but Leigh felt sure the man must be disappointed that Byron and Ella had not wed, and felt slightly uncomfortable with him. He and Uncle Jonathan appeared to be good friends and the two walked a small distance away to talk some business.

Leigh was very nervous meeting Byron's friends and neighbors and wished desperately that she could speak with the slow, easy drawl of the others present. Her English accent sounded strange and out of place here with these people. And she noted the cool appraisal she was given by many. She attributed it to her English heritage not realizing that she had dashed the hopes of many present to marry a daughter, niece, or cousin to the handsome Byron Marsh and share in the Marsh fortune and good name.

Byron saw Jack and Emily Cummings taking the children to the carriage and then coming their way. He braced himself.

"Byron, I ought to have you horse whipped. Business indeed!" Jack said with a laugh as he tipped his hat to Leigh.

Introductions were made and Leigh found she liked Jack at once. Emily seemed very shy but nice. As the two women chatted somewhat nervously with one another, Jack pulled Byron a short distance away. Here it comes, thought Byron.

"When you were gone over seven weeks time," Jack said, "we all started to fear you had met with foul play. You have never stayed away from Royal Oaks that long before." Jack glanced Leigh's way and grinned. "No wonder you were gone so long!" he added with a wink. "I, ah, passed Ella a moment ago and her face looked like a sculpture," Jack arched a brow at Byron smiling, "a marble sculpture." Byron laughed. "Laugh if you like Byron, but by the stony look I saw on her face I suggest that if you want to keep your lovely wife, you keep her well out of Ella's path."

"Oh, Jack, though I know Ella has a foul temper, I do

believe you exaggerate."

Jack grinned. "Hell hath no fury . . ." Byron chuckled again. "You know Byron," Jack said with an appraising glance, "I did not expect to see you wed for at least another twenty years."

"Twenty years?"

"Yes," Jack laughed. "I had rather planned on saving you for Elizabeth."

Byron laughed hard. Elizabeth was Jack's infant daughter.

They returned to the women and joined in their conversation.

"Emily and I were in Richmond for a short time when you and Byron were there Leigh," Jack offered. "We had no idea he was on his honeymoon."

Leigh blushed and her eyes rose to Byron's. He smiled and placed an arm about her waist and gave it a gentle squeeze with his hand. Leigh was flustered by his touch and embarrassed by his show of affection with others present. She found that she did not so much fear his touch anymore, but rather that it made her knees wobble.

Ella was watching the couple closely from her carriage. She was livid at Byron's arm about his wife and wondered at his mood. He had told her often enough that one did not display affections in public.

"It is a cold day Jack, and Leigh and I have a long ride home," Byron said. "Would you and Emily care to join us for Sunday dinner?"

Byron realized too late that he had again invited dinner guests without first consulting Leigh. He turned and gave her a helpless look.

"Please do," she said. "I would like to get to know Byron's friends better."

"I do feel we should drop the children at home first," Emily said looking to Jack. "They will need to nap."

All was settled and soon everyone was on their way. Leigh had invited Uncle Jonathan to join them feeling she owed the man a return invitation with a more charming hostess.

Byron and Leigh chatted on the long ride home.

"Byron, I have met so many new faces of late, I fear I will never keep them all straight."

"Don't worry, pet," he replied with a smile. "I am here to help you and I am sure no one will think ill of you if you happen to forget a name. You know, Uncle Jonathan gives a ball every year at New Years, and many of the people you met today will be there, as well as friends that live farther away."

"Will I be going?" Leigh asked hesitantly.

"Of course," Byron replied, surprised at the question. "Who else would I take if not my wife?"

"I, ah, do not know. I just thought, well, it does not matter what I thought."

"It matters to me what you think," Byron said with a smile. He reached for her hand and gave it a squeeze.

Leigh's cheeks pinkened and in a moment she eased her hand from his and changed the subject.

So he is not ashamed to be seen with me, thought Leigh. He will take me to social functions just as Annie said he would. Most likely Ella would also be at the dance, she mused. It was still a long way off, it being only the first of December, but Leigh started planning exactly what she would wear. She bit her lower lip wishing she still had some of her jewelry. No doubt Ella would be decked out well in jewels.

"Leigh, you are not listening. What is the matter?"

211

"What? Oh, nothing. I guess I was just wool gathering. I fear it is one of many bad habits I have." Color rose in her cheeks. "What did you say?"

"I said, what do you think of Emily and Jack?"

"I like them very much. They seem extremely nice." She hesitated and nervously bit her lip.

"Is there something amiss, Leigh?" Byron asked in a concerned voice.

"No, but, ah, Byron mighten your friends disapprove of me because I am British?"

"Leigh, whatever would make you think such a thing?" he said kindly, giving her a shameful look. Then he smiled and took her hand in his and his voice was gentle and soft when he spoke. "Pet, most of us are from English decent. Though it is true there are those who still hold strong feelings against the British, my friends are not among them. The war is over and we now trade with the English. They buy my tobacco, as well as that of my neighbors."

Leigh was flustered at his kind words and gentle manner. She smiled weakly at him and let the subject drop. Mayhap he meant no insult to her or the English when he had taken her on the tour of Richmond.

Leigh shivered with the cold and Byron quickly placed an arm about her and pulled her close to his side.

"Cold, pet?" Leigh lowered her eyes and nodded her head. "We are almost home," he commented.

Leigh smiled inwardly thinking it was a shame the ride was not slightly longer.

They were the first to arrive at Royal Oaks, only slightly ahead of their guests. Leigh quickly sought out Ephraim to tell him there would be guests for dinner.

Byron stood watching her discuss the seating arrangements and other details with the man. It was going to be different with a woman in the house, he thought. He had been a bachelor so long, he must remember not to trespass on Leigh's rightful territory as his wife and hostess of his home.

She turned and smiled at him, dimples deep. Then a worried frown crossed her brow. "Byron you do not suppose the Cummings felt the children were not welcome do you?"

"No, pet. I am very fond of children, and the Cummings' ones especially. Emily and Jack know the children are most welcome here. I am sure it is just as Emily said," he assured her, "they needed to nap this afternoon."

"Good," she replied grinning at him, an odd look in her eye. She had no idea Byron was fond of children and the thought pleased her greatly. She turned her attention again to Ephraim and Byron walked to his study to pour himself a brandy to ward off the chill.

I think I am going to like being married, he told himself. Leigh pleased him more with each passing day. And it appeared she was going to be a most charming and able hostess.

The guests soon arrived and as the men departed for the study for brandys, Emily and Leigh entered the drawing room. They discussed Emily's children, a boy three named Jeffery, and an infant daughter Elizabeth.

"Emily, I do hope you know the children are very welcome in this house. Though there are those that prefer not to have children present when they dine, Byron and I are not among them."

"Thank you, Leigh," Emily replied with a shy smile. "I know the children have always been welcome here in the past and it is nice to know it is still so. Elizabeth does need to nap, and sometimes it is very difficult to get acquainted with an infant around." She laughed. "And a wild little Indian like Jeffery makes it nearly impossible."

Emily was nearly as tall as Leigh. She was petite in bone structure like Leigh and had a graceful way of moving. Her hair was a lovely shade of soft brown and she had large brown eyes that reminded Leigh of a frightened fawn.

Leigh was a good hostess and soon Emily got over some of her shyness and the two were talking comfortably together. They discussed Jack's and Byron's long friendship and Emily told her about some of the neighbors she would be meeting that were not present at church today.

The men joined them after a bit and the conversation grew more lively.

"Leigh, you have more than a few enemies marrying Byron," Jack said with a twinkle in his eye. "He was a most sought after bachelor."

Byron frowned at Jack askew. Jack appeared to be jesting but Leigh knew there was truth in his words. Ella was her enemy for sure.

"I could say the same of you Jack," Byron said curtly, then he smiled slowly. "I seem to recall you having your fair share of young ladies fluttering their eyelashes at you."

Jack laughed hard as Emily smiled lovingly in his direction.

"Enjoy your memories gentlemen," Jonathan said with merriment in his voice. "Someday you will be old and gray like me and everyone will doubt you ever turned a pretty lady's head."

"Why Uncle Jonathan," Leigh said looking hard at the man, "you are still a striking man and were I not married to this nephew of yours, I would flutter my lashes at you anyday." She coyly looked at him and gave her eyelashes a flutter.

Jonathan laughed heartily, as did the others, and bowed low in front of Leigh, taking her hand. "Leigh, my dear, it is going to be a joy, indeed, having you in the family."

Ephraim came to announce dinner and they retired to the dining room. Leigh glanced in Byron's direction and found a warm smile on his face. He was wishing that Leigh would flutter her lashes at him in that manner.

The meal was delicious and after it was over, the women excused themselves and left the men to smoke their cigars.

Leigh was worried Emily would ask how she and Byron met but the subject never came up, much to her relief.

The afternoon was soon spent and the guests left with gracious thanks and fond farewells. Leigh had greatly enjoyed herself and felt that she had made a friend in Emily.

As Byron and Leigh stood in the doorway waving goodbye, the old awkwardness again rose between them. Byron turned to Leigh smiling and after a moment announced he thought he best go to his study and catch up on some work. Leigh smiled timidly and retired to the bedroom.

That night Leigh was asleep when Byron came up to bed. He stood a long time looking at her sleeping form.

How much longer must I wait? he asked himself. She was so tempting laying there close by him every night. He thought of sleeping in the guest room next to his bedroom until things were more relaxed between them, but he'd be damned if he would let her run him from his room. He had even thought of having her things moved to another room, but then how would he ever get her back to his bed? It was definitely an awkward situation.

He sighed and climbed in bed beside her, careful to make sure their bodies were not touching in the huge bed. He would not have to wait much longer, he told himself.

A week went by and Leigh found when Byron was not working at his desk, he was often out with his men at some labor. There was more than ample help on the plantation, Leigh knew, and Byron did not need to toil with his men, but preferred to do so. She found this a good quality and admired him for it.

She had noted that here of late, he worked long hours in his study every night and never came to bed until she was already asleep. The man was definitely devoted to his home, she decided.

One morning as Leigh sat reading, she heard a great deal of noise coming from the foyer. She rose to see Ephraim and some other men pulling large trunks up the stairs.

"What is all of this, Ephraim?"

"These just arrived by river, Miss Leigh. Master Byron says they are the remainder of your clothes purchased in Richmond."

"Oh, yes, thank you."

She left the men to their task with a smile and later she and Annie went upstairs to unpack the large trunks.

As they started the task, Leigh again thought of Byron's generosity to her and wondered at his motives.

There were so many gowns. For some reason now that she knew Byron slightly better she doubted her earlier thought that he had purchased the gowns trying to purchase her affections as well.

"These sore are lovely gowns, Miss Leigh," Annie said putting the gowns in the wardrobe. "Bet Masser Byron was tickled pink gettin' um for you."

Leigh studied the woman but said nothing knowing that more than likely Annie would continue.

"Yes sir, that boy always did like to gift people," Annie chuckled. "As a boy he was forever making things for his mama and pa. Me and Ephraim too. They were usually things made of wood and mud." Annie placed her hands on her thighs and bent over laughing hard. "I 'member once he made this here bracelet out of mud." Annie paused and got a faraway look in her eye as she remembered the long past days. "He was just a tot and he mixed straw with the mud to gives it some body, and then he carefully shaped it into a circle. He took some quartz and chipped it and stuck the pieces in the bracelet so when it dried they looked like jewels. He came and took my hand in his own little one and led me proudly to see it." Annie turned to Leigh and chuckled, the look now gone from her eyes. "He didn't makes it big enough and it wouldn't go over my hand, but he never knew. Still got them pieces of quartz in a drawer somewhere though the mud crumbled long ago."

There was a misty look in Leigh's eyes and a gentle smile on her lips as she sat thinking of Byron and what Annie had said.

The gowns were lovely and well made and Leigh could not decide which one was her favorite. Again she found numerous items she did not remember them buying.

Shoes, nightgowns, muffs, hats, gloves, evening bags, the list was endless. So many things in fact, that she was sure she could not have possibly forgotten. She would have to speak to Byron about it.

That night as they sat eating dinner she mentioned it to him.

"Byron, my gowns arrived from Richmond today."

"Yes, I know. Is everything as it should be?" he asked not looking her way.

"Yes, everything is fine, but," she hesitated. "There is one thing," she added in a small voice.

Byron looked her way waiting for her to continue and when she didn't, he frowned. "What?" he snapped.

Leigh could see that Byron was not in the best of moods. "I-I thought you should know," she said timidly under his glare, "that-that there are numerous items I do not recall you purchasing."

Byron quickly looked away and now he seemed the one ill at ease. His frown deepened as he ate in an irritated manner.

"Byron," Leigh pleaded, "I fear the clothier took it upon herself to add numerous items to your order."

"I assure you, madam, she would not have done so," he snapped in an impatient tone. "Our order was rather large as it stood, and the business has been there for years and has a good name. It would not be so if the owner were not honest."

He again studied his plate and Leigh was confused by his manner. "But, Byron," she insisted, "there are numerous items I do not recall. I could not have forgotten so many."

"Very well!" he shouted. Then he sighed and laid down his fork turning to glare at her. "Leigh I had little to occupy me when we were in Richmond. I, ah, purchased a few items when I was out of the hotel alone and when you were being fitted." He quickly glanced away, picked up his fork, and refused to look her way.

"Oh, I see. Thank you."

The only time Leigh could recall Byron being alone was in the mornings when she bathed and the day he left her at the clothier's while he made arrangements for them to leave the city. She smiled at his averted face. She found it quite charming, and rather amusing, to think of Byron frequenting the shops alone and buying items for her without her knowledge.

There were deep dimples in her cheeks as she thought, just one more item to add to the list of qualities concerning the man.

It was now ten days till Christmas. Leigh and Byron had fallen into a routine. They had their meals together and Byron sometimes came in the afternoon and joined Leigh for tea, only he had coffee. Each evening they would sit and talk for a short time and then Byron would retire to his study. Leigh was always asleep when he came to bed.

A fondness was growing in Leigh's heart for the man and Byron often felt his body urging him to make her truly his wife. But Leigh seemed so happy and content, he feared to push too soon and ruin the progress they had made.

They had just finished another of Aunt Mary's delicious meals and went to the drawing room. Leigh seated herself and watched Byron begin to pace. She was perplexed, he had not paced in her presence for some time now, and she could think of nothing she had done to cause him worry.

"Is there something amiss, Byron?" she asked concerned.

"No, Leigh," he replied giving her a troubled glance. "But there is something I think we need to discuss. I, ah, have not broached the subject before this because I did not wish to recall unpleasant memories."

"Yes, Byron," Leigh stated nervously, apprehension now on her face.

"I wish to know what happened to you after we parted ways in Richmond."

"Oh," Leigh said with wide eyes. She quickly lowered her gaze to her folded hands in her lap. She was extremely ill at ease under Byron's close scrutiny. She told him exactly where she had stayed and worked, everything. Byron paced angrily as the story unfolded realizing that he had continually missed her somehow in that blasted millinery shop. He frowned at her when she told him about the loan from Mrs. Marrow, but said nothing. There was a black look in his eye when Leigh got to the part about Samuel Jones.

"This Jones need be found and put to his rightful end!" he roared.

"He is most likely gone by now, Byron," Leigh replied in a small voice. She was upset and fearful of Byron's rage and felt sure it was directed toward her for leaving him in Richmond.

"No doubt he is, madam," he scowled. "Why did you not tell me of this before?"

"Y-You did not ask," she replied totally bewildered.

"I did not ask, madam, for the reasons I stated before. And you had been ill and I feared it would cause us to quarrel," he arched a brow at her. "It appears I was right!"

Leigh stared at him completely bemudled. Why should he wait until now to be so upset with her over leaving him in Richmond? She had been in his home for more than a fortnight now, it made no sense.

"I assume you still owe this Mrs. Marrow money?" he inquired sarcastically.

"Yes," Leigh replied completely bewildered and fearful of him when he was in such a foul mood.

"The loan needs be repaid at once! For no other reason than that, you should have told me!" He stood arms crossed, scowling at her. "I think you need write this woman a letter," he instructed. "I will send the necessary coin with it."

Leigh decided he was angry because she was in debt and immediately her own anger grew. "I am quite capable, sir, of handling my own affairs," she quipped.

"I am sure you are, madam," he answered sarcastically. "You handled them so well in the past," he shouted, "you ended afloat in the river!"

He stormed to the doorway and turned to glare at her with a fierce look in his eye. "When you have the letter completed I will have someone deliver it to Richmond. You may ask Ephraim for the proper coin to seal within, he knows where I keep it!" With that he turned and took angry strides to his study and slammed the study door so hard a portrait in the foyer fell to the floor.

Leigh sat fuming! The man was totally unpredictable. His foul moods came with such a sudden and frightening force it left Leigh's hands atremble. Every time she started to feel comfortable with the man, he did something like this! Well, she decided, he could rage all he wanted! She cared not!

She had already planned to write Mrs. Marrow, in fact, she had started several letters but torn them up. She found it extremely difficult to tell the woman of her previous deceit and the fact that her husband was alive and well. Alive and well and an oaf!

Leigh rose from the chair and stomped up the stairs and slammed the bedroom door hard behind her.

Byron paced his study. He had done it again. Lost his temper with her when he had meant to hold it in check. He was angry that he could have missed Leigh in Richmond that often, and that she owed this Mrs. Marrow money. He liked not the idea of his wife in debt. And who was this Thomas Whitefield? Some young swain trying to wittle his way into her life no doubt! Leigh had been lucky the man had not taken advantage of her the first night she met him. How could Leigh have been so foolish as to trust the man, Byron thought, preferring to ignore the fact that apparently Mr. Whitefield had behaved as a perfect gentleman. But what really had him raging was this Jones business. He had seen red when Leigh told him how the man had struck her causing her to fall overboard. Leigh most certainly would have drowned if Byron had not found her that morning in the river. If he ever found this Jones, he would wring his head from his shoulders!

When Byron went up to bed, Leigh lay on her side, her back to him. As he climbed into bed he thought her asleep, but when he lifted the covers and lay down she irritably jerked them back over her shoulder. Byron scowled at her laying at the far edge of the bed, turned on his side away from her, and jerked them back.

It took Leigh several days to compose the letter. She

wrote all to Mrs. Marrow except the circumstances of her and Byron's meeting, and subsequent marriage, and how she left the boat. She wrote to her that her father had been the one that recently died, and that she had married Byron still in a state of shock and had later regretted the match. She saw her error now, she wrote, and she and Byron were very happy together. Leigh's quill hesitated over the words, but she forced herself to write them. Though it was far from the truth, she saw no way to tell the woman the facts of the matter without telling her exactly how she and Byron met, and why they had married. And besides, she told herself, she did not wish to cause the woman future worry. She wrote that she prayed that Mrs. Marrow would find it in her heart to forgive her for her deceit. She asked the woman to inform Mr. Whitefield that her husband would now handle the matter of the deed. She really had no intention of mentioning the matter to Byron, they were hardly speaking. Someday she would find a way to look into the matter on her own.

It was nearly Christmas and that was Leigh's favorite time of year. She had many happy memories of Christmas spent with her father. Though Leigh doubted Byron would give her a gift, she decided to try to get something for him. Mayhap it would lighten his mood and they could again spend time in the evenings talking as they had before.

With her letter in her hand Leigh went to search for Ephraim. She found him in the dining room setting the table for the evening meal.

"Ephraim, I have a request of you."

"Yes, Miss Leigh," he said stopping his work and giving her his full attention.

"I would like for you to deliver this letter to Richmond for me and the coins I need to repay a small loan." She handed him the letter and with it her mother's cameo. "And while you are there I would greatly appreciate it if you would try to sell this cameo and purchase a Christmas gift for Byron for me."

"Miss Leigh," Ephraim said, a frown wrinkling his brow, "Master Byron keeps money in the study. You need not sell your jewels."

"I do not wish to use his money without his permission," she said giving the man a stubborn look. "Please, Ephraim."

"Yes, Miss Leigh, I will do as you request," he assured her, doubt on his face.

Leigh smiled at him and then got a thoughtful expression on her face as she chewed at her lower lip. "I do not know what to get for him nor how much the cameo will bring." She glanced to Ephraim undecided. "There are several books that he desires—If the cameo brings enough, will you try to find one or more for me?"

"Yes, ma'am," he assured her.

"It is the only gift I can think of he would truly like. Try please, and Ephraim, not a word to Byron."

"I will do my best," he said concern still on his face. "I will leave first thing in the morning."

They stood talking a few more minutes and then Leigh left with a smile and a thank you.

That night at dinner Leigh and Byron again sat in awkward silence as they had these past few nights. Leigh glanced his way from time to time still bewildered at his untimely anger at her for leaving him in Richmond. Well at least she would repay her debt and mayhap that would ease his mind some. It was a shame, she thought, that

Byron was so moody and had such a foul temper. In so many ways he was a charming man.

Byron sat at the far end of the table chewing his food in an irritated manner. Damn! he thought. This silence had been going on for over three days now and he had had enough of it. He knew he had no one to blame but himself and that made him just that much angrier. He looked up at Leigh's demure form and noted the lovely gown she wore that barely concealed her breasts. He sat staring intently at her breasts as they rose and fell with her breathing. He clamped his teeth tightly together as he felt his brow start to break out with perspiration and refused to look her way.

When the meal was complete he rose to help Leigh with her chair and as she stood, she bent to smooth her gown, her bust spilling temptingly over the bodice of her gown. Byron's eyes grew large and it took all of his self-control not to reach out and crush one of those pink, round breasts in his hand. Byron mumbled something and Leigh quickly glanced his way.

"What?" she inquired with large, innocent eyes.

"Nothing," Byron growled. Didn't she know what she was doing to him? Constantly flaunting her woman's body before him. "I, ah, have work to do in my study," he said stiffly. "Good night."

Leigh stood bewildered as she watched him take angry strides to his study and close the door firmly behind him. She felt as if she had done something to further anger him, but she did not have the slightest idea what. I will never understand his moodiness, she told herself. She frowned at the study door as she made her way upstairs to the security of the bedroom.

The next morning when Leigh awoke it was snowing.

She stood at the bedroom window looking out at the soft white puffs floating gently to the ground. She bit her bottom lip hoping Ephraim had dressed warmly before he started his journey. Annie came to help her dress and when she went to join Byron in the dining room for breakfast, he was awaiting her in an agitated manner, pacing to and fro.

She glanced his way nervously and scurried to her chair. He mumbled a morning greeting not looking her way.

"Good mornin'," Aunt Mary said as she came bustling into the room. Her large frame hurried to the table as she held a tray offering Leigh some ham and eggs. "Lordy, you see that snow?" She glanced to Byron and grinned. "It sore a blessin' to have that hallway from the cookhouse on a day like this Masser B."

"I am glad it pleases you Aunt Mary," Byron answered with a grin. "Where is Ephraim this morning?" he asked. Then he got a worried expression on his face. "He is not ill, is he?"

Before Aunt Mary could reply Leigh spoke. "I sent Ephraim to Richmond to deliver my letter," she said casually as she buttered one of Aunt Mary's fluffy biscuits.

"You what!" Byron said incredulously.

Leigh jumped at the loud tone of his voice and looked to him surprised. She started to repeat herself but Byron interrupted as he leaped up from his chair.

"You had no right to send anyone without my knowledge," he shouted, "and especially not Ephraim! Ephraim is no young man, madam, and the weather is most foul! There are many who could have delivered your letter!"

Leigh was totally dejected and quickly looked to her folded hands in her lap. "Byron, I only," she paused her voice trembling with fear. She took several deep breaths and reluctantly pulled her gaze up to meet his. "I am sorry, Byron," she said in a timid tone, "I was only trying to do as you requested."

"I did not ask you, madam, to send such a valuable servant on such a simple mission!" He was no longer shouting as he noted her frightened expression, but his tone was stern and full of anger still.

Aunt Mary stood there quietly witnessing the entire scene. She glanced to Leigh's sad face and then scowled at Byron. She had never heard Byron be so brisk before, not even when he was upset with one of the servants. Why Masser B. so hard on this pretty slip of a wife? she wondered. She glanced between Leigh's dejected face and Byron's angry one. She left the room quietly, a puzzled look on her face.

Leigh ate no more of her breakfast and as soon as Byron had finished she excused herself and ran upstairs to the bedroom.

Byron stood in the drawing room and swore. Hell! he thought. If I do not soon bed with her I will never control this temper of mine. But, he thought with a self-righteous expression on his face, she had no right to send Ephraim anywhere without his permission.

Leigh stood at the bedroom window, tears streaming down her face. She had not meant to displease Byron, she sobbed. She had tried to do as he requested, but it seemed no matter how hard she tried, she brought the man's anger down upon her. Was her life always to be like this? she wondered. Always in turmoil. She had left the home of her childhood, and her country, behind, and for endless months she had traveled. She had lost her father. And now she was forced to live with a man whose quick temper and foul moods she felt she would never understand.

She walked to the bed, and using the bed steps, climbed up on the bed and lay down burying her face in her arm. Her body shook with sobs. Was her life, and that of her child's, never to know any stability, any security? Was life always to be a game of guessing at Byron's moods—and she the loser?

She rolled over with a sigh and stared at the canopy overhead. It was nearly Christmas and she had so desperately hoped to have a pleasant holiday. This Christmas would be difficult enough, she knew, it being the first she would not share with her father. She sat up sniffing and wiped at her tears. She would just have to set the matter right, she decided. She wiped away her tears, and fetching her warm cloak from the wardrobe, she hurriedly left the room.

"Henry," Leigh called entering the stables, "would you be so kind as to make ready a carriage?"

"A carriage, Miss Leigh?" Henry repeated, surprised to see her there.

"Yes, if you please."

"You planning to go out driving on a day like this Miss Leigh?" he inquired. "It's not a fitting day," he added.

"I have an urgent errand. And," she added fearing Henry would mayhap refuse, "I need to hurry."

"Yes'um," Henry replied, his face showing his doubt. "If you would care to wait in the house where it is warmer, I'll bring the carriage about when it is ready," he offered.

"No, Henry, there is no need. I do not wish to take you

from your work."

"Master Byron is going with you then," Henry stated, relieved.

"No."

"Then, Miss Leigh, you'll need me to drive you."

"No, I'll not take the closed carriage. If you will hitch the smaller open carriage over there," Leigh said pointing across the stables, "I can drive myself."

Henry looked at her with wide eyes. "But, Miss Leigh, Master Byron have a fit I let you go out alone—and in weather like this—and in an open carriage!"

"I assure, Henry—he will not," Leigh replied, a determined expression on her face.

"Yes'um," Henry answered shaking his head slowly.

When the carriage was ready Henry helped her to board and then opened the barn doors wide.

"Miss Leigh, are you sure you won't allow me to drive you?" he asked one more time.

"I'm sure, Henry. Thank you," Leigh answered driving the carriage out of the barn.

Henry watched her leave, taking special note of the direction she took. He knew Master Byron was not going to be pleased but he felt he had done all he could to persuade her differently. He could hardly refuse her, he thought, she was the mistress of Royal Oaks.

"Master Byron ain't gonna like this," he said to himself slowly shaking his head as he pulled the barn doors closed.

Leigh took the lane that passed the slave quarters. She had only gone a short distance when she realized, seeing the endless stretch of land ahead of her, that she had not the slightest idea of which direction Ephraim would travel. Well, she thought stubbornly, I'll just have to

229

keep looking until I find him. He could not have gone too far. And though he is no doubt on horseback, even with the slower carriage I should be able to overtake him. He has no reason to push his mount.

Slapping the reins against the horse's rump, Leigh raced the carriage down the road. The cold icy wind whipped at her cloak and stung her eyes. Already her hands felt numb with cold and she found it difficult to hold the reins. The snowfall was increasing, covering the ground with fluffy white, and Leigh found it difficult to distinguish the path the road took, but she refused to slow her pace.

She had gone a good distance from the house when she finally slowed the carriage as her eyes roamed the countryside. Nothing looked familiar, but she thought, how could it? She looked back and the landscape was much the same. She could no longer see the outline of where the road lie, and by the manner in which the carriage was bouncing about, she had serious doubts that she was still on the road. And if she was not, she had no idea where or when she left the road. She noted the carriage tracks behind her were fast filling with snow. If they disappeared completely, and she did not find Ephraim—would she be able to find her way back to the house? she wondered.

I'll go a small distance more, she decided, beginning to feel apprehensive, and if I do not see Ephraim, I'll turn back. She wrapped her cloak closely about her, her body shaking with cold, and urged the horse on.

The carriage topped a hill and Leigh saw a deep incline ahead. She pulled hard on the reins trying to slow the horse, but with the numbness in her hands, she could not, and the carriage raced on precariously, out of control. Leigh screamed, somehow managing to retain her seat, the carriage bouncing wildly, and then she heard a cracking sound and the carriage bounced high and landed with a thud at a crooked angle at the bottom of the hill.

Leigh gasped trying to regain her breath and placed a hand to her head, feeling dizzy. When she had regained some of her composure, she stepped from the carriage and inspected the broken rear wheel. She glanced back up the hill at the path the carriage had taken and was thankful that the damage had not been greater and that she had not been seriously injured. Had she forgotten that she carried a life within her? If she had been injured, she could have lost the child. Again she gave thanks for her safety.

With a sigh, she began unhitching the horse. She knew she had come a good distance from the house. So far in fact, she was unsure of exactly which direction would take her back. And the shoes she wore were hardly enough to offer any protection against the snow laden ground. They were already wet and her feet were nearly numb now. What if she could not find the house? she thought with panic. No one knew where she was and only Henry knew that she had left. There would be no one searching for her for sometime—if ever!

Tears formed and she quickly brushed them away. She had no one to blame but herself for her predicament, she thought, and crying would serve no purpose. How foolish she had been!

She finished unhitching the horse, and leading the horse by the reins, she began climbing the hill. She slipped several times on the icy ground and was panting hard by the time she reached the top. She looked ahead and saw endless acres and again tears formed.

She glanced at the horse wishing desperately that she had a saddle. And though she knew it was thought unsafe for a woman with child to ride, she was an excellent horsewoman. But she had never ridden bare back, never ridden any way but sidesaddle, and if she tried it now, and fell, she thought, she could receive the injury she had so far avoided. No—she decided, it was best she walk.

Leigh had not been walking long, but already she felt the effort taking its toll. The hem of her gown and cloak were soaked and felt as if they weighed ten times their normal weight. Her face felt stiff, her hands and feet ached with cold. She looked again to the horse. I'll never make it on foot, she decided. Chancing a fall was less of a risk than she and the child she carried freezing to death, she surmised. She tried to mount the animal but found to her dismay that she could not without benefit of stirrup. She looked about for a stump, anything to stand on to give herself better leverage, but she saw nothing. Determined, she grabbed a handful of mane and tried again and again to pull herself atop the horse, but no matter how hard she tried, she could not manage the task. Frustrated tears ran down her face and she leaned her head against the warm side of the animal.

"Why, oh why, was I so foolish," she cried.

She heard the sound of thundering hoofs and she squinted her eyes trying to see through the thick blanket of falling snow. A huge stallion was racing toward her, the rider bent low in the saddle. Her hands began to tremble, now more from fear than cold, for she knew by the set of the shoulders, that the rider was Byron.

Byron reached her side, a concerned look on his face. "Leigh, are you injured?"

Leigh lowered her gaze and shook her head to the negative. Byron released a relieved sigh and made as if to dismount, but then thinking better of it, he sat back in the saddle studying her.

"I see you wasted no time in getting yourself afoot, madam," Byron said, a frown now on his face and anger creeping into his voice. "And where, pray tell, is my carriage?"

"I-I fear I broke a wheel," Leigh replied hesitantly.

Byron scowled at her and when next he spoke his voice was filled with rage. "Did I not warn you about trying to leave this plantation?" he barked.

Surprised, Leigh drew her eyes up to his. "I-I was not running away Byron," she offered meekly.

Byron arched a brow and glared at her. "It is hardly the type of weather where one chooses to go for a ride in an open carriage, madam," he stated sarcastically, doubting the truth of her denial. "It is small wonder you now find yourself afoot!"

Leigh again drew her eyes slowly up to his, and noting the intense scowl on his face, she nervously bit at her lower lip.

"I would think that if you care not for your own welfare," Byron continued, anger rumbling deep in his chest, "that you would at least consider the child you carry."

"Yes, Byron," Leigh agreed meekly. She took the reins of the carriage horse and again began walking.

Byron watched her a moment and then urging his horse into a slow walk, he followed behind her.

"Have you an explanation, madam?" Byron barked some moments later.

"I-I was searching for Ephraim," she answered in a

233

small voice.

Now it was Byron's turn to be surprised. His eyes roamed over her slight form trudging through the snow and he sighed. "Leigh, Richmond lies in the opposite direction," he informed her, his tone less severe.

Leigh made no reply as she maintained her slow progress. Byron sighed heavily several times and then steered his mount close to her side.

"Here," he said reaching toward her, "give me your hand."

Leigh slowly raised tear-filled eyes to his, hesitated, and then sniffing, placed her small hand in his. Effortlessly Byron lifted her across his lap and placed her securely in front of him. Leaning over, he grabbed the reins of the carriage horse, handed them to her, and with one strong arm on either side of her, urged his stallion into a slow trot.

Leigh sat erect, nervously chewing at her lower lip. She glanced at Byron askew and noted his still angry face close above hers, and they rode in silence. Leigh pulled at her cloak, trying to wrap it around herself more securely, and shivered. Without a word Byron pulled her back against him, her left side resting against his chest, and wrapped his cloak about her as well. With the warmth of the huge stallion beneath her, and Byron so close, Leigh soon began to feel warmth creeping back into her body. She relaxed slightly against him and eventually rested her head against the hollow of Byron's shoulder with a sigh.

When they reached the house Byron dismounted and then swung Leigh gently down.

Leigh stood timidly before him, her face downcast. "I-I am sorry about the carriage, Byron," she offered meekly.

234

"A-And I had not meant to displease you when I asked Ep . . ."

"It is of no matter," Byron interrupted, his tone cool.

They entered the house and Leigh immediately sought the solitude of the bedroom, tears again in her eyes.

Leigh did not appear for lunch or for dinner and Byron did not venture to the bedroom to ask why. When he went upstairs to bed that night she was sleeping and he could tell she had been crying. Her body still quivered with occasional sobs as she slept. The corners of his mouth turned down and he climbed into bed quietly with a long face. He put his hands behind his head and lay there a long time staring at the canopy overhead.

Aunt Mary had told some of the other servants about Byron's angry words to Leigh and in the following days he was given the cold shoulder by many—not to mention the mysterious fact that though Leigh's food came to the table still steaming, the food Aunt Mary served him was ice cold.

Byron's mood became even more foul with each day Ephraim was away. The relationship that had begun between Leigh and Byron did much backsliding in Ephraim's absence, and he was quick to notice on his return.

In the days that followed Ephraim's safe return, the house remained quiet. Leigh and Byron spent as little time together as possible and everyone was aware of Byron's sour mood. The Marsh house seemed full of gloom.

It was two days until Christmas. Leigh timidly approached the closed study doors. She nervously smoothed her gown and patted her hair into place. Chewing her bottom lip she lightly tapped on the door.

"Yes," she heard Byron reply.

Very carefully she opened the doors and took several steps into the room.

"B-Byron, have you a moment?"

"I believe so, madam," he said motioning to one of the chairs near the fireplace.

Leigh nervously sat on the edge of the chair and grasped her hands tightly together. She had planned exactly how she would approach the matter but she nervously ran the words through her mind again. She had no idea how Byron would accept her making suggestions concerning his family.

"You had something on your mind, madam," he said irritably when several moments passed and she made no move to speak.

"Yes," she said jerking her eyes up to meet his and seeing his frowning face. "I, ah, do not know what has been your practice in the past, but—ah—"

"Madam," he barked, "if you have something to say, I wish you would do so and be done with it. I have a great deal of work to do."

Leigh swallowed hard and quickly reverted her gaze to her hands. "I was wondering if you had planned on asking Uncle Jonathan to Christmas dinner?"

Byron swore under his breath and rose from his chair. "Is this the foolishness you bother me with when I am working? I beg you, madam, use your wits! If you would like to invite Uncle Jonathan to dinner, then do so! But do not in the future bother me with such trivial matters when I am in this room!"

"I-I," Leigh started. Then covering her face with her hands she ran from the room crying.

Byron swore and kicked the desk. He looked to his

father's portrait and he stood staring into those stern brown eyes for some time before he slowly sat down and rubbed his brow with one hand.

It was Christmas Eve and Leigh sat reading in the drawing room. Ephraim and Henry came in carrying a large pine tree and Leigh watched the strange procession with round eyes. Finally her curiosity got the best of her.

"Ephraim, Henry, have you gone mad?" she asked looking from the men to the tree.

"It is a Christmas tree," Ephraim replied with a grin. "It has become a custom here abouts."

The two men left and in a moment returned carrying a Yule Log. This Leigh recognized at once. Henry bid Leigh good evening and the two men left again. Ephraim returned a few moments later carrying a small bag of candles and some homemade ornaments for the tree. Annie followed close behind him with two large bowls of cranberries.

"Here, Miss Leigh," she said handing Leigh a cloth, "puts this over your gown so you won't muss it and you can helps me string cranberries for the tree."

Leigh smiled at the couple, and taking the cloth, spread it over her lap. Annie handed her a needle and thread and she began to string the fruit with a smile on her face. They were doing this for her, she knew. Byron still sulked in his study and she knew the kind couple was trying to lighten the holiday for her and she was very appreciative of their consideration. Soon they were all talking and gaily laughing, and Byron, hearing them from his study, came to investigate.

He saw Leigh and Annie sitting on the settee stringing cranberries and Ephraim working on the tree. He noted

Leigh's red hands and merry face and he saw that Ephraim and Annie had large smiles on their faces as well. It had been many days since anyone smiled in his direction.

He entered the room and the mood immediately changed to one more solemn. Byron began to feel the cad and moved to help Ephraim with the tree. The room remained silent and Byron began to feel extremely uncomfortable and awkward. He cleared his throat several times and then tried to jest with them. After several tries with no success he again fell silent.

He cleared his throat and walked to the fireplace and stood warming his back as his eyes roamed over their three averted faces.

"Leigh—Annie—Ephraim—I, ah, know I have been most unpleasant of late," he said in a soft tone, "and I, ah, humbly beg your forgiveness."

Annie and Ephraim had heard Byron apologize few times in the past and they were quick to accept. Leigh looked to him, hesitation on her face, but in a moment as she looked into his warm gaze and gentle smile, a smile also graced her lips.

The decorating continued again under a more cheerful note. Byron and Ephraim began humming Christmas carols as they placed the candles on the tree limbs.

"It is a shame I never learned to play the piano as my mother desired and did so well herself," Byron commented. "If I had we could sing carols proper."

"I can play, Byron," Leigh said in a small voice.

"Well then," he said approaching her side and smiling, "please do."

He offered Leigh his hand to help her rise and escorted

her to the piano. As Leigh sat down a soft flush appeared in her cheeks and she smiled shyly in his direction.

Soon all four of them were gathered around the piano. They sang carols together, Byron and Ephraim both having deep, rich voices. Annie had a beautiful soprano voice, and Leigh's was sweet and clear, and they harmonized well together. There was laughter and gaiety in the Marsh house again that night.

The next morning when Leigh awoke Byron was already up and dressing.

"Byron, you should have awakened me. I fear I will keep you waiting breakfast."

Byron smiled. "Sweet, I have told Annie to let you rest. I seldom eat when first I rise and I do not mind Annie serving you breakfast in bed. Besides," he said moving to the bed and looking tenderly into her eyes, "I am sure in your delicate condition you need your rest."

Leigh blushed and lowered her gaze.

"If you wish I will have a cup of coffee and await you for breakfast this day."

Leigh looked up and gave him a timid smile. "Yes, I would like that."

He walked to the door calling over his shoulder. "Very well, I'll send Annie up right away." When he reached the door he turned to her and grinned with a twinkle in his eye. "By the way, Merry Christmas, pet."

"Merry Christmas, Byron," Leigh smiled.

Byron found Annie and sent her to the bedroom and then made his way to the cookhouse. He greeted Aunt Mary with a Merry Christmas and then poured himself a cup of coffee. He went to sit at the old oak table and gave

Aunt Mary an appraising look.

"You know," he commented as if thinking out loud, "I'll have to have the walls checked in the hallway leading to the house. It seems here of late the area has become drafty."

Aunt Mary quickly looked away and literally flew into a cloud of flour as she made another batch of biscuits, though Byron noted two full pans waiting to be placed in the oven.

Byron casually sipped his coffee as he strolled from the room, and once he was a safe distance away, he chuckled.

Leigh dressed as quickly as possible. She hurried down the stairs wearing a lovely pink gown and entered the dining room to find Byron already seated. He did not look her way or rise to help her with her chair and Leigh stood a moment studying his mood. As she sat down she noted a small black box on her plate and she picked it up with a puzzled look on her face. She glanced Byron's way and saw a deep grin on his face.

"Merry Christmas, sweet," he chuckled. "Open it."

Leigh lifted the lid carefully and with large eyes gasped at the contents. Inside was the most beautiful necklace she had ever seen. There was a large emerald surrounded by diamonds and there were more diamonds scattered on the delicate chain and more still on the clasp. Leigh's eyes were round and her mouth hanging open as she looked up to Byron, but he was no longer in his seat but standing beside her.

"Byron, it is gorgeous," she said overwhelmed. She gazed into his deep blue eyes and searched them carefully. "I expected no gift," she said softly, "and certainly not one as costly as this."

His returning look made her blush and she lowered her eyes feeling awkward under his gaze. "I do not know what to say," she managed.

"It will look well with your eyes, my love," Byron said softly as his eyes caressed her face.

Leigh blushed even more deeply. Byron had never called her his love before and she found the words left her slightly light-headed and that her heart skipped a beat.

"Byron, I feel terrible," she said, a twinkle in her eye. "I have no gift for you in return." Leigh knew it was impish of her but she wanted to keep his a secret just a little longer.

"I expect no gift, pet," he said easily. He returned to his chair talking to her over his shoulder. "The child you carry is gift enough for me."

Leigh's eyes tenderly explored his face as he sat down. What a wonderful and sentimental thing to say, she thought. She was glad she had told the small fib about his gift.

Ephraim entered wishing all a Merry Christmas, grinning from ear to ear. He pulled a gold watch out of his pocket and polished it on his sleeve.

"Ephraim, have you something new there?" Leigh asked with a smile.

"Yes, Miss Leigh, as well you know," he answered, white teeth sparkling. "And I thank you and Master Byron for the gift of it."

He served them their breakfast and left the room, a smile still on his face.

"He thanks me?" Leigh said looking to Byron.

"It was our gift to him," Byron replied enjoying a warm meal for a change. "I did not think to tell you before, I apologize."

"Byron, there is no need to apologize. It was very thoughtful of you to include me in your giving."

Byron glanced her way and they exchanged a smile. Several moments passed before Byron added; "By the way, we gave gifts to all the other servants as well. We gave Annie three new dresses."

"It is nice to know I choose so well," Leigh replied.

Byron quickly glanced her way to see if he had misread sarcasm in her voice, but she was smiling at him with a most tender look. His heart started to beat rapidly and he felt a tenseness growing in his loins. He looked away trying to think of something, anything, except Leigh's lovely face and round breasts rising temptingly above the bodice of her pink gown.

After the meal was over they went into the drawing room to sit by the fire. When Byron was settled, Leigh turned and pointed to a package wrapped with ribbon and cloth under the tree.

"Now I wonder what that could be," she said giving Byron a wicked smile. "Byron, would you see please?" she added with round, innocent eyes.

Byron rose with a wrinkle on his brow and retrieved the package and offered it to Leigh.

"No, you open it."

Byron again settled himself on the love seat and slowly unwrapped the package as Leigh watched him with anticipation. Inside were three books he had mentioned wanting.

His face was full of surprise and he looked up to her.

Leigh let out a small delighted giggle. "Merry Christmas to you, Byron. Are you pleased with the gift?"

"Oh yes, Leigh. However did you come by them?"

"I got Ephraim to . . ." Leigh's voice slowly lowered until she was whispering, "get them for me when he was in Richmond." She looked anxiously into Byron's eyes fearful that he would again be angry with her.

"I see," Byron said coming to her side. He took her hands in his and gave them a gentle squeeze. "And I had to act the cad about Ephraim going to Richmond," he offered in a low tone, his face full of remorse. "Will you forgive me?"

"Byron," Leigh said, the corners of her mouth turning up, "as long as you like the gift, all is forgiven."

"Indeed I do," he said running his hand affectionately over the books. He opened one book and a painting appeared on the page edges. "Edge painting!" he exclaimed excitedly.

Leigh gave him a puzzled look and then glanced quickly to the open book he held. An intricate, detailed painting now appeared on the edge of the pages of the book. Edge painting? Yes, now she recalled. It was quite an art. Water color paintings were done on the fanned edges of the pages of the book and were only visible when the book was opened, for when the book was closed, they disappeared inside the gilded outer edge of each page. Leigh had never seen such a book before but she did recall that fore edge painting had been quite the rage in London. She knew such books were quite expensive and again she was surprised that her cameo had brought so much.

Byron looked at her with a warm smile. "Thank you, Leigh," he said sincerely. "I have wanted a book with these edge paintings for years now but have not been able to find one. Thank you again."

Leigh gave him a dimpled smile in return. She was delighted that he was so pleased with her gift.

"Would you like for me to read to you?" he asked.

"Oh yes, please," Leigh replied fidgiting like a small child.

Byron chuckled and picking a book, placed an arm about her shoulder and began to read. Leigh snuggled a little closer to him and smiled to herself. She enjoyed the closeness of him, and his clean, manly scent.

Ephraim was coming down the hall when he saw Aunt Mary's huge rump in the doorway leading from the dining room to the hall. He walked up quietly behind her and tapped her on the shoulder nearly scaring the daylights out of her. She turned and gave him a fierce scowl but quickly lowered her eyes at the stern look received from Ephraim at being caught eavesdropping on Byron and Leigh. She mumbled something under her breath and hurried back to the cookhouse.

Ephraim watched her go and then looked about to make sure no one could see him. When he was assured that he was completely alone, he edged the door of the dining room open just enough to peek in with one eye.

Leigh had passed the morning so content and relaxed that she was shocked when she noted the hall clock had just struck one. She jumped up from the settee and practically ran for the door.

"My goodness," she said excitedly, "Uncle Jonathan will be here any minute and I need to change my gown."

"I think you look lovely as you are, pet," Byron said with a smile, a soft caressing tone in his voice.

Leigh started for the door and then stopped and

whirled about taking no notice of Byron's words. She hurried back to the tea table, picked up the box containing her necklace, whirled about again and hurried for the stairs.

"Byron, will you send Annie up please," she called as she turned the corner.

Byron chuckled. "Yes, my love."

When Jonathan arrived Leigh was still upstairs changing. Byron poured his uncle a glass of brandy and they went into the drawing room so Jonathan could thaw out by the fire. They were talking easily when Leigh entered the room.

"Uncle Jonathan, forgive me for not being ready when you arrived," she said gliding into the room with a smile.

Both men stood admiring her beauty with their mouths hanging open. She wore a gown of deep green velvet. It had a low bodice which left no doubt that Leigh was nicely endowed. The gown had long fitted sleeves that were worn off the shoulders, and the skirt was full and hung in soft folds about her, making her long, slender, limbs even more attractive. Annie had wound and wrapped her hair atop her head and small ringlets bounced from the back of her head. And around her neck was the emerald necklace Byron had given her for Christmas.

Both men spoke at once and then laughed as Byron smiled at his uncle and indicated he should speak first.

"Leigh," Jonathan said, "you are a Christmas gift in yourself. It is a gift just to stand here gazing at your beauty."

Leigh blushed, but she rushed to the man and placed a

soft kiss on his cheek. "Merry Christmas, Uncle Jonathan."

Jonathan smiled and reached for the package he had set on the tea table. "And Merry Christmas to the both of you," he replied handing the package to Leigh.

Byron motioned for Leigh to open it and she complied without argument as both men watched her with grins. It was a large silver bowl and Leigh quickly thanked him most graciously and placed it on the bookshelves beside the fireplace. Byron in return gifted Jonathan with a set of mint julep cups.

"Leigh, Byron, how did you know I have been wanting a set like this for years?" he said smiling to them both.

Byron cast a smile to Leigh and she looked at him warmly in return. It was very thoughtful of him to include her name on this gift card as well.

Leigh placed her hands on her necklace and excitedly showed it to Uncle Jonathan.

"A most suitable gift for a woman as lovely as you, my dear," Jonathan said admiring the necklace.

"And Leigh gave me not one, but three books," Byron added proudly.

"You could not have chosen better," Jonathan chuckled. "There are few things Byron treasures as much as his books." He winked at Leigh. "And he has so many things, he is quite difficult to buy for."

During dinner Jonathan commented how nice it was to have them to share Christmas with. His own daughter, Margaret, was soon expecting her first child and was not able to make the long journey home this year. Byron and Leigh exchanged looks and Leigh blushed at the expression she saw in Byron's eye.

After dinner the conversation turned to some of Byron's more distant relatives that lived in other areas of the country and Jonathan also spoke much about Byron's deceased parents. It was obvious to Leigh that Jonathan still greatly mourned his dead brother and Byron often got a melancholy expression when recalling some, shared happy event.

Leigh had thought of her father numerous times throughout the day and now she fought hard to hold back tears.

Byron noted the faraway, misty-eyed look on Leigh's face and came to her side. "Leigh, sweet," he said placing his hand over hers and giving hers a gentle squeeze, "would you be so kind as to grace Uncle Jonathan and myself with your skill at the piano?"

Leigh gazed into the warm blue eyes, and nodding shyly, agreed. Jonathan and Byron exchanged a look and Jonathan immediately chastised himself for being so foolish. Had Byron not told him Leigh had recently lost her father?

Once Leigh began to play, and the three of them began to sing carols, the mood again became light and joyful. It was very late when Jonathan departed for home.

Leigh sat at her dressing table as Byron undressed for bed. She already wore her nightgown and sat admiring the emerald necklace.

"Byron, it is truly lovely. I am most fortunate to own such a beautiful piece."

"You are most welcome, pet." He glanced her way and grinned at her reflection in the mirror. "I enjoy seeing a beautiful woman wearing beautiful things, so be forewarned, I plan to gift you with more."

"Byron, I was not asking or hinting for more," Leigh replied quickly putting the necklace away and moving to the bed.

"I know you weren't, pet." He moved to where she stood at the side of the bed and placed his arms about her. Leigh's body began to tremble as she looked deeply into his blue eyes. His eyelids took on a hooded look and his blue eyes became even bluer and deeper in color.

"Merry Christmas, Leigh," he said softly.

"M-Merry Christmas, Byron," Leigh replied in a whisper. Slowly, ever so slowly, Byron's lips lowered to hers and Leigh's eyes fluttered closed. His lips were soft and gentle on hers and he kissed her long and tenderly. Leigh enjoyed the feel of him so near and was rather disappointed when the kiss ended. Not looking his way she turned and climbed into bed, a flush on her cheeks.

Slowly, Byron told himself. Don't push too fast or too hard. He had felt a certain amount of response in Leigh's kiss but that did not mean she was ready to play the wife in bed. He blew out the candle and finished undressing.

He lay beside Leigh in the large bed thinking. Soon she will accept me as husband. They had spent a most enjoyable day together and Leigh had seemed to truly enjoy his company. I must control my foul moods and play the suitor more, he thought. And then soon . . . soon . . .

Leigh lay awake beside him. She had enjoyed the kiss much. Her body still trembled from his touch. And it had been a most pleasant day she had spent with Byron. She was rather disappointed that it had ended. She realized, with some surprise, that she had grown to cherish Byron's company. When he was not in one of his foul moods, he was most charming. I must be more careful, she thought, to do nothing to displease him. I will seek out his company more often in the future, she decided, and coyly flutter my eyelashes at him. Of course, she thought remembering her upbringing, I must not appear *too* bold or Byron will think me the harlot. But if I play the woman more, soon he will forget his love for Ella. Soon he will want me as wife, soon . . . soon . . .

Chapter Nine

New Year's day was like a circus at Royal Oaks. Leigh found every person on the plantation crowding the foyer when she came down shortly before lunch.

"What in the world is going on, Henry?" she asked looking about puzzled.

Henry gave her one of his father's grins. "Master Byron is passing out the shares."

"The shares?"

"Master Byron shares the profit from the plantation at the end of each year with everyone on the place. Down to the smallest child everyone gets their fair share," Henry proudly stated.

Leigh thanked him for the information and made her way to the dining room nodding and talking to many as she went. I am ever finding new things to admire Byron for, she thought.

She spent the afternoon napping and getting ready for Uncle Jonathan's New Year's Eve Ball. She had chosen a gown of emerald green satin. It would look well with the necklace, she knew. It was cut low in front and had tiny puff sleeves worn off the shoulder. The skirt was full and hung fairly straight in soft folds from just below the bust. It was a style made popular by Napoleon's Josephine. Leigh was not really showing her pregnancy yet, but she noted her waist was not as trim and the dress would not stress the point.

She soaked a long time in the tub and now sat all perfumed and powdered wearing her matching shift. Annie just finished her hair when Byron entered the room.

"Leigh, I did not mean to slight you today, but there was much to do." He came and placed a small kiss on her bare shoulder and then smiled at her in the mirror's reflection as he exchanged some teasing banter with Annie.

"Annie, would please have water brought up for my bath."

"Sore thing, Masser Byron," Annie grinned, hurrying from the room.

Leigh turned her back as Byron disrobed and climbed into the tub. After he started washing Leigh glided up to his back and asked if he would like her to scrub his back for him.

Byron gave her a bemused look that changed slowly to a smile. "I do not wish you to muss your pretty hair."

Leigh laughed. "I won't muss my hair."

Annie had fixed Leigh's hair in a large twisted bun behind one ear, leaving small curls to circle her face and long ringlets to hang over one shoulder from the bun.

251

The bun was covered with a fine net sewn with tiny green jets, and her hair sparkled as she moved her head.

She knelt down behind the tub and started washing Byron's huge shoulders. Byron leaned forward slightly, a bemuddled expression on his face, wondering at Leigh's mood.

"Scrub it hard, will you, pet? It is a most difficult place to reach."

"Well then," Leigh giggled, "I will just have to help you more often."

There was a broad grin on Byron's face when Leigh rose and stared laying out his clothes. His eyes followed her about the room. The emerald green shift she wore was cut low in the bodice, the satin fabric shimmering in the candlelight as she moved, and Byron was struck anew by her beauty. He wondered why she was suddenly acting the wife. She had never done these small chores for him before and he found it charming, thinking to himself that tonight when they returned home he would take her gently in his arms and make love to her. He sat lathering soap on his hairy chest, his eyes dark and misty, and grinning as he watched her walk about the room.

"Which gown have you chosen to wear?"

"The satin green one, it will look well with the necklace."

"And your eyes, my love. Pet, get out my green waistcoat instead of the red one, and we will look well together."

"Byron, you do have the eye for details," Leigh chuckled. She thought it amusing that Byron should care. Of course, she had planned to get out the green all along.

Leigh again reverted her gaze as Byron stepped from

the tub. Once he was decently clothed she went to the door and called for Annie to help her finish dressing.

Her dress in place, she handed Annie her necklace to fasten. She looked at her reflection in the mirror and was pleased with what she saw. The gown's bodice was covered with tiny green jets like the hair net and she had a matching evening bag also covered with the jets. She had chosen none of these accessories and knew that Byron had done so. The man really did have an eye for detail. Her necklace sparkled as the light from the candles caught it and Leigh sighed as she looked at it.

Annie handed Leigh her long white gloves and she rose thanking her and turned to see Byron fully dressed and looking extremely handsome.

He wore black pants that came to just below the knee where they met black stockings. His shoes were also black and they had large gold buckles. His shirt was flawlessly white and had layers of ruffles falling over the green waistcoat. His coat was also black with long tails and had gold threads woven artistically on the stiff, high collar. With his still tanned skin and dark hair he looked wonderful. Leigh was glad Byron did not choose colorful clothes as many men did today. His clothes were always of the best fabric and very well made and he seemed to dress to suit his own high standards and not let fashions dictate.

Annie wished the couple a Happy New Year and smiling broadly told them how nice they both looked as she left the room.

Leigh walked to the bed to get her matching cloak and turned to find Byron before her, a small box held out in his hand. Leigh gingerly took the box searching his face. She opened it slowly and found earrings to match her

253

necklace. There was a diamond on the stud with an emerald dangling from it, surrounded by more diamonds. Leigh admired them with a long sigh. She had only the one pair of earrings she wore now, small gold loops, Jones had taken the rest, but she had never owned jewelry as beautiful as Byron had gifted her with.

"Byron, they are breathtaking. You spoil me, two gifts of jewels within a week."

"I gave you fair warning, pet. They will go well with the necklace and enhance your beauty this night." He smiled and looked deeply into her eyes. "Put them on so I may see."

He followed Leigh to the dressing table and stood behind her as she sat down and removed the gold loops. When she replaced them with the emeralds, she moved her head from side to side and her ears sparkled as she moved.

"Byron," she said softly with tears coming to her eyes, "you leave me speechless."

"Why, Leigh, what is it? I meant the gift to bring you joy."

She turned and gave him a soft smile. "It is tears of happiness that you see." She rose up on tiptoes and placed a soft kiss on his cheek. "Thank you Byron, and not just for the earrings."

Byron seemed flustered. His eyes rested on Leigh's low bodice, her breasts rising temptingly above it. He was aware of the alluring scent of her body, the silky feel of her lips against his cheek and he felt himself start to break out in a cold sweat.

Leigh noted where Byron's gaze settled and it served her purpose well. She planned for his eyes to stay right where they were all evening and off of Ella Borough.

Byron cleared his throat. "Come, pet, or we will be the last to arrive."

When the couple went downstairs Ephraim was awaiting them in the foyer. He complimented both on their appearance and made special mention of Leigh's earrings.

Byron helped Leigh on with her cloak. It was green satin like her gown, floor length with a hood, and the entire cloak was lined with mink. She also carried a matching mink muff.

Ephraim assisted Byron on with his cloak, and wishing them a good evening, said Henry was waiting with the carriage. They left the house with fond farewells. As they rode Leigh was aware of Byron's gaze upon her. He said nothing and only continued to study her with his eyes. Leigh tried several times to converse with him, but he seemed in a most reflective mood.

When they arrived at Uncle Jonathan's it was aglow with hundreds of candles. It was large, well built, and held furniture of good quality like Royal Oaks. There was a portrait in the drawing room of a woman that much resembled Byron and Leigh commented on it as they passed the room. Byron said it was his cousin Margaret.

Many guests were already present as Leigh and Byron entered the room. The ballroom was large with a high ceiling. A group of musicians sat in the far left corner playing soft music, chairs lined the walls, and a buffet table with a large silver candlelabrum and silver trays filled with food stood near the doorway. A huge crystal chandelier hung in the center of the room, numerous candles casting sparkling light about the room. The rainbow of colors represented in the gowns of the women gave the room a festive, gay appearance.

Leigh noted many glance their way as they entered the room and heads quickly came together in fevered whispers. Her cheeks pinkened and she shyly lowered her eyes as Jonathan came to greet them. Jonathan placed a fatherly kiss on Leigh's cheek as he complimented her on her beauty and then escorted the couple about the room introducing Leigh to his other guests. As more guests arrived, he excused himself and left Byron the honor of introducing his wife. Byron's hand slid to the small of Leigh's back as they walked among the guests. Leigh was introduced to many and given compliments by all, though some were given cooly.

The musicians began playing a waltz and Byron, smiling, bowed before her and escorted her to the dance floor. Leigh found him to be a most graceful dancer. Uncle Jonathan approached the couple as the dance ended and begged a waltz with his niece. Byron, smiling, handed Leigh over to him and stood watching his lovely wife as she whirled about the dance floor in his uncle's arms. Leigh also found Jonathan to be an excellent dancer and thought to herself how much she was going to enjoy this evening.

As Byron stood watching the pair dancing he was assaulted by men asking his permission to dance with his wife. Byron consented gracefully as any gentlemen would, but he did not like the idea of Leigh in another man's arms. Still, it would be rude to refuse. He had known the people here most of his life.

When the dance ended Jonathan and Leigh walked a small distance and stood chatting. Jonathan noted more guests arriving and quickly excused himself. Leigh glanced to the ballroom doors and saw Ella and her father just arriving.

Ella strolled into the room and stood looking about, and then her eyes came to a stop. Leigh followed her gaze and saw Byron across the room talking with Jack Cummings. She returned her gaze to Ella and found the woman now staring intently at her.

The two women stood glaring at each other across the room, each appraising the other's gown—and Leigh felt the victor.

Ella's gown was lovely and of good quality but it was daringly low in the bodice and with Ella's generous bosom Leigh thought it bordered on indecency. The gown was a soft mint green and Leigh felt with Ella's fair complexion, it did little for her. She wore a lovely diamond necklace about her neck, but again Leigh felt it did not compliment her gown nearly as well as her emerald did her own. Ella's hair was fixed similar to Leigh's and she wore a large white ostrich plume arranged in the coiffure.

Leigh saw Jack approaching out of the corner of her eye and turned and gave him a tremendous smile.

"Leigh, you are dazzling." Jack smiled.

"Thank you, kind sir," Leigh replied smiling warmly at him in return.

A servant passed carrying a large round silver tray filled with glasses of champagne and Jack took two, offering one to Leigh.

"Oh I don't know if I should Jack. I have never had champagne before. Papa would never permit it. He always said it went to a woman's head."

Jack chuckled. "I judge you may safely partake now, being an old married woman and all," Jack said teasingly. "Jonathan expects everyone to enjoy themselves immensely at this annual affair of his—so Mrs. Marsh,"

Jack said grinning and again offering her the champagne.

Leigh laughed and took the offered glass and she and Jack stood chatting as they sipped their champagne. When their glasses were empty Jack begged a dance and Leigh readily accepted.

Jack whirled her about the dance floor and Leigh was enjoying herself until she saw Byron dancing with Ella. They looked to be gaily chatting and Leigh's heart came up to her throat and she missed a step. She blushed profusely and apologized to Jack.

"Leigh, you are a most graceful dancer, there is no need to apologize." He smiled at her and they continued to dance as Leigh tried desperately to follow Jack and still keep an eye on Byron and Ella.

Byron noted Jack and Leigh waltzing and wished himself as lucky. Ella had hinted so strongly that Byron dance with her that it would have seemed most ungentlemanly to refuse to offer.

Ella studied Byron's solemn face. She did not know what had attracted him to his skinny wife, but she intended to do all in her power to woo him back to her bed, and remembering their past intimacies she had little doubt as to her power to do so. If she could drive a wedge between Leigh and Byron, she could most definitely take Leigh's place. She had not spoken to Byron since the day he informed her of his marriage and she knew she must make him aware that she was no longer angry with him. No doubt, knowing Byron, she mused, he had married the girl in a fit of passion. Well, she decided, she would use the same bait to get him back.

"Byron, sweet," she cooed, fluttering her lashes, "I have not seen you in simply weeks."

"I have been busy, Ella," Byron said briskly glancing at

her and then returning his gaze to Leigh and Jack across the room.

"Oh yes, that ridiculous matter of the shares. I had almost forgotten how you spend weeks working to prepare the amounts." She looked to him and stuck out her lip as if pouting. "Really Byron, when are you going to stop this ludicrous habit of paying slaves?"

He frowned at her and sighed. "Ella, we have had this discussion before and my answer has not changed. These people work the fields and without them my plantation would not prosper. Though it is true that I hold papers on most of them, I still feel they should share in the money they help to earn."

Ella's lip protruded farther. "But Byron, you provide food, clothing, and a roof over their heads. They could not afford to live nearly so well if they worked for someone else on a wage alone. And," she added with large eyes, "to give away ALL that money!"

"Ella, I have enough money so as not to go hungry, I assure you," he said in an irritated manner. He looked hard at her and frowned. "When will you learn you must allow people some dignity. Not to give them a share in their labor is just as deceitful as it would be if I were to feed them and house them in return for nothing. Either way, the people have no dignity."

Ella continued to pout thinking Byron would find it charming like he once had, but when the dance was over he quickly excused himself, much to Byron's relief, and went in search of Leigh.

Leigh and Emily stood chatting with their husbands when the musicians started playing a minuet. Byron smiled and bowed low in front of Leigh and she curtsied with a dimpled grin and accepted his hand. The couples lined up in two rows, the women to the right, the men to the left. The dance was done in quadrille with two couples coming forward and dancing together and then changing partners. Leigh looked down the line and discovered that Ella would shortly be Byron's partner. As Leigh and Byron walked forward, Ella and a handsome gentleman Leigh had not yet met came to greet them. When Ella curtsied low in front of Byron, Leigh gasped and her eyes nearly popped out of her head. She felt sure that Byron had seen the woman's navel at the very least. Leigh continued the dance with Ella's partner, watching Byron and Ella closely out of the corner of her eye.

When the dance ended, the man introduced himself as James Bradford, saying he had been a friend of Byron's for years. Leigh stood chatting politely with the man for a short time while glancing about for Byron, then excusing herself she went to stand near the buffet table and search the crowded room for him. When she could not see him or Ella, she nervously chewed at her lip wondering if they had gone to some more private place.

"Hello," Leigh heard someone purr. She turned to see Ella behind her. Little did Ella know it was a great relief to Leigh.

"Miss Borough," Leigh nodded.

"Oh, dear, please call me Ella," she said sweetly. She had no intention of addressing Leigh as Mrs. Marsh. "Simply wonderful party isn't it? Byron and I have been enjoying these parties of Jonathan's for simply years now."

"How nice," Leigh curtly replied. She turned away pretending to watch the dancers. She was quiet a moment and then whirled to face Ella with a grin. "Though to be truthful Ella, I truly can understand your enjoyment of

260

past balls, my husband is a wonderful dancer, don't you agree?"

Ella gave her a spiteful look and they stood side by side in silence, both of their chins high and backs stiff.

"Tell me dear," Ella purred, "wherever did you and Byron meet?"

Leigh quickly reverted her gaze and Ella noted the color draining from her face.

"We were staying at the same inn."

Both women turned in unison to see Byron standing a few feet behind them. He walked to Leigh's side and placed a hand protectively on her shoulder as Leigh smiled nervously up at him.

"How convenient," Ella commented looking from one to the other. Leigh appeared flustered and Ella's woman's intuition told her she had struck a nerve and she pressed on with a smile.

"Exactly when did you marry?" she questioned watching Leigh's face closely.

"Shortly after we met, Ella," Byron said easily, pulling Leigh closer. "Not that it is really any of your affair."

"Were you married in Richmond?"

"No, actually we were married at the inn," Leigh replied in a small voice.

"The inn!"

"Yes, the inn," Byron snapped, irritated with her questions. "The innkeeper and his wife had grown quite fond of Leigh during the period she stayed with them after the loss of her father." His hand casually caressed Leigh's shoulder in a comforting way as he spoke the last words. "They insisted we use their home for our wedding. The man was even kind enough to send for a minister that was an old friend of my father's."

Leigh raised her eyes to Byron's and the look she gave him was full of warmth and tenderness. He had told the truth, thought Leigh, yet he made it sound all so proper. The small fib about the minister being a friend of his father's she could overlook.

"Byron, old friend, may I have another dance with your lovely bride?"

They all turned to see James Bradford smiling at them. Byron reluctantly gave his consent. He liked not the idea of Leigh in James' arms, though he was a friend, he was handsome, charming, and a bachelor.

As Leigh began dancing with James, she glanced over her shoulder and saw Byron make a bow and excuse himself from Ella. There was a deep, dimpled smile on her face as she and James waltzed.

Byron stood off to one side scowling at his wife as she gave James a dazzling smile, and a muscle in his jaw started to twitch.

No sooner had the dance ended than Leigh was asked by another gentleman, and then another. And everytime she turned around someone was offering her more champagne, and with all the dancing she was doing, she was quite thirsty.

Leigh danced and danced having a marvelous time. She wondered several times where Byron was. She had not seen him in some time now. When she had seen him last he had been dancing with Emily Cummings and when she smiled in their direction, only Emily returned her smile.

Leigh stood chatting with Uncle Jonathan when Jack came to request another dance. Leigh commented it had been sometime since she had seen Byron and when the dance ended Jack spotted his tall frame across the room and took Leigh to his side. Ella stood with him looking longingly at his face.

"Byron, I believe this belongs to you," Jack said with a chuckle as he placed Leigh's hand in Byron's. Byron quickly snatched his hand away and frowned at both Leigh and Jack. Jack gave Byron a disapproving look and then glanced at Leigh.

"Lovely lady, thank you kindly for gracing me with a dance," Jack said. He looked at Byron. "You know not only is she beautiful, she is also a most graceful dance partner."

"I would not know myself," Byron said sharply with a frown. "It seems she has been much occupied this night."

Jack slapped Byron on the back with a chuckle. "That is what happens when you have a wife as lovely as Leigh."

Ella shot Jack daggers and then glared at Leigh. Leigh saw her admiring her necklace and casually placed her hand on it turning it so that the candlelight caught it many times and it sparkled. Leigh glanced at Ella beneath her lashes and thought Ella looked almost as green as the emerald in her necklace.

"Byron, dear, you simply must come and speak to Elizabeth Burton with me," Ella said moving to stand between Leigh and Byron.

"Later Ella," he answered not even looking at her. "They are playing a waltz and it appears I may finally get a chance to dance with my wife."

He held out a hand to Leigh and she took it with a smile. As they walked to the dance floor Ella stood fuming. Jack soon excused himself and left her to fume alone.

Leigh knew Byron was angry with her but she had not the slightest idea why, and by now she had had enough champagne that she did not really care. She was extremely pleased with Byron's words to Ella earlier and his behavior toward her just now. She decided if he was going to be in one of his foul moods, so be it. Nothing was going to ruin this night for her. She felt like the belle of the ball—and indeed she was.

As Byron took Leigh roughly into his arms and they started to waltz, his face was stiff. But in a few moments he relaxed with the sway of the music. Leigh smiled at him and they looked deep into each other's eyes. The loving look was caught by other pairs on the dance floor and many smiled at them as they danced by.

Jack was dancing with Emily when he noted Ella's keen interest in the couple. As he and Emily waltzed past Ella standing on the side, Jack commented overloud to Emily how nice it was to see Byron happily wed. When Ella turned and glared at him, he smiled and nodded his head in her direction.

When the dance ended Byron placed Leigh's hand firmly in the crook of his arm and escorted her to the buffet table to sample some of the delicious food. Jack and Emily joined them and they stood chatting as they all filled their plates. When Jack and Byron moved farther down the long table Leigh turned and whispered to Emily:

"See those two young ladies across the room," Leigh said with a motion of her head. "One of them has a lovely blue gown."

"Yes," Emily replied noticing who she meant.

"They have been giving me the most unpleasant looks all evening. I met them earlier and can think of nothing I have done to offend them."

Emily smiled. "Leigh, the one in the blue gown is Elizabeth Burton and the other is June Stockham. They both have been trying to gain Byron's attention for some years now. They were bitter enemies in the past but it appears they have now joined forces in their dislike of you." Emily glanced to the far end of the table and noted Jack and Byron in deep discussion with Fred Borough. "Pay them no mind, Leigh," she offered. "Jack was right when he commented on your husband's popularity."

Leigh grinned and thanked her for the information as the two women in question approached the table and gave both Leigh and Emily a wilting glare.

"You know, June," Elizabeth said in a loud tone as they both prepared themselves plates, "it is simply a shame that with all the lovely women in this area some men have to chose a Tory for a wife."

"Don't I know it, Elizabeth. And the English women are all so skinny and unusually unattractive," June commented.

Leigh quickly turned away as tears appeared in her eyes. Emily studied her sad face and then turned to give the spiteful pair a frown. As shy and meek as Emily was, she felt her anger growing.

"Elizabeth, June," Emily snapped, "I believe both of your families are of English decent, are they not?" The two women looked up to Emily's large, brown, angry eyes and blushed slightly. "It is a shame," Emily continued, "that you did not inherit any of their excellent breeding!"

Jack approached the women soon enough to hear Emily's last words and stared at his wife wondering what in the world had upset her easygoing manner. Leigh murmured something and quickly left the ballroom as Emily whispered to Jack. Emily followed after Leigh and Jack turned to appraise Elizabeth and June.

"You know ladies," Jack said casually, "if all the Tories had looked like Byron's wife, we would still be under the rule of the crown—and not a shot fired." He arched a brow at both of them and walked away.

It was several minutes before Emily and Leigh returned. Leigh seemed to have recovered herself and was again smiling. The two couples stood talking and all chuckled at Jack's jesting. James Bradford came up to them and requested another dance with Leigh, and though Byron frowned at him, he said nothing as James led his wife to the dance floor.

Leigh did not see Byron and went from partner to partner on the dance floor, each gentleman stating they wished a dance with Byron's bride. Before Leigh realized, someone was saying Happy New Year and she was again James' partner.

"Ah, madam, it appears I planned this well," James said with a grin. To Leigh's utter surprise he took her in his arms and kissed her passionately. "Happy New Year, Mrs. Marsh. You know I never did get to kiss the bride."

Leigh, slightly flustered, wished him a Happy New Year in return. James looked about and saw Byron across the room and there was a scowl on his face, and he was looking in their direction.

"I fear I must now deprive myself of your company," James commented. "Though Byron is an old and dear friend, I fear I may have brought his displeasure down on me." James smiled at Leigh, not showing a great deal of worry over Byron's frown and offering Leigh his arm, he led her to her husband's side. Just as they reached Byron, Ella came rushing up wishing Byron a Happy New Year. Byron looked at Ella and then arching a brow at Leigh, pulled Ella into his arms and kissed her long and extremely passionately. When Byron broke the embrace he again glanced to Leigh, the scowl still on his face. Leigh felt the kiss had only been to anger her, though she could not be sure, but Ella seemed to feel otherwise for she turned to Leigh and gloated. Taking Byron's arm in hers she pulled him to the dance floor saying it was time for the dance he had asked for.

Byron had requested no dance but he went along with Ella thinking it would serve Leigh right. After all she had gone from one man's arms to another the entire evening and she had spent a good deal of time dancing with James and smiling at him in a manner Byron considered coy. And to top that she had actually kissed the man! Well now, he thought, she can stand and watch me in another's arms.

Leigh hurriedly excused herself from James and went upstairs to one of the bedrooms to recover herself. Tears came to her eyes as she thought of Ella in Byron's arms and she quickly wiped them away determined not to let that woman ruin her evening.

She went to one of the guest rooms and sat down at a dressing table to freshen her hair. As she rose to leave, Ella walked in and Leigh quickly sat back down in front of the mirror.

Ella walked up behind her sharing the mirror. "My, my, dear, you do look wilted," Ella cooed patting her hair.

Leigh gave Ella's reflection a withering glare. "It is quite warm on the dance floor, Ella." Leigh patted her hair and glanced again to Ella, an impish look now in her eye. "I notice you look fresh, Ella."

Ella huffed at Leigh's implication that she had not been dancing. "It seems Byron prefers to, ah, *converse* with me," Ella cooed straightening the bodice of her gown, her look implying she and Byron had been doing anything but talking. She bent over behind Leigh to get a better view of her hair, her generous bust displayed in the mirror's reflection, and Ella noted just the hint of insecurity flash across Leigh's face. "You know, sweet," Ella purred, her smile laced with malice, "if you plan on keeping a man like Byron, there is much you need to learn."

"I assure you, Ella, I know exactly how to make Byron happy," Leigh replied trying desperately to sound self-assured. Her hands were trembling as she reached for her small evening bag and she forced herself to again confront Ella in the mirror's reflection. "In fact," she said arching a brow at Ella, "there is very little about Byron I do not know."

"Surely sweet Byron has not told you *everything*—about us."

Leigh quickly drew her eyes away, and rising walked toward the door. She knew that Byron had loved this woman, after all they had been almost engaged, but it had never occurred to her that they had been lovers. Was it possible? Mayhap, thought Leigh, remembering how she and Byron had met. But Mrs. O'Malley had explained that Byron had thought her a harlot, and Ella was a lady of breeding. Not excellent breeding, thought Leigh with a disapproving look in her eye, but still a lady. And if they had been lovers—were they still? Leigh's bottom lip began to quiver as she ran it through her mind. Byron was a man, and yet he had not laid a hand on her since they wed. He had shown her kindness—but not love. Had she not thought before that Byron still loved Ella? Leigh felt tears threatening to spill and she blinked hard several times forcing them back. Taking a deep breath, she spun about to face the woman, forcing her face to appear calm. She would not give Ella the satisfaction of knowing the worry she had caused her.

"If you were capable of making Byron as happy as you say, Ella," Leigh stated, her tone cooly self-assured, "then why do you suppose he married me?"

Ella opened her mouth to reply and then quickly snapped it shut. Leigh smiled at her frowning face and hurriedly left the room.

Once in the hallway the smile on Leigh's face was replaced by a look of sadness and rejection. Again she felt tears forming and she quickly brushed them away.

As Leigh descended the stairs she noted Byron below in the foyer, a dark scowl on his handsome face.

"Madam," he said briskly as Leigh neared his side, "I believe we failed to exchange New Year greetings."

"Happy New Year," Leigh said softly smiling and moving close to him. She knew that Ella would soon be following her down the stairs and she did not want the woman to find them quarreling.

"Happy New Year, pet," Byron replied taking her in his arms, forever at a loss at her dimpled smile. He gazed deep into the smiling emerald eyes and his lips lowered slowly to hers and when Ella reached the top of the stairs she saw them locked in an embrace. The kiss was long and tender and Leigh relaxed, giving herself totally to the warmth and security of being wrapped in her husband's arms.

"Here, here, enough of that," Jack chuckled from the doorway.

Byron looked up, his arms still around Leigh, and glared at Jack.

Jack took no note of the sour look on Byron's face as he approached the couple, two glasses of champagne in his hands. "Here Leigh," he said offering one to her, "drink your champagne, and then if you can pry yourself from this brute's arms," he said glancing to Byron and smiling, "come dance with me. They are playing a Virginia Reel and Emily is already occupied."

Leigh giggled and eventually Byron smiled at his old friend, and bowing low, he reluctantly placed Leigh's hand in Jack's. He watched Leigh's skirts swishing about her as she and Jack walked away, the faint smell of her perfume lingering in the air, and his eyes grew dark. He had felt response in Leigh's kiss. A familiar tightening gripped his loins as he again thought, and planned, the long night ahead.

Byron saw very little of Leigh the remainder of the night. It seemed Ella was ever at his side and he was growing weary of her constant attention and decided to seek Leigh and start for home.

Though it was approaching two in the morning, they left many couples still dancing when they departed. Some of the guests were staying several days with Jonathan and on the ride home Byron asked Leigh if she would object having them for dinner in the following days. He stated it had been a practice of his in the past. Leigh quickly agreed and chatted gaily about the ball and the dinner party to be planned.

Byron was not completely over his foul mood and with Leigh's gay chatter concerning the ball his mood grew even more foul. He had found no opportunity to dance with his wife after their New Year's kiss and it seemed she was constantly in the company of James Bradford. And with Ella plaguing him all evening after he had been the fool and kissed her so passionately, his mood had had little time to improve. Leigh, on the other hand, had had a wonderfully gay evening and by this time had had too much champagne and was completely unaware of his mood.

As they undressed for bed, Byron's mood remained silent and black.

"Byron, thank you for taking me. I had a mar-ve-lous time," Leigh said smiling at him in the mirror's reflection.

"I am well aware of that, madam," he snapped.

Leigh turned and stared at Byron, surprised. "Byron are you angry with me?" she questioned, her voice showing no sign of stress.

"I could not but help, madam," he scowled, "to take note of your obvious enjoyment of Mr. Bradford's company this evening."

The champagne made Leigh's mood carefree and light. "Why Byron Marsh, you're jealous," she teased.

"I most certainly am not!" he barked, the scowl growing deeper. He began to pace the room, the scowl growing ominous as he recalled his plans for this night when they returned from the ball.

He paced as he unfastened his shirt. He had already removed his coat, stock, and shoes, and he struck Leigh as funny pacing in his half-dressed state with such a fierce look on his face. She began to giggle and when Byron turned and snarled at her she quickly assumed a more solemn face and fought hard not to smile—but soon she lost the battle.

"I see nothing amusing, madam," Byron growled.

With that Leigh started to laugh, and the meaner Byron looked, the harder she laughed. She had learned that Byron's bark was worse than his bite, and now with the help of the champagne she no longer feared him, and roared with laughter.

"Not only do I have a wife who dances with every young buck in breeches," Byron said with a mean look, "but now," he stated throwing his hands in the air, "she makes jest of me as well."

"I am sorry, Byron," Leigh managed to say between giggles. "I am not laughing at you, really."

Byron mumbled something and finished undressing. He went to sit on the side of the bed in his robe. He sat watching her closely as she brushed her hair. His eyes became hooded and seemed to deepen in color as they caressed the soft curve of her back, the white skin at the nape of her neck. When their eyes chanced to meet in the mirror's reflection, surprisingly it was Byron who quickly cast his glance downward.

Leigh wiped tears of laughter from her eyes and carefully put away her necklace and earrings. As she walked to the bed, she tried desperately not to smile, but when she glanced in Byron's direction, she simply did not have the self-control and the giggling began again.

"Goodnight," she managed between giggles.

"Goodnight!" Byron snapped exasperated. He blew out the candles, removed his robe and climbed into bed mumbling something about women.

Leigh turned her head and buried it in the pillow so he would not hear her snicker.

They slept late the next day and when Leigh awoke her head felt as if it would fall off if she moved it too quickly, and the sunlight pierced her brain. She moaned and Byron awoke and turned to see her greenish complexion. He felt sorry for her, he had paid this price himself many times.

"Leigh, can I get you anything?" he questioned softly.

She winced at his words. "Byron," she whispered, "there is no need to shout. I am right here beside you."

Byron chuckled. Now it was his turn to laugh, but somehow he had not the heart. He rose and started to dress. "Stay in bed and I will have Annie bring you something to ease your plight."

"You best make it a gun," Leigh groaned. "I fear shooting me is the only thing that will ease this plight."

She turned her head gingerly and buried it in the pillow. Byron smiled at her and gently placed a kiss on her brow.

Soon Annie came with a mug and told Leigh to drink it all. Leigh became even a more sickly green when she placed it near her mouth, but under Annie's stern look she finally managed to get it all down and then let out a most unladylike burp.

"Now you sleeps Miss Leigh and when you wakes, you feel better," Annie assured her.

"Annie, please pull the drapes before you leave," Leigh said closing her eyes slowly.

Annie grinned as she gently closed the door. No need telling her the drapes were already closed.

Leigh woke late in the afternoon feeling fine and extremely hungry. She rose and dressed herself, mentally thanking Annie many times for the cure. When she looked for her gold loop earrings she found her mother's cameo beside them in the case. She slowly picked it up, then whirled and started for the door.

She searched for Annie and personally thanked her for the miracle she had performed and then went in search of Ephraim. She found him tidying Byron's study.

"Ephraim, I thought that you and I were friends," she said in a hurt tone.

"Why we are, Miss Leigh. What makes you doubt it?"

"This," she said holding the cameo out for him to see.

"Oh," Ephraim said looking away shame-faced.

"Ephraim, how could you? I asked you not to use Byron's coins unbid. I suppose I should have guessed when the cameo brought the value of three books."

"Miss Leigh, I did not break my promise to you."

"Then how did you purchase the books?"

"Well," he said looking down and shuffling a foot, "I, ah, had some coins of my own."

"Ephraim," Leigh exclaimed surprised, "you did not use your own money!"

"Miss Leigh, come and sit down and let me explain," he said taking her arm and directing her to one of the leather wing backs. Once she was settled he paused a long time to gather his thoughts.

"Miss Leigh, when Master Byron was a child he did not like to do his studies. The only way, or at least he said the only way, the old Master could get him to devote himself to his studies was to have me study with him. Though it is unusual, and I believe even unlawful, for a Negro to know how to read and write, I do. And I have Master Byron's father to thank for that." He looked at her and then drew his eyes up to the painting of Byron's father that hung over the mantel. "Before the old Master died, he gave Annie, Henry and myself our freedom. We can leave Royal Oaks whenever we wish. That was more than twelve years ago, and we are still here. We love this plantation, Royal Oaks is our home and everyone on it our family." He looked again to Leigh and there was a soft smile lighting up his old face. "Master Byron has taken care of me and mine. He sees we have a nice home, good food and clothing, and he still continues to pass out the shares. He is a good man, Miss Leigh, as well you know. Annie told me that that cameo was something that you cherished and I could not have you selling it to buy books for Master Byron. As I said, I love this place and everyone on it, and that includes you too, Miss Leigh. Please consider the books a gift from me to you and Master Byron. It would please me greatly."

Tears glistened in Leigh's eyes as she rose on tiptoes and placed a soft kiss on Ephraim's cheek.

"Thank you, Ephraim," she said softly.

"You are most welcome, Miss Leigh," Ephraim beamed.

Leigh went to eat in the cookhouse with Aunt Mary. They chatted as Leigh ate and she asked many questions of the old Negro cook. Leigh found Aunt Mary had a natural gift from God when it came to her skills in a kitchen. They talked and when Aunt Mary saw how great Leigh's interest was, she told her to come anytime and she would teach her all she knew about the art of cooking.

Leigh finished her light meal and thanking Aunt Mary graciously for her offer of tutoring, went to search for Byron. Ephraim informed her he was at the stables with Henry inspecting some new stock and she went and got a cape and headed for the stables to join him.

Byron seemed very surprised, but delighted, that she should seek out his company and he smiled broadly as she entered the barn.

"Feeling better, Leigh?" he asked.

"Yes, I swear Annie is a witch."

Byron and Henry laughed heartily and then Byron invited her to look over the horses that had just arrived.

Byron found Leigh knew her horseflesh and was impressed by her knowledge. They spent the remainder of the afternoon debating the qualities of two stallions and one particular filly.

As they sat eating dinner that night, Byron shook his head in wonder. At the far end of the table Leigh's graceful beauty shone. She was the epitome of femininity in both appearance and grace of movement and yet her head was full of all types of knowledge uncommon to most women.

"Pet," he grinned, "where did you gain your knowledge of horses?"

"My father loved them well," she said giving him a dimpled grin, her eyes slightly melancholy. "He often took me with him when he went to purchase new stock. I guess I learned much at his side," she said shrugging her arms as though she were somewhat embarrassed at the expression of admiration she noted in Byron's eyes. "I think," she added with a soft laugh, "he wished me a son."

"Pet, looking at you,' Byron said as his eyes softly caressed her face, "I doubt he ever wished you a male."

Color rose in Leigh's cheeks and she drew her gaze from his.

They spent the evening in the drawing room discussing several topics, including plans for the dinner party for Uncle Jonathan's house guests. They decided they would also invite all the neighbors that lived close by.

Leigh greatly enjoyed the quiet, domestic day spent with Byron, and as she sat before her dressing table mirror brushing her hair she thought about their life together. He was the father of her child, not matter how conceived, and the center of her world. She knew now that she loved him, foul moods and all. Shyly she glanced at his long, muscular body in the mirror's reflection as he undressed for bed. She felt a sudden pride in knowing that no other woman could lay claim to him. Ella may still love Byron, she thought, and he her, but Ella had no right to claim him as her own.

Byron watched Leigh askew. She was unusually quiet now, he mused. He wondered what would happen if tonight when they climbed into bed, he took her gently in his arms. Would she reject him? He had planned to do just that last night when they returned from the ball—mayhap tonight was the night to approach her in a gentle manner. He shrugged into his robe and went to sit on the side of the bed.

As Leigh climbed into bed the usual goodnights were spoken. Byron blew out the candles and then climbed beside her, but instead of turning his back to her as he usually did, he slid across the huge bed and now lay close to her side. Ever so slowly his hands went out to her and pulled her gently toward him. Leigh began to tremble realizing that this night Byron would at last be truly her husband. She realized that there was no feeling of fear where he was concerned, but instead a gentle yearning to be made truly his love. Byron's lips touched the nape of her neck and Leigh felt small shivers of delight ripple through her body. Slowly his lips moved toward hers and then suddenly Leigh gasped and sat straight up in the bed.

Byron frowned cursing himself for pushing too hard too fast. She had seemed so content with things as they were, he should have realized, he told himself. He felt a sudden anger building in him. He was now aroused, his manhood swollen, and he felt she had no right to constantly turn him away. He sat up with a jerk and reached for a flint to light a candle. Once lit, he turned to scowl at her but suddenly his face showed concern at her still form and the odd look on her face.

"Leigh, what is it?" he asked worriedly.

"Byron," she said in a whisper, as though her voice would break the spell, "it moved."

"What moved?"

"The baby."

"Oh."

There was a long pause as Byron sat studying her. Then her words seemed to register.

"The baby moved?" he asked again. She turned a grin in his direction and slowly nodded her head.

"Here give me your hand." She placed his large hand gently on her stomach and sat very still looking straight ahead. "There!" she exclaimed, "did you feel it?"

"No-o. Are you sure?"

"Oh yes," she said turning liquid eyes to his. "Isn't it wonderful?"

"Wonderful," he replied, slightly confused by the entire affair.

Leigh lay back with a contented sigh. Byron studied her a moment more and then blew out the candle and lay down beside her. Leigh lay thinking how nice it would feel to nestle close to his side. She was no longer thinking of what they may share in the bed this night, but rather of what a wonderful father Byron would make.

Byron lay with his hands behind his head staring at the ceiling. He wanted to turn to her again but now felt an awkwardness as to how to approach her again. He sighed heavily several times and then turned on his side, his back to her. He began to toss and turn with a fitfulness and eventually he rose quietly, and donning his robe, walked toward the door. There was a worried frown on Leigh's face as he left the room.

Byron went to his study and poured himself a brandy. He stood looking at his father's portrait and thinking of his own child soon to be born. He had been a bachelor so long. He knew little of motherhood. He was an only child, as were most of his neighbors. Jack had two older sisters but Byron had no memory of Mrs. Cummings carrying the girls. In fact, he had never been close to any pregnant woman other than Annie when she carried Henry and he had been only a boy himself then. Now he wished he were more knowledgeable on the subject.

Byron knew he had long built frustration, and though Leigh had seemed passive enough tonight to his embrace, mayhap she would not be so passive when he became more amorous. He doubted that once he became fully aroused he could change his mood even if Leigh fought him!

He poured himself another drink and sat down behind his desk and propped his feet upon it. He wanted nothing more than to take Leigh in his arms and it would be a long time, too long, before the child was born. He swirled the brandy in his glass and frowned, then he drank it in one long gulp and rose to get another.

Though Leigh was still trim and very lovely to look upon, he could tell when she wore her nightgown that her waist was becoming thicker and her stomach was starting to round. But, he mused, that did not mar her full, round breasts and the graceful curve of her hips. He felt his manhood rising as he pictured her form in his mind, and with an oath he poured himself another drink and returned to his desk.

I guess it is best to leave things as they are for a short

time longer, he decided. Mayhap Leigh will give me some sign when she's ready to accept me, he thought hopefully. If she should fight me, I could injure her or the babe and, he sighed, I will not take that risk. He sighed heavily several times as he sipped his brandy.

Leigh lay in bed wondering where Byron had gone. It was obvious to her that the mentioning of the child had upset him. He had said he liked children but it appeared he liked not the idea of having one of his own. Tears appeared in her eyes and she glanced dejectedly to the empty bed beside her. She started to rise several times and see where he had gone but decided against it. Then a long time later she heard him talking loudly below. She rose, frowning, and put on her robe. She lit a candle and started to make her way cautiously downstairs to see whom Byron was speaking with at this late hour. There was a light shining from the study door and Leigh could plainly hear Byron speaking. She tiptoed to the door and timidly peeked one eye around the corner of the door frame. Byron sat behind his desk, his feet propped upon it, he was smiling and toasting a drink with no one!

"And here is to the fool who takes a virgin wife," he laughed, "and then doesn't take her."

As he drank his eyes rose and he spotted Leigh's long curls in the doorway.

"Leigh, my dear, come in, come in." He rose unsteadily and motioned to her with his arm. "Come in, come in." He had a broad grin on his face and Leigh slowly entered the room watching him carefully. He took a step toward her with a crooked grin born of spirits, and Leigh became frightened.

"How nice of you to join me," he said making a small bow. When he rose his eyes wandered the room before he

280

again found her and his gaze came to rest. He took several steps toward her and his feet did a funny little hop. "Would you care for a dear, my drink?"

Leigh fought hard not to giggle and covered her mouth with her hand to hide her smile.

"Of course you would," Byron said merrily. He carefully walked to the table where the crystal decanters stood and with a wide sweep of his arm, snatched up one, and somehow managed to get a small amount in a glass. He turned with his crooked grin and again his eyes seemed to have trouble locating her.

Leigh knew he had had too much to drink, and though leary of him in this state, he did seem to be in a most jovial mood, and rather amusing.

As he walked toward her with the brandy, his foot caught in the carpet and he started to fall in her direction. She quickly stepped from his path and as he did an awkward pirouette on one foot, she reached out her hand and took the glass of brandy from him so it would not spill on the lovely Oriental carpet. He came to a rest away from her and looked about wondering where she had gone. He called her name and felt someone tap him on the shoulder and turned to see her standing behind him.

In Byron's mind he was being most charming and suave and he thought before this night was over he could persuade her into playing the wife.

"Shall we toast," he said looking to the ceiling, then back to her. "Here is to a fine boy," he said trying to tap his glass to hers. Leigh finally held his hand still and touched her glass to his and then took a small sip. Her eyes opened wide and she gasped as the brandy burned its way to her stomach. Tears appeared in her eyes and it was several moments before she could speak. Byron seemed not to notice and she gave him a studious look.

"Byron, do you look forward to our child?" she questioned uncertainly.

"Of course, madam," he answered with a grin as he rocked back and forth on the balls of his feet. "Fie on you for thinking otherwise."

Leigh stood quietly watching him and then a thought occurred to her. "What if your son is a girl?" she asked suspiciously.

Byron placed an arm about her shoulder and moved closer as if he was about to tell her something of great importance. "Leigh," he said in all seriousness, "sons are never girls, they are always males."

Leigh studied his face, and fought hard to keep from laughing. "You don't say," she commented.

"Oh, but I do," he said standing back and looking hard at her. "If the babe is a girl, she will be a daughter."

Leigh stood looking at him in disbelief. He was dead serious. She laughed and shook her head. She placed her brandy glass on his desk and when she turned again to face him he was frowning at her.

"Really Leigh, I would expect you to be more knowledgeable on these matters. You are soon to be a mother yourself."

Leigh stared at him a moment and then picked up her candle and started for the door.

"Where are you going?"

"To bed, Byron, the hour is late."

"Good idea, I'll go with you," he said making a small bow and giving her a devil-may-care expression.

In reality he bowed so low his head nearly touched his knees, and when he stood up grinning, his eyes roamed the room and never did find her. He took several careful steps toward her and his feet became tangled.

Leigh laughed. "Byron don't you think we should extinguish the candles on the mantel before we leave?"

"No doubt we should," he agreed winking and spinning smartly about on one foot. He stood in the center of the large room blowing hard in the direction of the mantel.

"Byron," Leigh said with a sigh and a smile, "you can't blow them out from there!" She started walking toward the mantel as Byron turned and looked to where she had been standing.

"I most certainly can," he boasted. He turned back to the mantel and blew hard just as Leigh reached the candles and blew them out herself. As she turned and walked to his side, he had a broad grin on his handsome face.

"See, I told you I could," he announced proudly.

Leigh giggled and taking his arm in hers, led him from the room. When they reached the stairs Leigh guided him carefully. He missed his footing several times and she began to fear he would fall and injure himself, mayhap dragging her along with him. She stopped with a sigh, and laying her candle down on the steps, placed one of his arms about her shoulder, then picking up the candle, she wrapped her free arm about his waist.

"Now, Byron," she instructed, "hold tight to the railing and be very careful. Look down at the steps."

He grinned at her and nodding his head studied the steps intently as they climbed. She is most anxious to bed with me, he thought. First she suggested we go to bed and now she hugs me tightly as we climb the stairs. And to think I was afeared she would fight me if I tried to bed her. He was grinning from ear to ear when they reached

283

the bedroom.

Leigh helped him to bed and then told him to lay back as she removed his slippers. She looked at his robe, hesitated, and then pulled the covers over him leaving it in place. He was still grinning at her and as she turned, he sat up suddenly and grabbed her arm.

"Ah, my lusty virgin," he slurred pulling her to him and placing one of his large hands over her breast.

Leigh gasped and pushed against him with all her might. To her surprise he fell back on the bed with hardly any resistance. He gave her a surprised look and started to rise again as she placed her hand on his chest and stared hard into his blue eyes. Byron stared back at her in a confused manner and Leigh opened her mouth several times to speak, but said nothing. She crossed her arms before her in a disgusted manner and paced briskly to the fireplace, her face full of anger. She whirled about, glaring at him, and Byron began to snore. Leigh flounced to the dressing table and pulled off her robe with one swift jerk. She glared at his long, muscular body relaxed in drunken slumber and stomped to his side of the bed.

"You oaf!" she said in a harsh tone. "I am not some strumpet to be treated in a crude fashion," she sneered with a toss of her curls. She bent low over his sleeping form, jabbing at his massive chest with one finger. "I am your wife! Do you think you can drunkenly force your vile ways on me again?" She straightened, hands on her hips, and her eyes caressed the smooth handsome features, the full lips, the thick dark lashes resting against the tanned skin, and she sighed. "Am I never to have any tenderness or soft words of love from your lips?"

Walking quietly to her side of the bed, she lifted the

covers and climbed in close beside him. With a sigh she nestled her head on his shoulder and there was a smile on her face as her eyes fluttered closed.

The next morning Byron studied her closely. He remembered her joining him in the study and he remembered they had walked to bed together—but after that he drew a complete blank. He had awakened with his robe still in place and he knew she had helped him to bed. He could not remember if he had said or done anything, but he knew he had not bedded her. His body still felt tense and tight. Leigh made no mention of the incident, though her attitude and manner toward him was cool and aloof the following day, so Byron decided to let the matter be.

Two days later they had dinner guests. Leigh spent the day in the cookhouse with Aunt Mary. She begged the woman to shoo her out if she got in the way. She was so interested in the cooking, that soon Aunt Mary had an apron on her and had her helping. Leigh could not have been more delighted. Byron searched for her once and found her in the cookhouse, apron on, and a kerchief wrapped about her head, hanging onto Aunt Mary's every word. He chuckled to himself and closed the door quietly, returning to his study.

When Aunt Mary reminded Leigh of the time, her eyes grew round and she rushed from the room to get dressed, leaving Aunt Mary laughing at her hurried pace. She burst into the bedroom where Byron was just finishing dressing and he too laughed when he saw her. She still wore the kerchief and was evidently unaware of it. He placed a kiss on her cheek as he left the room and promised to send Annie to help her change.

The gown she wore was a soft, rich, brown, almost the color of her hair. It was high waisted and had a full flowing skirt and long puffy sleeves. Annie arranged her hair in a bun on top of her head and she wore the emerald earrings dangling from her ears. She looked charming as she descended the stairs. Byron stood below in the foyer wearing a dark brown suit and a rich gray waist vest, sipping a brandy while awaiting Leigh.

"I feared I would not be ready in time," Leigh said nearing his side. "And to be quite truthful," she added with a giggle, "I never expected such a busy social season. Do you often entertain?"

"Life on a plantation is demanding, Leigh. Once spring arrives, and with it the time for planting, there is small time for anything else, so we do our socializing during the winter months," he explained.

Leigh smiled up at him and again felt her composure slip under the penetrating gaze of the deep blue eyes. "I-I need see Ephraim for a moment," she said. "If the guests start arriving I will most likely be in the dining room."

"I'll call you should they arrive," he assured her. "You look most charming," he added, his smile warm.

"Thank you," she replied with a curtsy and Byron noted just the hint of a blush enter her cheeks.

Leigh returned to the foyer just as Uncle Jonathan and his ten house guests arrived. She and Byron stood together in the foyer welcoming their guests as Ephraim took their cloaks. When James Bradford came to take Leigh's hand and placed a kiss on the back of it, Byron frowned and the look was caught by his uncle who quickly escorted the guests into the drawing room. Ephraim entered the room carrying a large silver tray with wine and glasses for the ladies and for the men who

286

wished stronger refreshments, several decanters of excellent brandy and bourbon.

The Cummings arrived shortly after and Leigh was delighted to see Emily again. She had grown very fond of the woman and Emily had lost almost all of her shyness where Leigh was concerned. The Cummings were followed almost immediately by Ella and her father.

Ella swished into the foyer and gave Byron a toothy smile. Her father approached Leigh and complimented her on her lovely gown. As Ephraim helped Ella with her cloak Leigh noted Ella's beautiful blue gown and had to admit the color looked well on her.

"Leigh, Byron, I want to thank you for your kind dinner invitation," Fred Borough said smiling to the couple.

"The honor is ours," Leigh replied. She felt Byron's large hand wrap warmly about hers and looked up to see an engaging smile on his lips. She smiled back with a squeeze of his hand and the loving look was not lost on Ella who frowned at Leigh as her father escorted her to the drawing room. When she saw James Bradford the frown instantly disappeared.

Leigh and Byron mingled among their guests and Byron gave James little chance to converse with Leigh, or even stand near her for that matter, though the man had little opportunity as it was the way Ella hung onto him.

Several times the guests' attention was drawn to Ella. She laughed loudly several times at some witty remark made by James and then looked askew in Byron's direction. Byron paid her small attention and Ella became even bolder in her flirting, thinking to make Byron jealous.

When Ephraim announced dinner Ella was disappointed to find Leigh had seated her a good distance from Byron and put Emily to his right instead. Ella glanced Leigh's way heatedly, and Leigh glanced back, dignified and cool. The dinner conversation soon seemed to settle around Leigh, her feelings for this land and her new home, the state of affairs in England when she left, and present turmoil in France. Ella found the entire matter boring and spent the majority of the meal trying to gain Byron's attention but he seemed most engrossed in what Leigh was saying, though Ella could not imagine why.

The meal was another of Aunt Mary's masterpieces and Byron commented to one of the guests that Leigh had helped to prepare the meal. Leigh blushed as Byron explained her interest in Aunt Mary's skills.

As the meal ended the men's conversation again turned to the turmoil in France and politics in general, and the women excused themselves and retired to the drawing room, leaving the men to smoke their cigars and pipes. The women settled themselves comfortably, all but Ella who found herself at odds now that there were no men for her to flirt with. She glared at Leigh through hooded eyes and casually strolled about the room.

"Tell me, dear," she commented, "however do you find time for cooking? I would think a man like Byron would demand most of your time—at least I always found him so demanding of mine."

An awkward silence filled the room and Leigh's face became stiff. She quickly lowered her gaze to her lap, embarrassed by Ella's statement implying to all that she and Byron had once been more than just neighbors and friends.

"It appears, Ella," Emily said in a brittle but polite tone, "that Leigh is capable of running a household and still finding time for her husband. Why Jack commented just the other day on the happiness he sees in Byron of late."

Ella glared at Emily not acknowledging her statement. "I would think such dull matters as cooking better left to servants," she quipped.

"I, for one, hardly consider excellent food dull," one matronly guest commented and several others nodded in agreement. "Not many of us are blessed with such an outstanding cook, but I assure you were I so blessed, I would jump at the opportunity to learn from such an artist."

Ella saw that none were going to allow her to taunt Leigh easily and thinking of no further comment she fell silent.

When the men joined the ladies in the drawing room Ella again divided her attentions between Byron and James completely ignoring all others present. As the evening wore on she tried desperately to find an opportunity to be alone with Byron but found when he was not talking with his other guests he was at Leigh's side. He had never been this attentive to her at social gatherings and Ella felt an uneasiness seeping into her body as her hatred of Leigh grew stronger.

"Leigh, do you by chance play chess?" Uncle Jonathan asked.

"No, but I would enjoy learning if that is an offer of tutoring."

"Indeed it is," he laughed. "I mistakingly taught that husband of yours many years ago and I have won few matches since."

Byron approached and casually placed a hand on Leigh's waist.

"If you think Leigh will offer less challenge allow me to give you warning, she has an excellent head on her shoulders."

"Of that there was never any doubt," Jonathan agreed as Leigh turned a bright smile in Byron's direction, "but I have a feeling she will be gracious and occasionally allow an old man a game."

Leigh smiled. "Gentlemen, before you decide the outcome of the games, do you not think first I should learn how to play? I could prove most inept."

Jonathan laughed. "I am at your disposal, my dear."

"I shall also assist in this tutoring," Byron offered.

"Now I have little doubt as to the outcome," Jonathan chuckled and Leigh and Byron joined him.

The evening was growing late but all the guests seemed to be having an excellent time and no one appeared anxious to depart. Byron and Leigh stood chatting with Jack.

"Leigh, Byron, Emily and I insist you join us next Sunday after church for dinner," Jack said.

"Thank you Jack, we would be delighted," Leigh replied after glancing to her husband and receiving his nod of approval.

"Good, it is settled. You know Leigh, Emily has spoken of little else but you since the two of you met. She is very fond of you."

"I am most fond of her also," Leigh replied with a smile.

"It is nice that the two of you have each other's company," Jack continued. "I fear in the past Emily had regretted that there were no women neighbors close by for her to keep company with."

"But Jack," Leigh said without thinking and glancing

in Ella's direction, "Ella is a neighbor."

"Yes, that is true," Jack said glancing to Byron and looking slightly uncomfortable, "but Ella and Emily have never gotten on well together."

"I am sorry to hear that, Jack," Leigh replied. "I find it hard to imagine anyone not being fond of Emily."

"Nor I," Byron added. He and Jack exchanged a look over Leigh's head and Byron knew it was Emily who was not fond of Ella. He had never known that before and now it was also apparent to him that his best friend, Jack, also cared little for Ella. He knew that as children growing up Jack and Ella had never gotten on well together, but he had thought them long over childhood quarrels. Strange that in all their adult years Jack had kept hidden from him his dislike for Ella.

When it appeared the guests would soon be leaving Byron excused himself and made his way to the cookhouse. He found the drivers of the guests' carriages gathered around the oak table in merry conversation with Annie, Aunt Mary, Ephraim and Henry. He chatted a moment with the group, and then informing the drivers their masters would soon be ready to depart, he started back toward the drawing room. Ella met him in the hallway, a large toothy smile on her face.

"Is there something you require, Ella?" Byron asked politely.

"No," Ella replied taking one finger and tracing it lightly across Byron's chest. "That is, nothing but your company. I overheard father and Jonathan speaking earlier and father is invited to your uncle's tomorrow for one of their day-long chess matches." She fluttered her eyelashes giving Byron a bold glance. "I'll be home all alone the entire day," she added invitingly.

Byron's eyes hooded and roamed over her body, pausing at the generous breasts, tiny waist, rounded hips, as if judging the worth of her offer. "Ella," he started, his tone cool, but he was interrupted when Ephraim opened the door from cookhouse, heading in their direction. Placing a hand on Ella's elbow, he hurried them toward the foyer. The guests were just leaving the drawing room and Byron quickly let loose his hold on Ella's arm and joined them.

As the guests departed they all thanked the host and hostess for a most enjoyable evening and complimented Leigh again on the delicious meal, that is all but Ella. She lavished praise on Byron saying his parties had always been ones she especially enjoyed and completely ignored Leigh. The slur was caught by her father who frowned at his daughter's rudeness and generously thanked Leigh for her invitation and kind consideration of her guests.

Byron and Leigh stood in the doorway together as the last carriage pulled away.

"It went well, don't you agree?" Leigh asked with a grin.

"Indeed so, madam," Byron smiled. "But then how could it not with such a charming hostess."

Leigh gazed into Byron's blue eyes and sighed contented, feeling suddenly exhausted after the tension of hosting her first dinner for Byron's friends—and being witness to Ella's displays all evening.

Noting her tired appearance Byron placed an arm about her shoulder. "Come, pet," he said walking her toward the stairs. "The hour is late. We have all of the morrow to discuss your success as hostess."

Leigh grinned up at him, and wishing him a goodnight, made her way to the bedroom.

"I need see Ephraim for a moment," Byron called after her. "I'll not be long."

Leigh was in bed, curled on her side, the covers pulled snuggly about her when Byron entered the bedroom. Thinking her already asleep, Byron walked to the side of the bed and stood quietly gazing down at her lovely face. Leigh's eyes fluttered open and she gave Byron a sleepy smile.

"Goodnight, pet," he said bending over to place a fleeting kiss on her brow.

Leigh murmured a soft reply as Byron turned to blow out the candle and he did not see the warmth of her tender smile or the soft glow of love in her eyes.

Chapter Ten

Sunday came and Leigh and Byron attended church and then stopped at the Cummings' plantation as planned. As they descended the carriage Leigh commented what a lovely place it was. Byron offered her his arm and they started for the house. They were talking when Leigh looked up and saw a huge beast running toward them. She stood, rooted, her eyes wide with fear.

"Leigh, look out!" Byron shouted blocking her body with his own. The beast ran straight for him and knocked him to the ground and Leigh let out a small scream and now stood horrified watching Byron struggle with the beast as Jack came running from the house.

"General, you mangy dog," Byron said still struggling, "I am going to wring your neck proper one of these days!"

Leigh saw to her amazement that it indeed was a huge

dog and that he was licking Byron's face. Jack stood at her side laughing but Leigh still wore a worried expression on her face.

"Byron, are you injured?" she asked.

The dog sat down next to Byron, wagging his tail. His face almost looked as if he was smiling at them.

"I am sorry Leigh," Jack said with a grin. "I hope General did not frighten you. He has an unusual fondness for Byron, though I cannot imagine why," he added with a wink.

"That mangy brute," Byron said rising and brushing with angry swipes at his clothes. "I can never come and visit with Jack that he does not greet me overhard. Why can't you have normal size dogs as everyone else Jack?"

Jack knew that Byron was not truly angry with him or the dog, and taking Byron's arm in one of his and Leigh's in the other, he escorted them to the house. General followed close at their heels, tail wagging. Jack explained that General was a breed called a Great Dane. His father had brought a pair of them from England many years ago and General was their descendant.

"They always grow quite large, but I feel General is unusually so," he said. "General has always been fond of Byron and runs to greet him whenever he comes to call." Jack laughed. "He is so large that when he stands on his hind legs he is taller than your lengthy husband and carries much weight as well. I know Byron tires of being knocked down, but I fear there is little I can do. Byron is the only guest that General greets in this manner." Jack placed a finger to his lips and made a show of studying the dog. "It is beyond me why any dog of mine should show such questionable taste."

Leigh laughed and Byron gave Jack an evil look and

then too laughed. Emily came to greet them on the steps of the veranda and soon all were in the foyer talking as Leigh and Byron were helped with their wraps. A small boy came running and leaped into Byron's arms.

"Uncle Bywon," the boy said placing a smacking kiss on Byron's cheek.

"Well hello there, young man," Byron said giving the child a big smile. "Now I wonder who you could be. You much resemble Jeffery Cummings but he is not nearly as big as you, or so strong either," Byron said making a show of feeling the boy's muscles.

"It's me Uncle Bywon, Jeffery," the boy said laughing, his face alight with a smile.

"Well so it is," Byron agreed with a grin.

Jeffery turned to Leigh and smiled. "Hello," he said.

"How do you do, Master Jeffery," Leigh said with a curtsy as Byron placed the boy on the floor in front of her.

"Jeffery, this is Mrs. Marsh, my," Byron stopped when Jeffery turned to give him a wide-eyed look.

"Are you Uncle Bywon's new mommy?" he asked of Leigh.

"No," Leigh chuckled, "I am his new wife."

Jeffery looked from Leigh to Byron slightly confused by this, but then he smiled at Leigh and placed his small hand in hers. "You're pwetty."

"Thank you kindly, sir," Leigh replied with a grin.

Jeffery motioned for Leigh to bend down closer and then whispered in her ear that they were having lemon meringue pie for dessert today, licking his lips and smiling.

"How wonderful," Leigh exclaimed, "that is my favorite kind."

Jeffery gave her a beautiful boyish smile and taking her hand in his escorted her to the drawing room, the others following and smiling at the boy.

They all sat in the drawing room chatting and General lay near the fireplace watching them with his eyes. Leigh saw the dog was very well-behaved here in the house. Jeffery sat beside her and told her stories about the dog and himself and how they fight the Indians and the British every day out behind the big barn. When he mentioned the British, Emily looked flustered, but Leigh glanced her way and smiled and pretended to be most interested in Jeffery's mock battles and complimented both him and General on their bravery.

When dinner was announced Jeffery insisted he sit next to Leigh and Byron smiled at the two of them chatting during the meal.

When the meal was over and the men sat smoking their cigars, Leigh asked Emily if she could help put Jeffery down for a nap and take a peek at Elizabeth still sleeping. Emily readily agreed and as the woman climbed the stairs General followed.

Leigh rocked Jeffery and told him a tale of knights and shining armor. Emily sat nursing Elizabeth and also listening to the tale. Once the children were settled, the women went below to again join the men. As they reached the foyer Emily walked on as General came close to Leigh's side. Leigh stopped, studying the huge dog. She had no intention of being knocked down as Byron had and timidly put out her hand to the animal.

"Good General," she said in a small voice. The dog licked her hand and again looked as if he were smiling. Leigh patted his large head and his tail wagged from side to side as he walked with her to the drawing room. When she sat in one of the chairs, he came and sat at her feet.

Leigh loved dogs, and once she saw General meant her no harm, she enjoyed his company and sat stroking his head. Byron noticed the attention General gave Leigh and her return lavish attentions to the dog.

"It appears you also will be plagued by the beast, Leigh," Byron said with a grin.

"Now I can understand General's fondness for Leigh," Jack added with a chuckle.

Leigh looked to the dog and caressed his head. "I love dogs and General seems an especially nice one."

Byron saw that Leigh did indeed love dogs and he made a mental note to do something about that in the future.

"Emily, Jack, thank you again for the delicious meal and the hospitality of your home," Leigh said as they made to leave. "I greatly enjoyed myself and the time spent with the children. I quite hate to depart."

The Cummings assured her that their home was always open to both she and Byron. They walked with them to their carriage, and when they reached it Leigh turned to General. "Goodbye beast, it was most pleasant meeting you," she said in a jovial mood.

General sat wagging his tail and at Leigh's words he lifted one paw as if offering it to her. All present were highly amused.

Several weeks passed and Leigh and Byron grew closer still. Byron was busy most of the day with the plantation but each evening they spent together in the drawing room, Byron reading to her from one of his favorite books or tutoring her in chess. And each night when it was time to retire Byron would walk her to the stairs and then bidding her a goodnight and placing a fatherly kiss on her cheek, would retire to his study until she was asleep.

Leigh often wondered about his nightly work in his study. And she worried often if he was truly that busy each day with the plantation, or mayhap visiting Ella instead. The man had made no advances toward her and though once Leigh feared his touch, now she yearned for it. She was determined not to show her insecurities and continued to play the part of the contented, timid wife, fearing that if she acted otherwise she would lose all chances of winning his affections.

Leigh received a letter from Mrs. Marrow stating she was forgiven all. She had been a frightened bride herself once, she wrote. She also wrote how grateful she was for Leigh's letter. Only yesterday, the letter stated, she had learned that they found the crew of the boat Leigh had taken from Richmond dead and afloat in the river somewhere down near the mouth of the river. Mrs. Marrow stated that she would have been frantic to receive such news had she not received Leigh's letter first and known that she was safe. She also stated how fortunate it was that Leigh had left the boat before misfortune had struck.

As Leigh read the words she had little doubt that Samuel Jones was the misfortune!

Mrs. Marrow's letter closed by saying that she and Thomas Whitefield were keeping company now. Leigh smiled as she read the words. And the letter continued to say that though she had never met Byron, she understood he was a quite attractive man and that he carried a good reputation in Richmond and she wished Leigh and Byron only the best.

That same afternoon Leigh sat in the drawing room, a

lap desk before her, and was writing another letter to Mrs. Marrow when Byron entered the room. He stood watching her with his hands behind his back and rocking to and fro on his heels.

Leigh glanced his way several times and smiled but he said nothing and eventually she began to feel quite uncomfortable. She sat aside her quill and paper and looked in his direction nervously.

"Is there something amiss, Byron?"

"I have a surprise for you," he stated with a twinkle in his eyes.

Leigh's eyes lit up like a child's at Christmas and she rose and tried to see what he was hiding behind him but he kept turning with her and not allowing her to see his hands.

"Byron, you cad," she laughed. "Do not tease me so."

"Very well, madam, sit down and close your eyes."

Byron chuckled as Leigh scurried to a chair, closed her eyes and figited.

"You may look now if you wish."

Leigh opened her eyes and saw a large puppy held out in Byron's hands. "Oh, Byron," she sighed as she held her hands out to the dog. She smiled into his eyes as she placed the puppy's head close to hers and rubbed her cheek into the soft fur. "Oh, Byron," she repeated, "I cherish this gift above all others."

"I am happy it pleases you so," Byron said caressing her face with his eyes. He came to sit beside her and scratched the puppy behind one ear. "You may regret the gift I fear," he warned as Leigh gave him a bewildered glance. "Though the pup is not large yet, he is but two months old and General is his sire. I fear he will grow much larger."

"I shall call him Major," Leigh replied hugging the pup and grinning at Byron, then a slight gasp escaped her lips and she looked quickly in the dog's direction. "It is a him, isn't it?"

"Yes," Byron chuckled, "and Major is a fitting name."

Byron did not know what had possessed him to take this pup from Jack. Jack had offered pups numerous times in the past, but always Byron had declined. Byron loved animals, and dogs he was especially fond of, but he had never wanted one of Jack's brutes. Seeing Leigh that day with General, her so small and delicate and General so large and powerful, he had slowly changed his mind.

Leigh stroked the pup's back gently. "He will be a great comfort to me, Byron, thank you again. He will be grand company now that you are so busy with the plantation— and before long I shall be confined to the house."

"Leigh, you shall not be confined. You can go visiting whenever you wish," Byron quickly assured her.

"I know and I plan to visit with Emily often, but when I am larger with child it will not be acceptable for me to be seen in public."

"I find this confinement of expectant mothers quite silly myself. You have no reason to hide your condition, Leigh," he said irritably. "And I assure you everyone is quite aware of where children come from."

Leigh laughed. "Byron it is just not acceptable for a woman to go about displaying her large belly, you know that." She took his hand in hers and looked deeply into his eyes. "You would not want your friends to think ill of me, would you?"

"No, of course not—but I still think it is ridiculous."

That night Byron waited his usual time before retiring to bed thinking Leigh asleep. But when he entered the

301

bedroom he found her comforting the puppy where it lay on a blanket at the foot of the bed.

"Leigh, do you not think Major should learn to sleep outside?"

"But Byron, he is just a pup—and I do not want him to cry and disturb anyone," she begged.

Byron agreed though there was a frown on his face. During the night Leigh was up and down continuously with the dog. Byron did not point out to her that the dog was disturbing someone greatly—him, and by morning he regretted the gift many times.

As the weeks rolled by Major grew in leaps and bounds and Leigh's shape began to round. Often when she lay sleeping, she would roll next to Byron and he would awaken at the feel of her silky flesh next to his. He thought often of taking her into his arms and making sweet, gentle love to her—but each time he feared her rejections. She seemed so content with things as they were and she was rounding rapidly with the shape of his child. He often felt the fluttering in her stomach now and the first time he felt the baby move strongly it helped to cool his mood more permanently. There will be many years to share once the child is born, he told himself.

Major was still just a pup and not nearly as large as General, but at the fast rate he was growing he showed every chance of gaining his sire's great size. He was quite clumsy and Byron and Leigh laughed at his awkward attempts at fetching and jumping. Major followed Leigh wherever she went and when she went to visit Emily he howled and barked the entire time she was gone. When Leigh was made aware of this by Byron she took Major with her on her visits and let him run and play with the

302

dogs on the Cummings' plantation.

It was nearing the end of March and now quite evident that Leigh was with child. She sat on the veranda, sewing a gown for the baby, Major at her feet. A contented sigh escaped her lips as she took in the pleasant day. Her eyes roamed over the front lawn taking in the budding trees, the new grass, the fresh beginnings of spring. She thought again how truly lovely Byron's home was—of the friends she had made—of her life, her future, and that of her child's. Her eyes began to mist and she chided herself for her melancholy moods, attributing them, as was their due, to her pregnancy. She felt the child move strongly, and patting her belly, she smiled.

"It shall be a fine, strong son I give my husband, Major," she said to the dog.

Major looked at her, cocking his head. Leigh giggled and Major wagged his tail, and then watching her with his eyes, he returned his large head to rest on his paws.

A sound drew Leigh's attention and she looked down the long, tree lined lane that led to the house and saw an approaching landau. There was one passenger, a woman, and as the landau rolled to a stop in front of the house Leigh saw that it was Ella. Though Major was barely five months old, he was already larger than most dogs in the area, and he stood and growled at Ella as she approached his mistress.

"Major, it is alright," Leigh said patting the dog's head. Major stopped immediately and lay again at Leigh's feet watching Ella closely with his eyes.

"Good day, Ella."

"Leigh," Ella said with a nod of her head as she gave the dog a hateful look. "I see you have acquired one of Jack's brutes. Really dear, you should discuss these things with Byron first," Ella quipped. "I have known Byron longer than you, dear, and I happen to know he cares not for this particular breed of dog."

"Byron gave him to me," Leigh replied sweetly as she reached down and again patted the dog on the head.

Byron opened the french doors from his study and started walking toward the two women. "I thought I heard voices out here," he said moving to stand by Leigh still seated in the chair. "To what do we owe this honor, Ella?" he asked, his voice carrying the slightest bit of sarcasm.

Evidently Ella missed the tone in his voice, for she kept right on giving him a large smile.

"Daddy sent me over with a message for you, Byron, concerning the tobacco crop this year." She fluttered her eyelashes boldly at Byron and then turned to frown at Leigh. "Why don't you run along, dear, this business will no doubt seem very dull to you."

"Ella, Leigh is most welcome to stay right where she is," Byron said, his voice irritable.

"No, Byron," Leigh said allowing him to help her to rise, "Ephraim will have my tea ready anytime now anyway." She turned to face Ella. "Come and have tea when you finish with your business, Ella," she added. Though Leigh despised the woman, she would not be a poor hostess.

Ella watched Byron's careful attention to his wife and pangs of jealousy formed a frown on her brow. Her eyes were drawn to Leigh's large shape and the frown slowly disappeared. So she is with child, thought Ella. Well it will not be long before Byron tires of her now. Soon her large belly will interfere with the more intimate life of husband and wife and Byron will lose interest in the strumpet. A snide smile spread slowly on Ella's lips. Yes, this suited her just fine.

"Come into my study," Byron commented to Ella once he had assisted Leigh into the house. Byron opened the study doors leading from the veranda and preceded Ella into the room continuing on to his desk. "Just what is your pressing business, Ella?" he asked bluntly.

Ella stood casually glancing about the handsome room. "Papa wants to know how many acres of tobacco you plan to plant this year."

Byron frowned and sat down at his desk. "Same as these past two years though I cannot imagine why Fred is concerned. If we planted twice the normal amount, the English would take it all. They are greedy for tobacco in England."

Ella took one of the wing backs near the fireplace and sat smiling at Byron. Ella thought Byron rather cool but attributed it to his work. He had found no time to sneak away from this possessive wife of his, but she was sure it would soon change. The man obviously still cared for her. Had he not kissed her long and passionately in front of his wife and others at the New Year's Ball? In fact Ella had now convinced herself that Byron had somehow been tricked into marrying this little slip of a girl. Why seeing Leigh's large belly, she thought, she was probably with child when they wed—and who was to say if the child was indeed Byron's?

"I see you wasted no time in fathering a child," Ella said sweetly. "Judging Leigh's size Byron, I fear there will be much talk that the event occurred before the marriage."

Byron glared at her. "No one but you, Ella, would have such poor manners, or the courage, to gossip on such."

Ella laughed. "Now, Byron, do not act the innocent. You forget, I know you only too well."

Byron frowned at her and walked to the veranda doors. "Ella, if you are quite finished, I have much that needs my attention."

"Tell me, Byron," Ella said ignoring his last comment, and his frown, "can you be sure the child is yours. I mean, you cannot have known her long before."

"Quite sure!" Byron interrupted. "Which is more than I can say," Byron growled arching a brow at Ella, "were the woman in question someone other than Leigh."

Ella studied him carefully. Had she seen just the flicker of doubt cross his face?

"Now if you will excuse me," Byron said leaving the room and slamming the door firmly behind him.

An evil smile curled the corners of Ella's mouth. She stood up slowly, smoothing the skirt of her gown. I think I'll take tea with Leigh after all, she decided. I owe that harlot a large amount of trouble. Why not start delivering it this day? With a malicious grin, Ella walked toward the study door leading to the foyer.

Byron stood on the veranda steps frowning. He had no doubts that he had been the first to bed Leigh, but what of after? Had she had another when they were parted in Richmond? Could he be assured that the child was his? He started toward the field, his pace brisk. Leigh had denied being with another, but could a man trust a woman—any woman? The frown on his face softened when he thought of her lovely face and gentle manner. But then the frown reappeared when he remembered her in the arms of James Bradford at the ball—and had she not flirted with the man, even allowing him to kiss her?

Could he be sure? The image of large emerald eyes, innocent and unselfish, penetrated his thoughts. He had had no reason to doubt until Ella had planted the seed. And Ella was hardly the one to call the kettle black! He would drive Ella's spiteful words from his mind, he decided. The child Leigh carried was his, and until proven otherwise, he would think on it no more.

Casually Ella strolled into the drawing room. Leigh was seated on one of the love seats and when she noted Ella enter she poured her a cup of tea, handed it to her, and without a word picked up her own cup.

"My, my, dear, I guess it will not be long before the babe interferes with your wifely duties," Ella commented.

Leigh looked at Ella's trim waist and graceful form and thought of her own large shape and awkward movements, but she would not give Ella the satisfaction of seeing her insecurities.

"Why, Ella," Leigh said with large, innocent eyes, "I cannot imagine what would make you think such a thing. I guess it is because you have never carried a child."

Ella's spine stiffened and she looked to Leigh with hatred. "No doubt it will just ruin your figure, dear," Ella purred as she ran her hand over her own shapely waist and hips. "And husbands do so hate unattractive wives—especially a man like Byron."

Leigh drew her eyes from Ella and sipped her tea, determined to ignore the woman's spite.

"It must be quite dull for you, dear, confined to the house like this," Ella continued.

"No, Byron is grand company, Ella, and I also have Major here to keep me company—and then of course, Emily Cummings visits quite often."

Leigh smiled at Ella and Ella frowned in return. It

surprised her that a meek little thing like Emily had made friends with Leigh. Emily had never shown any willingness to be friendly with her. And though that had never bothered Ella, she needed no women friends, it was one more reason to hate Leigh. She sipped her tea, on outward appearance calm, but inside Ella's anger grew.

"I had a simply wonderful time at the ball, didn't you? I declare, Byron simply could not get enough of dancing with me," Ella said sweetly while watching Leigh for the smallest reaction.

The tea cup in Leigh's hand began to rattle and she quickly placed it on the table before her and picked up her sewing.

"You must grow rather weary of sewing those little garments for the child."

"No, I enjoy preparing for Byron's child," Leigh replied glancing to Ella and arching a brow.

"Is Byron quite sure the child is his?" Ella asked with bitterness.

Leigh gasped and rose from the seat. She would not let this insult go unanswered. "Ella, I ask you to leave this house. You have forsaken the good graces due a guest."

"I dare you ask me to leave!" Ella snapped loudly, also rising from her seat. "This is Byron's home and you have no right!"

"I have every right," Leigh replied, her voice rising with anger. "I am Byron's wife," she said with another arch of her brow, "and this is also my home!"

"What you need, miss priss, is a slap in the face!" Ella snarled—and with that she reached out her hand and slapped Leigh hard across the cheek.

Major was on her in an instant. He grabbed the hem of her gown growling, and literally pulled her about the room causing her to bump into the furniture.

Ephraim heard the loud voices and then someone squealing and came to see what was about. As he came into the room he saw Ella struggling with the angry dog and it was all he could do to keep from laughing until he noted the angry red mark on the side of Leigh's face.

"Major, heel," Leigh called. The dog released Ella's gown at once and came to stand by Leigh, still growling. He had done the gown great harm.

"You mongrel!" Ella screamed. "Look what he did to my gown!" she yelled holding the gown out and inspecting the damage.

"I am sorry, Ella," Leigh said with no sympathy in her voice. "He is just a pup and I am sure he meant no harm." Though Leigh tried to hold it in, a small smile played around the corners of her mouth.

"No real harm!" Ella roared. "You idiot! Why if he were as large as General, he would have killed me!" She gave Leigh an evil look with squinted eyes. "You need have him destroyed, and if I have any say in the matter—he will be!"

"Miss Ella," Ephraim said, anger in the old man's voice for the first time Leigh could remember. "You have no call to talk to Miss Leigh that way. I fear I must ask you to leave this house."

"Well—I never!" Ella said stomping from the room, her torn gown swishing about her.

A short time later Byron entered the room. Leigh and Ephraim stood talking quietly and looked up in unison to see his angry face.

"What is going on in here?" he snapped. "Ella comes to the field screaming," he said throwing his arms wide, "and says she has been insulted by the two of you and that Major attacked her and needs be destroyed." He frowned at the two of them, crossed his arms and stood waiting for one of them to speak. "Well," he snapped looking from one to the other and tapping the toe of his boot on the floor.

Leigh and Ephraim both started talking at once and with a large, heavy sigh, Byron sat slowly down in a chair. He studied first one excited face then the other and in bits and pieces the story began to make sense. When all was told Byron was angrily pacing the room.

"Byron, please," Leigh begged, tears in her eyes, "do not destroy Major."

"Leigh," Byron said surprised, "I have no intention of destroying him. In fact, if I could think of a just reward, I would give him one." He held out an arm to her and she rushed to his side and was taken protectively into his arms and hugged closely. "And Ephraim, I thank you sir for doing my job and further protecting my wife and home."

"You are most welcome," Ephraim said with a grin. He turned and leaving the room, called over his shoulder; "There is a mighty fine ham bone in the cookhouse that Major might like."

Byron and Leigh laughed and Byron called after him to see that Major got it.

Chapter Eleven

It was now almost May and Leigh was heavily burdened with child. Byron cast many a weary eye at her round belly. He questioned Annie about Leigh's large size and was told that some mothers just get larger than others and since Leigh was so delicately boned and slight of frame it most likely just appeared she was larger than she really was. Annie assured him she had never seen a mother-to-be in better condition.

Leigh's complexion had become even more lovely and her eyes seemed to shine. She was always smiling these days. She had spent many hours altering some of the gowns Byron had purchased for her and commenting how lucky she was to have so many in the Josephine style. When the gowns were completed she could usually be found sewing some garment for the child or playing with Major. Byron, Annie, Ephraim, or Aunt Mary seemed to always be close by and wherever Leigh went she found a helping hand or arm to lean on. She laughed many times when she found she had difficulty rising from a chair without assistance and she found that now she needed Annie or Byron to put on her stockings and shoes for her. She could sometimes see her feet, but never reach them.

Byron was busy with the plantation and absent from the house most of the day. He returned early one afternoon and found Leigh sitting on the steps of the veranda surrounded by some of the Negro children on the plantation. All of the children's faces were intent on Leigh. He walked closer, curious, and smiled when he realized that she was telling them a story of knights, witches, and fair young damsels. He stood listening for a while and it was all he could do to keep from laughing out loud as he watched the children's awed faces. Leigh would assume a different voice for each of the characters in her story and was acting it out in a most charming way. His eyes roamed over her body leisurely and admiringly before he tiptoed quietly away, a grin on his handsome face.

Each evening now that the weather was so lovely, they would stroll about the grounds after dinner. They were doing so this night just as the sun was setting. A majestic sunset of pink and lavendar blending to a deep coral. Clusters of scarlet honeysuckle grew along the fences, the dogwoods and crab apple trees were in bloom lending their pink and white flowers to the splendor of the season, and the magnificent white blooms of the magnolias seemed as an artist touch to complete the beauty of the scene. A soft breeze was blowing, carrying the scent of the flowers.

"Byron, I just cannot get over it. What a lovely climate you have. One day it is cold and gray and the next the weather is warm, the sunsets are breathtaking, and there are flowers in bloom wherever the eye looks. The view from here is simply overwhelming," Leigh sighed as she breathed in the sweet, fragrant air.

"Yes, pet, the seasons are quick to change," Byron said with a grin, "and I judge spring to be the loveliest of all."

Byron reached up and snapped a large white magnolia bloom from a tree and handed the flower to Leigh with a smile, then taking her hand they strolled slowly, Major running about their heels, both enjoying the beautiful bounty of nature.

"I will have to pick some flowers for the house," Leigh commented placing the magnolia near her nose and inhaling the pleasant scent.

Byron glanced askew at Leigh's belly. "Have Ephraim or Annie go with you, pet. You need not be alone."

"I will." Leigh glanced at his handsome profile and hesitantly chewed at her lower lip. "Byron, ah, we need to discuss the nursery," she said fearing his reaction. For though Byron seemed solicitous of her condition, they had not actually discussed the child since that night in Byron's study when they had toasted to the expected birth of a son. Leigh stopped, and turning to face him, took a deep breath. "The babe will be born around the end of June I judge, and we have no room prepared."

Byron cast another glance to Leigh's shape. How could her body stand the burden for two more months?

"I thought mayhap if it was agreeable with you," Leigh continued, slightly nervous how Byron would react, "we could have the bedroom next to ours redone."

"Whatever you desire, pet, is fine with me. There are

cradles and such in the attic, have Ephraim get them down for you on the morrow."

"Thank you, Byron," Leigh replied with a smile to take one's heart. "Would it also be agreeable if I have new drapes made and the walls redone?"

"If you wish," he said reaching out and caressing one of the shining curls laying over her shoulder. "Make a list of what you require and what we do not have here at Royal Oaks, I will send for from Richmond."

"Byron, you make life so pleasant, I fear you spoil me terribly."

"Sweet, I doubt that. Your nature is too gentle and kind to ever be spoiled."

She looked at him with liquid eyes as he caressed her curls and placed a gentle, warm kiss on her lips.

The following day Leigh and Ephraim were busy in the attic. They found a lovely old cradle, a rocking horse complete with saddle, bridle, and stirrups, and several other items Ephraim said had belonged to Byron. They brought them all down with Henry's help and thoroughly scrubbed them clean. Leigh insisted on helping and no words from Annie or Ephraim could change her mind.

In the following days the house was a bustle of activity. Leigh and Annie supervised the thorough cleaning of the room, bolts of fabric kept in stock at Royal Oaks were gone through and cloths were chosen for the drapes. Annie solicited the help of two of the best seamstresses on the plantation, Ephraim supervised the workman painting the room, and the nursery began to take shape.

Leigh had trouble deciding on a color for the room and finally chose a soft golden yellow, leaving the wide woodwork white. She and Annie helped in the making of the drapes, also white with a profusion of wide ruffles, and made to be tied back at about midpoint of the window. Leigh decided she would trim the ties in either rose or blue once the child was born.

Henry gave the rocking horse a fresh coat of paint and further supplies were sent for from Richmond. Byron could find Leigh almost anytime working in the nursery.

He stood quietly in the doorway one evening watching Leigh slowly turn in circles as she patted her large belly and inspected the freshly painted room.

"Need some help?"

"Oh, Byron," she giggled, "you startled me. Yes, please sir, some assistance would be appreciated. I cannot decide how to place the furniture."

He strolled into the room and stood beside her surveying the room and the furniture. "How about the chest over there on the wall by the windows?"

"No-o-o," Leigh said looking at the chest and then the area of the room Byron had indicated. "Try it over there please," she said pointing to the wall next to the doorway.

Byron moved all of the furniture and then moved it all again. Each time he arranged it under her direction, he commented how nice the room looked—but each time Leigh bid him move it all again saying it was just not right. Finally she seemed to have the furniture the way she wanted and Byron sighed and then chuckled at her frowning appraisal of the room.

"Mayhap we should . . . ?"

"We tried it that way," Byron interrupted.

Leigh looked to him and laughed. "Now Byron, you do not even know what I was about to say."

He came to her side with a grin on his face and placed his arms about her pulling her near and enjoying the sweet scent of her body. He rubbed his nose in the soft, shining curls as he caressed her back. "It does not make the slightest difference, my love," he said in a soft voice. "We have tried it every conceivable way—and I like it the way it is now."

Leigh looked up to his handsome face and laughed. "Then," she said hugging him tight, "this is the way it shall remain."

The day the room was finished Jack and Emily came to call.

"Oh, Emily," Leigh said in an excited voice as she grabbed Emily's hand and pulled her along, "come and see the nursery."

Emily laughed and followed dutifully behind Leigh. She stood in the doorway taking in the charming room.

"Leigh, it is lovely," Emily said.

The walls were the softest golden yellow. The wide woodwork was left white and there were white drapes at the windows with layers and layers of ruffles. A cherry cradle stood before one of the windows, yards of netting above it. There was a rocking chair near the cradle with a rose pink and blue print cushion. A brass crib stood against one wall, again with the netting, and there was a rocking horse freshly painted near the center of the large room on a lovely carpet of blue with a rose pattern bordering its edges. A large chest of drawers, also in cherry, stood next to the door. The room was bright, sunny, and totally charming.

Leigh walked from piece to piece lovingly stroking it with her hand. "Most of these were Byron's but the brass crib is new. He surprised me with it." She turned to Emily and smiled. "I could not resist the few touches of rose and blue. I fear Byron's son will have to grow fond of the rose," she laughed.

"The room is just lovely, Leigh," Emily said as she looked about. She remembered well how she had felt after fixing Jeffery's room for him. She opened one of the drawers in the chest and saw the numerous small gowns Leigh had sewn for the baby. "You are very talented with a needle, Leigh. We will have to spend a day doing needlework together. I fear my skill is not nearly your measure and mayhap you could give me some tutoring."

"I doubt that you need any tutoring, Emily, but I would greatly enjoy your company."

"Major is growing in leaps and bounds I see," Jack was saying as the two women entered the drawing room.

"Yes," Byron laughed, "and it would do your black heart good to be greeted by him as General greets me."

"The weather is so lovely, let us go sit on the veranda," Leigh offered.

Everyone agreed and Leigh bid Ephraim bring them some refreshment. They sat chatting until Ephraim arrived with tea for the ladies and mint juleps for the gentlemen. Leigh sipped Byron's drink and made a face.

"I cannot understand how you find that refreshing," she commented to Byron.

"Nor I that iced tea," Byron answered with a small bow.

Jack chuckled. "That reminds me of a story." He glanced to Leigh. "Did Byron ever tell you about the time he decided to liven up his parents' summer ball?"

"No," Leigh smiled.

"Now, Jack, Leigh does not . . ." Byron started.

"Yes, I do," she said, surprised to see Byron flush.

"Well you see," Jack started, "years ago, we were just boys, Byron's parents were giving this summer ball. My

317

parents had allowed me to stay the night with Byron. In all truthfulness I think Mr. and Mrs. Marsh insisted I stay hoping it would keep Byron out of mischief. Well anyway, a punch had been prepared for the ladies and your mischievous husband here decided to have some fun and put some stronger spirits in the ladies' beverage." Jack laughed hard and even Byron chuckled. "He snuck out to the cookhouse and took what he thought to be wine and added it to the punch, only he had gotten vinegar instead!"

Leigh and Emily laughed hard.

"You should have seen all those dignified ladies," Jack laughed, "trying not to spit while they sputtered and turned scarlet."

"It was a rather sour brew," Byron chuckled. "But Jack found it more amusing than I. You see, I had to answer to my father and it was some time before I sat down without the most tender care."

"Oh, Byron, how shameful," Leigh snickered.

"You think that was shameful, let me tell you about the time Jack . . ."

They passed the afternoon talking of childhood pranks, crops, and children. More than once Byron turned to find Leigh's gaze focused on him, and there was a tenderness in her gaze that he had never noted before. And more than once Leigh felt Byron's large hand reach for hers and give a gentle squeeze, or his hand resting tenderly on her shoulder. Everyone seemed to enjoy the quiet Sunday afternoon spent with friends—but Byron and Leigh seemed to enjoy it immensely.

That night Byron awoke to a loud noise from below and was alarmed to find Leigh not in bed beside him. He quickly rose, donned his robe and slippers, and hurried from the room. When he reached the foyer he again heard a loud noise that sounded as if it came from the cookhouse. He knew that Major would have barked were something amiss, but nonetheless, he hurried to investigate. He opened the cookhouse door to find Leigh intent on cooking, a kerchief on her head, and flour covering her pert little nose. Major lay at her feet watching her with his eyes.

"Leigh, what in the world?"

"Oh!" Leigh exclaimed dropping her bowl to the table with a thud. "Byron, you gave me a start."

"What are you doing?" Byron asked incredulously, arching a brow and grinning.

"I am making sweet bread," she answered with a smile and a matter of fact air.

"Making sweet bread! Leigh, it is the middle of the night!"

"Yes, I know. I could not sleep and I was hungry. I have seen Aunt Mary make it many times," she said, busily returning to her work.

Byron walked in and stood beside her, studying her. "Why did you not wake someone?"

"Byron, I can hardly wake anyone," she replied giving him a shameful look. "It is the middle of the night. I cannot disturb anyone's sleep."

Byron did not point out to her that she was disturbing his sleep. "Can you make coffee?"

"Of course."

He smiled at her shaking his head. "Then if you will make me some, I shall keep you company until your sweet bread is ready."

He went to sit at the old oak table and Major came to his side. He sat scratching the dog behind one ear and watching Leigh as she puttered about the kitchen in her robe and slippers. She had a white apron tied over her large belly and her stomach preceded her wherever she went. As he watched her he realized how much he loved her. He did not know why it took him so long to realize that he needed her and wanted her in his life—but now he realized that he could not live without her and had loved her almost from the beginning. He could still see her sitting on that blanket and turning to him with large frightened eyes saying; "Mighten there be heathens about?" A warm smile crossed his lips as he watched her. He, Byron Marsh, loved this woman—who at the moment with apron on, flour on her nose, and kerchief askew, looked very much like a clown!

They sat in the large cookhouse, Leigh sipping tea and Byron sipping coffee, chatting while they awaited Leigh's bread. The coffee was good, Byron noted. Byron grinned at her and vowed to have Ephraim seat them closer together at the long dining table in the future. He liked having her near and not having to talk loudly to her down the long expanse of the table.

At last Leigh announced the bread was done and went to get some for herself and Byron. She turned to Byron with tear-filled eyes when she discovered it was better suited for building houses.

Byron rushed to her side at the sight of her tears. "There, there, sweet," he said hugging her as close as her stomach would allow and gently patting her back. "I will have Aunt Mary make you some on the morrow."

"But Byron," she sniffed, "I do not understand. I did exactly as I have seen Aunt Mary do, and I did so want some this night."

"Come, pet, we will find something else to ease

your hunger."

He pulled out a chair for her and as she sat down he offered her a napkin to dry her tears. He found some pecan pie left from dinner and cut them each a generous slice. They sat at the table eating pie, Byron looking lovingly at Leigh's sad face.

"Aunt Mary makes the best pecan pie I have ever tasted," Byron commented, trying to cheer Leigh up.

"Yes, she does," Leigh agreed forlornly, "but I still wish I had the bread."

Leigh and Byron now sat across from one another at one end of the long dining table. They talked often through dinner and both seemed to enjoy the more intimate dining arrangements.

Leigh could not remember the last time Byron had lost patience with her. His manner was always courteous and Leigh found she loved him more each day. Byron felt less urging from his body, and had for some time, but he still kept reminding himself that the child would soon arrive and then they could at last begin a life together truly as man and wife. He felt sure now that Leigh loved him as he did her.

Mrs. Marrow and Leigh now exchanged letters regularly. After consulting with Byron, Leigh invited her and Mr. Whitefield to visit later in the summer. A letter arrived from Mrs. Marrow stating that she and Thomas would be delighted to accept their invitation.

It was a warm June evening. Leigh and Byron strolled the grounds after dinner discussing the planned visit. There was a dull ache in Leigh's back and she felt as if her burden had lowered. She walked slowly at Byron's side, leaning heavily on his strong arm. Suddenly she stopped

321

dead still, eyes wide.

"Byron, my water broke!"

Byron had been wool gathering and not giving Leigh his full attention. He heard her say something about breakage and patted her hand. "Do not fret, Leigh. I will have Ephraim fix it or buy you another."

When Leigh did not comment or move, Byron turned and noted the strange expression on her face.

"Leigh, what is it?"

"My water broke!" she repeated.

Byron stared at her with a stupid look on his handsome face. He did not have the slightest idea what she was talking about and continued to stare at her in confusion until he noticed that the hem of her gown was wet.

"It is the baby, isn't it?" When Leigh nodded her head, his eyes grew large, he stared at her a moment longer, and then began to pace around her in a circle. "But Leigh you said the last of June, this is the first!"

"Byron, sometimes babes come early."

"But one month early!"

Leigh was trying to watch him but he was making her dizzy with his pacing. She waited until he walked behind her and then started for the house.

"Wait!" Byron yelled. "Don't move!" He ran to stand in front of her waving his arms as if she were a herd of stampeding cattle. She gave him a merry look as he repeated his earlier statement. "But Leigh, you cannot have the babe yet, it is too soon!"

"Byron," she smiled, "I assure you I can."

"Oh."

Again Leigh started for the house and again Byron hurried to stop her. Major ran along beside them and when they stopped, he stopped and sat wagging his tail and looking from one to the other.

"Don't move, Leigh!" Byron said in a panic. He stood nervously wringing his hands as Leigh grinned at him. "What should we do now?" he asked in a helpless manner, holding his hands out wide.

"I thought mayhap we would go to the house," Leigh chuckled.

"Leigh, we should get you to the house immediately!" Byron said as if he had not heard her words. He walked about Leigh as if to pick her up but acting as if he thought she would break if he touched her. "But how?" he said in a helpless manner.

"Well," Leigh said smothering a laugh, "I rather thought we would walk."

Byron frowned at her and his voice was scolding. "Walk! Leigh, you can't walk! You are having a baby!"

"Byron, I assure you many expectant mothers walk about." She placed a hand on his arm and looked hard into his worried and anxious face. "I would really prefer to walk, Byron."

Byron rushed to her side, doubt showing on his face. He took her hand in his and placed his other hand on her elbow. "Now go very slow, Leigh, and take little steps," he instructed.

"Yes, sir."

They started walking very slowly toward the house, Byron watching the hem of Leigh's gown intently.

"Slower, Leigh, slower."

Leigh slowed to a crawl.

"You are taking too large a step!" he yelled. Then he quickly raised his eyes to hers and cleared his throat before continuing in a softer tone. "Smaller steps please, sweet."

323

Leigh released a sigh and stopped altogether. She turned to look into his deep blue eyes, merriment in her own. "Byron, if I go any slower, I will be standing still—and if I take smaller steps, I'll go backwards."

Byron frowned at her and his voice was stern. "Leigh, this is not the time for jesting. Now do as I ask."

Leigh sighed and began again but after a few steps was gripped with a contraction. That settled it. Byron very carefully picked her up in his strong arms and rushed with her to the house. When they reached the foyer he stood turning in circles with her still in his arms, a look of complete confusion on his face.

"Byron, please put me down," Leigh urged.

He gave her an odd look and rushed to the drawing room and gently sat her on the sofa.

"I meant on the floor in the foyer," she said smiling at him.

"Leigh, the foyer floor is hardly the place to have a baby!"

Leigh giggled. It was obvious to her that the man had come completely unglued. She took his hand in hers and caressed it gently. "Byron, please go and call Ephraim and ask him to go get Annie."

He rushed to the foyer and bellowed for Ephraim. If the man had been at Uncle Jonathan's, he would have heard. Ephraim came hurrying down the hall and the moment Byron laid eyes on him he started shouting:

"Ephraim, quick, go get Leigh! Annie is having the baby!"

Ephraim chuckled and went to get his wife. Byron glared at his receding back and called after him:

"I see no humor in the matter, Ephraim. This is serious business you know."

Byron quickly returned to Leigh and knelt by her, looking worriedly at her face. "Would you like a cup of tea, Leigh?"

"No, Byron," she laughed as she caressed his face with her hand. "But I would like to go to the bedroom."

"Well, why did you not say so before," he said picking her up and starting for the stairs.

Leigh decided if she was ever to get there she best let him carry her. She looped her arms about his neck and studied his worried face as he carried her up the wide, curving stairs.

"I love you, Byron," she said in a soft tone.

He stopped in the middle of the stairs and turned to look deep into her emerald eyes. "And I love you," he said pulling her close and placing a soft, fleeting kiss on her ear.

Small tingles of delight ran through Leigh's body as she pulled back and searched those deep blue eyes and she knew he was telling her true. Tears came to her eyes and Byron quickly kissed them away. They stood in the middle of the stairs, Byron placing fevered kisses all over her face when another contraction gripped her.

"Oh Lord!" Byron said rushing the rest of the way up the stairs and to their bedroom. He placed Leigh gently on the bed and stood looking at her wringing his hands.

Leigh awkwardly pushed herself to a kneeling position on the bed and put her back to Byron. "Byron," she said pulling her long curls out of the way, "would you please unfasten my gown?"

Byron's large hands fumbled nervously with the delicate catches on the back of the gown. When the gown was at last undone, Leigh thanked him sweetly with a smile, and taking his hand, made as if to step down from the bed.

"Leigh," Byron shouted, "don't get up!"

"Byron," Leigh laughed, "I need remove the gown."

"Here, I'll do it," he said grabbing the hem of the gown. "Hold your arms up."

Leigh sighed and with a giggle, put her arms in the air like a small child waiting to be undressed. Byron easily slipped the gown from her and when he noted the wet and clinging shift beneath, small flecks of blood staining it, his color paled considerably.

Leigh looked at his worried face and thought it best to give him something to do. "Byron, would you get me a gown from the bureau please?"

Byron whirled and hurried to the highboy and threw clothes about the room as he searched the numerous small drawers for her nightgowns. At last he found one and returned to the bed with it just as Annie and Aunt Mary entered the room, Ephraim waiting discreetly outside the door. The two women quickly took command and shooed Byron from the room saying he could return when Leigh was settled in bed.

Byron paced outside the door still clutching Leigh's gown in his hand. Ephraim came with sheets and firewood. He returned again with a large kettle of water. Each time Byron questioned him as to the need of the objects and each time Ephraim shrugged his shoulders.

At last Aunt Mary opened the door and bid Byron enter. Leigh lay on the bed wearing a soft peach colored nightgown and held out her hand to him. Byron went to her side and took her hand noticing that she trembled slightly. Annie and Aunt Mary were seated in the wingbacks near the fireplace in quiet conversation and Byron glared at them. One would think this was an everyday occurrence, he thought, the way the pair of them sit there so calmly talking. This is the birth of my son!

Ephraim had built a fire in the fireplace, and with the warm summer night, the room was stifling. The night grew old and as the hours crept by Byron's anxiety grew. With each contraction Leigh had, he grew more pale. He was covered with perspiration, as much from worry as the heat, and his face was haggard. He questioned Annie many times as to Leigh's condition and was assured that all was well. He kept insisting that it was too soon, but Aunt Mary told him babes come in their own sweet time.

"If ours insists on coming early, then I wish it would do so and be done with it. Leigh is in pain!"

"Byron," Leigh said taking his hand and squeezing it, "it is the way of life. All mothers have pain when they bear their child."

Byron smiled at her and bent over and kissed her brow. How brave she is, he thought, braver than I.

As the contractions grew stronger and stronger, Leigh held tightly to Byron's hand as he mopped her brow with a damp cloth. Byron went from pale to white and Annie decided it was time for him to leave before he fainted and they would have his large bulk to worry over. She and Aunt Mary each took one of his muscular arms and gently led him to the door and pushed him out, securing the door behind him.

Byron paced outside the door for a while, running his fingers through his hair, and stopping now and then to place an ear to the door. Ephraim sat below in the foyer on the small love seat, Major at his feet. He had had to pull the large dog from the room and now the two of them waited together. Byron went to join them, first getting a brandy from his study.

"Ephraim, women die in childbirth," Byron said staring at the floor.

"Now Master Byron, I will hear none of that talk," Ephraim said, his voice stern.

"But they do. And the babe is near a month early. I could even lose them both."

"Yes, it is true that sometimes women die while bearing a child," Ephraim said placing a comforting arm about Byron's huge shoulders, "but Miss Leigh will not, nor will the child. Annie and Aunt Mary have helped to birth many a child, and I do not recall them losing one yet."

"I do not know what I would do if I lost her now, Ephraim."

"Master Byron, if you continue with this I am still not so old that I can't turn you over my knee as I did when you were a boy."

Byron gazed into the old, friendly eyes and saw that Ephraim was perfectly serious. A smile twisted the corner of his mouth and he nodded to the old man assuring him he would dwell on the matter no more. Major came and nuzzled his hand and he scratched the dog behind one ear as he sipped his brandy.

"How I hate this blasted waiting!" he said rising to get another brandy from his study.

A short while later Aunt Mary opened the bedroom door and all eyes turned to watch her slow decent down the stairs. Byron felt fear reaching up and tearing his insides at the solemn look on Aunt Mary's face. But she did not even glance their way as she continued on down the hall toward the cookhouse. They again settled themselves to wait, Byron and Ephraim exchanging worried looks.

"I bet it will be a fine boy, Master Byron."

"It is more likely a girl," Byron commented exasperated, "they always keep you waiting!"

Ephraim laughed and patted Byron's arm. He had never seen Byron in such a state. If the babe did not soon arrive he was going to be fit to be tied, thought Ephraim, not to mention drunk at the rate he was consuming his brandy.

Byron began to pace the foyer and Ephraim remained still, watching him with a worried expression.

"What time is it, Ephraim?" he asked.

Ephraim pulled his gold watch from his vest pocket and opened the lid. "Three minutes later than the last time you asked," he commented.

Byron sighed and continued to pace, glancing every so often to the bedroom door at the top of the stairs.

Aunt Mary returned and climbed the stairs without so much as a nod in their direction. Byron swore and went to get yet another brandy.

Upstairs in the bedroom Leigh was straining hard. Her body was covered with sweat and she was exhausted. Annie was not nearly as calm as she pretended. She was concerned that the babe was so early and Leigh appeared to be having a difficult time with the birth.

At last Annie saw the end nearing. "It is almost over, child," she said holding tight to Leigh's hand. "I can sees the head. Now push. Push hard as you can," Annie instructed.

Leigh pushed and strained to force the child from her. It felt as if someone had her hips and were trying to force the bones to either side of the room. She tried hard to hold in a scream, but a scream did escape her lips as the baby's head and shoulders emerged.

Byron and Ephraim heard the scream and Major jumped to his feet with a whine. Byron was halfway up the stairs, Major leading the way, when Ephraim stopped him. They looked into each other's eyes and sat slowly down on the steps together. Major stood outside the bedroom door whimpering. It seemed like hours before Aunt Mary came to the door and motioned for them to enter. Major bounded into the room as Byron and Ephraim looked at each other and slowly climbed the steps. They both hesitated outside the door before entering the room.

Leigh lay on the bed, a soft smile on her face as she held a hand weakly out to Byron. Byron cautiously approached the bed noting Leigh's tangled hair and the dark circles under her eyes. There was a small wiggling bundle wrapped in a blanket under her left arm. She gave Byron a bright smile and pulled back the blanket to reveal a tiny baby, red and wrinkled, waving its tiny hands in the air.

"It is a boy, Byron. Isn't he beautiful?" she said, her voice sounding hoarse.

Byron gazed at the red wrinkled face and was not sure of exactly how to answer. "Yes, beautiful," he said. He leaned over and placed a kiss on her lips. As he raised up he noted another bundle under her right arm.

"And this," Leigh said turning to where he looked and pulling back the blanket, "is our daughter."

The girl was smaller than the boy and had a full head of soft dark curls. Byron's eyes grew round as he looked from one to the other.

"Two!" he said amazed, running his fingers through his hair.

"Yes, twins, isn't it wonderful?" Leigh beamed.

"Do you see, Ephraim?" he said turning to the man with pride. "Twins!"

"Yessah, Master Byron," Ephraim grinned, "and handsome babes they be."

"And healthy too," Aunt Mary added. "A little small, but healthy. And that boy the spitting image of you, Master B. You looked just the same when you mama brought you into the world," she laughed, "excepting you was a big babe."

"Twins!" Byron repeated looking from child to child.

Annie motioned for them to leave the new parents alone and everyone quietly left the room. Major sat next to the bed, his head resting on the mattress, and every time one of the babes made a small cry or grunt, he would cock his head from side to side, ears standing straight.

Byron gazed down at the trio. My children, he thought. How could I have ever doubted Leigh, even for an instant? he wondered. He realized now that even if the children were not his it would make no difference. He knew Leigh would not have willingly given herself to another man, and loving her as he did, the child she bore would mean as much to him no matter who the father. He looked at the son Aunt Mary said so resembled him and he grinned. And his daughter, he thought, she would be as striking a beauty as her mother. He sat down on the side of the bed taking Leigh's hand in his.

"Thank you for my son and daughter, Leigh," Byron said gazing deep into her eyes before he kissed her tenderly. Leigh sighed and closed her eyes and Byron realized she was already asleep. He called softly to Major but at first the dog seemed not ready to leave. At Byron's stern tone he eventually followed him from the room. Annie waited outside the door and went to take the children to the nursery so Leigh could sleep undisturbed. She had worked mighty hard this night, thought Annie, and she needed her rest.

Byron stood outside the door and stretched. "Come, Major," he said grinning at the dog, "let's go find something to eat. I fear I am starving and I think there just might be another ham bone about."

The dog wagged his tail and followed happily behind Byron to the cookhouse.

Byron and Major shared one of the guest rooms that night and awoke to the sound of wailing babes. Byron hurriedly dressed and went to the nursery, Major close at his heels. Annie was changing the boy's diaper and softly cooing to the babe.

"You gonna be with your momma in a minute, little one," she said grinning at Byron when he entered the room.

Byron stood quietly watching her and gazing at his children. "Annie, may I change the girl?" he asked looking to his crying daughter.

Annie gave him a doubtful look but nodded her head. Byron studied Annie's skilled hands carefully as she changed his son and then tried to repeat her movements. He stuck his finger twice with the pin, but finally the diaper was in place.

"Well I seen a neater diaper in my day," Annie chuckled, "but I guess it'll do. You can carry her to the bedroom if you wants, Masser Byron."

Byron looked to his tiny daughter and then back to Annie. "Oh Annie, I, uh, don't think that I should. I might drop her or, uh, she is so tiny."

Annie laughed at Byron's uncertain face. "Sore you can. You just puts one hand behind their head like this," she said placing her hand behind his son's head, "and the other behind their little back like this—and pick um up. It ain't hard."

Byron stared at his daughter and then took a deep breath and rubbed his hands briskly together. Slowly and very carefully he mimicked Annie's movements. He picked up his daughter as though she were shaped of dried leaves, and with great care, he followed Annie into the bedroom holding his daughter stiffly out in front of him, his eyes glued to her crying face.

Leigh was sitting up in bed, pillows behind her back, her hair brushed and tied loosely with a ribbon allowing it to fall about her shoulders in soft, shining curls. She wore a frilly yellow gown and though there were still dark circles under her eyes, Byron thought he had never seen her looking more beautiful. She smiled at him and then giggled at his awkwardness with their daughter. Annie handed her her son and there was a slight flush in her cheeks as she undid her gown and placed the baby near her breast. Her eyes grew round as the baby clasped fiercely to her nipple and then she smiled. A smile that only a mother has as she caresses her infant with her eyes.

Byron sat beside her on the edge of the bed still holding his daughter stiffly out in front of him and watching Leigh out of the corner of his eye.

"Masser Byron, hold her closer," Annie instructed. "She won't break."

Byron cradled his daughter closer with Annie's help and was surprised when she started nuzzling his massive chest. He turned to Leigh with concern.

"Leigh, can you feed both, or should we get a wet nurse?"

Leigh blushed and then laughed at her daughter rooting the hairy, muscular chest. "I am sure, Byron, that nature will provide enough for twins," she said shyly.

Annie left to get Leigh some breakfast and she and Byron sat silently together on the bed, each with their own private thoughts concerning the children. When she finished nursing her son she handed him to Byron and took her daughter to nurse.

"What shall we name them?" she asked, smiling at her nursing daughter and fluffing her dark curls.

"I would like to name the boy Jonathan if you have no objection," Byron said as he watched his son still making small sucking motions. "I have always been fond of the name and my cousin Margaret had a girl." He raised his eyes to Leigh's. "We could call him Nathan."

"Yes, I like that. And the girl?"

Byron grinned at his daughter's tiny hands kneading Leigh's breast. "I am partial to Amanda."

"Amanda, Ammie. Yes, I like that also. Nathan and Ammie it shall be." Leigh gave Byron a dimpled smile looking deep into his blue eyes. She saw a warmth and a love there that made her heart skip a beat and she thought to herself that she would capture this moment and hold it forever in her memory, this picture of Byron holding their son in his arms and smiling at her with love. She felt an unexplained oneness with the man—a sharing—that she had never felt before with any human being.

When the babes were fed, Annie came with Leigh's breakfast and then returned the sleeping twins to the nursery while Byron bathed and changed. Leigh and Byron chatted while he soaked in the brass tub and Leigh ran her eyes admiringly over the broad shoulders, the powerful chest covered with soft hair, thinking how truly magnificent the man was, this man, her husband, the man no other woman could call her own. And this time when Byron stood up, wet and dripping, the sunlight glistening off his long, muscular body, Leigh did not look away.

"I will send word to Uncle Jonathan that the babes have arrived," Byron said as he lathered soap on one side of his face to shave. "Do you feel up to his visit this afternoon?" He chuckled. "I fear we will be hard put to keep him away once he knows."

"Yes, I feel wonderful. Please send word for him to come."

Byron grinned and returned to his shaving. As Leigh watched him with hooded eyes it reminded her of the first time she had watched him shave. How things had changed since then. She sighed as her eyes lingered over his handsome form.

When Byron finished dressing he opened a drawer in the highboy, extracted a black box, and approached Leigh with a deep grin, making a great show of offering it to her.

"A gift?"

"Open it and see, madam."

Inside was a large diamond and pearl broach. Leigh recognized it at once as the one Byron's mother wore in the portrait hanging in the drawing room.

"Byron, it is lovely, thank you," she said holding a hand out to him.

He quickly accepted her hand and sat beside her on the edge of the bed. "It was my mother's. She loved pearls and there are many more pieces that belonged to her that now are rightfully yours." He bent over and placed a fleeting kiss on her lips and when he raised up Leigh still held his hand and seemed reluctant to release it.

"I'll, uh, go and send someone to inform Uncle Jonathan of the birth," Byron said clearing his throat and rising slowly from the bed.

He turned to smile at her as he left the room and Leigh blew him a kiss. He was whistling as he descended the stairs.

That afternoon Jonathan came to visit. Leigh sat in the center of the large bed wearing a peach colored bed jacket that came to just below the waist. It was layered with large, full ruffles that overlapped one another and she had pinned the broach just below the collar. The blankets were modestly pulled up about her waist and she made a striking portrait sitting there with a babe in each arm and a beautiful smile on her face.

"My dear, motherhood definitely agrees with you," Jonathan said as he walked toward the bed with a grin from ear to ear. "You look radiant."

"Thank you Uncle Jonathan. I assure you it is great happiness that you see."

"Twins, I can't get over yet," he said beaming at the children and then turning to smile at Byron. "My Margaret will be green with envy," he added with a wink. "May I hold one, Leigh?"

"Yes, of course," Leigh said offering him her son. Byron anxiously instructed his uncle and Jonathan laughed as he took the baby confidently in his arms.

"I assure you, Byron, I remember quite well how to hold an infant. I held you often as a child, and believe me that was no small feat. You were forever squirming about." Byron and Leigh chuckled as Jonathan explored the tiny life with his eyes. "And which do I have here, the boy or the girl?" he asked.

"You have Jonathan, Uncle Jonathan," Byron replied with a grin.

"Jonathan!"

"I hope you do not mind having another Jonathan in the family," Leigh added.

"Mind! I am honored," he answered looking to his grandnephew with love. He pulled a handkerchief from his jacket pocket and loudly blew his nose. "I, uh, seem to be coming down with a summer cold."

Byron and Leigh exchanged a subtle look. They had both seen the tears that came to his eyes. Byron's eyes grew even bluer as he gazed at his wife and smiled.

"He is a most handsome child," Jonathan commented, his voice slightly hoarse. "He must take after his grand-uncle," he chuckled. He looked to the tiny girl asleep in Leigh's arms. "And the young lady's name?"

"Amanda, Ammie," Leigh replied.

"Well it is plain to see she will be as striking a beauty as her mother." He turned to Byron with a laugh. "It will do your heart good to someday drive the gay young bachelors from your door."

Leigh was startled to see color rising to Byron's face and she realized that the ways of young swains did not sit so well with him when his daughter was the fair young maiden. She smiled to herself and gazed at her sleeping daughter's face.

A short time after, Byron and Jonathan left Leigh to rest. Byron talked of nothing but the babies all afternoon. Jonathan smiled and shook his head as he listened to his nephew. He was no longer the wild young bachelor, thought Jonathan, but now the doting father.

Byron invited Jonathan to stay for dinner and afterwards they sat playing chess.

"Leigh should be done nursing the twins soon. Would you care to visit your grandnephew again?"

"Most assuredly," Jonathan agreed with a chuckle. "You are truly happy, aren't you Byron?"

"Of course," Byron replied, giving his uncle a surprised glance. "Why do you doubt it?"

"Oh, I don't," Jonathan replied with a matter of fact air. Then he gave Byron a solemn look and leaning back in his chair he continued. "In the past months I have grown very close to Leigh. We have spent many an afternoon together while you have been busy with the plantation." He chuckled. "Chess lessons, remember?" Byron nodded his head. "We talked often of the child to come and—of you. Sometimes Leigh gave me the impression that she thought you did not care for her." Byron quickly reverted his gaze and Jonathan noted a sheepish expression on his face and quickly leaned forward, again studying the chess board before he continued. "There was a time, Byron, when I too, doubted you loved your wife. I am glad to discover I was in error." He looked Byron straight in the eye. "You are very fortunate indeed, son, never forget that. Leigh is a jewel, Byron—never treat such a treasure casually."

"I assure you, Uncle Jonathan," Byron stated just as seriously, "I know my great fortune and I will never do anything to lose Leigh's love. I love her with all my heart."

Jonathan made a non-commital grunt and again studied the chess board. Byron looked down to the board with a puzzled look in his eye, not exactly sure of why his uncle had broached the subject, and wondered how much Leigh had told him of their life.

Jonathan gazed at his nephew's profile, and smiling,

arched a brow. "I believe it is your move," he commented with a twinkle in his eye.

That night Byron again resided in the guest room and he decided that he should continue to do so until Leigh was recovered from the birth of the twins. He tried to get Major to leave the bedroom, but the huge dog would not budge, and finally Byron left him with a sigh to sleep at the foot of Leigh's bed.

In the days that followed Byron would sit beside Leigh on the bed as she nursed the twins. Then he would be gone all morning and return to have lunch with her. She napped every afternoon and then Byron would join her again for dinner. Ephraim had brought a table to the bedroom so the couple could share their meals. Annie insisted Leigh stay abed for no less than a fortnight and was herself sleeping in the adjoining nursery to help with the babes at night and to keep a close watch on Leigh.

Byron talked of nothing but the twins. He told everyone and anyone on the plantation how they smiled at him whenever he was about. They were extremely clever children, he boasted, especially considering they were less than a week old. Annie laughed and tried to explain to him that days old children do not smile and recognize people but Byron would have none of it. Everyone smiled and shook their heads as Byron told them of the latest fantastic feat his children had accomplished.

Leigh was becoming more and more restless lying abed. When the twins were a week old Annie came into the bedroom to find Leigh climbing out of bed.

"Miss Leigh, you gets back in that bed this instant," Annie scolded as she rushed to Leigh's side.

"But Annie, I feel fine," Leigh pleaded.

"Now Miss Leigh, I ain't gonna argue with you. You gets back in that bed now!" she said pointing to the bed and arching a brow at Leigh.

Leigh slowly turned to the bed and climbed in with a sigh. Annie bent over the bed tucking the covers in neatly about her.

"Annie, please," Leigh said bending down so she could gaze up into Annie's stern face. "Lots of mothers are up after only a short while. Why some are even working in the fields!"

"Not on this here plantation they ain't! Now if you don't stay in bed, I gonna go and gets Masser Byron."

"Yes, ma'am," Leigh sighed with a forlorn expression.

Several days passed and Annie again caught Leigh out of bed. This time she was tiptoeing to the nursery when Annie entered the room.

"Miss Leigh!" Annie yelled. "All right, I done warned ya."

Annie left the room in a huff. Leigh stood shamefaced in the center of the room when she returned moments later with Byron.

"Leigh, just what are you doing out of bed?" Byron asked, his voice scolding. He stood with his arms folded and his weight resting on one foot as he tapped the floor with the other. Annie's expression was much the same as she stood behind him with her hands on her hips.

"Byron, I feel fine, really," Leigh said looking hesitantly up to his stern eyes. Byron frowned deeper at her and she looked to the floor shuffling one small foot.

"Madam, you are the most stubborn woman I have ever seen."

"Byron," Leigh said turning pleading eyes to him, "I

spend all my days alone in this room."

Byron smiled and came to her side placing an arm about her waist. "Sweet, I have all my meals with you here in this room. And Annie is here most of the day— you are hardly alone."

"I know," Leigh agreed with a sigh, "but I never see the babes except when I feed them. And I never am allowed to help bathe them or change them." Her sooty-lashed emerald eyes gazed deeply into Byron's. "Please Byron, I promise not to overdo. I will only grow weaker lying abed."

Byron laughed and cupped her face in one of his large hands and placed a light kiss on the end of her pert little nose. Then he turned and he and Annie exchanged a look.

"You will probably just be sneaking out of bed anyway," he said with a chuckle. "But you must promise not to tire yourself and to nap every afternoon."

"I promise."

"And if you show any signs of ailing, you is going backs to bed," Annie added sternly.

"Agreed, Annie," Leigh said with a smile.

Byron laughed and hugged her close enjoying the feel of her now trim body next to his own. He felt a familiar stirring in his loins and he released her abruptly clearing his throat. He placed a fleeting kiss on her lips and left the room as Annie helped Leigh to bathe and dress.

Leigh's movements were slow and awkward and Annie had her doubts concerning Byron's wisdom in letting Leigh out of bed. Byron had insisted Leigh not climb the stairs, so she was confined to the upper floor, but once she could come and go from the nursery as she wished, she was content.

Several evenings later Byron stood in the doorway watching her as she rocked and sang to their daughter. Leigh was unaware of his presence and cuddled her infant girl as she sang. How much I love her, thought Byron. I wonder how much longer I must reside in the guest room? He planned in wasting no time once Leigh was recovered from the twins' birth in making her truly his wife, and he hoped he would not have to wait too long. With Leigh's figure recovering to its former splendor he often felt the urging from his body and was again having a hard time controlling his moods.

She is a striking beauty, thought Byron as he quietly walked away from the doorway, and motherhood has served to make her only more beautiful.

Chapter Twelve

The twins were now two and a half weeks old. Byron and Leigh spent each morning together while Leigh bathed and dressed them and often Byron helped. Ammie would scream loud and hard whenever her curls were washed and Byron would stand back laughing at his daughter's show of temper. Except for this time shared with the babes, and the meals they shared together, Byron stayed away from Leigh as much as possible. He found himself dwelling more and more on Leigh's trim figure, waist small, hips round, breasts full and tempting, and it was sorely testing his moods.

Leigh was now permitted access to the lower floors and they again sat across from each other at the dining table.

"Do you feel well enough to have the Cummings over?" Byron asked as they sat eating dinner.

"I feel fine, Byron. We should have had them over

before this," Leigh quipped, not looking his way.

He frowned slightly at her. "Though I know they have been most anxious to see the twins since Uncle Jonathan informed them of their birth, I did not deem it proper for us to entertain them in our bedroom." He arched a brow at Leigh and then quickly smiled when she looked in his direction.

"I could have come downstairs before this," she retorted, her manner cool.

Byron was determined to be pleasant though Leigh's moods seemed irritable of late. "It is of no matter. Would you like to have them over tomorrow?"

"If it suits you," she said briskly.

Byron nodded his head, more determined not to argue with her. I guess a woman has a right to be irritable shortly after the birth of a child, he thought.

To a slight degree Byron was correct concerning Leigh's moods. But Leigh was beginning to doubt Byron's words of love the night the twins were born. He had not spoken them since and somehow they did not seem as close as they had before. He still slept in the guest room and Leigh was hurt by his lack of attention. It was obvious that he worshipped the children, and that greatly pleased her, but his lack of attention to her was making her wonder if she had misjudged the man. Mayhap he only wanted the children and needed her to gain them, she thought. Could she have been so wrong about the man? Was her first judgment of him those many months ago the right one? It hurt her more than she could bear, for even if he loved her not, she loved him with all her heart.

The Cummings arrived the next afternoon.

"Well, Ephraim, how are you doing with babes in the

house? Do they disrupt your well-run ship?" Jack asked with a chuckle.

"Lordy no, Master Jack," Ephraim laughed, "those are two of the best youngins I have ever seen."

Leigh and Byron entered the foyer from the drawing room as Ephraim took Emily's jacket and parasol.

"Leigh, you look marvelous," Emily said.

"Yes, you do," Jack agreed taking her hand in his.

"Please," Leigh said slightly embarrassed, "come into the drawing room."

"I think I'll get Jack and I a brandy first," Byron said.

"I'll go with you," Jack added.

Leigh asked Ephraim to bring tea for she and Emily and the two women entered the drawing room as the men headed for Byron's study.

"Leigh, you really do look wonderful. Are you feeling recovered?"

"Yes, I do feel just grand." Leigh laughed and held out her gown. "Though I find I must still wear my high-waisted gowns. The fitted ones are still too tight in the waist."

"It will only take a short time longer," Emily commented. "It was the same with me after Jeffery's birth, and Elizabeth's as well."

"I hope you are right, Emily, I am beginning to fear I will never again regain my waist."

"I would have thought to see Major about," Jack was saying as he and Byron joined them.

"He is no doubt upstairs in the nursery," Byron chuckled. He turned to Leigh and winked. "It seems he now splits his loyalties between Leigh and the twins. I heard him barking as your landau arrived. He is no doubt guarding the crib fiercely at this very moment."

345

"Can we see the twins now?" Emily asked.

"Of course," Leigh smiled. "I thought you would never ask."

They all laughed and went to the nursery. Major was with the twins and stood and growled as they entered the room, but when he saw who it was he quickly went to Emily's side to be petted.

Jack and Emily approached the crib and stood gazing at the two, tiny, sleeping infants.

"Oh Leigh, they are beautiful," Emily said, a soft smile on her sweet face.

"You must be very proud," Jack commented to Byron.

"Yes, we are," Byron said placing an arm about Leigh's shoulder and pulling her close.

The four turned and started to tiptoe quietly out of the room.

"They are wonderful children, Jack," Byron whispered as they reached the steps, "and they . . ."

Leigh stopped and drew back, Emily watching her, and then suddenly Leigh burst into tears.

"Leigh, dear, what is it?" Emily asked.

Leigh just shook her head and continued to sob. Emily glanced to the men at the bottom of the stairs and quickly placed an arm about Leigh and lead her to her bedroom. Leigh sat down in one of the wing back chairs before the fireplace and Emily sat in the other studying Leigh closely. She leaned forward and took Leigh's hand and looked worriedly into her sad eyes.

"Do you wish to discuss it?" Emily asked softly.

"Oh Emily, please do not think ill of me. I am sorry." Leigh wiped her tears on the hem of her gown and sighed. She looked up into Emily's huge brown eyes. "Emily, I fear that Byron no longer has any feelings for me."

Emily's large eyes grew even larger. "Leigh, I have known Byron for some years now and I think you are in error. I see love in his eyes when he looks at you and he has changed more since your marriage than you can ever know. What makes you feel this way?"

Leigh nervously wrung her hands and turned her gaze from Emily. "I don't know. It is many things." She rose and began to pace to and fro. "I am fat and unpleasant to look upon."

"Leigh," Emily laughed, "you are not fat, and certainly not unpleasant to look upon."

Leigh gazed at Emily and hesitated many times before she spoke. "Emily, Byron, ah, still, ah, sleeps in the guest room and has done so since the birth of the children."

Emily blushed slightly and drew her eyes from Leigh's. "Leigh," she said softly, "Jack slept in one of the guest rooms for weeks after Jeffery's birth. I was, uh, much too shy to ask him to return to our bed and went through much the same thing as you are now." Emily looked up to Leigh, her cheeks pink. "As it turned out he was afraid it would seem most ungentlemanly to return to our bed so shortly after Jeffery was born."

Leigh stood quietly listening to her words. She knew how difficult it was for this shy woman to share her feelings with her like this and she greatly appreciated Emily's willingness to do so.

Emily cleared her throat and looking away, blushed profusely. "Leigh, men sometimes forget that beds are also just for sleeping and that a man can hold a woman close and . . . and . . ."

Leigh also blushed at Emily's words. And sleep was all she and Byron had ever shared in the large bed—but perhaps Emily was right. She would hold her judgment of

Byron's attentions, or rather lack of attentions, for a while longer. She chewed at her lower lip, knowing that she had been most rude of late. I will do all in my power, she mused, to woo him back to my bed.

Jack and Byron returned to the study to refresh their drinks. Byron thought of asking Jack what was a reasonable time to wait before approaching Leigh, but he decided Jack would give him the ribbing of his life, and think him a fool, so he dismissed the idea.

The men stood chatting for a few moments, and when the women didn't join them, Byron became concerned. He excused himself and walked to the foyer.

"Leigh," he called up the stairs, "is there something amiss?"

"No, Byron," he heard her call back, "we are on our way down now."

Leigh walked to Emily and took her hand and giving her a smile said softly, "Thank you, Emily."

Emily grinned shyly in return.

"Do you plan to have your Independence Day party this year?" Jack was asking as the two women entered the drawing room.

"It is up to Leigh. I don't know how she will feel about having house guests so shortly after the children's birth. You know I had not planned to have the party this year, but since the twins were born early, perhaps it is possible." Byron turned at the sound of the swish of the women's gowns and saw Leigh and Emily standing in the doorway. "Leigh, sweet, Jack and I were just discussing something."

"Yes, I overheard part of what you were saying. What kind of social did you say?"

"Independence Day," Byron answered.

"When is it usually held?"

"On Independence Day," Jack said with a chuckle.

Byron smiled and took Leigh's hand in his. "Leigh, the fourth of July is Independence Day. It is the date we declared our freedom from English rule."

Leigh laughed and smiled back at the smiling faces around her. "You must forgive my ignorance, but the date is little thought of at home. Of course we will have the party—that is if Byron agrees."

"Then it is settled," Byron said with a wink and a squeeze of her hand.

Leigh smiled into her husband's deep blue eyes and the day became immediately lighter for Leigh.

The four sat discussing the party and Leigh found that Byron usually invited many of the same guests that came to Uncle Jonathan's New Year's ball. Since Leigh knew little of the celebration, she and Emily passed the afternoon discussing the coming festivities.

That night at dinner, after the Cummings had left, the conversation again turned to the coming party.

"In the past, several of the guests stayed here at Royal Oaks," Byron commented, "but I am sure they would understand if you did not feel up to having house guests. I could ask Uncle Jonathan to have them at his home."

"I will not hear of it, Byron. I do truly feel grand, and I am looking forward to it."

They exchanged smiles before returning to their meal. Leigh gazed at Byron's handsome profile under her lashes and smiled to herself. How well this served her purpose. If all the guest rooms were occupied, Byron would have no choice but to return to their bed.

"There is one item that bothers me," Byron said disrupting her thoughts. "I am at a loss as to how to handle the Boroughs."

"The Boroughs?"

"Yes, in the past Ella and her father have always been invited to this gathering, but I do not favor the idea of having Ella as a guest in our home, yet I have no ill feelings for Fred. He is a gentleman and a friend of Uncle Jonathan's, and I do not wish to offend him."

Leigh studied Byron's face closely. Was he indeed worried over having Ella because of Ella's behavior in the past—or mayhap he was concerned that if Ella came, it would be obvious to all that she and Byron were still carrying on an affair? Leigh wondered. Byron had not touched her since the day they were married—she wondered. Then she scolded herself for being so distrustful, and gave Byron a large smile.

"Of course they must be invited," she said.

"I guess they must," Byron agreed, "but I still do not relish having Ella as a guest after the way she behaved on her last visit."

Neither do I, thought Leigh. But perhaps she would be able to put her fears concerning Ella to rest if she saw Ella and Byron together again.

Royal Oaks was a flourish of activity in the days prior to the party. Leigh and Annie supervised the preparations of the guest rooms and Ephraim took charge of the men caring for the grounds, making sure all of Leigh's careful requests were met and that the lawns were manicured to perfection, and before Leigh knew it the fourth of July arrived, and with it the guests.

It was mid morning, Byron still working in the fields with the men, when the first of the far traveling guests arrived, James Bradford among them. Leigh welcomed

350

them warmly, they chatted briefly, and then Ephraim showed them to their rooms where they could rest and change before the afternoon festivities began.

Leigh had just finished dressing when Byron came in from the fields. She had his bath prepared and was laying out his clothes when he came hurrying into the bedroom.

"I am sorry to be so late, pet. Ephraim tells me several of the guests have arrived," he said.

"It is of no matter," she said giving him a bright smile and continuing with her task.

Byron's eyes followed her about the room as he stepped into the brass tub. She had chosen a gown of soft yellow for the occasion. It had a high neck all of lace and the sleeves were full and stood up on the shoulders, ending just below the elbow. The full flowing skirt had layers of lace near the hem and she wore the diamond and pearl broach pinned on the bodice of her gown, and a pair of pearl earrings, also belonging to Byron's mother, dangled from her ears. Byron's eyes shone as he watched her. He noted the fitted gown, and thought Leigh looked more beautiful than he could remember. In fact, he thought her figure even better than before. Though her waist was again tiny, her hips seemed slightly larger accentuating the smallness of her waist. A more womanly figure, thought Byron, and he found her graceful beauty, her willowy form, very seductive. He knew they would again be sharing a room this night and he wondered, it being only one month since the twins' birth, if it was too soon to approach her. Perhaps, he decided, he would speak with Uncle Jonathan before the day was out.

"I need see to the children for a moment," Leigh said passing the tub and running her hand across the broad expanse of Byron's shoulders. "I'll not be long."

Byron's eyes followed her as she left the room and his shoulders seemed to burn where her fingers had delicately traced their path. He began humming to himself, his eyes dark and hooded.

Byron had nearly finished dressing when Leigh returned. She picked up his white coat matching his suit and held it for him as he slipped it on, smoothing the cloth over his shoulders and back. Byron felt her touch, light and caring, and a sparkle appeared in his eyes as a slow smile spread across his lips. A familiar stirring came alive in his body and he clamped his teeth tightly together. A man could hardly take his wife while guests awaited on the front lawn!

"Thank you, sweet," he said turning and placing a soft kiss on her lips. He bent and picked up Leigh's matching yellow lace parasol from the bed, handed it to her with a smile, and offering her his arm, they went to join their guests.

The guests were beginning to gather on the front lawn and Leigh and Byron mingled among them making all feel welcome. Byron's eyes shone with pride as he walked the grounds with his hand on Leigh's trim waist and Leigh watched him carefully from beneath her lashes. All the guest rooms were taken, she thought, and the thought made her giddy and slightly lightheaded as she realized that this night Byron would again be beside her in the big bed.

Leigh was standing chatting with Emily and several other women when she saw the handsome black landau of the Boroughs coming down the lane. Byron hurried to greet them and in a moment Uncle Jonathan also joined the threesome. He and Fred stood talking casually, and then laughing hard, the two walked away leaving Byron

352

and Ella to stand alone.

"Do you like my gown?" Ella asked coyly, placing a hand near her large breasts and smiling up at Byron.

"It is very pretty," Byron commented as he looked about for an excuse to leave Ella.

Ella was sure, now that the twins were born, that Byron would tire of Leigh and she could talk him into ridding himself of his skinny wife and returning to her. Leigh would be busy with the babes and unable to devote herself to her husband and Ella knew what a demanding man Byron could be. And even though Byron had done nothing these past months to encourage Ella, Ella was used to getting her way, and felt sure Byron was still attracted to her. In fact, Ella had convinced herself that Byron had stayed with Leigh only till the child was born. She knew how fond Byron was of children and how desperately he had wanted a son, and though Ella had wanted nothing more but to marry Byron, she had never wanted his child, or any child for that matter. Now Byron had his children and they could get rid of Leigh, marry, and Byron would have his heirs.

"I do love these parties so, Byron," she said fluttering her lashes at him. "Remember last year's party?"

"Yes," Byron said uncomfortable with her presence. "It was very nice as I remember."

Byron knew very well to what Ella was referring. He and Ella had strolled away from the other guests and spent a passionate afternoon alone together. The memory only made him long for Leigh all the more.

"Nice as you remember," Ella giggled, trying to sound shy. "Shame on you, Byron," she said placing a hand possessively on his arm.

Byron saw James Bradford standing alone and he

quickly grabbed Ella's arm and steered her in his direction. Ella thought Byron was again taking her to a more private place and she cast a smug look around for Leigh and saw Leigh watching them closely. Ella nearly collided with Byron when he stopped abruptly before James. The three stood chatting a moment and then Leigh saw Byron excuse himself and walk away. Ella gave his back a hurt look and then turned her attentions to James with a broad grin.

Leigh gave Byron a tremendous smile as he approached her side.

"Ladies," he said to the gathering of women who had been conversing with Leigh, "would you excuse us please?"

"Of course, Byron," one of them commented as she looked to Emily and smiled at the way Byron placed a hand on Leigh's waist. It was apparent to all the ladies that Byron loved his wife and they thought them a most charming couple.

"Leigh," Byron said after they walked a small distance away to talk in private, "many of the guests have asked to see the twins and Uncle Jonathan is having a fit to show off his namesake."

"I plan to go and feed them shortly," Leigh assured him, "and then Annie is going to bring them out in their buggy."

They talked a few minutes longer before he placed a kiss on her lips and returned to his guests. Leigh went to check with Ephraim concerning the beef roasting in the open pit at the far corner of the front lawn and then stopped to chat with their guests as she made her way to the house.

Ella still stood with James. She had watched the

354

exchange between Leigh and Byron closely and as she watched Leigh's graceful movements among her guests and the smiling faces that greeted her, her hatred for Leigh grew.

"Ella," James said for the third time.

"What?"

"I do believe I am boring you."

"Don't be silly, James," Ella purred. "Why you know how much I enjoy your company." Ella took a step closer to James and then laughed loudly at some jest he made.

Leigh saw Ella flirting outrageously with James and overheard many of the guests commenting on her behavior.

After she finished nursing the twins she helped Annie to dress them in beautiful gowns of pink and blue, respectively. She had made the gowns especially for today. Annie pushed the buggy from the house and Leigh walked beside her as the guests came to admire the children. Major walked with them and stayed close by watching the guests suspiciously as they approached. Byron joined them and placed an arm about Leigh, smiling proudly as all commented on the handsomeness of the children.

"You must be very proud. Such beautiful children," one guest commented.

"Oh, aren't they adorable," said another.

James came to see the babes, but Leigh noticed that Ella stood back glaring at her.

James smiled down at the two sleeping infants. "Leigh, Byron, you have two most handsome children." He looked up to Byron and winked. "But then seeing how lovely their mother is, that should come as no surprise."

"Leigh is indeed a lovely woman," Byron agreed

placing a soft kiss on her brow.

Leigh blushed at the compliment and James smiled. When he turned to speak with Ella she was no longer there.

Uncle Jonathan strolled about the grounds with Annie showing off the twins to any and all until Ephraim announced the beef was done. The guests lined up in front of the roasting pit as Ephraim sliced off thick juicy pieces of the delicious smelling beef.

"Annie, let us leave the children out a while longer," Leigh said. "The fresh air will do them good."

"I'll just sits here with um under the shade of the tree," Annie agreed.

Annie pushed the buggy under the shade of a large oak tree as Leigh went to join Byron and their guests near the roasting pit.

"Major," Annie said looking to the dog, "you stay with the babes. I gots to get some diapers."

The dog looked to Annie and wagged his tail as she walked away toward the house.

Ella stood a small distance away and saw Annie leaving the twins alone. She was livid at Byron's words of praise for Leigh and determined to do something to ruin Leigh's day. She glanced about and saw that everyone was at the roasting pit.

"I'll go and pinch the brats," she said to herself, "and when they cry hard Leigh will have to return with them to the house."

There was a sly smile on Ella's lips as she made her way toward the twins. She did not see Major lying in the shade behind the buggy and she stopped with a gasp as the huge dog came from behind the buggy, his head lowered, teeth showing, as he growled a warning to her.

Ella stood dead still. The dog was much larger now and Ella had no intention of confronting him again. Very slowly, and very cautiously, she backed away with large frightened eyes.

"Leigh, what is so amusing?" Byron asked.

"Nothing, Byron. I often smile when I am so happy," Leigh replied as she casually took his arm and turned him so he would not see Ella's hasty retreat across the lawn.

Around dusk Ephraim hung lanterns in the trees and the party continued well into the night.

"Leigh, Byron, the food was delicious and the host and hostess most charming," Jack said as he helped Emily into their landau.

"We are pleased you enjoyed yourselves," Byron replied merrily.

"Indeed we did," Emily agreed, "and as soon as you feel the twins are up to it, we insist you come and spend the day with us."

"Thank you, Emily, we will," Leigh said.

Byron placed an arm about her and they stood a moment waving to Jack and Emily and then turned and went into the house, arms still wrapped about one another.

Many guests still lingered on the lawn and more still were chatting in the house. James Bradford was one of the guests that would be staying on for a few days and he stood in the foyer chatting with Ella when Byron and Leigh entered.

"Still here, Ella," Byron said glancing her way and then continuing toward the drawing room. "I thought you left some time ago."

"James has kindly offered to see me home after papa left so early."

As Byron turned to face her, his arm still wrapped securely about Leigh's waist, Ella brushed boldly against James thinking to make Byron jealous.

"That is nice of you, James," he commented. "I will have Ephraim leave a candle for you in the foyer in case we are in bed when you return."

"Fine, Byron," James grinned.

James noted Ella turn with a huff. He was not fooled. He knew Ella was flirting with him only to get at Byron and he also knew it was a hopeless cause. Why would any man turn to Ella when he already had someone as lovely as Leigh. Ella had flirted with him boldly all day. James smiled to himself. On the long buggy ride home tonight, he planned to find out just how far Ella was willing to go to make Byron jealous.

It was late when all the guests said their goodnights. James had been gone a good deal of time and still had not returned from seeing Ella home.

"Ephraim, Mr. Bradford will most likely be very late," Byron said. "Please leave a candle burning for him in the foyer."

"I will, Master Byron. Goodnight."

"Goodnight, Ephraim," Leigh and Byron said in unison as they climbed the stairs hand in hand. They looked at each other and laughed and Leigh thought Byron's eyes looked even bluer and there was an odd expression in them. Nervously she drew her eyes from his and her hands began to tremble as they neared the bedroom. When they reached the door Leigh drew her hand from his and continued on down the hall to the nursery.

"I'll just see to the children. I won't be long," she said.

Byron nodded his head and entered their bedroom and stood staring at the bed, the covers turned back for the night. He remembered the words spoken by his uncle today once he had gotten the courage to speak to the man.

"Byron, it has been many years since your aunt passed away, and many more since Margaret was born. I truly do not know if there is a certain time. I would imagine it is different with each woman." His words were serious and Byron had been thankful that he did not make sport of him for asking. "I am sure," Jonathan continued, "that Leigh will give you some sign when the time is right."

Now that Byron stood staring at the bed, he wondered. He had never told his uncle of their relationship, or rather lack of one, and he doubted that Leigh would give him any sign. He felt himself very awkward and nervous at the thought of them again sharing a bed and he cursed himself for his school boy feelings. Why you would think me some young buck that never before tasted a woman's charms, he thought. He wondered what Leigh's reaction to him would be after the months they had lived together as anything but husband and wife—and he still worried it was too soon after the birth of the twins, that mayhap he could injure her in some way. And if she did reject him, would it be because it was too soon, or simply because she did not desire him? But she had said that she loved him— did she know what love really meant? He knew how shy and innocent she was.

When Leigh finished nursing the children she walked slowly toward their room on wobbly legs, thinking of Byron and the night ahead. Timidly she did not glance toward the bed as she quietly disrobed, donned her gown, and brushed her hair. Taking a deep breath she neared the bed and then stood staring at her handsome husband fast asleep. She roughly jerked the blankets as she lay down and glared at Byron's sleeping form. He did not move and his breathing remained slow and steady. Leigh turned her back to him and quietly wept into her pillow.

Byron lay awake beside her unaware of her crying. He was furious with himself. Now I resort to feigning sleep in my own bed—and with my own wife! Why do I feel so awkward with Leigh in this bed? he asked himself. Lord knows I felt no hesitation with any other woman or in any other bed. Is this what love does to a man?—takes away his confidence—his masculinity? I never felt such awkwardness with Ella, he mused. But Ella was not as shy or as innocent as Leigh, though she had tried to pretend she was. And Ella had not just had twins—and he had never attacked Ella or any of his other charming bedmates against their will.

He sighed. Was their marriage to always be like this? Having her near, loving her, wanting her, but never touching her! Why do I feel so awkward with Leigh in this bed, he kept asking himself over and over?

He eventually fell asleep wanting nothing more than to turn to his beautiful wife and take her tenderly into his waiting arms.

Chapter Thirteen

Three days after all the guests had gone, Leigh was in the nursery just laying Ammie down for her nap when Byron entered the room and then motioned to her to follow him.

Puzzled, Leigh followed him to their bedroom.

"I have something for you," he said pointing to the bed. Leigh gave him a surprised and somewhat amazed look and then turned to stare at the bed wondering what was so special. Laying there, spread neatly on the dark blue bedspread, was the most beautiful riding habit Leigh had ever seen.

"Byron," she said amazed, as she inspected the habit and the high brown riding boots, "wherever did you get them?"

"I had them made when we were in Richmond. I remember once you telling me you could ride."

"Yes," Leigh smiled, remembering that first awkward breakfast they had shared together at the O'Malleys. "Though it has been two years since I last rode, I do greatly enjoy it."

"Well, madam," he said with a grin and a small bow, "if you would care to change, we will go riding now."

Leigh gave him an excited, dimpled smile and started to unbutton her gown.

"I'll await my lady's pleasure below in the foyer," Byron said with a grin as he turned and left the room.

Leigh noticed that he was never in the room when she bathed or changed. She had been thankful when she was so misshapen with the twins, but now that her figure was trim again, she would not have minded his manly presence. And mayhap it would help to entice him to treat her as wife, she thought.

She stood in front of the oval mirror and admired the lovely habit. The skirt and vest were tan. There was a white ruffled blouse and a dark forest green jacket. A matching green hat with a tan band and feather completed the attire. Leigh especially liked the hat. It was shaped like a man's tricorn, only smaller, and it tied beneath the chin with a dark green ribbon. The outfit looked stunning on her. The green jacket looked well with her eyes and the hat, tilted slightly on her head, looked most charming. Everything fit perfectly, even the boots.

When Leigh descended the stairs Byron was awaiting her. He whistled and winked at her as she smiled down at him.

"If I had known it would look that grand on you," he said, "we would have gone riding before."

Leigh reached his side laughing. "I somehow doubt it

would have looked nearly as nice when I was large with the twins." She stood before him and held her skirt out turning slowly about for his inspection. "But it does fit well now, don't you agree?"

"Yes, pet, it most certainly does," Byron agreed as his eyes lovingly explored her face and body.

She had braided her hair in one large braid and wrapped it in a circle at the base of her neck. Small, willful curls surrounded her face and her eyes sparkled as she smiled up to him. Byron felt his brow breaking out in a cold sweat and he cleared his throat as he drew his eyes reluctantly from her.

"Come, sweet, our steeds await us," he said offering her his arm.

Byron's huge stallion and a white-faced filly, the one they had discussed the morning she joined him in the barn, awaited them at the front door. Byron helped Leigh to mount and then handed her her riding crop. He mounted his stallion and they rode away from the house at a slow trot, Byron studying her horsemanship closely.

"Now be cautious, Leigh," he warned, "the filly has some spirit."

"I assure you, Byron, I do know how to ride. I used to ride to hounds in England."

Byron noted that Leigh said England instead of home as she usually did and he wondered if perhaps she at last was beginning to think of Royal Oaks as home.

They came to a fence and Leigh gave Byron an impish look, kicked her filly's sides, jumped the fence and took off across the field at a run.

Byron's face lost all of its color as he hurriedly pursued her. "Leigh, wait!" he yelled, but she rode all the harder.

In the open field it did not take his huge stallion long to

overtake the filly. Byron cut his horse across her path, forcing the filly to slow. When the horses were again slowed to a trot Byron turned to Leigh with a deep and worried frown.

"Leigh, you should not be so reckless," he scolded, his face full of concern. "It has been a long time since last you rode, you said so yourself, and not long since the twins were born."

"Byron, I am fully recovered from the birth of the twins," she laughed, "I keep telling you so. And I did greatly enjoy the run."

Her face was slightly flushed and full of dimples as she smiled at him and Byron's eyes became hooded and seemed to grow even darker blue as he caressed her form. They rode on at a slower pace, Byron taking special note of her words. Mayhap she was completely recovered from the birth of the twins, he thought. Her horsemanship certainly made it appear so. He smiled to himself.

They came to a stream and Byron stopped and dismounted and then went to help Leigh. As she slid off the filly and into his arms they gazed hard into each other's eyes. Byron slowly lowered his lips to hers, kissing her tenderly, lovingly, softly. Then the kiss grew more passionate and Leigh's arms crept up and about his neck and she held him tightly. Surprisingly, it was Byron that broke the embrace. He stood looking at their surroundings for a moment and then went to his horse and took a blanket from the saddlebags, spreading it under a tree. He sat down and motioned to Leigh to join him, patting the inviting space beside him. As she sat down by him she studied his mood. He did not look her way as he picked a blade of grass and began to nibble it watching the stream before them.

"I used to swim here as a boy," he said in a soft voice.

"The water doesn't appear deep enough," Leigh said glancing to the stream and then back to Byron.

"It is. And it is sweet and cool."

He turned and gazed into her eyes and his betrayed an odd emotion that Leigh could not quite make out, but she had seen that look before on the night she ran away from him in Richmond. It was that look of pain, and yet pleasure.

"Yes, sweet and cool," he repeated drawing his eyes from hers. "I enjoyed this stream much as a boy. There are several deep pools." He turned to face her again and this time his eyes had a devilish quality. "Let's go swimming now."

"Byron, we have not the right clothing."

At Byron's continuing, devilish look, Leigh blushed realizing his intent. She quickly looked about.

"Someone will see us," she said.

"No one will see us," he assured her. He rose and started unbuttoning his shirt. "We are still on Royal Oaks, pet, and no workers ever come around here."

Leigh sat watching him in indecision for a moment and then rose and walked behind the tree. Color rose to her cheeks as she removed her clothes and felt the soft summer breeze fresh against her skin. Byron is my husband, she thought blushing, and I do want to intice him to my bed, don't I? She was nervous and shy as she peeked from behind the tree, but Byron was not there but already splashing and swimming in the stream. Leigh waited, shyly, until Byron dove beneath the surface, and then half ran and half dove into the cool, refreshing

365

water. She came up laughing and shaking her head. The water really did feel grand.

Byron gave her a devilish grin and started swimming toward her. Leigh squealed and swam as fast as she could in the opposite direction, but it did not take Byron long to overtake her with long, powerful strokes of his muscular body. He grabbed one of her dainty feet and as she laughed and splashed in his direction, he tenderly pulled her to his side. They looked into each other's eyes laughing and then Byron's arms went about her pulling her tight against him.

"I love you, Leigh," he said in a soft and caressing voice.

Leigh could feel his nakedness next to her own, her breasts pressed firmly to his chest. Her heart was beating wildly and she found it hard to breathe. They stood in water up to Leigh's shoulders as Byron's mouth lowered slowly to hers. He kissed her long and passionately, pulling her closer still. Leigh could feel his manhood and knew Byron's passions were high. Her knees began to tremble and she feared they would not hold her when Byron picked her up in his arms, never breaking the embrace, and carried her to the blanket. There kisses grew more and more fevered as his hands caressed and fondled her breasts. Leigh moaned with pleasure as he placed fevered kisses on her lips, her neck, her breasts. Finally Byron could contain himself no longer and Leigh could feel his manhood searching as he whispered endearments, his large hands exploring her body. Leigh felt a warm, tender glow passing through her body as she and Byron made love and she clung to him calling his name. Byron tried to go slow at first but soon his long denied body would not allow him, and as their passion grew Leigh was amazed at her own desire. She moaned and moved beneath him, her hands ran possessively over his strong, muscular back, and she delighted in the feel of his powerful body next to hers. As passion consumed them both, Leigh clung to him, calling his name. Byron let out a satisfied sigh and sank down heavily upon her. They lay wrapped in each other's arms, both enjoying the aftermath of love's glow.

It was some time later when Byron rolled from her and looked deeply into the emerald pools. "I love you, Leigh. Never leave me again for I do not know what I should do without you."

"Byron, my dearest love, I shall never leave you. I love you more than life itself."

He gazed into her deep emerald eyes as his hand casually fondled the nipple of one breast and he kissed her tenderly. His kisses were warm and tender and his hands made Leigh tingly as she delighted in his touch. She felt an odd contentment she had never felt before and a memory from long ago began to stir within her. She was running in the woods, Samuel Jones close behind her. Ahead was a mist and as she ran into the mist there was a dark figure waiting, inviting arms spread wide. And as she ran into those arms they wrapped about her, lovingly, protectively, not only giving her a feeling of security, but also a feeling of pleasure and delight. Leigh looked into Byron's deep blue eyes and knew now that that figure had been him.

"I love you, Byron," she said softly.

Byron pulled her close and kissed her passionately and it was a long time before they swam in the stream again.

When next they left the stream they were laughing and shaking water on one another. They quickly helped each other to dress and started for home.

"Annie will probably be frantic," Leigh said giving Byron a shameful look. "You made me forget the twins and it's most likely well past time for them to be fed."

"I am sorry, pet," he grinned, riding close to her side. He leaned over in the saddle and placed a kiss on her lips. "I did not mean to make you forget your motherly duties."

"Had I known my wifely duties would be so pleasant," Leigh said with a smile, a slight blush coloring her cheeks, "I would have insisted on them much sooner."

Byron threw back his head and laughed hard, then kissed her again. "I assure you my love, I will give you no cause to insist in the future."

They rode on with Byron glancing Leigh's way and smiling. He kept looking at her as though he feared she would disappear if he did not watch her closely.

"You know, pet, you look so striking wearing that riding habit I think I will send for a portrait painter and have a portrait done of you wearing it. It would look very nice over the mantel in the drawing room."

"Byron, your mother's portrait is there."

"Yes, and rightly it should have been. She was mistress of Royal Oaks. But now my beautiful Mrs. Marsh," he said with a grin, "you are mistress. I'll hang mother's portrait in my study if that eases your mind and move father's to the foyer along side those of my grandparents." He grinned at her and nodded his head indicating the decision was made.

"Well then it is only fair that I insist that we also have

your portrait painted."

Byron turned to her with surprise and she laughed. "And I also insist that I choose your apparel as you have mine," she concluded with a grin.

Byron laughed and they sealed the bargain with a kiss.

They were chatting gaily when they entered the foyer and confronted Annie's stern presence.

"Miss Leigh," Annie said frowning at Byron, having little doubt who was at fault, "you is doing too much now, riding this long, and them babes just barely borned. You should be ashamed of yourself, Masser Byron, keeping her astride a saddle all afternoon."

"My most humble apologies," Byron said making a small bow to hide his grinning face. He fought hard not to laugh and heard a giggle escape Leigh.

"Ain't nothing funny about it, Miss Leigh," Annie scolded, "you is going to makes yourself sick."

"Yes, Annie," Leigh agreed. She and Byron exchanged a look before she went with Annie to attend the twins.

That night when Byron helped Leigh with her chair at dinner, he noticed her movements were slow. It concerned him but he said nothing. As the night progressed he became more and more worried, and when Leigh climbed the stairs for bed, he watched her closely.

Once she was settled in bed he came to stand beside her, his face full of remorse.

"Leigh, did, ah, I, ah, do you harm today? Was it too soon after . . ."

"Byron, my love, you did me no harm," she said taking his hand and looking up to him with love. "I am a little stiff after the ride today, that is all." She smiled and slowly rose to her knees on the bed so her face would be

369

level with his. "I should not have raced so across the fields when I had not ridden in so long." She placed a light kiss on his lips. "I am only a little stiff," she repeated pulling him into bed beside her.

Byron found Leigh was right. She, indeed, was only a little stiff.

Chapter Fourteen

The days grew long and lazy, the oppressive heat of summer spread over the land, and July turned into August.

Leigh and Byron rode together every morning. Sometimes they would ride as far as Uncle Jonathan's and stop to visit for a while. Jonathan noticed the new found closeness the couple now shared. He did not know what had brought on the change, for now they were always holding hands or touching in some manner. Leigh looked even more beautiful than before and Jonathan found it charming the way Byron's eyes seemed to follow Leigh about a room.

And Jonathan wasn't the only person to notice a change in the couple. There wasn't a servant at Royal Oaks who hadn't noted the happiness they saw when they looked at their master or mistress. Ephraim, Annie or

Aunt Mary was always about to shoo the children away from the veranda in the late afternoon when Byron and Leigh would come out to sit in the cool shade of the porch. Often they would spend hours there in quiet conversation or sometimes in total silence, each requiring nothing more than the comforting closeness of the other.

Byron leaned back against one of the large, white pillars and sighed. Leigh turned liquid eyes to his and smiled and then snuggled her head more securely in the hollow of his shoulder. He tightened his arms about her, pulling her back tighter against his chest. They sat both gazing at the beauty surrounding them. Byron nibbled lightly on Leigh's ear and placed a fleeting kiss on it.

"Wench, what shall I do with you," he said softly. "A man tries to spend a quiet afternoon enjoying his home and you come and lean against me as if I was this sturdy pillar here. And not only is the scent of your hair enough to drive a man wild, but you even taste good," he added again nibbling her ear.

Leigh giggled and squeezed his hand, then pretended to rise, but Byron quickly pulled her back to his embrace.

"I do not want to disturb you, me lord," she said impishly.

"Leigh, my love, there shall not be a day of my life that goes by that you do not disturb my every waking thought, and I would have it no other way."

Leigh turned in his arms and placed a kiss on his lips and then settled herself again in his embrace.

"Byron?"

"Umm," he replied nuzzling his nose in her hair.

"Don't forget that Rose Marrow and Thomas Whitefield are due to arrive tomorrow."

"I won't forget, my love."

"Rose said they would try to arrive by late afternoon. Please try to stay close to the house, I do so want you to be here to welcome them."

"I promise, my love. Is there anything else you require of me till then?"

"Only your company," she smiled.

"That, madam, I can guarantee," he said giving her a hug.

"Byron, I am so happy sometimes I fear I will wake up and find it was all a dream, or that something will happen to threaten our happiness."

"Never, my love." Byron turned her gently in his arms and looked deeply into her emerald eyes. "Leigh, I will never let anything or anyone spoil this happiness we share, never my love."

Leigh threw her arms about his neck hugging him fiercely. "Are all wives so blessed with such loving and passionate husbands?"

Byron chuckled. "If they have a sultress for a wife as I do, they are."

Leigh blushed at his words remembering their love making of the night before. She was thankful that Annie no longer stayed in the nursery as she had when the twins were first born. She would have been quite embarrassed if anyone were in the house to hear their love play. Just last night Byron had helped her with her bath washing her back. One thing had led to another and before she knew it he was sharing her bath. He had carried her to their bed laughing and wet, and it had been a most enjoyable night of love. Even today Leigh was still surprised at her total abandon where the man was concerned.

Byron pushed Leigh away and stood up slowly stretching. Then he looked down at her with a devilish grin and offered her his hand to help her rise.

"It is such a lazy afternoon," he said casually, "I think I'll go take a nap. Care to join me?"

Leigh took note of the passionate look in his eyes and hers were shaming in return. "Byron, it is the middle of the day!"

"No better time to take a nap," he said with a wink. "And with guests arriving tomorrow you need your rest, sweet."

Leigh laughed and took his hand and they strolled into the house.

It was shortly after lunch the next afternoon when Rose and Thomas arrived. Leigh heard the carriage out front and rushed to the door where Major stood growling, and then out onto the veranda. She ran to Rose the moment she saw her.

"Oh, I am so glad you are here," she said, tears of happiness appearing in her eyes. "I have missed you terribly."

"Leigh, you look marvelous," Rose replied. "You must indeed be as happy as your letters imply."

"I am, truly happy. I never knew such happiness existed." She turned a large dimpled smile to Thomas and warmly grasped his hand. "I am so glad you both could come."

"Rose is right, Leigh," Thomas said, "you do look grand."

"Thank you. Oh dear, here I am keeping you talking on the veranda, please come in."

"Are you quite sure this brute here will let us?"

Thomas said looking to Major askew.

"This is Major," Leigh said giggling and petting the large dog. "I assure you he is quite gentle."

"I should hope so," Thomas replied giving the dog a weary look. "I would hate to think what would happen if he were not. Why he is nearly as large as a pony!"

Leigh laughed. "He is not even full grown yet, or near the size of his sire."

Thomas and Rose both looked to Major with some amazement and Leigh laughed again, and taking one of their arms in hers, escorted them into the house. Byron came hurrying down the hall to greet them and introductions were made.

"Mr. Marsh, thank you so much for your invitation," Rose said.

"Byron, please."

"And please call me Rose," she said glancing to Leigh and smiling. "Leigh and I are too dear of friends for this Mrs. Marrow formality."

Leigh noted Thomas give Rose an odd look just as Ephraim appeared and was also introduced.

Byron escorted them to the drawing room and Leigh sent Ephraim for refreshments.

"Was your journey pleasant?" Leigh asked.

"Yes," Thomas answered, "and we have enjoyed the lovely countryside surrounding your home."

"Leigh tells me you are a silversmith, Mr. Whitefield," Byron said.

"Yes, and Thomas please."

The conversation turned to Richmond and business. Ephraim brought tea. Leigh gracefully poured four cups and as she handed Byron his cup he leaned over toward Thomas.

"Thomas, could I perhaps interest you in something a little more refreshing?"

Thomas laughed and he and Byron headed for Byron's study.

"Tell me, Leigh, how are the children?"

"Oh, Rose, they are growing in leaps and bounds, and healthy as can be. I can't tell you what a joy they are."

"Well it is certainly a joy to see you again. I've missed you terribly." Rose paused and again gazed at Leigh in wonder. "I just cannot get over how wonderful you look. Marriage certainly agrees with you dear, and," she said in a whisper, "Byron is a striking man. I had heard he was handsome, but . . ."

Leigh laughed. "You are pretty striking yourself. Thomas' company must agree with you."

Rose blushed slightly and laughed. "He is a wonderful man," she agreed.

"Tell me, Leigh," Thomas said entering the room, a snifter of brandy in his hand, "where are those twins I have heard so much about?"

"They are napping now, but I will bring them down shortly."

"I can hardly wait," said Rose. "Who do they resemble?"

"Ammie much resembles Leigh," Byron answered coming to sit at his wife's side, "and I am told Nathan resembles me," he added proudly.

They chatted easily with each other and Leigh smiled at Byron, grateful for his courteous hospitality to her friends.

"Tell me, Leigh, how are you coming with the matter of the deed?" Thomas asked.

"Well," is all Leigh replied and looking flustered,

quickly changed the subject.

Thomas and Rose exchanged puzzled looks but let the matter drop. A short time later Annie came to tell Leigh the twins were awake and she excused herself to go upstairs and nurse them. She nervously bit at her lower lip hoping the matter of the deed would not be brought up again in her absence. In all truthfulness she had forgotten the matter of her father's missing deed these past months, but she knew she should have told Byron before. By law, once she and Byron were married, the land actually belonged to him and Leigh worried over his reaction to the fact that she had kept the information from him.

When she returned to the drawing room carrying Nathan, Annie following with Ammie, Byron rose with a grin and took his daughter from Annie's arms. Leigh noted no tension in his manner and breathed a sigh of relief. Perhaps the subject had not been broached in her absence.

"Oh, Leigh, they are precious," Rose said admiring the baby in Leigh's arms. "May I hold one?" Leigh smiled and handed her Nathan. "I had forgotten how good it feels to hold an infant," Rose said grinning at the cooing baby.

Thomas cleared his throat. "Do you suppose you would trust me to hold your daughter?"

"Of course," Byron said handing Ammie to him.

Thomas was awkward with the child and Byron quickly gave him assistance.

Leigh laughed hard seeing Byron's tutoring. "Thomas, do not let Byron give you the impression he is a master at holding babes. He was much more ill at ease than you when first he held one of the twins."

Byron turned to Leigh and feigned insult, then he smiled a warm smile and winked.

They spent some time with the twins but when it became evident that Ammie would soon follow Nathan's lead, and also fall asleep, Leigh and Rose returned them to the nursery.

Thomas and Byron were chatting easily when the women returned.

"If you like I will show you your rooms now," offered Leigh. "I imagine you would like to rest before dinner."

Thomas and Rose agreed and Byron and Ephraim carried their bags as Leigh led the way to the guest rooms.

"I hope this room will be comfortable, Rose," Leigh said entering a room in soft greens and roses, the furniture of French design.

Rose followed her into the lovely room and looked about. "Leigh, it is beautiful, as is the rest of your home. I am sure it will be quite comfortable."

Leigh smiled. "If you need anything, just pull the bell cord."

Leigh turned to leave to show Thomas his room, but Rose stopped her. "Thomas can share this room with me," she said.

Leigh, Byron and Ephraim all turned in unison to stare at Rose with wide eyes and mouths agape.

"I assure you it is quite proper," Rose continued with a laugh. "You see Thomas and I were married several days ago."

Thomas chuckled and walked to his wife's side and placed an arm about her and smiled at the surprised faces before him.

"You are married?" Leigh asked amazed. As the two smiling faces slowly nodded their heads, Leigh rushed to them and gave them each a kiss. "Why did you not tell us before?"

"We wanted to surprise you," Thomas said. "And it appears that we did," he added with a chuckle.

"And besides," Rose added, "I would not have missed the looks on your faces just now for anything."

Everyone laughed and Byron and Ephraim also offered their congratulations.

Leigh whirled to face Byron, an excited look on her face. "We need have a party for them."

"That's a grand idea," Byron agreed.

"No, no, dear," Rose said, "we do not wish to cause you and Byron any inconvenience."

"Now I insist," Leigh said flatly. "And this time I shall have my way," she added with a wink in Rose's direction.

That night Byron and Leigh lay in bed discussing the party. They had decided on a summer ball.

"I will have to have someone deliver the invitations on the morrow," Leigh said. "Rose said they cannot stay too long." Leigh stared at the ceiling, a thoughtful look on her face, as she ran the details through her mind.

"Um," Byron offered as he reached over with one hand and lightly traced the outline of Leigh's breast beneath her flimsy gown.

"Now, Byron," Leigh said giving him a dimpled grin, "how can I plan a summer ball if you cannot keep your hands to yourself?"

"And how can I keep my hands to myself when you lay so close beside me, tempting me with your round, rosy breasts pressed firmly against that veil you call a nightgown."

Leigh laughed and Byron leaned over her and placed a

soft, fleeting kiss on her neck and then progressed to her shoulders.

"I will take care of the arrangements for the musicians," he said, pausing to kiss her again. "And I will see to the champagne on the morrow," he added kissing her again. "Anything else you require, madam?"

Leigh smiled warmly up at him and placed her arms about his neck. "Not concerning the party," she replied in a caressing tone.

Leigh invited the Cummings, Uncle Jonathan, and all of their friends and neighbors that lived close by. James Bradford and some of their other acquaintances that lived great distances reluctantly could not be invited since plans were made to hold the ball two days hence. They worried again over the matter of the Boroughs, but Byron finally gave in and they were also invited.

Rose and Leigh spent the day before the ball picking flowers for the house. They made numerous arrangements and the ballroom looked like a summer garden. Byron brought up many bottles of champagne from the wine cellar and Leigh spent long hours with Aunt Mary deciding on the perfect foods for the buffet table.

Leigh chose a gown of white silk. It was cut low in the bodice and scalloped along the edge of the neckline which was worn off the shoulders. There were tiny roses shaped of silk in a pinkish mauve bordering the scalloped neckline, and more still scattered about the full, flowing skirt, and more still along the scalloped hem of the gown. She wore a long strand of pearls and a lovely pair of pearl drop earrings with diamonds on the studs. She wore her hair in a large twisted bun at the base of her neck, small curls about her temples and ears, and Annie helped her to arrange two white roses in the bun, just behind her left ear. The effect was outstanding.

Byron wore a white suit with a dark blue waistcoat, and with his dark hair, deep blue eyes, and tanned skin, he looked even more handsome than usual.

Byron stood beside Leigh greeting their guests and he could not keep his eyes off of her. She had knotted the strand of pearls once just above her breasts and the resulting loop hung tantalizingly between her breasts, the warm glow of the pearls flattering the whiteness of her skin. Byron marveled at her beauty anew, and thought to himself that if he lived to be a thousand he would never see a more beautiful woman, and not just in appearance either. I'll be hard pressed, he thought, not to take my ravishing wife upstairs and enjoy her charms before my guests depart. He felt his passion growing as he watched the pearls resting against her breasts and reluctantly he drew his eyes from her and cleared his throat several times trying to regain his composure.

When the Boroughs arrived, Fred complimented Leigh on her outstanding appearance, but Ella was less than courteous.

Ella wore a gown of pink and Leigh had to admit the color looked well on her. The gown was cut extremely low and the bodice was inset with lace. Leigh marveled at the gown's ability to contain Ella's generous proportions, and made a mental note to tell the musicians not to play any minuets this night. If Ella were to curtsy in that gown, thought Leigh, she would lay herself bare!

The Whitefields were introduced to all as they stood with Leigh and Byron in the reception line. Once all the guests had arrived Byron announced the ball was in the Whitefields' behalf because of their recent marriage. As the evening progressed Thomas and Rose were congratulated again and again by all those present and they found the Marsh's neighbors and friends to be warm and generous people.

Rose saw Ella approaching and Ella's face looked anything but friendly.

"Miss Borough, how nice to see you again," Rose said.

"Miss Marrow," Ella nodded.

"Whitefield, dear, and this is my husband, Thomas."

"Yes, Whitefield," Ella said giving Thomas a half-hearted smile. "Allow me to congratulate you on your recent marriage," Ella continued in anything but a gracious manner.

"Thank you, dear," Rose said though the congratulations were given rudely and Thomas murmured his thanks bowing politely and placing a gracious kiss on Ella's offered hand.

An impish look appeared in Rose's eyes. "Tell me, dear, are you still engaged to, ah— Do forgive me but I am afraid I have forgotten the name of your betrothed."

Ella's face became even stiffer and slightly flushed. "James Bradford," she said quickly.

"Odd. I do not recall that name. Oh well, is the gentleman here tonight?"

"No," Ella snipped. "He was unable to attend."

"What a shame. I would have enjoyed meeting him."

Ella walked away with no further comment and Thomas gave Rose an appraising glance. "I do not know what all was just said," he commented, "but I do believe it was more than I heard."

Rose grinned up at him taking his hand. "Thomas, dear, I have not the slightest idea what you are talking about."

Byron insisted the newlyweds grace them with a dance and everyone stood aside as Rose and Thomas waltzed. Leigh smiled deeply as she watched the couple dance and the loving looks they gave to one another. The guests applauded when the dance ended and stood chatting in small groups when the musicians began another waltz.

"Leigh, may I have the honor of this dance?" Uncle Jonathan asked with a low bow.

"Why, suh," Leigh replied fluttering her eyelashes and mimicking the slow draw of the other ladies. "The pleasure is all mine, I'm sore."

Jonathan and Byron laughed heartily and Byron pulled Leigh close and gave her waist a squeeze. Jonathan offered Leigh his arm, and smiling, they made their way to the dance floor.

"I promise not to keep her long, nephew," Jonathan called over his shoulder.

Byron nodded with a chuckle and stood a moment watching his wife glide about the shining oak floor in his uncle's arms. He noted again how lovely she looked, the flattering gown, the roses in her hair, the sparkling, dimpled smile on her face, and he felt himself begin to perspire. She will always have this affect on me, he thought with a warm smile. I thought once I had tasted of her charms I would not find myself thus again, but the wench is a sultress. I never thought to find myself feeling love for any woman, but God how I do love her. His eyes glowed as they followed her about the dance floor, then clearing his throat, he went to refill his brandy glass.

He chatted with his guests and made sure everyone had the refreshment of their choice and that all were having a pleasant time. He saw Jack near the buffet table and walked his way.

"It is nice of you, Byron, to give this ball for the Whitefields," Jack said. "They seem a very nice couple."

"They are and actually the ball was Leigh's idea."

"Well, I compliment you both on your taste in friends," Jack chuckled. "And on the excellent champagne."

"Thank you, friend Jack," Byron grinned. Then raising his glass to Jack's, he toasted to a pleasant evening.

Jack gave Byron an odd look. Byron had not been this light of mood with him in years. He had no inkling as to what had caused the change in Byron since he and Emily had visited after the twins' birth, but something most definitely had. Byron was more relaxed than Jack had seen him in years, and there was a happiness in his eyes that almost sparkled. Byron had changed much after he and Leigh had wed, Jack remembered. He had seemed much less irritable and much more satisfied with his life. Then when the twins had been born, Byron appeared extremely happy and even more at peace with himself— but the look of him now made Jack marvel. Jack glanced Leigh's way and grinned. Thank you, Leigh, he thought. Thank you for returning my boyhood friend. I had begun to think I had lost him forever. Jack smiled at Byron and raised his glass for another toast.

"Leigh has been quite nervous wanting everything to be just right for this occasion," Byron said.

"I assure you it is a complete success and everyone is enchanted by the guests of honor." Jack winked at Byron. "As well as the beautiful hostess and charming host."

Jack and Byron again toasted, and grinning at each other, downed their drinks. Jack glanced about still grinning and then suddenly his face grew serious and stiff.

"Excuse me please, Byron," he said walking briskly away.

Byron frowned following Jack with his eyes. Jack went toward Emily standing and chatting with Ella, and there was an uncomfortable look on Emily's face. Byron took long strides and caught up with Jack just as he reached the women's side.

"It must have been Leigh's idea," Byron heard Ella say. "Byron is much too well bred to give a ball for mere merchants."

Jack glanced at Emily askew. "Excuse us, Ella," he said curtly. "This melody is one of my favorites and I wish to dance with my lovely wife."

Ella noted Byron out of the corner of her eye and whirled to give him a toothy smile. "Darling, it is a marvelous party."

"For mere merchants, you mean," Byron replied with a sneer. He scowled at her. "Ella, let me remind you, this is not the old world. There are no class distinctions here, Ella. The Whitefields are friends of mine, as well as my wife's, and are honored guests in my home."

He turned abruptly and walked away in angry strides leaving Ella to stare with her mouth hanging open. She glanced about and saw that Leigh was nowhere around. Probably gone to feed those brats, she thought. A snide smile appeared on Ella's lips. With hurried steps she caught up to Byron, grabbed his arm, and pulled him through the foyer to the veranda.

"Ella, what is it?" he asked impatiently. "I have guests to attend."

"Now, Byron, I just cannot have you angry with me." She smiled giving her eyelashes a flutter. "I assure you I meant no insult to the Whitefields or to you."

"Very well," Byron said turning to leave.

"Wait!"

Byron watched in amazement as Ella boldly stepped to him and pressed her generous breasts against his chest.

"Byron, love, do not pretend to be angry with me. You forget I know you only too well." She smiled coyly and raised up on tiptoes placing her arms about his neck and acting as if she expected Byron to kiss her.

Byron stared at her upturned face. The woman was incredible! How could I have ever thought I would be content with this woman, even for an instant? he wondered.

"I know you still want me, Byron, and that you still love me as I love you. How that harlot trapped you is a mystery to me, but it is of no matter now, my love."

She rubbed her large breasts teasingly against him. At Byron's continued silence she grew even more bold.

"Surely, darling, you have not forgotten all those wonderful nights we spent together." Thinking Byron enchanted by her seduction, she plunged recklessly on. "We can rid ourselves of that skinny wife of yours and . . ."

Byron reached up and jerked her arms from about his neck. He scowled at her and his voice was low and threatening when he spoke. "Ella, hear me well," he said looking hard into her eyes. "I love Leigh with all my heart. She is everything any man could wish for in a wife. I cherish her love, and I will never, NEVER, do anything to lose the love we share."

Ella whirled, turning her back to him and her voice was full of bitterness. "You loved me once—and you can again."

"Ella, I never loved you," he stated firmly. "And I think you are unable to love anyone other than yourself." She turned and gave him a hateful look. "We enjoyed each other's bodies, Ella, that is all," he added in a matter-of-fact way.

"You did love me once," she screamed at him, "and you will again!"

He looked at her as though she were a stranger and his voice took on a level, matter-of-fact, tone. "Never, Ella. Leigh is the only woman I shall ever love so do not set your hopes on another end." He turned and walked back into the house leaving Ella alone and livid with rage.

There was an evil look in Ella's eyes as she watched him go. "We will see, Byron," she whispered. "We will see."

Ella and her father left early that night. Leigh was relieved to see Ella depart. The woman had glared at her in an odd manner ever since she returned from nursing the twins. When Rose and some of the other guests had insisted that she and Byron grace them with a dance, Leigh had felt Ella's eyes piercing her back while she and Byron waltzed. She had finally managed to dismiss Ella from her thoughts as she and Byron gazed into each other's eyes and swayed with the music. A quiet hush fell over the room as the guests watched their blissful dance and the music had stopped before Leigh and Byron noted the stillness of the room. They turned to see all the guests smiling at them and then as the guests applauded Leigh made a small curtsy and Byron a bow. Ella left shortly after they waltzed.

It was late when the last of the guests departed and Thomas and Rose had a last glass of champagne with Leigh and Byron.

"We cannot thank you enough," Thomas said. "We feel we have made many new friends this night."

"I am sure you have," Byron said. "Everyone spoke of how much they enjoyed meeting you."

"Leigh, Byron, it has been a night I shall never forget," Rose smiled. "Never."

"It was our pleasure," Leigh said wrapping an arm about Byron's waist and smiling.

When they reached their room Byron helped Leigh to remove her beautiful gown and as soon as he finished undressing, he sat on the side of the bed watching her brush her long, thick hair.

"Have I told you I love you today?" he asked.

"Yes," Leigh replied giving him a smile in the mirror's reflection. She finished with her hair and rose going to his side. "But I have no objections to hearing it again."

"I love you," he grinned.

"And I you."

He took her in his arms and lay back on the bed, her atop his chest and body.

"How nice you feel," he said snuggling against her.

"Shhh. Thomas and Rose will hear," she giggled.

"I doubt that, pet. Their room is way down the hall and this house is well built I assure you. But if it eases your mind," he commented with a twinkle in his eyes, "I plan to do very little talking." He chuckled as she gave him a shameful look and then laughed softly holding her close. "Even if they should hear us, pet, they are newlyweds themselves."

"Byron, we are hardly newlyweds," she teased.

"Leigh, my love, we shall always be newlyweds."

They spent a passionate night, very quiet, but passionate.

Two days later the Whitefields had to return to Richmond.

"Leigh, dear, Thomas and I have shops to run. Believe me if we did not, you and Byron would never be rid of us," Rose said seeing Leigh's sad face.

"I know," Leigh sniffed. "I am just being selfish. But I so enjoyed your visit and I shall miss you terribly."

"We shall write each other, and you and Byron must come and visit as soon as you can. Our home is always a place where you are welcome," Rose said, tears appearing in her eyes now as well.

"And our home is always open to you," Byron said shaking Thomas' hand. "Mayhap we will be able to visit you in Richmond before the winter sets in."

"Anytime, Byron, anytime at all," Thomas said with a grin. "Rose and I think the world of Leigh and we find she had chosen well in the area of husband," he added with a wink. "Your home and your hospitality have made us feel most welcome and I thank you."

Final goodbyes were said and Byron assisted Rose into their carriage.

"Now, Leigh, you take good care of those babes and do write often," Rose said.

"I will, Rose."

Byron came and placed an arm about Leigh's shoulder and hugged her close. They stood with arms wrapped about each other and waved goodbye as the carriage pulled away from the house.

That night as they sat eating dinner, Byron studied Leigh's face. He laid down his fork and circled the table to come and sit beside her.

"Leigh," he hesitated, "why did you not tell me about

your father's deed?" At her surprised, and slightly embarrassed face he took her hand in his and patted it. "Thomas and Rose and I talked that first day when you went upstairs to tend the children. They do not know that you never told me, though I am sure for a small time I appeared quite the fool. But eventually I understood without giving away the fact that I had not known about the deed before."

Leigh drug her eyes from Byron's and folded her hands in her lap looking ashamed. "I am sorry, Byron," she said softly. "When first we wed, I, ah . . ." She looked him straight in the eye, and taking a deep breath, squared her shoulders. "I should have told you before, I apologize."

"Well, now I know," he said giving her hand a squeeze and rising to return to his chair. Once seated again across from her, he continued. "I will do all in my power to gain information about this land your father acquired, and then we can decide what shall be done."

"Thank you for being so understanding," she whispered.

"I love you, Leigh, never forget that."

She smiled tenderly in his direction and the remainder of the meal was passed talking about Leigh's father and her childhood in England.

They lay in bed that night, Leigh's head on Byron's shoulder, his arms wrapped about her, discussing the Whitefields.

"They are indeed wonderful people, Leigh," Byron said thinking of the many kindnesses the couple had shown Leigh when they were separated in Richmond.

"Yes, they are, and I miss them already," she said, a sadness in her tone.

Byron idly rubbed the small of her back delighting in

the feel of her body pressed tightly to his. "Would you care to go to Richmond the first part of September?"

Leigh sat up and looked to him excitedly. "Could we really?"

Byron grinned and nodded his head and his eyes were drawn from her excited face to her breasts barely concealed by her flimsy gown.

"But Byron, what about the twins?"

"We will take Ephraim and Annie and the twins with us. They will be nearly three months old and with the weather still warm, I judge the twins will be well able to make the trip. We shall go by boat."

"Oh, Byron, do you really think we can?"

"Undoubtedly," he said smiling and lowering her to his waiting arms.

Chapter Fifteen

They spent the remainder of the summer riding, frolicking in the stream, and making love. Their love-making was sometimes tender and sometimes so passionate that Leigh was amazed at her own abandon and the effect Byron had on her. She began to think of Byron as a god-like knight in shining armor. Her knight. She found she not only loved him, she worshipped him and delighted in the joys he brought her and the amazing way he could make her entire body tingle at his slightest touch.

In the afternoons Leigh sat for her portrait. Byron insisted she wear the riding habit and the artist posed her standing holding her small hat and a riding crop in one hand. Her long hair was allowed to hang free, again at Byron's insistence, and she was painted with her hair in slight disarray, as if blown by the wind. Byron loved the pose and the way the portrait was developing and he was like a child at Christmas waiting for its completion.

They would spend long hours talking in the evenings after dinner or as they lay in each other's arms at night. Leigh asked many questions concerning how this vast land was governed. Byron explained democracy to her and they often debated many of its principles. The debates were sometimes heated, but they never truly argued or lost patience with one another. Byron found he enjoyed her mind as much as her body.

The twins grew more adorable with each passing day. Nathan finally got a thicker covering of soft, wavy hair, and Ammie's curls grew fuller and more luscious like her mother's. They became cheruby and had full pink cheeks, dimples at their wrists and ankles. They laughed and giggled when Byron played with them and seldom cried, though Ammie still disliked having her hair washed. They were old enough to take to church now and all the parishioners admired the handsome children and their doting parents. Uncle Jonathan would strut about after services first with Ammie, and then with Nathan, and he was a frequent visitor in their home.

Leigh's portrait reached the stage where she was no longer required to pose as the artist finished shadowing of clothes, skin, and hair tones. He promised the portrait finished by the end of October and then agreed to begin Byron's. Leigh discussed Byron's pose and clothing with the man and they decided on a painting of Byron wearing tan breeches, a white ruffled shirt open at the throat, and high leather riding boots. Major was also to be in the portrait standing at Byron's side. The artist agreed with Leigh, it would make a most stunning portrait.

The day arrived for their trip to Richmond and Byron

stood by wide-eyed as his men loaded the boat for the journey.

"Leigh, dear," he said turning to her and arching a brow, "did you by chance forget the cookhouse?"

Leigh giggled. "Byron it takes much to travel with infants."

Byron cast an eye askew at the boat. "No doubt."

The boat was fairly large and had two cabins. As Leigh and Byron lay in the bunk of their cabin, Leigh commented what a nice boat it was.

"I am glad it meets with your approval, pet. Jack and I purchased it last week."

"It is our boat!"

"Ours and the Cummings'. Jack and I thought when all the children are older, the four of us, you and I, Jack and Emily, might like to travel to Richmond more often or mayhap even further up river. We were both weary of trying to find a trustworthy captain and crew, much less a sturdy boat, so we bought this one."

"How nice, it is a lovely boat." She snuggled closer, her round breasts pressed firmly against his hairy chest. "Though the bed is much smaller than ours at home."

"Ah, madam," Byron said giving her a wicked grin, "now you know why Jack and I chose this particular boat."

Leigh laughed and kissed his cheek. "The truth be told, sir," she teased, "you just wanted to keep me close at your side."

"If that is what it takes to keep you near me, then I confess my guilt."

Leigh smiled tenderly at him. "Byron, my love, were our pallet as large as Royal Oaks itself, I would still be close at your side."

"And I yours," he said gently brushing her lips with a kiss. He pulled her fiercely against him and kissing the nape of her neck, whispered, "And I yours."

Leigh sighed, contented. How she loved to feel his presence next to hers. As the river gently rocked the boat and the moonlight danced on the ceiling overhead, Byron made sweet, passionate love to his wife.

The trip was very pleasant and the children well-behaved. When they arrived in Richmond Byron hired a carriage to take them to the hotel where they had stayed in the past. The manager gave them a broad grin as Byron walked in with Leigh, Annie and Ephraim each carrying a twin. When Leigh and the others started upstairs to their rooms, the manager turned to Byron and gave him a wink.

"I see, Mr. Marsh, that you won the quarrel over your wife visiting England."

"Yes," Byron answered slightly miffed at the man's familiarity. Then a grin broke out on Byron's face and he laughed as he took the man's hand and gave it a hardy shake.

Byron and Leigh shared a room, and Ephraim and Annie another with the twins, as they had on the boat. Once everyone was settled in their rooms, Byron came to Leigh and picked her up swinging her about.

"There is a play in the city. What say you I go and purchase some tickets and we invite the Whitefields to join us?"

"That's a grand idea." Leigh grinned and gave Byron an impish look. "Though it is a surprise to find a play in these back woods."

"I will have you know, madam," Byron said feigning insult, "that even us backward Americans enjoy a play now and again."

When Byron left to purchase the tickets, Leigh went to surprise Rose and invite them to the play. She had not written Rose as to exact time they would arrive in Richmond, only that it would be sometime this week, and she giggled to herself in anticipation of Rose's surprise. When she entered the small shop memories assaulted her. She glanced about and saw Rose standing behind the counter, her back turned as she arranged some hats on a shelf.

"I'll be with you momentarily," Rose called over her shoulder.

"I am a Federalist come to purchase guns."

"Leigh!" Rose exclaimed turning to her with joy. "Why did you not write me you would be arriving today?"

"We wanted to surprise you and to be truthful Byron was not sure exactly when he would be able to leave the plantation. He has gone now to purchase tickets for the play that is in town. We are hoping that you and Thomas will join us."

"Oh that would be nice. Thomas and I had hoped to be able to take in the play while it was here and I would greatly enjoy going with two of my favorite people."

"Then if Thomas agrees it is all settled."

"I feel sure Thomas will be delighted," Rose said leading Leigh through the curtained doorway in the rear of the shop. "Come, dear, let's have tea."

When Rose bustled into the kitchen to prepare the tea, Leigh stood alone in the small room and looked about. She thought about the first time she had sat alone in this room. How things had changed. Tears came to her eyes and she was removing a handkerchief from her bag when

Rose returned and noted her tears.

"Leigh, dear, why the tears?"

"Oh, I am just happy at seeing you again and looking forward to seeing Thomas." She sniffed and wiped her tears. "Walking through that doorway just now I thought of all that has happened since I worked here for you." Leigh looked up to Rose, and again her large emerald eyes filled with tears. "Rose, I am so happy and I love Byron so much I sometimes get teary-eyed just thinking of him. Please do not think me foolish."

"Leigh, sweet, I would never think any woman foolish for being sentimental over the man she loves."

Leigh sniffed and wiped her tears and then turned a bright smile to Rose. "Have you found a suitable clerk?"

"Yes," Rose sighed, "but she is not nearly your measure. She is off today. Had I known you were coming, I would have never given her the day's leave."

They chatted over their tea and Leigh much enjoyed the afternoon shared with just the two of them. Leigh now thought of Rose as the mother she never knew and it was clear that Rose loved her in much the same way.

Several times when the shop was busy with customers Leigh helped to wait on them as Rose stood aside smiling and shaking her head.

That night as Leigh's and Byron's carriage pulled up in front of the theatre, they saw Ella waiting in the crowd.

Byron groaned and made a face. "I wonder what she is doing here?"

"No doubt, my love," Leigh teased, "she has come to see the play."

Byron frowned at her. "I just hate a witty woman."

Leigh gave him a startled look and Byron laughed and quickly placed a kiss on her lips.

"Byron, you should not look so fierce when you are teasing."

"Pet, I did not think you would take me seriously," he said placing a hand over hers. "You know how much I enjoy your quick mind."

She laughed. "But Byron, you can look most unpleasant when you wish."

Ella stood watching the entire exchange and her eyes burned holes into Leigh's back. As the couple walked beneath the awning at the entrance of the theatre, Ella approached them with a snide smile on her face.

"Hello there," she said to Byron.

"Good evening, Ella," Byron said curtly as Leigh nodded her head in Ella's direction.

"I am waiting for James Bradford," Ella commented casually looking about. "I swear, he just can't get enough of my company here of late," she sighed, as if bored with the entire affair.

"How nice for James," Byron commented sarcastically.

The Whitefields arrived and Byron quickly excused himself and he and Leigh went to greet them. Ella stood alone watching the two couples as they chatted gaily.

"Enjoy yourself, Leigh," she said with malice, "for this is going to be the last social function you attend."

Leigh thought she heard someone mention her name and looked about. She saw Ella giving her such a hateful look that it made all the hair on the back of her neck stand up. She shivered and drew Byron's attention.

"Come let us go inside," he said. "Leigh seems to feel a chill in the warm evening air." He offered Leigh his arm and the four of them made their way inside passing Ella still standing alone.

Byron noted how much Leigh enjoyed the performance and he promised himself that once the twins were older, they would travel to Richmond more often when such fine entertainment was in town. The Whitefields, too, seemed to enjoy the play, and at its conclusion the four of them went to partake of a late supper.

"Byron, it was simply beautiful," Rose said. "Thank you so much for taking us."

"Yes, indeed," Thomas added. "And we insist that tomorrow you both come to the house and bring the children. Rose and I shall prepare you a fine meal."

"Agreed," Byron and Leigh said in unison and then laughed.

That night when they were in their hotel room, Leigh again thought of the last time she and Byron had been in Richmond. She had been a frightened girl then, and now she was a happily married mother of twins. What unexpected joys fate sometimes offered, she thought. She lay in Byron's arms idly rubbing the hair on his chest. They had just made love and there was a contented smile on Leigh's lips.

"Isn't life wonderful, Byron?"

"Wonderful, pet," he agreed. She turned liquid eyes to his and they smiled at each other as Byron placed a fleeting kiss on the end of her nose.

Leigh again nestled her head on Byron's shoulder and sighed. Yes, life was indeed wonderful when you had a man like Byron to share it with.

The following day they took Nathan and Ammie and went to visit the Whitefields. As they rode through the city toward Thomas' modest home on the outskirts of town, Leigh suddenly became very pale. She gasped and turned her head following something with her eyes.

"Pet, what is it?" Byron asked alarmed. "You look as if you have seen a ghost." He turned to gaze where Leigh was staring but saw nothing unusual in the passerbys that strolled along the walks.

"I, ah, thought I saw Sam . . ." her voice was strained and trailed away. She looked nervously into Byron's concerned and loving eyes and some of the color began returning to her cheeks. "It is nothing, Byron. I'm fine, pay me no mind."

Byron placed a comforting arm about her shoulders and continued to study her closely as they rode. She did appear recovered and by the time they reached the Whitefields, he too had dismissed the incident from his mind.

They spent a wonderful day with the Whitefields. After the twins had been fed and seemed ready to nap Rose went and got a large downy comforter and placed it on the floor of the cozy drawing room. She and Leigh laid the twins down and sat quietly for a few moments to see if they would fall asleep.

"Now come keep me company in the kitchen," Rose whispered. "They cannot roll off of that and injure themselves."

Leigh and Rose entered the kitchen where Byron sat chatting with Thomas as Thomas prepared their meal.

"I have been a bachelor so long," Thomas was saying, "I have grown quite fond of cooking. I think Rose prefers I leave the kitchen to her or a cook."

"Nonsense, dear," Rose said going to help him. "And I fear you are the better cook."

400

Everyone laughed and Rose turned to wink at Leigh as she joined Byron at the table to watch their two chefs at work. They sat holding hands, both enjoying the domestic scene. Thomas and Rose often got in each other's way in the tiny kitchen, and one was constantly shooing the other from their path.

Byron chuckled commenting on how at home he felt.

"You should, Byron. Thomas and I both think of Leigh as our very own. I hope you don't mind if we think of you as a son-in-law, and the children as our grandchildren."

"Rose, Thomas, I am honored indeed," Byron grinned. "Thank you."

Leigh gave Byron's hand a squeeze and when he turned to her she smiled at him with such a tender look he felt sure he would be hard pressed not to rush her back to the privacy of their hotel room.

The wonderful aromas of Thomas' cooking proved to be an accurate appetizer to the delicious meal placed before the couple. Much to Leigh's regret, before they knew it the day was spent and it was time to leave.

Thomas and Rose escorted the couple to their carriage.

"Write us often and keep us informed as to your welfare and that of the babe's," Rose said.

"I will," Leigh replied, her eyes filling with tears.

"Mayhap you can come again soon for a visit," Byron commented. "You know you are both always welcome at Royal Oaks."

"Thank you, Byron. We will try," Thomas said. "You know how highly we think of you both but it is very difficult to get away from our two businesses."

Byron shook Thomas' offered hand. "We understand, but do come when you can."

Leigh tearfully kissed them both goodbye and then

handed Ammie to Byron as she entered the carriage. Byron took the seat beside her, settling Nathan in his lap and turned understanding eyes to his wife.

"Please do not cry so, my love," Byron said soothingly. "I give you my word as soon as we are able, we will return to Richmond. I cannot stay longer, there is much to do at home."

"I know, Byron," she said, trying to give him a smile and wiping her tears. "If we stayed a fortnight, I would still shed tears on departing."

"And besides," Byron said with a grin, "we cannot stay longer in Richmond if we are going to visit the O'Malleys."

"The O'Malleys!" Leigh exclaimed with large eyes.

"I hesitated to mention it before Leigh, and I am still uncertain as to whether it is a wise decision. It is a hard day's ride to the O'Malleys—but if we hire a coach and leave before the sun, we can arrive by sunset I judge. Do you think you and the twins are up to the travel?"

"Oh yes, Byron," Leigh said grabbing his hand.

"We will only be able to stay one day," he warned her.

"Will Ephraim and Annie go with us?"

"No, we need leave them here to finish purchasing the supplies we need at home. I'll hire a driver." He glanced at her uncertainly. "Are you quite sure it will not be too much for the children?"

"Quite sure. They are healthy and happy. One day's ride in a coach will do them no harm," she smiled.

"Then we leave before the sun on the morrow," he concluded placing a kiss on her lips. He took her hand in his and they rode back to the hotel laughing at Nathan waving his tiny arms in the air in excitement as he watched the city roll by the carriage windows.

They arrived at the O'Malleys' at dusk of the following day. John opened the front door and stood peering out when he heard the carriage pull up. When he saw Leigh, his face lit up with excitement.

"Mary!" he called. "Mary, it's Leigh. The lass has come home!"

Mary came rushing from the house wiping her hands on her apron. When she saw Leigh before her, Ammie in her arms, she rushed toward her with tears. "Leigh, child," she said weeping.

The two women embraced and John came and placed a kiss on Leigh's cheek and then hurried to welcome Byron, noting the sleeping infant in his arms.

"Mary, let's not be leaving them here in the yard," John said smiling to his wife.

Mary ushered the couple into the inn as John gave quick instructions to their driver. Once inside, the inn was full of excited conversation as John and Mary made over the twins like doting grandparents.

"Oh my," Mary exclaimed, eyes wide, the thought just occurring to her, "have you eaten?"

When Byron and Leigh, smiling, shook their heads that they had not, Mary bustled from the room clicking her tongue against the roof of her mouth. Leigh laughed, and handing Ammie to John, went to join Mary in the kitchen and help to prepare the meal.

"Saints be praised," John exclaimed, as he watched Leigh's graceful form following his wife, "but the lass does look grand."

"You'll get no argument from me," Byron replied smiling to the man.

A few minutes of awkward silence passed and then John cleared his throat and turned a serious face to

Byron. "Son, I hope that no ill feelings still linger betwix us."

Byron looked at the old weathered face, goodness and kindness shining from John's eyes, and he smiled warmly. "Mr. O'Malley, rest your fears. Though there was a time I resented your interference, those days are long since passed. You are wise beyond your years. If you had not forced the issue, and I had left here without her, I have little doubt that I would have soon returned. My head would have soon discovered what my heart already knew—that I love her."

John's eyes misted with a look of fatherly love and pride. "Ah, son, 'tis good to know," he said patting Byron on the back.

Ammie reached up one small hand and grabbed on to John's white whiskers holding fast. Byron laughed hard as John, his face twisted in a painful grin, loosened the hold of the tiny fingers.

Leigh and Mary worked well together in the kitchen, and as they prepared the meal, Leigh answered all of Mary's questions, filling her in on all that had happened since she had left their home.

"You are truly happy aren't you, Leigh?"

"Yes, Mrs. O'Malley," Leigh said softly, gracing Mary with a beautiful dimpled smile. "You were right. He is a good man—and I love him with all my heart."

Mary smiled knowingly and gave Leigh a hug. "I am so happy for you, lass."

The coach driver entered the kitchen and Mary placed a plate before him making arrangements for the man for the night. The three chatted briefly and then Mary and Leigh went to join Byron and John in the common room.

John and Mary sat at the table with the couple, holding

the twins and talking merrily, while Leigh and Byron consumed the delicious stew Mary had prepared for them. Everyone seemed to enjoy the night, and it was very late when Leigh and Byron climbed the stairs, each carrying a sleeping child.

Byron opened the door to Leigh's old room allowing her to precede him, and as Leigh stepped through the doorway she was assaulted with memories. This is where it all began, she thought. This is where fate decreed I should meet my knight. She turned to Byron with love in her eyes but found his own eyes distressed.

"I fear, madam," he said somewhat awkwardly, "that this room will bring back unpleasant memories."

He laid his sleeping daughter in the center of the bed and Leigh put Nathan down next to his sister and stood staring at Byron across the bed, but he refused to look her way. Leigh, smiling, walked around the bed and stood looking up at her husband's handsome face.

"Byron, love," she said in a soft one, "all is forgiven. Never has a woman had such a loving and devoted husband, and," she continued standing on tiptoes to place a fleeting kiss on his lips, "never has a wife loved her husband as I love you."

Byron gazed into her eyes, and pulling her close, hugged her fiercely. "Oh, Leigh, I think that I should die if I were ever to lose your love."

They stood, arms about each other, gazing into each other's eyes, and in a moment Byron chuckled. "Pet, I fear you do torture me," he said seeing a glow in her emerald eyes much the same as her look after they had just made love. "You looked at me with an expression to melt any man's heart, and one I have seen often before, knowing full well," he smiled glancing to the bed and their sleeping children, "that this night we sleep with babes between us."

Leigh giggled and kissed him again. "Ah, but m'lord, there shall be many more nights."

Byron laughed. "Indeed there shall," he said holding her close. "Indeed there shall."

When Byron awoke the next morning the bed was empty. He hurriedly dressed and made his way to the common room. He found Mary and John there tending the twins and when the babes saw their father, they smiled, waving their tiny arms in the air with delight. Byron picked up each child in turn placing a kiss on their cheeks and then his eyes roamed the room.

"She is out by her father's grave," John said to Byron's unasked question.

Byron thanked him and went to search for Leigh. He had wanted to bring Leigh to visit the O'Malleys because he knew the couple would be concerned as to her fate, and being common uneducated folks, he knew Leigh had not written them knowing that they could not read. But also he wanted to bring Leigh here for this—so she could visit her father's grave. He had often found comfort in standing over his parents' graves, but when he saw Leigh standing alone and quiet, her head bowed, he wondered, and his heart ached for her. Would it bring back too many unhappy memories? Would it cause her to relive those lonely days following her father's death—the night he had . . . had . . .

He walked up quietly behind her, his eyes roaming over her slender form. "I wish I had known him," he said softly.

Leigh turned tear-filled eyes to him and then flung

herself into his arms, weeping. Byron held her close soothing her tears with gentle words.

Mary and John stood at the window watching the couple.

"Does a body good to see them so happy," Mary commented. "You can rest your fears, John," she added.

"Ah, Mary, 'tis a blessing," he smiled. "I do believe the lad loves our Leigh nearly as much as I love you," he said placing a smacking kiss on Mary's cheek.

"Oh, go on with ya," Mary laughed.

Ammie and Nathan noted the smiling faces, and like all children, giggled their childish delight, and Mary and John laughed, hugging them close.

"Not only do I feel that God has given me the child I always prayed for," said Mary looking at her husband with love, "but now we have two beautiful grandbabes as well."

"Aye," John said taking Mary's hand and gazing out the window at the couple. "God in his wisdom . . ."

Leigh sighed, her tears spent, and looked up to Byron with a melancholy smile. "I miss him so," she sniffed.

"I know, my love," Byron said taking his handkerchief from his pocket and wiping away the last of her tears.

"I wish Nathan and Ammie could have known him. He was such a good man, Byron."

"Of that I have no doubt, my love."

"Father would be so pleased knowing how happy I am now and how much I love you."

"He knows," Byron said kissing her brow and smiling into her eyes. "He knows."

"I would like to pick some flowers."

Byron nodded, and taking her hand, they strolled through the surrounding woods and Byron helped Leigh to pick a large bunch of wild flowers and then stood quietly by as she placed them on her father's grave. When they went again to join the O'Malleys, they were walking arms wrapped about each other's waist.

They spent a pleasant and happy day visiting with the O'Malleys and all retired early that night knowing Byron and Leigh would have to leave before the sun rose the next morning to return to Richmond.

John and Mary kissed Nathan and Ammie goodbye and the two women wept upon parting while John and Byron exchanged hearty handshakes. Byron gave John detailed directions to Royal Oaks and the couple promised to visit first chance they had.

As the carriage pulled away from the inn Byron smiled at Leigh. "Nathan and Ammie will have no shortage of doting grandparents between the Whitefields and the O'Malleys."

"Yes," Leigh agreed. She glanced to her father's grave one last time, her smile a little forlorn. "I think both of our parents would be pleased and honored to be replaced by such dear and kind friends."

Byron took her hand and gave it a gentle squeeze. "We are indeed fortunate, my love," he smiled.

Ephraim and Annie were waiting to greet them when they returned to the hotel. Pleasant greetings made the round and then Ephraim and Annie took the twins to their room while Byron escorted his sleepy wife to theirs.

The supplies Byron had had Ephraim purchase were delivered the following day and as Byron watched the boat being loaded for the return trip he wondered if he was going to require a second boat to get them all home.

Once home they quickly regained their habit of riding

together in the mornings. Occasionally Leigh had the feeling they were being watched as they rode. She would glance about, the hair on the back of her neck standing up, but she never saw anyone or mentioned the feeling to Byron.

"Leigh, a buyer will be here on the morrow to inspect the tobacco," Byron said as they walked their horses across the field after a morning ride.

"Will we be entertaining him?"

"No, he will be here only the one day and will be staying the night as a guest of the Cummings. But I will have to deny myself your company and spend the day with him. I am afraid I shall be gone most of the day, pet," he said turning to her with a helpless smile. "After he finishes inspecting Uncle Jonathan's tobacco, he will come here, then to the Boroughs', and lastly to the Cummings'. It has been customary in the past for all four of us to make the rounds with the man." He arched a brow at her. "Sometimes buyers have been known to offer less than a fair price if others are not present to insure quality and compare your tobacco with theirs."

"I will ask Emily to come and spend the day with me."

"She may have to decline, sweet," he said glancing at her. "Jack said they plan to travel to Richmond the following day, and I am sure Emily will have much to keep her busy preparing. As a matter of fact, they plan on taking the buyer back to Richmond on the boat."

"It is of no matter," she said giving him a dimpled grin. "I am sure I can entertain myself for one day and I have sewing to do for Ammie and Nathan."

That night after dinner Byron and Leigh strolled into the ballroom and stood at one of the windows gazing out at the moon and the lovely clear night full of stars.

409

"May I have this dance, madam?" Byron asked with a grin and a slight bow.

"I would be honored, my gracious sir," Leigh replied with a giggle, curtsying low.

Byron laughed and taking her in his arms, whirled about the empty moonlit room humming a waltz. They smiled into each other's eyes as they danced.

"We will have to teach Ammie or Nathan how to play the piano," he winked, "then we will have proper music to waltz to."

"Yes, that would be grand," Leigh smiled, caressing the back of his neck with her hand. "Though to be truthful, my love, I do find your humming most pleasant."

Byron smiled and held her tighter as they danced.

Ephraim passed the open ballroom doors as he made his nightly rounds. He was reaching to close them when he saw the couple dancing their blissful, silent dance.

"Yes, sir," he chuckled walking quietly away, "there is going to be lots of babes at Royal Oaks now."

The following day after breakfast, Byron kissed Leigh goodbye and rode off in the direction of Uncle Jonathan's.

Leigh was not fond of the idea of Byron spending the afternoon at the Borough plantation, but Uncle Jonathan and Jack would be present, as well as Fred Borough, and she doubted that Ella would be included in this man's business.

She spent the morning sewing for the children and doing small chores about the house. By afternoon she had grown restless, missing Byron's company. She had thought to see the men as they rode here to Royal Oaks, but as of yet there had been no sign of them.

She went upstairs and changed into her riding habit. Major sat watching her and she talked merrily to the dog.

"Now, Major, you stay with Ammie and Nathan. I shall not be long."

The dog wagged his tail and when she went into the nursery to check on the sleeping twins, he laid down beside the crib and followed Leigh with his eyes as she tiptoed from the room.

"Annie," Leigh called descending the stairs and seeing the woman below in the foyer, "I plan to ride for awhile. Mayhap I will meet Byron and the other men as they make their way."

"Now, Miss Leigh, don't you go riding too far by yourself," Annie instructed.

"I won't, Annie, promise." She turned to Annie with a smile when she reached the door. "Most likely I shall not be long unless," she added with a twinkle in her eye, "I should meet Byron along the way."

Annie chuckled and returned to her dusting. "It sore do a body good to see them two so happy."

Leigh decided she would ride to the stream that she and Byron favored. From there she would ride home by the path that took her nearest to the Borough plantation and if she saw the men she would invite them back to the house for some refreshment.

Before she reached the stream she again had the feeling of being observed. She became more and more uncomfortable and slowed her filly to a walk as she glanced about nervously. The filly seemed to sense Leigh's anxiety and became skittish and restless.

"There, there girl," Leigh said patting the horse's neck and reassuring herself as much as her horse. She thought of turning about and going back home but then she decided that she was acting foolish and she spurred her mount and rode on toward the stream at a faster pace.

When she reached the stream, she dismounted and stood staring at the sparkling water and remembering all the happy, passionate times she and Byron had spent here. It was a magical place to Leigh and very dear to her heart.

She heard a rustling in the trees behind her and again the hairs on her neck bristled. With apprehension, she slowly turned her head, and when she saw him standing there smiling at her, she screamed dropping her reins. As her filly bolted away, Leigh sank limply to the ground in a faint.

When Byron and the other men finally reached Royal Oaks, Byron thought of returning to the house to place a quick kiss on Leigh's lips not knowing she had left only moments before. The buyer had been late in arriving at Uncle Jonathan's and it looked as though the entire day would be spent with the man. He, Jack, and Fred, had already spent long hours haggling with the man over Uncle Jonathan's tobacco and now they must do so again here and then again at Fred's and Jack's. I'll be lucky if I make it home by dark, he thought disgusted.

As the men walked to the large barns filled with curing tobacco, Jack and Byron exchanged weary looks.

Leigh opened her eyes and looked about. She was in a small, dingy, wooden house of some kind. It looked old and near collapsing. There was a table and a chair and she lay on a filthy blanket on the dirt floor. Her eyes roamed the room and came to an abrupt halt on the face of Samuel Jones.

412

"About time you come to," he said smiling at her and showing black, rotten teeth.

Leigh lay perfectly still, only her eyes showing any sign of life. She prayed she was having a nightmare and that soon Byron would wake her and take her gently into his strong and reassuring arms.

"Hee, hee. Ain't it funny," Jones sneered. "I had no ideay it would be you I'd be taking."

He stood up slowly, stretched, and then walked to her side. Leigh quickly sat up and scooted back against the wall, watching the man with disbelieving and frightened eyes.

"You got more lives than a cat, you do. I thought sure you drown that night you fell in the river. If I'd known you didn't, I might of come back and looked for ya." He leaned over her smiling broadly and Leigh quickly turned away at the foul smell of his breath and unwashed body. He laughed and walked a few paces away before turning to again leer at her.

"To think I spent a whole night searching for you in them woods that night your daddy told you to run, and now I find you twice without no looking at all." He threw back his head and laughed heartily. "Fate is a funny thing, ain't it?"

"You killed those men on the boat that night, didn't you?" Leigh asked in a fearful voice.

"Maybe I did," he replied frowning at her. "You done rob me twice of the money you was to bring when I sold ya." He came at her angrily and stood glaring at her. "I needed money from the sale of them goods on that there boat."

"But you took my father's money and our deed as well."

413

He shook hard with laughter. "Your father didn't have enough money in that box of his to keep a body for a week."

"You lie. That box contained all of the money from the sale of our estate in England."

"You best watch that temper of yours, missy. I got ways of making you wish you had." He leaned closer to her face and closing one eye, leered at her. "Your precious daddy was a fool!" he spat at her.

Leigh gasped and had to use all her self-control not to reach out a hand and slap the man's face. He laughed at the anger he saw in her eyes.

"Yes, missy, a fool. I thought you would have known by now but I can see by the look of you that you don't. That land your foolish father bought already belonged to another."

He turned and walked back to the chair, laughing and slapping his thigh. He sat down, lounging, his fingers hooked in his belt, and stared at her. Leigh thought she would scream at the man in rage. He knew he was torturing her with this knowledge and that his very presence frightened her beyond belief.

"Your father, the fool," he finally said, "paid his coins for Royal Oaks." He sneered when Leigh looked to him amazed. "That's right, missy. I ought to know." He frowned at her. "I nearly got hung when I lost that deed in a wager and the man that won it returned with some of his friends. It seems one of the gents knew that the land stated in the deed was this here Royal Oaks, and knew the gent that owned it too."

Leigh remained still, watching him. She could see his anger building as he sat thinking about what he had told her.

"When that Borough woman come to me in Richmond and offered to pay me to take a woman from Royal Oaks, I agreed right enough."

"Borough woman!"

"Yeah. Neighbor I reckon. She wanted you gone from here mighty bad and offered me a tidy sum to do the job. I figured this here Royal Oaks owed me something, so I agreed right enough. Of course," he added with an evil grin, "I would have agreed anyway seeing the sum she was willing to pay. Now I get a bonus besides, seeing that it's you."

Leigh sat running it all through her mind. So Ella hated her so much she had paid to have her taken from Byron, she thought. Oh Byron, my love, please hear my prayers. She could see his loving, handsome face before her and at the thought of Ammie and Nathan, tears came to her eyes.

"Stop that sniveling!" he yelled. "I hate weepy women and I ain't putting up with it. Keep it up and I'll beat you good," he warned.

Leigh hurriedly wiped her tears and fought hard to keep new ones from forming. She glanced about the small room. I must get away from this crazy man, she thought, but how? There was only the one door and he lounged near it.

"Yeah, fate sure is a funny thing," Jones repeated. "Keeps throwing us together. I had no ideay it was you she wanted to be rid of. This here Borough woman didn't seem to care much what became of you after neither."

He laughed at her frightened look and his eyes slowly raked her body from top to bottom.

"You don't look none the worse for wear from a year ago, missy. In fact, I think you look even better."

Leigh noted the lusty look in his eye. Keep him talking, she told herself. Give Byron time to find you.

"You are very clever, Mr. Jones," she said meekly, straining to sound anything but horrified as she was. "However did you know I would be riding alone today, and where I would ride?"

"Beginning to appreciate me, ain't ya?" he said with a snicker. Again his eyes roamed over Leigh's body as he spoke. "That woman told me how you two ride together every day and where you most often ride to. Seems she has been watching you for a while. Been watching myself the past couple days. She said you would be alone today."

So Ella had planned well knowing that Byron would be busy today. If only, she thought, I had stayed home today.

"Where are we now?"

He looked hard at her before answering. "Guess it do no harm to tell ya, seeing how you ain't getting away from me." He casually leaned back in the chair with a grin. "We are a bit away from that there Royal Oaks. I found this here shack and been staying here. Gonna be on our way as soon as it is dark. That damn filly of yours was too skittish, couldn't catch her. Guess will have to walk to the river. Got a boat waiting there." He stood slowly and walked to the door, turning his back to her. "Have to find something to pass the time till then."

When he turned to her with a lusty grin and took a step toward her, Leigh jumped to her feet and inched away from him.

"Ain't no use trying to run this time, missy," he laughed. "You ain't getting away from me again."

Leigh backed away as far as the room would allow. She stood with her back pressed against the crumbling walls of the shack and her eyes belayed her terror. He took slow, stalking steps toward her and Leigh frantically searched the room for a way of escape. Her hand touched on a loose board in the wall behind her and as his steps brought him ever nearer, she frantically clawed at it with her fingernails. Just as he grabbed her arm, the board came loose and Leigh swung it around with all her might catching him aside the head. He released her with a curse, and Leigh ran for the door sobbing Byron's name.

Byron arrived home at dusk. He strolled into the foyer to find Ephraim and Annie talking rapidly in hushed tones.

"Master Byron, thank goodness," Ephraim said looking up and seeing him. "We were becoming quite concerned."

Byron gave Ephraim a somewhat startled look. "Ephraim, you know these things usually take the better part of a day, I don't understand why you . . ."

"Where is Miss Leigh?" Annie interrupted staring at the closed entry door.

"Leigh?" Byron repeated in confusion. "Why she is here, isn't she?"

"Oh Lordy," Annie exclaimed, her knees crumbling beneath her.

Ephraim quickly supported Annie against him and looked to Byron with worry on his old wrinkled face. "Miss Leigh left right after lunch to go riding," he explained. "She said she was going to ride for a while and then mayhap meet you on your way from the Cummings' plantation. When she didn't return, we assumed . . ."

Byron panicked. "I haven't seen her!"

They stood staring at one another in silence, each face

more worried than the next.

"Quickly, have Henry saddle me a fresh mount and gather the men in front," Byron ordered.

"I knew," Annie cried burying her face in her hands. "I knew when it got past time for the twins to nurse—I knew."

Byron stared at Annie, his concern growing greater with each passing instant.

"The twins are fine, Master Byron," Ephraim assured him. "Annie got a wet nurse for them until Miss Leigh comes home." He turned to Annie and looked her square in the eye. "Now Annie," he said as much for Byron's sake as his wife's, "let's not think the worst. Mayhap she just lost track of the time enjoying her ride."

Byron heard the doubt in Ephraim's voice. They all knew that Leigh was not at all likely to forget the time. Byron feared she had been thrown and at this very instant lay somewhere hurt in need of his help.

When the men were gathered in front of the house, Byron stood on the veranda shouting orders to them. He divided them into several groups to search in different directions. Ephraim handed out torches since it would soon be dark.

"Ephraim and I will search with the men to the south," Byron concluded. "If you find her or her filly, send someone immediately to inform me."

The men nodded their heads in understanding and then started off in their designated directions.

Annie and Aunt Mary stood side by side on the veranda. They exchanged worried looks and began to pray as they watched Byron and Ephraim gallop across the field, Major close at their heels.

Within half an hour one of the men found Leigh's

horse grazing in the far east pasture. When Byron saw the man racing toward him on Leigh's filly, his heart rose up in his throat.

Ephraim looked to the filly and then to Byron. "Now Master Byron," Ephraim said soothingly, "she is most likely just fine. Mayhap the horse wandered away. At this very moment she is probably trudging back to the house angry with the filly." At Byron's disbelieving look, Ephraim continued. "Even if she was thrown Master Byron, it does not mean she is hurt bad."

"Please, God, let it be so," Byron whispered. "Please, God."

Leigh ran as fast as she could. She could hear Jones' angry curses as she bolted from the shack. She stopped to catch her breath and looked nervously about. She was lost, not knowing which direction would take her home. The sunlight was all but gone and she noted the dwindling light with panic. She could hear Jones yelling again and knew that he was pursuing her.

"You little hell cat!" she heard him yell. "I will find you and when I do, you will regret hitting me. Before I'm done with ya, ya wish you never was born!"

Leigh could tell he was not far behind her, and sobbing, she picked up her skirts and started running. She ran aimlessly, crying Byron's name over and over.

The night grew black and still Leigh ran. She could see nothing before her and prayed the dark would be to her advantage and Jones would have trouble finding her tracks. She prayed harder than she had ever prayed in her life.

She would run a while and then stop to listen. She tried desperately to quiet her sobbing and the rapid beating of

419

her heart. I must hear him if he is near, she told herself. She was near exhaustion and did not know how much longer she could go on. Several times she heard twigs snapping nearby, and her fear helped her to reach deep down inside and find the strength to run some more.

She tripped over a fallen branch and fell to the ground with a thud. She lay sobbing into her hands. Eventually she pushed herself up and stumbled to a grove of trees. She sat at the base of a tree, breathing hard, and listened. The minutes ticked by like hours but she heard no other sound than that of her own labored breathing. Mayhap I've lost him, she thought hopefully. She sighed and leaned back against the tree.

When the two arms came snaking around the tree trunk, Leigh screamed loud and long.

Even though Byron's man had found the filly some distance from the stream, Byron still judged it the most likely spot Leigh would have ridden to and he and Ephraim continued in that direction. When they reached the stream Major ran about in an excited manner and appeared to have picked up a scent. He whined several times and then took off at a run.

"We will follow Major," Byron said. "Mayhap he can find her for us. Pray it is the right decision, Ephraim."

They had only followed the dog a short distance when a spine chilling scream floated over the night air. Major's ears perked and a low growl rumbled in the huge dog's chest as he stared in that direction. Byron quickly dismounted and grabbed the dog by the collar, motioning to Ephraim. Ephraim came to his side taking both sets of reins in his hand.

"Ephraim," Byron whispered, "secure the horses and

then you and Major circle around that way. And whatever you do, keep Major still," he said looking to the growling dog. "I do not know if that was Leigh we heard scream but something is definitely amiss up ahead. I'll go this way. And Ephraim, be careful."

Ephraim nodded his head in understanding and taking the dog by the collar, started off in the direction Byron had indicated. Byron was frantic but he knew that panic would serve no purpose. If Leigh is in danger, he told himself, I must remain calm and use my wits. I cannot help Leigh, or anyone, if my brain is muddled with panic.

Leigh heard Jones laughing, his hot, foul breath touching her face.

"I told you you wouldn't get away," he sneered. He placed a hand roughly on her breast and squeezed hard. "Now, missy, it is time to pay."

Leigh struggled and tried with all her strength to free herself from his grip. Dear God, she prayed, take my life before this vile man has his way with me. She was struggling fiercely when she heard a voice cut through the night air.

"Leave her be."

"Byron," she gasped. She could not see him but now she knew that he was near. "Thank you, God," she sobbed.

Jones pulled a knife from his boot and placed it at Leigh's throat. He looked about nervously, seeing no one. "Gent," he yelled, "I got a knife at her pretty white throat and unless you want me to split it from ear to ear, you best show yourself!"

"Leigh," Byron called, "are you all right? Has he harmed you?"

421

Leigh looked at Jones and he nudged her and nodded that she should answer.

"I-I'm all right, Byron," she called weakly.

Byron could hear the fear in her voice and he struck a flint and lit his torch and stepped from the darkness.

Leigh sobbed pitifully when she saw him and her knees seemed to buckle beneath her. The muscles in Byron's cheek were vibrating with his anger and he looked as if he was ready to do battle with the devil himself. Jones roughly jerked Leigh to her feet and held the knife closer against her throat.

"Let her go," Byron growled in a low and threatening tone. "If you harm her in any way, I'll see you in hell!"

"I can't do that, gent," Jones said relaxing some when he saw that Byron had no weapon. "You might attack and kill me, true, but not before I've slit her like a pig. That there Borough woman paid me good to see her gone and there is more acoming after I finish the job. Besides this little lady owes me," he said smirking at Byron and fondling Leigh's breast with his free hand. Leigh winced at the pain he caused her, her breast being full of milk for the twins and Jones laughed at the look he saw in Byron's eyes.

"Samuel Jones at your service, gent," he said with an evil laugh.

When Byron heard the name he took several steps toward them.

"Now I'd watch myself, gent," Jones said jerking Leigh back and pressing the knife firmly against her throat. "This here knife can split a hair."

"You can't get away with her now," Byron said. "I give you my word that if you set her free, you will not be harmed."

"No," Jones chuckled, "can't do that."

He appraised Byron. It was going to be hard to get away with her now, that was true, he thought. If I could get him to charge me out of control, I could stick him with my knife before he knows what hit him, Jones decided. He is a big one, but I got my knife and I figure that makes us even. Yeah, if I can just cause him to act foolish and lose his head, it will be small trouble to put him to his end.

The matter settled in his mind, Jones looked at Byron and slowly started to unfasten Leigh's blouse. Byron snarled and took another step toward them.

"Now gent, I done warned ya," Jones said grabbing Leigh's hair and giving it a savage jerk, snapping her head back.

He did not want Byron to charge him until he was completely beyond reasoning. Then, and only then, would he feel the odds in his favor. He grabbed the front of Leigh's blouse and ripped it open exposing her breasts and slowly he squeezed them watching Byron carefully all the while.

Byron yelled and lunged for the man. Jones flung Leigh from him and turned his knife so Byron would land on it. Jones did not see the huge dog leaping through the air toward him, but Byron did. Byron twisted his body in mid-air and reached a long arm out to Leigh pulling her to the ground with him. He took the impact of the fall on his body and held her to him as they rolled away from Jones. Quickly he leaped to his feet, guarding Leigh with his body, and ready to do battle.

Jones was on the ground struggling with the huge angry dog. Ephraim came running out of the darkness, and Byron took off his coat and placed it over Leigh to hide her nakedness before helping her to rise. They all stood as if hypnotized, watching Jones struggling with Major. The light from the torch caught on Jones' knife as it flashed through the air, and Major let out a yelp and then lunged at Jones' throat and shook him as though he were a rag doll. Leigh clung to Byron, horrified. Byron and Ephraim both seemed to find their wits at the same time and rushed toward the pair. Byron pulled the furious dog from Jones and Jones laid perfectly still, his head at an odd angle.

"He is dead," Ephraim said bending over the man. "Appears his neck is broke."

Major whined and on unsteady feet started in Leigh's direction but he collapsed on the ground after only a few steps. Leigh rushed to the dog and cradled his large head in her lap. She saw blood gushing from a slash in his side and she began to rock to and fro sobbing.

She turned pleading eyes to Byron. "Byron, don't let Major die," she begged with tears streaming down her face.

Byron came to squat beside her and inspected Major's wound. His eyes were sad as he gazed into her tear-filled emerald ones.

"Leigh, my love, I love you more than life itself and there is nothing I would not grant you." He paused taking her hand gently in his own. "Major is a fine dog, and I cherish him dear. He has most likely saved both our lives this night." He placed a hand on Major's neck and looked lovingly at the dog and then slowly drew his eyes back to Leigh's. "Leigh, do not ask this of me for he has fought bravely and well, even after the blow was struck, and he has lost much blood. The wound is deep, Leigh." He caressed her hand and looked deeply into her eyes.

"My love, I cannot grant you what is not in my power to do so. It is in the hands of God now."

Ephraim brought the horses and Byron picked Leigh up in his strong arms and carried her to the horses and placed her astride the saddle.

"I'll send someone with the wagon for you and Major Ephraim," he said. "Stay with him and give him as much comfort as you can," he added looking to the suffering dog.

Byron and Ephraim exchanged looks and Leigh knew they did not expect Major to live.

"What about him?" Ephraim asked pointing to Jones.

"He is in no hurry now," Byron said looking to the man with disgust. "I will send someone for the body later. Scum like him need not share a wagon with you or that fine animal."

Ephraim cradled Major's head and was speaking softly to the dog as Leigh and Byron rode sadly away.

Chapter Sixteen

A week passed. Leigh's portrait now hung above the mantel in the drawing room. Leigh sat on the veranda, leaning against one of the large white pillars, and watched Byron playing with the twins. He had spread a blanket on the front lawn and he and the babes lay on it playing. He was on his back holding first Ammie and then Nathan high in the air over his head. They were all laughing. Leigh marveled that his strong hands could be so gentle when need be. As she watched them she thought of all that happened in the week just passed.

That night they had returned to the house and Byron had sent Henry with the wagon to fetch Ephraim and Major. He had calmly asked Leigh what had happened. He repeatedly questioned her if Jones had harmed her in any way, and Leigh repeatedly assured him she was fine except for her concern over Major.

Byron had noted Jones' words about Ella and he questioned Leigh in a lengthy manner until the story was straight in his mind. He had been very patient with her but now that he had it all clear, he was raging about the house cursing Ella. His anger was so intense, it frightened Leigh.

"Annie," he yelled, "stay with Leigh. I will be back shortly."

He rushed from the house to his horse still at the veranda steps.

Leigh followed him and pleaded with him not to go. "Byron, I have not been harmed, please," she begged clinging to him.

"Leigh, Ella needs be confronted with her foul deed!" he growled with a fierce gleam in his eye.

Byron had the look of death about him and Leigh feared he would do Ella great harm, mayhap even kill her! She begged him again, but all to no avail. He would not hear her words and rode off at a gallop in the direction of Borough plantation.

Leigh paced nervously, wringing her hands. By the time Henry and Ephraim returned she was near hysterics.

"Ephraim, please, you must stop him! I fear he will harm Ella," she weeped.

"He needs wring her neck!" Ephraim replied in anger.

"Ephraim, please!"

"I'll go after him, Miss Leigh," he said, his old face now also showing concern. Ephraim knew Byron's temper only too well.

Leigh thought they would never return. She paced the bedroom wringing her hands and crying. She prayed that Ephraim would arrive in time. She had never seen Byron so angry. He had been in a rage when he left the house. Her anxiety grew as the minutes turned into hours.

Much later she lay on the bed crying when Byron quietly entered the room. She lay a moment studying his face and then rushed to his side.

"Byron?" she whispered.

He took her in his arms and held her tightly. "Rest your fears, Leigh. I did Ella no harm."

They stood a moment embracing and then Byron led her to one of the chairs by the fireplace and took the one opposite hers and told her what had happened.

"At first Ella denied her part and I could tell that though Fred knows me well and could see my anger, he wanted to believe that Ella was innocent of such a terrible deed. But when Ephraim arrived and he spoke with him too, he no longer could deny the truth of the matter. He questioned Ella himself and eventually she admitted her guilt. She cried and begged her father, and me, but Fred would not hear her words." He paused taking Leigh's hand and looking hard into her eyes. "Leigh, he has sent her from his home and stated he never wants to lay eyes on her again."

"Oh, Byron, how sad," Leigh said as tears came to her eyes. "She loved you so much and now she has lost her father's love as well as yours."

"Leigh, I never loved Ella. Feel no sympathy for her. She got her just reward. Women of her kind are much like cats," he said. "They somehow always manage to land on their feet."

It seemed Byron had been right about Ella. Jack and Emily had left for Richmond as planned, not knowing of Leigh's kidnapping. When they returned several days later and learned what had happened, they came themselves to see that Leigh was indeed unharmed. Jack told them that they had seen Ella in Richmond and that she had left the city on the arm of a traveling drummer who sold his wares to one of the dress shops there.

Mayhap she would find happiness with the man. Leigh hoped that she would.

Nathan was giggling at his father and Leigh smiled as she watched them. Major came and nuzzled Leigh's hand and she gently petted his large head, cradling it with her arm. He was not completely recovered from his wound, but now they knew that he would live and one day soon be himself again.

As Leigh petted the dog and watched her husband and children, she thought of Samuel Jones' words concerning fate. On that the man had spoken true. Fate had most definitely played a large part in her and Byron's lives.

It had been fate that Leigh's father sell their home and travel to America. And fate again that he purchased land already belonging to Byron. Leigh knew now that one day she and Byron would have certainly met. Mayhap they would have fallen in love and wed anyway. But fate had been given a turn by Samuel Jones and so had chosen another path. And that path had led Leigh to fear Byron and flee him, and her fleeing had brought together Rose and Thomas, now happily wed.

It surely must have been fate, she mused, that led her to take the same boat from Richmond as Samuel Jones. And fate again that Byron left Richmond when he did and stopped that morning to sit on the riverbank.

And it must have been the hand of fate that persuaded Byron to bring home that large puppy those many months ago, for without Major things might have turned out much differently.

Leigh looked to Byron and the children. Byron was rolling on the blanket with the twins and they were giggling their delight.

"I love you, Byron," she called.

Byron looked her way and smiled, a twinkle in his deep blue eyes. "And I love you, Leigh—more than words can say."

Leigh rubbed her cheeks against Major's large head and gave Byron a dimpled grin. What was fate after all, she thought, if not the hand of God.

FASCINATING, PAGE-TURNING BLOCKBUSTERS!

BYGONES (1030, $3.75)
by Frank Wilkinson
Once the extraordinary Gwyneth set eyes on the handsome aristocrat Benjamin Whisten, she was determined to foster the illicit love affair that would shape three generations—and win a remarkable woman an unforgettable dynasty!

A TIME FOR ROSES (946, $3.50)
by Agatha Della Anastasi
A family saga of riveting power and passion! Fiery Magdalena places her marriage vows above all else—until her husband wants her to make an impossible choice. She has always loved and honored—but now she can't obey!

THE VAN ALENS (1000, $3.50)
by Samuel A. Schreiner, Jr.
The lovely, determined Van Alen women were as exciting and passionate as the century in which they lived. And through these years of America's most exciting times, they created a dynasty of love and lust!

THE CANNAWAYS (1019, $3.50)
by Graham Shelby
Vowing to rise above the poverty and squalor of her birth, Elizabeth Darle becomes a woman who would pay any price for love—and to make Brydd Cannaway's dynasty her own!

THE LION'S WAY (900, $3.75)
by Lewis Orde
An all-consuming saga that spans four generations in the life of troubled and talented David, who struggles to rise above his immigrant heritage and rise to a world of glamour, fame and success!

A WOMAN OF DESTINY (734, $3.25)
by Grandin Hammill
Rose O'Neal is passionate and determined, a woman whose spark ignites the affairs of state—as well as the affairs of men!

Available wherever paperbacks are sold, or order direct from the Publisher. Send cover price plus 50¢ per copy for mailing and handling to Zebra Books, 475 Park Avenue South, New York, N.Y. 10016. DO NOT SEND CASH.